Aurora:

Between Heaven and Earth

by

L.Lynn Eckert

MICK ART
PRODUCTIONS LLC
PUBLISHING
www.mickcartproductions.com

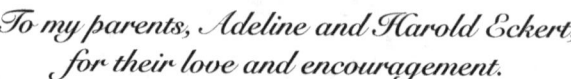

To my parents, Adeline and Harold Eckert,
for their love and encouragement.

Aurora: Between Heaven and Earth
All Rights Reserved
Copyright © 2017 L. Lynn Eckert

Mick Art Productions, LLC
www.mickartproductions.com
ISBN: 978-0-9915660-6-8
Library of Congress: 2017906607

PRINTED IN THE UNITED STATES OF AMERICA

Content

Preface

Science fiction engenders a compelling arena in which to explore all the "what ifs" that tug at the emotions and the intellect, a place where ordinary people tend to fall into extraordinary circumstances. It becomes enjoyable to escape into another world and vicariously take a journey into uncharted territory.

All of the characters and a number of the geographical locations in this narrative do not actually exist. And though some of the technologies described herein are couched within the fluid context of fantasy, one must consider the amazing devices of today. Such things would have seemed like magic to our ancestors.

The three central characters in this account are caught between the earth and the sky, the known and the unknown, and even between inner and outer space. One is reaching for something beyond planet Earth, another is searching for a place in the world, and yet another finds shelter under the wings of two flawed people. Although this chronicle flows out of a pool of dreams, it nevertheless attempts to shoot an arrow of truth through an onslaught of specious darts to hit the real target: The human heart.

Chapter One: Event

Where do hopes and dreams come from?
How does an event conspire to shape our lives?
Although I am but fashioned of the earth,
I dare to ask.
Mari

Neil Clayborn spent his days in a wheelchair. However, neither his mind nor his dreams were on such a tether. He also realized early in life that his older sister Celeste had a kindred spirit in the truest sense. This created a lasting bond, which became evident during an innocent, though remarkable moment in time; the day he asked her if she might not like to take him on an evening stroll. Delighted by the request, she wheeled him down a meandering path through a sublime park near Fairbanks Alaska. By nightfall the stars had become exceedingly radiant, and over those lofty diamonds spread the most vivid array of the Northern Lights they had ever seen. Gazing up at such a remarkable sight, Celeste, always captivated by any aurorean display, declared, "Neil, what a marvelous part of God's creation they are! Oh, how wonderful it would be to sail among those dancing colors of the night!"

The years passed swiftly, the wheelchair was gone, and so was the life Neil had once known. Nevertheless, the vivid memories of that night long ago were still with him as he stood by the starboard railing on the forecastle deck of the research vessel *Aries*. Presently, the ship remained motionless on the waters of the Pacific, approximately five hundred miles southeast of Japan; for this was July 22, and the much awaited solar eclipse was about to unfold.

Neil was driven by an alchemy of vision and intrepid curiosity, although he stubbornly embraced an elusive thing called nostalgia. The field glasses he held in his hands, circa 1912, attested to the fact; a gift from his sister as a token of their shared interest in the sky. With them he scanned the northern part of the oft obscure line which divides the land and sea from the atmosphere arching above. The weather was clear and a temperate breeze tussled with the long dark raincoat that covered his wiry frame.

While evaluating the conditions at the distant but alluring horizon, and noting the aesthetics of the scene in which he found himself, he became aware of a man standing among a small group of people assembled amidships. The man was wearing a bright green T-shirt and a red jacket, and he was gesturing toward Neil as he spoke to the woman next to him. Moments later he left the group and sprinted his way toward the bow along the outer railing of the ship. In a burst of youthful energy he hopped up the six steps leading to the forecastle deck. The man was nearly shouting when he said, "How are you, good sir?"

Neil, not quite sure what was up, responded cordially to the greeting, saying, "I am doing very well, thank you! And, you?"

"I'm doing great!" replied the man, brushing back a palm full of thick blond hair. "As a matter of fact this is a fantastic day."

"Indeed," acknowledged Neil, "it is."

"Hey, you must be a Britisher!" declared the impetuous gentleman, gripping the railing with one hand and pointing at Neil with the other. "I can tell by your accent."

"How observant," informed Neil, "but you will need to adjust your assessment."

"Why is that?" he asked.

"I am an American," stated Neil.

"Well, me too and proud of it!" declared the man, adamantly. "So, you must have been born over there?"

"No," returned Neil, "but I was there in my youth."

"So," he said, still persisting, "you're a member of the crew then?"

"No," returned Neil, resetting his gaze on the horizon, "I am not."

"Oh, I see," replied the man. Then, not to be deterred any longer, he offered up his hand for a vigorous shake, saying, "I'm Ted!"

"Pleased to meet you, Ted," acknowledged the resident of the forecastle deck. "You may call me Neil."

"Hey, Neil, nice ring you got there!" remarked Ted, immediately taking note of the leather band around the little finger on the hand he just shook—the ring was unusually wide, with the imprint of an ancient crest on it, and if it were to be examined closely the delicate design would reveal a shield, two lions, the sun, three arrows in a circle, and a dove with an olive branch—but Ted wasn't aware of that, he was only struck by the fact that it was leather, and confessed, "I once tied a leather string on my wrist so I wouldn't forget my wife's birthday."

"Did it work?" asked Neil.

"Yeah," sighed Ted, "but she never let me forget that string!"

"Hmm," returned Neil. "I see."

"Say," queried Ted, "you're not going to look at the sun with those binoculars are you?"

"That would be extremely unwise," informed Neil, dryly.

"For sure!" declared Ted. "Anyhow, isn't the sky clear?"

"On that I must agree," replied Neil.

"This is super!" added Ted. "I've been waiting a long time for this. I can't believe it's really here."

"It is quite an opportunity," replied Neil, putting the glasses to his eyes again.

"You bet!" declared Ted, now pointing up into the sky. "Just think, it's really going to happen. You know, right up there. Its like being an eye witness to creation!"

"I suppose you might use those terms," agreed Neil.

"I can't help but think about it," continued Ted, still voicing his excitement. "Do you think about it? You know, space, the planets, the universe and all that?"

"Actually, Ted, I do," remarked Neil, as he stopped to check the time on his phone.

"Why do you ask?"

"Oh, I don't know," returned Ted. "Hey, you must be an astronomer like some of the other guys!"

"Physicist," returned Neil, tersely.

"Well, I'm just an average guy with an average job," remarked Ted. "Look, that's my family down there on deck. The only one on the boat!"

"I see," returned Neil.

"Yeah," replied Ted. "Anyhow, whenever we go on a cruse or something I always get to know the crew. They've always got lots of interesting stories to tell, you know what I mean?"

"I believe you will discover a very fine crew here," informed Neil. "Stories they will surely have."

"Yeah," agreed Ted, then he glanced back at the group gathered amidships and saw his wife, Angela, motioning for him to return. "I'd better get back down there, it's just about show time!"

"Of course," replied Neil.

"Nice meeting you, man!" added Ted, as he turned to go.

"Have a good day," replied Neil. "Oh, and I must say, Ted, you are indeed fortunate to have your family with you."

"You bet!" replied Ted, as he scurried down the steps and followed the railing back to the small group. Neil kept his eyes on the man until he was reunited with his wife and daughter, then he politely raised his hand to them after the entire group cheerfully acknowledged him with a wave.

Excitement always runs high regarding the total eclipse of the sun. It also seems to draw out a fair degree of unease, yet it never ceases to trigger the imagination. The spectators watched the moon as it journeyed between the earth and the sun and as the brilliant light of midday grew dim. At the totality, an area of darkness called the umbra engulfed the ship and a verity of stars became visible to proclaim the mystery of the heavens one more time. But it was during the very apex of night at midday, a moment for which so many had prepared during the long months leading up to the event that interlopers appeared. They were almost imperceptible at first, becoming mere pinpoints of light traveling in slow motion across the sky through the eerie darkness and across the face of the eclipse. Neil observed them, as did many others on board the *Aries*. The first appeared like a shooting star with a slight tint of blue. Then a second phantom followed, a green point of luminescence tracing across the blackened disk of the moon. Both disappeared from sight shortly thereafter.

Neil searched for any lingering evidence of what he had just witnessed and remarked to himself, "Of course, even now they appear." He made a check of the time and pulled a pencil and small notebook from his pocket to make some calculations.

Ted immediately left the group amidships and headed for Neil. Even before his arrival he was firing questions in rapid succession. "Did you see those things? What do you suppose they are? Are they shooting stars? Are they meteors?"

"I cannot say exactly," answered Neil, with a relative calm.

"That was strange!" exclaimed Ted, "They couldn't be meteors could they?"

"Hmm," quipped Neil.

"What do you think they could be?" pressed Ted.

"I must only speculate at this point," returned Neil, as he made more marks on the pad.

Ted watched as Neil maintained his silence. Then seeing Neil was preoccupied, he said, "Hey, man, I see you're busy. I'll catch you later." Neil acknowledged Ted with a nod as the man reluctantly rejoined his family.

With no satisfactory explanation for the appearance of the strange lights the shipboard conversation quickly returned to the eclipse. Everyone was riveted to the spectacle as the moon pulled its vale from the sun. Soon midday would again be bathed in the full glory of the planet's nearest star.

An hour or so had passed and most people were still on deck to witness the diminishing effects of the eclipse. However, something else was about to command the attention of every person on the *Aries*. Ted was the first to notice it. A large circle had formed on the surface of the water about 600 feet off the starboard side of the ship. It appeared as if the sea itself had come to a boil, and Ted shouted, "Hey, look over there! Look at that!"

Neil observed the changing characteristic of the water through his glasses as everyone on the open decks surged to the starboard side of the ship to see what was taking place. Low frequency sound waves reverberated through the entire vessel as a small blue ethereal orb pierced the surface of the agitated water. The orb became part of an elongated cone or mast, this was followed by an assemblage of square gossamer sails but, unlike any ship of the sea, these sails pointed in all compass directions and were glowing with blue light. An identical arrangement could be seen on the underside as the thing steadily rose up out of the water. Although ethereal in appearance, it possessed an aural presence not unlike a thunderous melange of musical chords. Suddenly an object measuring more than 200 feet in diameter was free of the water. Once airborne, it became shrouded in mist. Then it rapidly accelerated away to the northwest, leaving wisps of vapor trailing behind it.

"Did you see that!" shouted Ted, as he came stumbling up the steps to where Neil stood.

"Indeed," replied Neil, looking out over the sea, seemingly with a mix of astonishment and confusion.

"What was that thing?" blurted Ted.

"Most unusual," replied Neil, squinting through the field glasses once more.

"Man," replied Ted, excitedly, "where do you think it came from?"

Neil took the glasses from his eyes and seemed to be at a loss for words as both men tried to process what had just happened, but then they noticed a small green point of light low on the horizon to the north. It steadily grew in size, because it was heading right for the ship at great speed. To the astonishment of everyone on board a massive green luminescence shot directly overhead. All of the people on the open deck instinctively ducked the menacing object, but Neil stayed glued to his spot, apparently unfazed, even as seconds later the object shot upward and vanished. Angela came running to the foot of the steps at the forecastle deck but made no attempt to climb up. She franticly pleaded for Ted to return with them to their cabin. He was about to oblige, but something was in the distance.

"Look out," cried Ted, "another one's coming!"

Within moments a churning mist thundered over the ship with an instant burst of wind. Everyone on deck cried out as warm droplets of water fell like a spring rain. By now the strange objects were no longer a novelty.

"Okay," remarked Neil, speaking to no one in particular, "I have some serious questions."

"What did you say?" asked Ted, not quite catching the words.

"We want to go inside," demanded the woman at the bottom of the steps. "We want to go now!"

"Come on, Daddy," cried his daughter. "I'm scared, I want to go in!"

"Okay," cried Ted, "okay, we'll go inside."

The voice of Capt. Nathaniel Harris was suddenly heard over the loud speakers, "Everyone must clear the deck and return to their cabins immediately. I repeat, for your own safety please return to your cabins immediately!"

The crew assisted in the evacuation, making sure no one was left on any of the open decks. Although Neil was hesitant, he responded to the captain's orders and followed behind the others as they flocked toward the main doorway amidships. He was the last one to reach the door, but just as he stepped inside Ted came up and grabbed his arm. It was with bewilderment in eyes, that he asked, "Do you think they're from outer space?"

"I cannot answer your question. I can only speculate," replied Neil.

"Speculate?" questioned Ted. "Somehow, you act like you've seen all of this before!"

"You are right, Ted," admitted Neil, "I have seen these things before but not quite in this context."

"You have?" replied Ted, excitedly. "When? Where?"

"I don't have the answers you are looking for," Neil replied. "This may be the first time for you, and in many ways it is for me. Right now we must do as the captain says."

"That's it?" replied Ted, exasperated.

"Forgive me if I am at a loss to explain," said Neil, sharing the man's frustration.

"But what could they be?" replied Ted.

"Actually," returned Neil, "we are both searching for the same thing."

"We are?" asked Ted. "And what is that?"

"The truth," remarked Neil.

"Truth?" questioned Ted.

"Yes," replied Neil.

"Yeah," groaned Ted, "well, if you say so."

Daylight was in abundance over the sea but all anyone could do aboard the *Aries* or, perhaps, all anyone wanted to do was to peer out of the windows and portholes in their cabins, feeling like so many prisoners bound for the unknown. Before long the captain set a course for the island of Oahu. In due time the bewildered passengers would be allowed to resume their normal routines without restrictions. Neil, however, remained cloistered in his cabin for the rest of the voyage.

Chapter Two: Reverie

In the cradle of the night I find repose,
Yet I am wide awake upon my bed,
Quite given to daydreams,
Ever captured by a divine reverie of heart.
Mari

Perhaps it was the heat, or it might have been the subtle fragrance of morning, or a gentle whisper from deep within her soul, nevertheless, Mari was awake. Her summer nightclothes felt much too warm, yet she lingered in her bed with a soft cotton sheet pulled up around her. By July 24, Wyoming had settled into a mid-summer swelter. The air outside of the partially open bedroom window barely animated the sheer white curtains hanging from the slender rod above it. A single night light created a gentle chiaroscuro effect in the room, leading the pensive young woman to gaze up at the delicate pattern stitched on the pure white canopy as it spread between the four tall bedposts.

Occasionally Mari would stay in bed to muse about things, but this time her thoughts returned to the new journal she had tucked away in her secretary desk. She stayed connected to the world by contemporary means, but the old desk provided a place of refuge when she was apt to find a few quiet moments alone. A small lamp with an amber glass shade occupied the right hand edge of the open writing surface. Next to the lamp sat a crystal bud vase with a single pink rose. By the vase lay yesterday's newspaper, but the wire frame glasses resting on it could not obscure the oversized letters on the front page: "Objects sighted over Bighorn Mountains, Wyoming on edge."

The sole occupant of the sumptuous bed and quiet chamber rose up to switch on the lamp. She adjusted the glasses on the bridge of her nose then rummaged through the bottom drawer of the desk, finally locating the leather bound book under a pile of loose paper. After pulling up a chair she let her lithe fingers stray through the virgin pages, slowly turning each leaf as if it were part of a volume already written. It beseeched her for words, but unlike a year ago she would answer: "Alas, another birthday has come and gone and I have yet to venture very far from home. So it is here within these blank pages where I will set free my captive thoughts and give chase to my elusive dreams...."

Although she was encouraged by the warm illumination of the lamp she was inclined to let her mind wander, now feeling quite unready to broach so many unwritten things. Her clear blue eyes turned their gaze on the glass doors of the desk to contemplate the contents within. She collected books and many other things as well, and the old shelving unit in the corner of the room stood as proof. On top were several aged hardcover editions carefully propped up by two angelic figurines, each of which appeared to be serenely watching over her small domain. The very bottom shelf burgeoned with several oversized copies on such subjects as music, architecture, and astronomy. But, curiously, with the exception of an ancient Bible, the two center shelves supported an odd variety of musical instruments. There where three tarnished silver flutes, one dented trumpet, a dulcimer without strings, one imperfect french horn, a piccolo, and one venerable clarinet. All of which had come to retain a certain romance for the eye, however, they no longer blessed the ear.

The old paper on the walls carried a busy pattern, but she still found a place for six framed pictures of wild flowers, a large Art Nouveau print of four young maidens depicting the four seasons of the earth, and three poignant photographs of her family. She had recently placed two used dresses over a petite wooden rocker and set a new pair of shoes near her closet door. The dresses needed to be taken in and the shoes had to wait for some reorganization to find a home.

Thoughts were still adrift as she swept several locks of dark brown hair behind her right ear. An ear of delicate form, youthful and fair with a single white pearl in the lobe. Even as her comely features were highlighted by the lamp, neither this, nor any other light would have revealed her unsolicited quietude. For her, silence was a virtue, yet on occasion she would lament, because she was profoundly deaf in the left ear and nearly so in the right. Mari could never hear the song of a meadowlark, even if it perched among the leaves of the towering ash that overshadowed her window to the east. Given this, her eyes were exceedingly sharp and very aware of the fragile daylight as it began to filter into the room.

The morning rays now combined with the light of the desk lamp and overpowered the night, causing the black form of a lonely violin case to become evident as it leaned against a rather heavy blue vase. The vase contained one umbrella that vividly displayed a field of stars in the clear night sky when fully open and one white parasol of delicate proportions leaning next to it. There were ten more umbrellas of varying designs residing in her closet, but the single parasol with a finely carved wooden handle had become her favorite. Yet, she regarded the violin above all else. She loved its smooth sensuous shape, rich finish, and savored the vibration of its strings when on occasion she guided her bow across them. Now lured by the thought of music she closed the journal. With unspoiled delight she floated across the oak floor to retrieve the instrument.

Recently, Mari had been informed that the music which flowed from the lustrous wooden body would at times provoke irritation on the part of those who loved her. Even so, she gently placed the case on the bed and retrieved the instrument with quiet anticipation. This was an early hour so for the moment she would use an imaginary bow. Sound was largely a tactile experience, but somehow music represented a special kind of freedom, just as she told herself she would someday travel far beyond the familiar walls of her room. When finished with her performance she carefully returned the instrument to its case.

Thus constrained only by the liberty of her own mind she returned to the journal, where, at the consummation of a few fleeting paragraphs she closed the cover. A new day beckoned, so she felt prompted to tiptoe over to the south facing window and part the curtains. She sought the ready handle on the sill and let her fingers grasp the smooth knob, then she confidently cranked the sash all the way open with a few deft turns. A scant breeze came drifting through the screen as the sun touched the horizon. All too soon the day would become clear and hot, but from this time forward Mari Abigail Cygnet was determined to keep a chronicle of reverie.

Chapter Three: Paradise

I long to board a ship and sail away to some far and distant land.
I would sit on some enchanting shore to watch the sea and sky,
And it would feel like paradise.
Mari

On July 27, in the early morning hours and one day ahead of schedule, the *Aries* docked at its home port, which was in a small harbor on the island of Oahu. The return voyage was uneventful and everyone disembarked shortly after the arrival of the ship, though Neil made sure he was the last passenger to leave the ship. Before disembarking, he spoke to Capt. Harris to express his appreciation for the voyage.

Later that same day he arranged for a ride to a remote location on the north side of the island. He located an obscure trail that twisted its way up the side of one of the steep mountain slope then began a vigorous climb. Eventually he reached a flat outcropping of rock near the summit. Once there, he pulled out a communication device and made a call.

He heard a clear voice ring out, saying, "Happy birthday old man!"

"Marcus," replied Neil, "thank you for remembering! Although, as you surely know, my birthday was days ago."

"On the sixteenth," replied the voice, "I know, but we missed you."

"I am glad someone did," returned Neil.

"We've had a rather peculiar time of it," came the reply.

"I would imagine," said Neil.

"But all is well," replied Marcus. "Specific information still eludes us and we would like to get your take on things."

"I cannot wait," returned Neil. "As you know, my perspective may vary a little."

"I bet," replied Marcus.

"You do not know how much I regret this self imposed exile," added Neil.

"Actually," affirmed Marcus. "I think I do."

"I am looking forward to returning to the fold," admitted Neil.

"We're on our way," encouraged Marcus.

"Good," replied Neil, expressing relief, "you know where to find me."

"Paradise?" asked Marcus.

"Of course," said Neil, as he keenly surveyed the view from his lofty vantage point.

The sun was well below the horizon as the man on the mountain top slipped his communication device back into his coat pocket and waited.

Chapter Four: Home

Although I follow The Bright and Morning Star,
I am still learning about faith, hope, and love,
And the blessings of home.
But I still wonder,
Will I find love on this terrestrial ball?
Mari

The chalk-line contrails of military aircraft had faded from the skies of Wyoming and a collection of orange tinted mare's-tales had taken their place. It is said this type of cloud often foretells a coming storm or a drastic change in weather, but this time they failed expectations, for there had been very little in the way of rainfall and it was close to becoming a season of drought. There were days of moderation but a second wave had arrived to oppress the land as temperatures in the flatlands and valleys contributed to cases of heat related illness among both man and beast. The dust of the parched land had invaded even the simple things. It coated windshields and dashboards and farm equipment. It sifted lightly through window screens to settle on every exposed surface within businesses establishments and homes. People and air conditioners struggled all across the wide expanse of Wyoming. Sturdy men in soiled work clothes wiped their brows, cold drinks were sold in generous quantities by pretty young ladies in company uniforms. It seemed as though everyone was feeling the pressure and longed for some kind of relief.

On August 23, one month from the time of the eclipse, moderate southwest winds once again carried dust from afar to create color in the atmosphere at the last light of day. By evening the eastern slopes of the Rocky Mountains cast enigmatic shadows and the forest hollows had succumbed to the disappearing light. In Campbell County, approximately fifty miles east of the Bighorn Mountain range, a stretch of rural pavement called Seven Mile Road ran serpentine across the land for twenty miles between highway 50 and 59. An unpretentious structure known as Grace Community Church stood on the outside of one of the gentle curves in the road. This thoroughly inviting nineteenth century house of God rested prominently on a generous knoll of scorched grass. The orange glow creatively painted on the uppermost part of the steeple had long since departed, but the light within the sanctuary brought to life each one of the stained glass windows.

On this particular Sunday the last chords of a jubilant melody trumpeted from a series of grand pipes nestled at the back of the church. The front doors were open wide and only a handful of people remained inside as Mari's bantam profile became framed within the entryway. A stout figure appeared behind her. Rev. Sterling protectively followed behind as she stepped out of the vestibule into the heavy night air. The reverend's usual coat and tie were absent because of the heat and he lingered in conversation with his newest parishioner, even though he found it difficult at times to communicate with the deaf. Mari was very aware of this and put him at ease with her gentle spirit and kind words. The evening message was about unmerited favor and the presence of God. Mari pondered those things as she drove her small white sedan out of the parking lot onto Seven Mile Road bound for Stone River.

A glorious host of stars were beginning to make themselves known but Mari's quick eye caught the movement of one small wayward light traveling over the mountains ahead of her. Suddenly two jets raced over the car. An instant later the light and the speeding planes vanished into the night. The presence of the Air Force signaled that the much appreciated respite from the noise in the sky had come to an end and there remained a nagging incertitude, especially when recalling recent news reports.

The welcome sign for Stone River came and went as she approached the town. Found to be typical of the region it supported its own school system, a grocery store, post office, hardware, tavern, and a few other essential businesses. A number of new lampposts had been placed on Main Street but very few improvements had been made through the years. These cast their light on old store fronts and dusty cars all through the night. Newly planted trees dressed up aging the sidewalks but each spindly wisp had wilted from the heat and only provided a limited amount of shade for the weary pedestrian.

Very little activity could be seen within the three story red brick Stone River Hotel as the white sedan rolled by. Then coming up on the right side of the street were some orange neon letters blazing the word Midway, shedding its light above the entryway of the local tavern. The large windows on either side of the door were clean and clear and the blinds were open to the night. This allowed its interior light to profile the six people gathered on the sidewalk, all of whom seemed to be talking at once and pointing to the sky. The gathering caught Mari's attention because she waited on tables at there the better part of each week. She was thankful for the employment but now she was just glad to have the day to herself.

South of town she made a right turn onto Landings Road, where the paved surface soon became gravel as it burrowed through a section of fertile agricultural land. Bales of hay loomed like giant wheels in the open fields. A little farther down the road a yard light shone brightly between a barn and a two and a half story house reminiscent of the Victorian era. The aging wooden barn had received a new coat of red paint and the house was the color of a clear Wyoming sky.

Mari traveled down the long drive toward the house and she could see her father standing prominently in the center the ample front porch. A light breeze had developed and there was just enough movement in the air to catch the blades of the old windmill in the back yard and it turned them with a noticeable squeak. She parked her car under the generous canopy supplied by three large ash trees and headed to the small east side porch. A flurry of insects buzzed around the yard light, but the warm glow from the kitchen window was as inviting as ever. She let the screen door shut with a notable clap as she entered the kitchen and was promptly greeted by the aroma of baked apples. In her lilting, somewhat breathy voice, she called out, "Mom? I'm home!"

When her mother heard the door and her daughter's voice she immediately left the living room and returned to the kitchen, saying, "Hi, dear, what took so long?"

"I know, I finally made it," stated Mari.

"Home so late?" questioned her mother, speaking softly, but reinforcing with deft sign language.

"The evening service started later than usual because of the heat and I stayed around to talk for a while," explained Mari, adding her own lively gestures to the conversation.

"How was it this evening?"

"I'm glad I got to stay and visit a while."

"Well, good for you, Honey, you need to get out more."

"It's really hot in this kitchen!"

"It's all this baking!" declared her mother, for it had been a long day and she was tired. Jennifer's graying hair was somewhat out of place and her usually neat appearance was disheveled. Yet, her only thoughts were of her daughter, so she gently combed back ample amounts of Mari's hair with her fingers, while her daughter carefully removed her hearing aid and slipped it into the pocket of her jeans. She always did this when she got home, like taking off a pair of tight fitting shoes after a long day.

Both mother and daughter supplemented their speech with visual communication. Sign language was almost akin to a private language between the two of them. Her father preferred not to be bothered by any outward display but her mother became skilled in their use. Mari's gestures literally danced with expressive hand movements and were often a pleasure to the observer.

When Mari inquired as to why her father was on the front porch, her mother heard the question but she didn't answer, instead, she pulled something out of her pocket and kept it wrapped in her hand, saying, "Mari, I have something for you. It's something I found this afternoon."

Jennifer now had her daughter's complete attention, and Mari quizzed, saying, "Mom? What is it?"

With signs and gestures only, Jennifer instructed her daughter to close her eyes and hold out her hands. Her daughter obediently cupped her palms as her mother dropped something into them. When Mari opened her eyes she was astonished, but she immediately recognized the small gold Mariner's Cross as it lay in her hands.

"Where ever did you find this?" replied Mari. "It's been years!"

Before Jennifer could answer the question the conversation was broken by the roar of low flying aircraft and a voice blared from the living room, saying, "Them!"

"Now, William," called Jennifer.

"What?" questioned Mari, unaware of her father's comments, still busy examining the pendant.

"Those planes," sighed her mother, "they irritate your father."

"They're only trying to help," replied Mari.

"Just wasting their time and our money!" cried her father, preaching from the dining room arch. "They can send those planes and those agents back to where they came from. Now they're crawling all over the place. Some guy was asking questions in town yesterday out in front of the hardware."

"You've been getting worked up all week now, dear," cautioned Jennifer. "Sarah Craig said she saw something the other day, some lights by her house and you know she's not one to tell stories, but she's not all worked up about it."

William countered, saying, "She's probably just seeing things. Why don't they spend their time on the real issues? Take the local rabble for instance, like that guy Toller and those buddies of his. They can come out here and break into our barn and guess what? Nobody cares! And who knows what happened to our cattle? And what about the horses? They're still spooked. If I'd been here they wouldn't have gotten away with it. My shotgun would have done them some good!"

"Now, William," admonished Jennifer, sitting down at the table, "you don't know if it was those boys. What if you're wrong?"

"They're always up to no good," replied William

"What do you think about it, Mari?" signed Jennifer, turning to her daughter.

Mari shrugged her shoulders. Trouble was the last thing she wanted to think about. Her mind was elsewhere as she wrapped the fine gold chain of the pendant around her fingers, savoring distant thoughts and pleasant memories.

"So what about the Sanders?" scowled William in rebuttal. "Did you know they lost a couple of horses a few weeks ago? They just up and died. I wouldn't put it past some people around here. Who knows, Jennifer, who knows?"

"I didn't hear such a thing," countered Jennifer. "I saw Clara yesterday and she never said anything."

"You can't depend on anybody anymore," added William. Then he looked his daughter squarely in the eye and shook his finger at her. "Mari, I don't want you to go off riding like you do. No more riding in the back country! Hear me?"

"What's wrong with my riding?" answered Mari, with instant irritation.

"The horses are out of sorts," replied her father, "and you don't know who might be out there."

"King is okay!" protested Mari.

"Maybe so," enforced her father, "but I don't want you out there by yourself. Things aren't exactly right, you never know what you're going to find."

Jennifer added sign language to make sure Mari got the warning from her father.

"Okay, okay," replied Mari, recoiling at the scolding, "if you say so."

"You be careful, young lady," instructed her father again. "Sometimes you're prone to wander, you just keep it close to home for now."

"Wander?" questioned Mari, with irritation evident in her voice. "I might be deaf, but I'm not a kid anymore."

After his final admonition her father disappeared into the living room. Mari didn't try to defend herself any further, yet she felt her father's accusation was unfair. He thought she was given to bouts of aimless wandering but she considered her excursions to be a form of independence and adventure.

"I know you can take care of yourself, dear," encouraged Jennifer, knowing her daughter could be stubborn at times. "This is all going to pass. They'll find out what's going on. Give it some time."

"But," countered Mari, "it's just that—"

"Now, your father is worried about you," injected her mother, "and frankly, I am too, and that's just how it is."

Mari's attention returned again to the pendant for it had been a long time since she held it in her hands. There was no great monetary value involved, but the pendant was a well crafted representation of a ship's wheel with an anchor and rope. After a few minutes she returned to the conversation, and asked, "Mom, where ever did you find this?"

"I was helping your father clean up in the barn this morning," replied her mother. "Something shiny caught my eye and there it was, it was just hanging on a hook by the sliding door to the corral!"

"How strange!" replied Mari, still thinking about the time she lost it. "Grandpa gave it to Grandma before they were married and she kept it all those years. Grandma gave it to me when I was a kid and I lost it. I always wondered what happened. Why would it turn up now?"

"I don't know, dear," returned her mother, mystified, but unconcerned.

"I wonder what it means?" returned their ever inquisitive daughter.

"Oh, Mari, you think about things too much," cautioned her mother. "Just be glad you got it back."

"I'd just like to know that's all," she replied softly, still gazing at her lost treasure, but her face suddenly fell to the concern for her mother who was now sitting at the kitchen table looking far older than she did only moments before. Jennifer had become lulled by the rhythmic sound of the old clock by the back door and hypnotized by the images of the slow blades of the fan overhead as they reflected off the curved neck of the faucet on the sink.

"What is it Mom?" asked Mari.

The gaze of mother and daughter chanced to meet, then Jennifer asked rather sheepishly, "Do you think those things are really from outer space?"

Mari put the pendant in her pocket and examined the checkerboard pattern of the black and white floor tiles as she thought about what her mother said, then replied, "I don't know what to think, I don't like the thought of aliens from outer space any more than you do. There's enough trouble down here. Anyhow, somebody came into the tavern the other day and asked me if I'd seen anything. I said no, Mom, and that's the truth." Mother and daughter communicated at times with words unspoken, but there seemed to be an uncomfortable distance growing between them. Mari had returned from college with an expanded view of the world and she was still trying to piece it all together. "I did see something tonight though, while I was on my way home, a small light in the sky over the mountains. Then I saw some of those planes. I've never seen any of the stuff like they've been showing in the news."

"Well, we won't worry about it," consoled Jennifer, "if there is anything out there, they'll find out what it is and they'll take care of it."

Mari approached the open window over the sink and looked out at the barn across the driveway where she happened to notice Meadow, her cat, stalking something in the yard so she ran to the door and called out to her. The animal immediately came running into the house. Mari picked up the pet and cuddled it in her arms, stroking the pure white fur. Then becoming introspective, she said, "I know Meadow doesn't care much about space, but I think humanity still has the need to explore. There's so much we could learn about the universe and ourselves. God willing, someday we might explore far and distant worlds. I'd like to study science or something but I like to be down earth too." The cat meowed and flashed its big blue eyes at her owner then squirmed, so Mari let the cat jump to the floor and run into the living room. "Still, there are times when I feel like a total stranger. Its as if I don't belong anywhere. People are always so suspicious, they don't like it when something or someone is different. Especially when they find out that I'm deaf or if they see me using sign language. They all run the other way or something. I haven't found my place yet, but I guess only God knows what the future holds. As the Bible says, '...we know that all things work together for good to them that love God, to them who are the called according to his purpose.'" (5)

"Now, Mari, you can't mind what other people say," cautioned her mother. "You're our daughter and we're proud of you. You're a dreamer and that's okay, but you just need to be more practical sometimes. Like you say, its all in His hands."

"I'm doing some reading," returned Mari, "and I'm learning. I don't have it all put together, but someday I'll figure it out."

The pendulum of the wall clock swung back and forth between the past and the future as she bent down and peeked through the oven door. The pastry needed a little more time so she lingered in the kitchen. The oscillating fan on the counter made little headway against the heat as it occasionally whisked warm air over the young woman's face, only managing to imperceptibly rearranged a few delicate strands of her hair.

Jennifer got up to give her daughter a hug, and said, "I try not to let things get to me too much, but there is one thing I do worry about."

"What's that, Mom?"

"I worry about you working at the tavern all the time."

"Why?"

"I wish you would find something different."

"But—"

"Honey, it isn't the best place for you."

Mari could read the concern in her mother's eyes, but she countered, "I know, but it's only for a little while longer. I'm waiting to hear from an architectural firm in Cheyenne, they promised to call next week. Besides, Peg keeps order around there."

"Didn't you say there was something in Casper?" asked Jennifer.

"I'm going to take a look next week if I don't hear anything from Cheyenne."

Her mother got up and checked the oven. "Maybe you ought to find something in Gillette, one of your friends moved over there not to long ago. You could do better that's all."

"Believe me," replied Mari, "I'd like to get out of that place but Peg says she re-

16

ally needs me."

"There are other things in life to think about," said her mother, "you can't wait forever to start a family."

"I don't want to rush into anything," said Mari. "It'll all work out."

"Maybe so," returned her mother, "but you've got to consider it."

"How are those things doing in there?" asked Mari, nodding in direction of the oven.

"Yes, my dear," remarked her mother, "it is time."

Now glancing around the kitchen, Mari found the counters laden with dishes and pans. "I'll help you clean this up, Mom, you just rest."

Mari ran water in the sink while she gathered the mixing bowls, tins and utensils as one by one her mother removed the delicately browned pastries from the oven and placed them on the table to cool. Three tins happened to slip out of Mari's hands and landed on the hard floor with a clatter. One rolled into the dining room but the other two fell nearby resting rim on rim.

"I'll get those," declared Jennifer.

"No, no, I'll take care of it, Mom," insisted Mari. " You just relax." She recovered the tins and sunk them into the water as a sweet aroma found their way into the rest of the house and out through the open windows into the heavy night air. Air that would take the entire night to cool down.

The Cygnet ranch was one of many scattered across the expanse of open land, a land now covered by a large dome of stars running from horizon to horizon. The house possessed a dignified charm as it stood prominently in the well manicured yard surrounded by beds of flowers. A fence with a white arbor of red and white roses divided up a portion of the lawn in the front yard. Beyond the western edge of the yard stood acre upon acre of forest land. And, between the dense living timber and the side of the house were twelve pear trees, which encircled a large gazebo reminiscent of an era that seemed long gone. At his daughter's request, William found an old mailbox somewhere long ago and attached it to a post by the southern entry of the structure. Here in this humble shelter Mari would draw and write, occasionally filling the mailbox with secret letters, pretending to receive lengthy correspondence. She also spent many hours talking with imaginary friends and curious members of the animal kingdom. Although her imagination was free to roam, the ranch itself was very real and she did her share of the work when called upon. She highly regarded the center of the family's economy and appreciated the living they derived from livestock and rotation crops.

Mari had been adopted at the age of two and remained an only child, but her parents loved her and considered her as their own flesh and blood. Her features even reflected the dark hair of her father as well as the bright blue eyes of her mother. When she was a teen, Mari was mercilessly taunted by her peers for her slight frame, the silence of her ears and incessant daydreaming. What she lacked in natural endowments she made up for in stamina and uncommon poise. She loved Wyoming and her roots were deep, however, it was hard for her to entertain thoughts of staying on the ranch or in the same small town for the rest of her life.

The Midway Tavern always seemed to be a hive of activity and Peg Moore toiled long hours to further the business. She made no specific changes to the structure after she acquired it, but her industry kept good food on the table. She relied heavily on her capable staff, one of whom was Linda Bain. The woman took over the duties of head cook nearly two years ago when business began to increase. Old photographs of the town hung on walls of aging green paint and vintage tools were secured on high shelves. Several large fans hung from the ornate tin ceiling to move hot air from one corner of the dining room to another. An early twentieth century bar with eight stools occupied the south side of the room. A large mirror surrounded by an ornate frame was mounted behind the bar and the two shelves near the bottom were always overstocked with the bottles of the trade.

On most Sundays it wasn't unusual for people to fill up the dining area or arrive alone to sit at the bar. So it was in the lingering warmth of the evening when Neil Clayborn came in to take a seat. His plaid shirt, jeans, and leather boots allowed him to blend in with the resident population. The wide brimmed hat he used to keep the sun at bay rested on the bar next to him and his eyes were soon hidden behind a pair of reading glasses. He scanned the local newspaper as he sipped on a cup of black coffee. The only remnant of his shipboard attire was the leather band on his finger.

He had only been there about twenty minutes when a man by the name of Frank Niverson came walking through the front door and found a seat at the bar next to Neil. A woman immediately arrived behind the bar to wait on her customer. Her short unnaturally blond hair seemed to make her eyes look overly large, but she cheerfully greeted the newest arrival, saying, "Hi there, how are you this evening?"

Frank instantly read her name tag, then boldly commanded, "Nancy, how about one of those dark beers." She obediently recited the selection on hand and he responded. "Make it that last one."

"Good choice," returned the bar keeper as she reached for a bottle in the cooler. Then she filled a glass and pushed it towards her customer with a flirtatious smile. Frank grabbed the foaming brew and the woman disappeared into the kitchen. He first gave Neil a penetrating look then turned his eyes to the mirror, where he intently studied his own ruffled image. Nancy returned from the kitchen and busied herself by shuffling bottles around on the shelf by the mirror, but she had one eye trained on Frank as he lifted a pack of cigarettes from his pocket. When he opened the box Nancy admonished him. "We're nonsmoking in here you know."

"Yeah, yeah," said Frank, "maybe I like the smell of fresh tobacco."

"Just so you know," returned Nancy.

"Fresh," repeated Frank, appearing a bit agitated. Then he pulled a cigarette out of the pack and slowly ran it under his nose to catch all of the aroma. Neil tried to mind his own business as the man next to him rolled the soft aromatic stick between his fingers and located the lighter in his pocket. Next, he put the cigarette between his lips and provocatively ignited a flame on the lighter while eyeing Nancy. Nancy stared back. Frank smirked in defiance then put out the flame, after which, he carefully slipped the unlit cigarette back into the pack and tossed the lighter on the bar. Then he glared at Neil, saying, "What about you, have you seen anything unusual lately?"

Neil took his eyes from the paper, and said, "You're asking a question?"

"Yeah, I'm asking you," replied Frank, as he snatched the lighter back. "I'm interested in people and I'm interested in things."

"Is that so?" commented Neil, remaining cordial, but keeping his distance. "What kind of things?"

"Objects. Objects in the sky," stated Frank, casually.

"Hmm," returned Neil, not committing.

"You must have some opinions?" declared Frank.

"Of course," replied Neil, hesitating a bit, "I would like to know what's going on just like anyone else."

The two men gazed down at their drinks as the six people who had been standing on the sidewalk in front of the tavern finally decided to return inside. They were giving up in mild frustration, having not seen anything of substance. There were no lights in the sky, there were no more planes thundering overhead, and the excitement had evaporated.

"So," inquired Neil, "what have you seen?"

"You presume there are things I haven't said," replied Frank, "well, they say the people around here don't like strangers, but I don't mind asking the questions. Well, such as it is, what do you know of that incident in the Pacific?"

"The ocean?" asked Neil, appearing surprised.

"Is there another?" condescended Frank. "It was all over the news world wide."

"Yes," replied Neil, "something flew over the water out there."

"And out of the water," added Frank.

"Oh, Yes, of course," replied Neil. "I get the feeling you are not from around here."

"You could say I'm a visitor," remarked Frank. "By the way, I wonder if you might know someone by the name of Jed Mullen?" A wrinkle appeared on Neil's brow but he let man continue with his questioning. "How about Elias Parson?"

"No," replied Neil, "I don't know him."

"I haven't paid Parson a visit yet," said Frank, "but I spoke to Jed about a month ago...just before he died."

The brown liquid in Neil's cup had grown cold but he drank it anyway, then said to Frank, "It looks as though I cannot be of much help to you."

"Mullen predicted the appearance of those objects at the time of the eclipse," informed Frank.

"I didn't hear anything of that in the news," replied Neil, blankly.

"No," said Frank, "you wouldn't have. I have my sources."

"I see," was Neil's only response.

"There was some kind of connection," revealed Frank. "He also mentioned someone by the name of John Shepherd. He said he died on Thunder Peak some years ago along with some others. Did you ever know Shepherd?"

"I believe I heard something about it," replied Neil. "I guess it was big news at the time, yes, some of the locals told me about it. This may be a poor excuse but I have not been out here for very long. I am still getting to know the folks in this area."

"Everyone has an excuse," replied Frank, turning to the mirror again.

Neil folded the newspaper and laid it aside as Frank retrieved the pack of cigarettes from his pocket and opened the box. Then Neil said, "Well, on that note, I must add one more excuse to your list. I really must be going."

"So soon?" countered Frank as he closed the box.

Nancy cleaned the bar in front of Neil, scrubbing it with long aggressive strokes, saying, "More coffee?"

"No," replied Neil, "thank you, everything's fine."

"Hey," cried Nancy, glaring at Frank, "you know what I said about that."

"Yeah, yeah," muttered Frank as he slipped the box back in his pocket.

"Another beer?" asked Nancy, with a stern face.

"Beer," he replied.

"Okay then," returned Nancy.

"As you know," added Frank, "the dust gets thick out there."

"Right you are!" returned Nancy.

"How about your name?" questioned Frank, directing his attention back to the man about to leave.

"It's Neil. And yours?"

"Frank. So, Neil, where are you from?"

"Out East."

"How far east? You may look the part, but your speech doesn't seem to go with that plaid shirt of yours."

"Hmm," grunted Neil. "You may not prefer the manner in which I speak, nonetheless, my words serve me."

"All I was saying—" returned Frank.

"I'm just stating a fact," continued Neil.

Nancy pushed a cold brown bottle toward Frank, saying, "Here you go." And the man impatiently grabbed the bottle as Nancy shook her head.

"I like facts," said Frank, engaging Neil. "Will I see you again?"

"Maybe," replied Neil, putting on his hat. Then after placing several bills on the counter he got up from the bar. "Have a good evening Frank and good luck quitting."

"I don't give up on things easily," replied Frank, as he put away the cigarettes.

"No doubt," agreed Neil.

Frank gazed back into the mirror. Although, as soon as he heard the front door click shut Frank ran to over to the front windows to watch the man as he crossed the street, lingering on his subject as he got into a dark blue Jeep and pulled away.

Flickering images played across a video screen mounted high in the back corner of the room. Several lights were moving through the night sky as a local reporter was interviewing someone who seemed willing to talk. Lips were moving without sound as informative crawls traced the bottom of the screen. No one in the tavern seemed to be paying any attention, for the Midway always reverberated with the sound of popular music and the din of local gossip.

The Jeep rolled to a stop by one of the pumps at a small gas station and repair center outside of town called Al's. Lights were shining brightly overhead, chasing the night away from the gas pumps as Neil got out and promptly began to service his vehicle. The building was in mild disrepair and old car parts spilled out from the back of it. Used tires filled an open shed next to the building and there was a truck parked nearby with the hood ajar. The garage consumed nearly half of the building and both doors were up. A red car missing a grill and a fender could be seen inside one of the bays. While Neil was at the pump a man in greasy overalls and a yellowing T-shirt strolled out carrying a fresh supply of paper towels for one of the dispensers. He called out to Neil, "How are you doing over there?"

"Okay, how about you?" replied Neil.

"Real fine," replied the man, as he jammed the towels into the small box on a post between the pumps. "You know, I haven't seen that Jeep of yours around here before. You aren't one of them investigator guys are you?"

"No," returned Neil, "I am not one of them."

"There's a guy been poking his nose around here asking lots of questions about them lights," said the man. "You haven't heard about those lights or what have you?"

"Well, Yes," said Neil, "I heard some things. What about you?"

"About them lights?" answered the man. "I only heard about them, I haven't seen anything. I heard some crazy stuff though. Some people around here say they seen things but not me, nope, I don't go around spreading nonsense."

Neil returned the nozzle to its slot in the pump and walked over to the man and handed him some crisp currency, saying, "Keep the change."

"Thanks," replied the man, quickly counting the money and sporting a broad smile. "So, I see you're not from around here?"

"That is correct," said Neil. "Are you the owner?"

"Yeah, I'm the owner, I'm Al," returned the man. "Say, are you out here on vacation then?"

"No," said Neil, "actually, I just bought a place not to long ago. I have only been out here a few weeks."

Al's eyes grew wider, saying, "Well, there's good land out here, hope you like the territory."

"I do," informed Neil, "very much so."

"Say," said Al, "you might find some folks are kind of funny around here. They're a different sort. Most don't talk much, some do and some are saying some crazy stuff, jumpy, you know what I mean?"

"Care to elaborate?" replied Neil.

"Nope," returned Al, "I'm just saying."

"Well, Al," said Neil, with a friendly return, "thank you for the gas and the heads up."

"You take it easy," added Al, "and if you ever need that thing repaired we can do it here!"

"I will be sure to remember that," replied Neil.

Al put his hands in his pockets and slowly sauntered back to the garage as Neil pulled away. He grabbed a broom and began to sweep the dust and stones from the oily floor of the open bay out onto the cracked and pitted asphalt. Small clouds of dust puffed up from the broom as he swept. He mumbled to himself, "I just don't know about some of these people. I just don't know."

Chapter Five: Occurrences

I never weary of the grandeur.
I love this land,
But what of these strange occurrences?
I pray for rain.
Mari

On Monday, August 24, the heat continued to plague the land, while high above the earth in the cold vacuum of space satellites were still providing insufficient data, which relegated any anomalies to the unknown. Yet, the armed forces had several opportunities to pursue a number strange objects over the Bighorn Mountains but there was little to show for their effort. Be it hearsay or provable fact, anything of note was voraciously eaten up by the anxious press. Some people braved ridicule, insisting they saw strange creatures or described the beings as looking like small children. Others, it seemed, insisted the creatures were dark and hidden by the shadows of the night. Still others said they saw silver men without faces. All this played against a backdrop of conjecture, but it was the distance between knowing and not knowing that kept nerves on edge.

A thread of truth could usually be uncovered in an honest report, which usually turned out to be known aircraft or some kind of man-made object. However, simple explanations were often given by the authorities to convince the untrained observer that he or she may have mistaken everyday objects for something else. Fears could often be put to rest and the observer consoled by the realization that the thing they saw was a common occurrence. Even so, various countries and nations saw a marked increase in unexplained sightings. Each reacted differently, some were wary, and others extended friendly invitations to any would-be alien visitors. As time went on the reports concerning green or amber objects received the most favor by the press, but the singular blue light as seen of late had been regarded with a high degree of suspicion.

Many agencies around the world were commissioned to look into such phenomenon and the United States Air Force was conducting its own investigation as well. The task was to some extent reminiscent of past efforts by the military to get answers. This time their search put several of its personnel on a circuit to interview a sampling of the local population. It was in the early part of the afternoon of the 24th, when the investigation took two officers to the home of a six year old boy on a ranch located 60 miles south of Stone River. Colonel Robert Hanover and Lieutenant Stanley Kilborn had just arrived in Wyoming to look into some of the possible sightings. It had been reported that Edward and Martha Durnat's grandson, Timothy, had seen a light come down from the sky. The young boy insisted he saw something land on his grandparents property. He also said he saw a creature of some kind.

The sun scorched the ground and the air felt hotter than ever as Col. Hanover and Lt. Kilborn drove the large important looking sedan down a country lane that passed some dilapidated buildings and a weather beaten barn, finally rolling to a stop next to a small white house. The men looked at one another with lingering doubts, both sharing the same skepticism over what they might find. They mounted the small front porch and Lt. Kilborn knocked on the door. Soon they were greeted by an elderly couple. The lieutenant introduced himself and with some reluctance the men were let inside. The crisp military uniforms were impressive as well as intimidating, but the residents were courteous and offered their guests comfortable chairs in their modest living room. The couple explained they had not seen anything of consequence and that the boy, now playing outside somewhere, had made up the entire story.

Conversation was cordial but it was fast becoming another dead end, when, suddenly the playful laughter and the whoop of a child echoed through the front yard. A pair of small hurried feet scampered up onto the porch. Then, totally unaware of the guests inside the house, a young boy flung open the front door and nearly jumped into the room. The play and laughter faded when he saw his grandparents and the men in uniform staring at him, so he decided it was time to hide behind his grandmother's large rocker.

"Now, Timmy," admonished his grandmother, "you go back out and play, you let grandma and grandpa talk to these officers."

"He looks like a nice young man," said Col. Hanover "Won't you please let us speak to the boy?"

The youngster peeked out from behind the rocker momentarily, only to duck back out of sight as each person studied the face of the other in the room. The colonel was about to state his case once more when, still unseen behind the chair, the boy blurted out, "I saw monsters!"

Everyone grew quiet, then the boy's grandfather scolded, "Now, Timmy, don't you go talking such nonsense. You go back out and play."

"Sir," begged Hanover, "if you don't mind, we would like to ask the boy some simple questions. It won't take long."

"He likes to make up stories," said his grandmother, "you know little boys, how they are."

"I'd like to speak with him all the same if you don't mind," insisted Col. Hanover. "We'll let him tell us in his own words then we'll be on our way." The grandfather nodded his approval so Hanover turned to the boy, and said, "Now, son, won't you come out so we can see you and we can talk?" There was silence behind the chair. "Would you like to tell me your name?"

"Timmy," declared the boy, from behind the chair.

"Timmy," replied Col. Hanover, "why, that's a nice name, and you look like a very fine young man. My name is Robert and I heard about your story. Wouldn't you like to tell me all about it?"

The grandparents began showing more apprehension but kept to themselves as Col. Hanover politely said, "Please, tell us about what you saw. Don't be afraid, I'm sure you would like to tell us all about it and we would like to hear your story."

Timmy crawled out from behind the chair and stood next to his grandmother, his clothes and his bare feet were covered with dust and dirt from hours at play. He fidgeted as though he would bolt for the door when he got the chance, occasionally scratching his left toe against his right foot. Keenly he eyed the men who sat so very stiffly in the overly soft chairs, after which, he looked up to see his grandfather's stern face. Then a boyish grin spread from ear to ear and he turned to the officers and stretched out his arms from side to side as far as he could reach, saying brashly, "It was big. It was really big and I was by the pond and I saw a really big light way up high!"

"You did?" replied Hanover, responding to the boy's enthusiasm. "Then what happened?"

"It came down and it was like a big monster!" cried Timmy. "I hid behind a tree!"

"Were you scared?" asked the Hanover.

"Sort of," returned Timmy.

"Did you run away?" asked Lt. Kilborn.

"I stayed behind the tree," said Timmy, proudly.

"What kind of monster was it, son?" asked Hanover.

"A sea monster!" declared Timmy.

There was a moment of nervous silence, then the boy's grandfather broke in with an unexpected twinkle in his eye, and said, "Jellyfish."

"A water creature?" questioned the colonel.

Edward injected. "The boy pointed it out to me in one of those kid books of his. He's always in those books. He's got a big imagination, makes stuff up all the time, probably saw the picture and made up the whole thing."

"Timmy," said Hanover, "you aren't making up the story are you?"

"Nope," insisted the boy, shaking his ruffed head of hair.

"Is that all you saw?" asked Hanover, again trying to clarify the story. The boy looked around at the adults without saying anything more so the officer continued the questioning. "Son, what else did you see?"

Timmy's grandfather took this opportunity to get up from his chair and head for the boy's room. He soon returned, paging through a colorful children's book on creatures of the sea, then came up to Col. Hanover and opened the book somewhere in the middle, he pointed to a glossy picture and handed it to the officer, saying, "That's it."

Col. Hanover took the book from the man and studied the photograph, turning the book sideways, then righting it again as his eyes scoured a large picture of a Solmissus suspended in deep blue water. Other examples of sea life appeared on the opposite page, all with detailed captions. Hanover held the book up for the boy to see and pointed to the jellyfish, saying, "Is this what you saw?"

He slowly nodded his head in affirmation, saying, "It was really big!"

"Was it like any of these others?" asked Hanover, showing the boy pictures of the creatures on the opposite page.

"Nope," returned the boy, "not those."

"Timmy," said Hanover firmly, "would you tell us about it?"

"Yup," replied Timmy, now realizing the men were actually listening to him.

"They waved to me."

"They?" asked the lieutenant. "Who waved to you? The jellyfish?"

"Two silver men," replied Timmy. "They went by the pond. Then they went into the monster and then it went up in the sky again. It went up really, really fast!"

"Well, at least we have friendly monsters!" laughed Hanover, nervously, but he continued his questioning. "What did the silver men do by the pond?"

"They walked around," answered the boy, as a matter of fact.

"Then what?" added Hanover.

"They waved goodbye," returned the boy.

"Son, you don't want to lie do you?" demanded Hanover as he looked to the lieutenant in disbelief. "Is it the truth?"

"Yes, mister," insisted the boy.

"You're not telling us big stories from this nice book?" asked Hanover, giving the boy his most important looking face.

"Nope," replied Timmy, meekly shaking his head again.

"Was anybody else there with you?" asked the lieutenant. "Did anybody else see it?"

"Nope, just me," said Timmy, then he looked down at the carpet and dragged his big toe playfully across it as he smiled broadly.

Col. Hanover cleared his throat and was about to ask another question when the boy raised his arms above his head, and exclaimed again, "It went way up in the sky!"

"How far?" asked Hanover.

"Way, way up!" exclaimed the boy,"

Then Col. Hanover pulled a small photograph from his pocket with evidence of the misty blue object witnessed by those aboard the *Aries* during the eclipse. He showed it to the boy, and asked, "Did it look like this?"

Timmy shook his head no, saying, "It was a jellyfish!"

"See," said the boy's grandfather, "he makes up stories from those books of his."

Hanover handed the picture to Edward, saying, "Have you ever seen anything like this?"

Edward handed the photograph back to the colonel, saying, "No sir, we've never seen anything like that."

Col. Hanover turned to the young child, saying, "Thanks, Timmy, you've been a good boy."

Timmy then took off running, pretending to be a jet plane as he darted through the living room and out the front door, sailing down the porch steps to run in the yard.

Lt. Kilborn turned to the Col. Hanover, and remarked, "Should we wrap this up?"

"Definitely," replied Hanover, then he tuned to the old couple. "Now, Mr. and Mrs. Durnat, are you absolutely sure you did not see anything that evening?"

"We're sure," said Edward. "Like I said, the boy's got a big imagination these days."

"When did he first tell you the story?" asked the colonel.

The woman tried to recall, finally she said, "Oh, it was about a month or so ago, I suppose."

Lt. Kilborn gave Col. Hanover a doubtful glance, then Hanover looked at his watch and said, politely, "Well, we must be on our way. Thank you for your cooperation. If any thing develops we may be back. We'll let you know."

"Of course," returned Mr. Durnat, cheerily, "come again anytime."

Both men bid their hosts goodbye. The intense heat of the sun penetrated their dark uniforms as they walked to the car and all the more so as the men entered the smothering vehicle.

Kilborn took off his hat and wiped the sweat from his face, and complained, "What is it with this heat?"

"I don't know," replied Hanover, "but it needs to end right along with all this nonsense. This is a useless waste of time. I don't think we'll find any answers here. A jellyfish in Wyoming?"

At three p.m. special investigator Frank Niverson had some unfinished business. He decided it was time to see Elias Parson, a resident of the region near Thunder Peak in the vicinity of White Lake. Elias was known to chase off trespassers with a gun but Frank wasn't about to let that thwart his efforts. He located a rarely traveled road and followed it as it twisted its way upward at a fairly steep grade. The dark green pickup was working hard as it cut through heavily forested areas. The road forked off twice to locations unknown until it became a two-track path, the tires churning up large amounts of dust with each labored revolution.

About the time he began to wonder if he had the right trail he came to an opening and stopped the truck. After rolling down the dust covered window he cast his eyes on old gray shack surrounded by some twisted pines. The shelter was covered with an uneven distribution of boards and tarpaper along with several other kinds of building material added into the mix. It appeared as though it was struggling to remain upright and would collapse from the next mischievous wind. Quite possibly the thoroughly rusted antique truck sitting by the side of the building was helping to hold it upright. Odd pieces of scrap metal were scattered around the property, likely the remains of old machinery scavenged from other refuse piles miles away.

Only a few seconds had passed before a black Lab bolted from behind the shack barking and snarling at his perceived intruder. Frank grimaced at the dog and knew its owner would appear shortly. Sure enough a bearded man with gray hair, ragged overalls, and a sleeveless shirt emerged from the shadow of the open doorway. He came ambling toward the truck with a double barrel shotgun in his hand. In no time at all the gun was pointed squarely at Frank's face, which was conveniently framed by the open window of the truck.

"Your on private property, Mister," growled the man.

"I'm looking for Elias Parson," replied Frank, squinting into the sun.

"Why do want to talk to him?" retorted the old man.

"I need to ask him a few questions," replied Frank, to the muzzle of the gun.

"Well, I'm Elias and I don't talk to strangers," said the man, now defensively waving the firearm in the direction of the road. "You better get off my property!"

"My name is Frank, I only need a minute of your time. We have reports coming in about some unusual activity around these mountains."

Elias eyed Frank, then directed a brief command at the dog, "Sonny, simmer down!"

Frank was determined not to leave without further inquiry so he slowly opened the door of the truck. Elias stepped back and the dog snarled as Frank calmly slid out of the seat to confront the man. The gun was now leveled at Frank's chest and he slowly raised his hands, saying, "Just a minute of your time, that's all."

"You got one minute!" demanded Elias.

"I want to know if you've seen anything unusual up here," said Frank.

"Why is that?"

"The government is interested in what's going on."

"Gov'ment, of course, but I'm legal!"

"Maybe so, but there are some things going on you might know about."

"Like what?"

"That's what I'm asking you," said Frank, as he slowly pulled out some identification, and said, "FBI. We've been looking into some reports concerning some unusual objects or lights in and around these mountains. I heard you might know something."

"I don't know what you heard," said Elias, "but you better never mind. Nothing's around here anybody wants."

"I saw a friend of yours the other day, a man by the name of Jed," answered Frank. "Jed Mullen...I talked to him just before he died."

Elias froze for a moment and said nothing. He lowered the gun and looked to the ground as if learning about the unexpected loss of a relative. Although the news seemed to catch him off guard, he said, "Well...he was up here for about five years on an' off till he got to wheezin'. He took sick a couple of months ago. Had to go find a doctor. They said he needed to go to the hospital. I Really liked that guy. Wait a minute, how'd you know him?"

Elias trained the gun on Frank again with renewed suspicion, but Frank continued, "The point is, he knew you. We had a short conversation and he kept repeating something, he said, 'There will be lights in the sky at the eclipse.' What do you make of it?"

"What's it to you?" replied Elias.

"It's my job to find out," said Frank.

"Well, the gov'ment is too nosy," replied Elias.

"What I'm saying is, he knew about the event before it ever happened," said Frank. "He knew about the objects during the eclipse. It was confirmed by witnesses."

"People is always seein' things," said Elias.

"It was verified," informed Frank.

The dog lifted a leg and moistened the left front tire of the truck, then Elias said, "Jed was always talking about strange things. I thought he was crazy in the head, you know, not right and all. He was kind of a professor once, but his drink got 'em. He said he met some people years ago and they was talkin' about that atomic stuff or whatever. He wanted to work with them people awful bad, but things didn't go so good." The old man relaxed his grip on the gun. "I like it up here and I don't want no company. Then one day he came along and he said he needed a place to stay for a while to sort things out so I let 'em stay. Nice guy though, but there came a time when he seemed different. I don't know, suddenly he wouldn't talk about nothing' and kept to himself, know what I mean? But we stuck together, we kept our word and we never told what we seen. I can't believe it, now he's dead."

"You just said, 'what we've seen.' What did you see?" queried Frank.

"I said too much already," countered the old man. "You better be movin' on."

"Then tell me, how can I get up into those mountains to see for myself? How do I get up to what they call Thunder Peak?"

"Not Thunder Peak, Mister," warned Elias. "You're asking for trouble. No one goes up there now, it's cursed, anybody who goes up there never comes back or they don't come back right. There was weird stuff going on. There was some mining operation going on up there one time, then one day the whole side of that mountain just slid down."

"You ever hear of John Shepherd?" asked Frank.

"Jed said he knew 'em," admitted Elias. "He said he was one of them miners that died up there with the rest of 'em. I say you better leave it be"

"I'll take my chances," returned Frank.

The dog wandered aimlessly back to the shack as Elias gave in to Frank's persistence, saying, "The only way to get there is on foot."

"Can you read a map?" asked Frank.

"Maybe," replied Elias.

Frank pulled out a topographical map of the area and had Elias point out the best route then hastily managed to get his truck turned around on the narrow drive. Elias just shook his head as he walked back toward the door of the shack, mumbling, "Gov'ment men don't know nothin'."

The vast envelope around the globe is always busy with contemporary aircraft, yet unexplainable things can and will be seen. Even on land ordinary objects can appear to be something they are not. But then there are the accounts which are truly unexplainable, such as the time when Clara and Henry Sanders were returning home late one evening after being gone for a few weeks. When their car entered their driveway they saw something out in the adjacent field. Henry stopped to take a closer look and saw a large spherical object glowing with a dull green light. As he approached the sinister glow he caught a glimpse of two small dark shapes near it, these promptly disappeared into the object and within seconds it darted upward with a sharp hissing sound. Sometime later he discovered unusual marks on some of his cattle consisting of small dots and lines behind the left ear. Although the animals were thoroughly examined by the local veterinarian the cause could not be determined.

Not long after this incident another sighting occurred in the middle of the afternoon over the state of Missouri. This time it was in full view of an ordinary passenger on a commercial flight from Dallas to Chicago. Jack Olson didn't like to fly, though he couldn't help but gaze out of the small window by his seat. He became totally engrossed in the checkerboard pattern of the landscape far below, and marveled at the thought of his own rapid transit, the dynamics of the commercial jet, and the effortless experience of air travel. Nevertheless, this wasn't without a nagging apprehension regarding the perils of flight. Yet it was as if he was on some armchair adventure, leisurely looking out at the sight of the great open fields of agriculture, where perfect rectangles of green were cut by roads and the ever snaking rivers and streams. The distraction was working for the most part, but he never failed to note every bump of turbulence, quick but agile tilt of the wing, or every stray sound of the mechanisms at work in the body of the plane. He longed to have his feet on the ground and to be savoring the moment when he was walking away from the plane.

The sky was clear and blue, the sun was shining and he had just begun to relax, when he happened to see something unusual pass less than a thousand feet below the plane. The disk was made up of a fluttering collection of blue shapes obscured by a cloaking mist. It was traveling due west at a speed only slightly faster than that of a commercial jet and was producing a noticeable vapor trail on its journey through the air. Jack was obviously startled by what he saw and watched in amazement until the object was gone. No evasive maneuvers were made by the pilots of the plane he was on, which he thought might be due to the fact the strange object was traveling at a relatively safe distance below them, or that it was not noticed until it was too late to take action. Jack was not necessarily frightened by what he saw because it happened so fast. Mystified, he desperately wanted to say something to his wife in the seat next to him, but she was resting with her eyes closed to the light in the cabin. As he looked around at the others, he found that none of the passengers were paying any attention whatsoever to what was going on outside the confines of the long slender tube. They had all settled down to take naps, were preoccupied with headphones, or engaged in reading their favorite book. When Jack's wife opened her eyes she found her husband's face to be rather pale, so she asked, "What's wrong, Honey?"

"I saw something fly under the plane," he replied.

"Oh?" replied his wife.

"It seemed awfully close," said Jack.

"Our plane seems to be okay," replied his wife.

"It just seemed awfully close," said Jack, not even attempting to describe the object he had seen only moments before.

The rest of the flight proved uneventful. The pilots never confirmed the sighting publicly, but the airline did listen to Jack's account once he reached his destination. He never got a response from his inquiry, and eventually decided it might be best to keep quiet about the whole thing, not telling another living soul, but he knew what he saw.

The evening of August 24 was set ablaze as the atmosphere gathered crimson hues behind the Bighorn Mountain range. There was movement in the sky above the peaks as two points of light traveled together. A single military aircraft scrambled after two unknown objects. The lone pilot brought himself within visual range by rocketing upward at a 45 degree angle and leveling off to maneuver below the objects at the speed of sound. This was the pilot's third encounter with such an anomaly and this time he was able to make a much more detailed observation. The lead object was cone shaped and covered with a green luminescence, but the one following it was a panoply of small sections fluttering within a churning mist. Also there could be seen a number of small orbs at stationary points around the perimeter with one on top and one on the bottom. After several minutes the two objects would attain speeds greater than any known aircraft. Both targets entered the upper atmosphere and the pilot was compelled to return to base. He would file a report, go through a debriefing, and provide an extraordinary visual record of what he had seen.

Night had fallen on the Cygnet property, Mari had gone to work at the tavern as usual. Her mother was washing the last of the dishes from the evening meal and her father was in his recliner reading the paper to catch up on recent news. Although, not without the hope for something positive, he grumbled about the lack of common sense in the general population. The day was ending and the ranch was settling down for the night, but in the corral behind the barn there was a momentary flash of green accompanied by a tumultuous and flickering orange glow. All of this was mostly obstructed from view by the other buildings in the yard. When Jennifer looked through the window above the sink she saw what looked like flames behind the barn. Alarmed, she dropped the dinner plate she had in her hand and it sank into the hot soapy water. She cried out, "William! Come quick, the barn's on fire!"

In the time it took for Jennifer to reach the living room to get William the orange flames had disappeared and a green light shot into the sky. Seconds later a serene blue mist settled into the very same spot.

"What?" cried William as he left the chair, not believing what he was hearing. They both ran to the kitchen window and saw an eerie blue light and a turbulence in the air that made the trees near the barn rustle.

"That's not fire," said William. "I'm going out there!"

"It looked like fire a minute ago," cried Jennifer. "I don't know what it is, oh, William be careful!"

Her husband first went to the bedroom to get his shotgun then returned to the kitchen. He told Jennifer to call the police while he went out into the yard to see it what was. A quarter moon shone brightly in a clear night sky and the stars were prominent. There was barely any wind in the region yet the troubled air surrounding the blue light forced the blades of the windmill in the backyard to revolve, sometimes fast, sometimes slow. Jennifer lifted the receiver of the kitchen phone to make a call for help but heard only static. The cell phone was no better.

She ran to the porch to tell William the phones were out, but by this time William was well on his way to the barn. He heard what sounded like low rumbling music. Once he reached the barn he looked through the small window next to the large sliding door and saw an odd light shining within. He slowly pushed the door aside. Then, in the illumination that came from the corral he made his way along the paving in the open area between the door he had just entered and the one that led to the corral. He could feel heavy vibrations occurring deep within the ground below his feet. The air was laden with moisture and the large tractor as well as everything else in the barn was covered by condensation. When he approached the sliding door to the corral he accidentally kicked an empty gas can but the clatter was arrested by the sound and vibrations invading the entire structure. William wondered about the horses in the other part of the barn, but he couldn't do anything for them now.

He grasped the metal handle on the large door in front of him and courageously thrust it aside. Its rollers rattled and squeaked on the track and his eyes met an object that resembled a great sea creature with twenty long tentacles moving about in an agitated mist. It had the rounded form of a jellyfish, much like a Solmissus, and it moved about as if it were underwater. The creature itself was more than 40 feet from the barn, yet some of the appendages came near the door and its entire body shimmered in its own luminosity. Each of the tentacles had a bulbous end, brightly lit, and moved as though they might make a venomous strike at anything that moved.

William then saw a humanoid form emerge from the center portion of the creature. The being was clad in a silver suit with a head covering that had no visible facial features and it remained within the confines of the moving appendages. At the same time one of the tentacles of the large creature began to penetrate the ground.

William cried out several times, saying, "Who are you?" There was no response from the silver being as the monstrous creature probed deeper into the soil, where it withdrew a three foot long cylinder. An intense blue sapphire glow then encased it. When the glow dissipated the silver being took the slender object into the center of the creature and was swallowed up by it. Within seconds the creature began to dissolve away and William stumbled backward into the open doorway of the barn. What had been a sea creature soon became a collection of sail-like shapes that regimented themselves in ranks of three top and bottom with small orbs forming around the perimeter. Then William, still gripping his gun, watched the object slide upward into the air until he was left standing in the dark. He reached for the switch by the door and the lights came on. His next thought was to check on the horses and to his surprise all of the animals were standing calmly in their stalls, seemingly unaffected by what had just taken place. After finding nothing amiss he went to the open door and switched on the two large lights in the corral. He cautiously stepped out to investigate and found a hole in the soil about six inches in diameter. Water was trickling into it from the puddles on the hard dry soil. This provided the only evidence of such an extraordinary event. A slight breeze had arisen and a chill came over him, it was then that he realized he was soaked to the skin. With nothing more to do he turned off the lights and shut the doors to the barn and headed back toward the house. The kitchen windows were still glowing warmly in the in the night.

Chapter Six: Vexation

Vexation and enchantment seem to coexist.
The valleys are dark and forbidding,
But the mountain peaks reach for the sky.
Mari

The next day proved to be bright and sunny, the outside air was pleasant, and Mari was sitting at the kitchen table enjoying a breakfast of black cherries and blueberries with cream and sugar before going to work. The kitchen was quiet and the clock chimed nine a.m. as her father stepped in from the side yard.

Mari casually glanced up and greeted him cheerfully but her father gave no reply. He walked on by as if she were not there and went to the cupboard and removed a small glass. He ran some water into it then put the glass on the counter without taking a drink then went back outside again to wander around the yard. As Mari finished the rest of her morning tea she saw her mother arrive from the living room with a blank expression, so she asked, "What's, with Dad? You both look like you've seen a ghost!"

"Oh, Mari," replied her mother, with a mix of anxiety and confusion, "it was last night!"

"What was last night?"

"We saw it."

"Okay?"

Her mother lowered her voice and her lips clearly formed the words as she said, "Your father saw them."

"Them?" asked Mari, "Who?"

Jennifer sat down and told her daughter about all that had transpired on the previous evening. Although Mari couldn't hear her mother's worried voice she saw the fear in her eyes. Her mother phrased softly saying, "It looked like a jellyfish. That's all he would say. He has been outside all night."

"A jellyfish?" repeated Mari, not quite apprehending her mother's words.

"I'm worried about your father," replied her mother, "he won't tell me anything more about it."

"It was in the corral by the barn?" repeated Mari, still confused.

"Yes," said Jennifer, "behind the barn."

"There was something on the news the other day but they said it was probably a hoax," returned Mari.

"I saw some lights behind the barn," said her mother. "I was in the house and your father went out there. He saw it, now he won't talk about it, but it looked like the barn was on fire and we heard strange sounds."

"On fire!" Mari ran to look out the window, but said, "It doesn't look like anything was on fire. Mom, are you okay?"

"Nothing was burned," replied her mother, "but it looked like fire and there was a green light, then it was blue, then there were strange sounds...oh, I don't know...Mari, maybe you could talk to him...I don't know what else to do!"

"What kind of sounds?" asked Mari.

"I...I don't know," stammered her mother. "It was like music, it was like a waterfall, it was like—I don't know...I'm just worried that's all. Maybe you can help, Mari, you have a way."

"What can I do?"

"If you would go talk to him, maybe he'll open up."

"I saw him go outside a minute ago."

"He's just wandering around and I'm worried."

"You know Dad," assured Mari, trying to calm her mother, "he won't let anything get him down. I'm sure he'll be okay."

"Why don't you try to talk to him, you have a soothing way. It might not seem like it, Honey, but he listens to what you have to say."

"I wish I could stay but I have to go to work."

"I know, but when you get home then?"

"When I get home, Mom," assured Mari. "I'll talk to him. Will you be all right?"

"I'm okay."

"Are you sure?"

"Yes, Mari, I'm okay."

"I'll see both of you later then and don't worry about anything."

Mari got to work on time as usual but she was not at ease. Having second thoughts, she was now worried about her parents, wishing that she had stayed home as her mother requested and the more she thought about it the more anxious she became. She hesitated to talk to Peg about it but she needed to confide in someone. Mari finally took Peg aside and made her promise not tell anyone else about what she was about to say. The woman agreed and Mari divulged the details of her father's encounter. Peg initially sympathized, but began to have doubts about the facts, thinking Mari's father might have made up the story for publicity, even though Mari insisted her parents would never make up such a thing.

Peg knew Mari was an exceptionally good worker and was as sweet as could be. She was able to do the job regardless of her physical limitations. It was for that very reason she hired her. Mari demonstrated she could be as effective as any person who could hear. Many of the customers and guests admired her, returning again and again just to have her wait on them. She was amiable, even philosophical, but there were other times when she seemed to be daydreaming. Her personality was often mystifying, which caused Peg some concern, yet her winsome spirit always seemed to prevail. But there was something about Mari Peg just couldn't put her finger on. When the time came for Mari to be sent to the market for some much needed produce, Peg and Nancy found themselves alone in the kitchen. Beset by her own confusion and frustration, Peg couldn't resist telling Nancy about what Mari had said. Nancy was all ears and listened to every word.

Mari resumed her duties after returning from the market and entered the dining room with some colorful napkins and seven red, white, and blue helium balloons tied to long strings. The balloons waved gently in the air as she walked to the back corner of the room and approached a set table for three. She carefully tied the balloons to a condiment tray and made sure all the decorations were properly set for a young child's birthday celebration. Once she was satisfied with the arrangement she returned to the kitchen. Nancy, on the other hand, could always be found tending the bar and chatting with customers. She was irreverent at times but fastidious when it came to keeping things clean. Today was no different as she vigorously worked in long sweeping motions with her bar mop to polish the long wooden counter. She was just finishing up when her boyfriend Dan came in. The young man was a welcome sight and when she saw him, she called out, "Hey, Dan!"

"Hey, Nan," was the reply as he sauntered up to the bar.

"I can't wait to get out of here," replied Nancy, with evident anticipation. "I want to go out somewhere tonight."

"That's what I came in about," said Dan.

"Yeah?" replied Nancy, alive with pent-up desires.

"I heard there was a man in here the other day checking things out," replied Dan.

"Yeah, there was," replied Nancy, wondering what was up.

"Frank, I think," said Dan. "Yeah, that's it, that's the name, he was talking to some guys in here."

"I guess," groaned Nancy, "who cares, it's all crazy anyway."

"No, there's something to all this and I got to find out," continued Dan.

"Yeah," agreed Nancy, "those investigators or what ever were already out to your place the other day. You said they didn't come up with anything so why are you looking for them?"

"I think there's something they're not telling us," replied Dan. "Remember what the vet said? Anyhow, I want to talk to the guy. I want to find out what he knows."

"I just heard about something," added Nancy.

"What did you hear?" returned Dan, becoming interested.

"I just heard it today so don't you go spreading this around," whispered Nancy. "Just so you know you're not the only one."

"What is it?"

"I heard Mari's father saw something."

"Cygnet?" cried Dan. "When?"

"Quiet," whispered Nancy. "Mari told Peg and Peg told me. I guess her father saw one of those jellyfish things by their barn last night. The phones were out and her mother thought the barn was on fire except nothing got burnt. I guess her father's going around acting kind of funny. Anyhow, I just found out so don't you say I told you this."

"Okay, is there anything else?"

"I don't know, that's all I heard. Mari won't tell me anything."

"Maybe I'll go see Cygnet myself."

"No! Mari says he's not talking. I think Mari might be making some of it up, you know how she is, a little out there sometimes. Just wait for a while."

"How about if I talk to her myself?"

"No!" exclaimed Nancy. She looked around to see anyone heard then lowered her voice. "She doesn't know I know about it. Peg said she wasn't supposed to tell me what Mari said. So just forget it."

"Well," added Dan, with a grin, "her old man must have seen something or she wouldn't have said so. See, Nan, I got to find that guy Frank."

"Just wait," urged Nancy, "there'll be all sorts of other people out here, especially if it's true about what her father saw."

"Maybe," replied Dan, now visibly impatient, "but that's what I came to see you about. I'm going to do some investigating on my own. Del says he's seen Frank around so I'm going to make the rounds and find out what's happening."

"Dan," whined Nancy, "you promised we would go out!"

"I know, but this is important," replied Dan, now more determined than ever.

"Come on!" pleaded Nancy. "All you've been doing lately is running around. Just forget that stuff, let's just get—"

"Hey, I got to look into this."

"But Dan, what about me!"

"Hey, Nan," replied Dan, now on his way to the door, "we'll do something tomorrow, I promise, I gotta go."

"Dan!" cried Nancy.

"Tomorrow, Nan!"

The front door slapped shut. Nancy threw her mop on the counter with a pout and strutted into the kitchen.

Dan made an impromptu stop at Al's service station and as it happened Del was there talking to Al. Both Del and Al were indulging in some of the latest information, so seizing the opportunity, Dan couldn't wait to fill Del in about the things Nancy had just told him. By the time Dan finished, Del slapped him on the back, saying, "Thanks man, this is just too good. The old boy's finally cracked!"

By early afternoon the tavern began filling up with people oppressed by the heat and Neil Clayborn happened to be one of them. He entered the tavern with two other people but each went their own way. There was a woman seated at the bar near the kitchen doors so Neil took a seat at the opposite end. Nancy immediately sprang over to him and he ordered black coffee, picked up a rumpled newspaper and settled in. The loud clatter of dishes in the kitchen caught his ears, then the swaying balloons at the back of the room caught his eye, and so did Mari, who was busy making sure the family celebration was going according to plan. Neil had become aware of her during one of his previous visits, but this time he was sure of something he had observed earlier. In some uncanny way she reminded him of his sister. He found the coincidence astonishing, right down to the diminutive details of her physical appearance and the contagious essence of her personality.

In the kitchen, Linda was focused on preparing a new order and when Mari returned she took time to thank her for preparing special sandwiches for the birthday

36

party. Then she headed for the cluttered back corner of the room, where everyone took their lunch break. There were two chairs and a small narrow table but she remained standing, finally finding the time to nibble on a ham sandwich and take a few sips from a bottle of water.

Nancy came in and carelessly deposited several glasses on the counter by the sink with a resounding crash. Relieved after finding the glasses had survived the careless tumble, she drew up to Mari to air her feelings, saying, "I wanted to go out to a movie or something tonight but Dan doesn't want to."

Mari set her bottle on the table, and casually answered, "Why not?"

Nancy only knew a limited amount of sign language and tended to speak rather loudly when talking to Mari. Flailing her arms, she said, "Oh, he's all worked up about stuff."

"Stuff?" asked Mari, taking another small bite of the sandwich and pushing her glasses back up on her nose.

"He's taking that UFO stuff way too seriously. He wants to go see one of those investigators or something."

"He does?" replied Mari, only half interested.

"That's what he says but I don't know," shrugged Nancy in reply, then curiously eyeing Mari and probing for a response, she said, "Well, I've never seen anything myself."

"I guess he has his reasons," offered Mari, remaining aloof.

"Have you seen anything unusual lately?" asked Nancy, sharpening the point.

"Of course not!" replied Mari, suddenly getting defensive.

"Anyone you know seen anything?" pressed Nancy.

"What are you saying?" said Mari, now suspicious.

"Oh, just thought I'd ask," replied Nancy.

"I don't want to talk about that now," stressed Mari, with a scowl.

"Well," returned Nancy, "I just wish I had a life that's all."

"Life," echoed Mari, turning to look off into the distance to daydream a bit, but then she turned to Nancy. "Do you ever think about what God might want for your—"

"Mari," Nancy cut in, "you ought to get out more. You got to get away from this place."

"Get away?" replied Mari. "Where to?"

"You should go out with us sometime," added Nancy.

"Just me?" replied Mari.

"Not just you, silly," countered Nancy. "Are you in space again? There's more to life than this old place."

"I wish," replied Mari, rolling her eyes and wrapping up the remains of her sandwich.

"Hey, Ken Sorley likes you," informed Nancy, "I could pass on the word."

"Who?" asked Mari, seemingly confused as she put the sandwich back in the lunch bag and put the bag into the small refrigerator under the table. The name eluded her and she was having a hard time with some of Nancy's erratic gestures. Nancy had also turned away before she finished speaking and Mari couldn't see her face.

"Ken," said Nancy, much louder, as if more volume would help. "You know, that big guy?" Mari just frowned, so Nancy made fists then she flexed her arm muscles, saying, "Are you in space again?" Mari was still confused so Nancy grabbed her phone.

Mari's phone vibrated and she pulled it out of her apron pocket to read the text: "Ken Sorley." She promptly shook her head, "No," then sent a text to Nancy: "I don't like his dirty jokes."

"He's better than Joe!" exclaimed Nancy.

"So?" cried Mari, raising her own voice a few notches.

"I warned you," mouthed Nancy, now pointing a finger. "So what about Ken?"

"It didn't work out," returned Mari with a shrug. "I broke it off."

"Mari?" cried Nancy.

"He gives me the creeps," returned Mari.

"You're too up tight," replied Nancy.

"Really?" said Mari, as her dark eyebrows went up.

"You're acting funny," accused Nancy.

"No, you are!" declared Mari, in a verbal rebuke.

There was a pause. The two women seemed be taking a time out, then Nancy sent another text: "I had a weird dream about you last night."

"What kind of dream?" quipped Mari.

"You sprouted wings!" replied Nancy, now feverishly punching the buttons like it was a game.

"Seriously?" questioned Mari, wondering what crazy thing her friend would say next.

"Like an angel or something," said Nancy.

"Come on!" cried Mari.

"You were standing in the school parking lot," added Nancy, then she got back to her phone to text: "You had an umbrella in your hand and you were going to hit me with it!" Nancy laughed, but Mari shook her head in disgust. Nancy sent another text: "Then you just flew away!"

"I wish I could fly away!" retorted Mari.

"To space?" mouthed Nancy, silently.

"Stop that space stuff!" replied Mari, now exasperated.

"Actually," returned Nancy, "you were kind of cute!"

Mari just rolled her eyes again as Nancy giggled, saying, "Oh, Mari!"

Trying to escape the irritating conversation, Mari changed the subject, and said, "What about Dan? If you care so much about him why don't you tell him exactly how you feel?"

"Easier said than done," replied Nancy, sending a text.

"Don't hassle him," returned Mari. "Just tell him—"

"He's all absorbed," added Nancy, voicing her feelings. "It's getting on my nerves."

"Maybe he wants you to think about him a little more," countered Mari.

"Peg doesn't believe in that UFO stuff," sent Nancy. "She thinks it's all crazy."

"Maybe it's not," countered Mari, crisply.

"I'm just telling you what Peg says!" said Nancy, emphatically.

"I don't care what Peg says," returned Mari.

But in the very next reply, Nancy sent: "Peg doesn't think your father saw them either."

Mari instantly looked up at Nancy and couldn't believe what she just read. Nancy suddenly realized what she did and pocketed her phone.

Mari's eyes blazed. Her face said it all, but she shot back, "Peg told you, didn't she?"

"Told me what?" said Nancy, turning away.

"About my father!" declared Mari.

"So what?" said Nancy, looking around for something else to do.

"I knew I should have kept my mouth shut!" cried Mari.

"She's worried about you," countered Nancy. Mari groaned in frustration, but Nancy continued. "You've been awfully dreamy lately and we're concerned about you. Why, even Dan said your father—" Nancy just realized she dug the hole deeper and ran over to the sink to pick up a large spoon to vigorously scrape some dried food off a dinner plate into the garbage bin.

Mari caught enough of the words and replied with sparks of indignation, "Dan? You told Dan?"

"Sorry, Babe," returned Nancy, half apologizing.

"Why did you do that, Nancy?" cried Mari, with incredulity.

"Dan won't make fun of you," soothed Nancy.

"I just knew this would happen," spat Mari. "He knows a lot of people. He'll make it sound worse than it already is."

"People are going to find out sometime," was Nancy's casual reply.

Mari walked out of the kitchen to reset two empty tables and check on the birthday party at the back of the dining room. She was trying to take her mind off of her troubles as she neatly adjusted table cloths and napkins. She had just replaced some of the flatware, when four men appeared at the front door. Del Toller and his three friends came marching single file into the tavern and headed for the large table at the center of the room that was assigned to Mari. She saw them, but instead of waiting on the new arrivals she deferred once more to the needs of the birthday party, hoping against hope the men might change their minds and leave the premises. When she headed back to the kitchen she met Nancy coming out of the swinging doors but Nancy only gave Mari a grouchy look as she promptly headed for the bar.

Del Toller, Pete Saar, Jack Barren, and Kenny Harmon were well known around town and they were no strangers to the Midway. Del had graduated from Stone River High School a year earlier than Mari and she didn't miss his absence from the halls. She did her best to keep her distance. Pete and Kenny were Del's contemporaries and all three men suddenly disappeared from Stone River for about a year. When they resurfaced, Jack was with them and the new arrival quickly became an insider. The men followed Del like shadows as he roamed at the impulse of what ever his piercing brown eyes rested upon, eyes which were somehow enhanced by his neatly trimmed beard and the straight black hair over his ears. Although restless, he somehow managed to hold down a part time custodial job at the Stone River High School. Pete was the shortest of the four by a couple of inches, though he was the most opinionated and kept his thinning brown hair under a ragged straw hat. Kenny had a large dose of charm, which he used to his advantage, and employed it often by talking Del out of his frequent conflicts. Jack had a ready sense of humor, but like Del, it usually exercised its leverage at the expense of someone else.

Del also nursed an ongoing grudge against Mari's father regarding an incident during the previous summer. William had at one time openly accused Del of stealing cattle and after that the family dog disappeared from the Cygnet ranch. William immediately suspected Del when it was found dead a few days later on the road.

The two women found themselves back in the kitchen and Mari had mostly recovered from her tiff with Nancy and looked to her for sympathy. She complained, saying, "Del's back."

Nancy peered into the dining room through the vertical slit between the two swinging doors of the kitchen, saying, "I see he's behaving himself." Mari made no immediate comment then Nancy muttered to herself. "At least she can't hear his stupid mouth." Glancing over at Mari with her big eyes, she said to her, "Well, maybe he'll leave early today."

Mari just smiled cynically.

Peg arrived back in the kitchen just as Nancy patted Mari on the back, saying, "You go girl, maybe you'll get an extra big tip this time!"

The proprietor eyed Mari sternly for a moment and caught the drift of the conversation then pulled another order slip from a stainless steel clip on a narrow white board by the door. Seeing Mari's hesitation, she said, "He's a customer like anyone else. I'm trying to run a business here and it's not easy, especially with all the stuff that's been going on lately."

"I got my hands full at the bar," remarked Nancy, pointing to the dining room.

"Come on now Mari," said Peg. "Just get out there."

"Four of them," added Mari, feeling out numbered.

"The customer comes first," reminded Peg. "Anyhow, you think about stuff too much."

Mari swallowed the advice, adjusted her glasses, then left the kitchen with one more red balloon for the young celebrity at the birthday gathering. She never made eye contact with the men and returned to the kitchen one more time to fidget with some clean silverware on a drying rack, taking time to find the proper place for each utensil in the storage bins.

Peg needed to clean up around the dumpster and she asked Nancy if she could take a moment to help her out, Nancy agreed and both of them headed for the back of the building. Someone or something had worked its way into the container only to drag out an ample selection of rancid food, filthy cans, stale bread, broken bottles, and greasy plastic jars.

Before leaving the kitchen, Mari muttered to herself, "Well, it could be worse...it will all work out somehow I guess." But, the ugly feeling in her stomach was still there when she left the sanctuary of the tavern's only food preparation room. All four of the men had taken ownership of the table and were impatiently waiting for service. Del, now sporting a toothy grin, inhaled every move their server made as she approached.

Upon arrival, Mari politely asked, "May I help you?"

In reply Del thrust a booted foot out from under the table, and rasped, "Yeah, you could help me a lot!"

Unruffled, Mari said, "What would you like?"

"I'd like something sweet," announced Del, after which, he turned to the others at the table and winked. The other men at the table laughed under their breath as they eyed her and eagerly anticipated what Del might say next. Del added, "Yeah, little girl, I'd like something real sweet!" Then Del, speaking very slowly to make sure Mari caught every last word, said, "But first, I heard your old man saw a jellyfish last night!"

"That's none of your business," countered Mari.

"I just like to keep up on things," said Del. "Them UFO's is crazy stuff."

Neil was still at the bar and within earshot of the conversation. He could also observe the scene by means of the reflection in the mirror.

"Hey," continued Del, grinning, "do you got any of them jellyfish on that menu?" When Mari didn't immediately respond, he said it a little bit louder. "Hey, do you got any of them jellyfish on this here menu?"

Mari understood well enough, and replied, "Of course not."

Del's face hardened, it progressed to a sneer, which became a sly smile, then went blank. Finally he flashed a relishing grin as he put his arm around her and pulled her in close. She couldn't hear the tone of his voice, but she read his lips when he spoke the words, "Hey, I was just kidding, Sweetie, I just want you to be friendly."

Mari struggled to get free of his grasp, saying, "Hands off!" She somehow managed to slip out of his grasp but she didn't run away, as she was still hoping to gain control of the situation.

"Come on," grouched Del, "don't you go sticking your nose up. I seen you at that party over there. How about you throw us a party? You must be getting some charity around here you being deaf and all. You can't be making it pay. Maybe you got other talents, know what I mean?" Del's eyes reflected his enjoyment as he picked up a menu and slowly paged through it. Then he pointed to something inside, and said, "Come on now, you play nice. Look right here, that's it, that's what I want!" He motioned for Mari to closely examine the selection on his menu, but when she did he pulled it away and mumbled something suggestive without moving his lips. Then facing the others with one hand to his cheek so Mari couldn't see, he filled the room with his voice when he said, "She talks funny, an' she may be a deaf, but I don't care about them ears!"

The men at the table laughed and played along with the game, but everyone else in the busy tavern had grown quiet.

"I don't need this," retorted Mari. "I'm going to get Peg!"

But in the next moment Neil appeared at Mari's side and delivered an admonition, saying, "She is quite correct. She does not need harassment from you. I suggest you leave her be!"

"Leave her be?" growled Del. "Who are you?"

"You might extend some courtesy," added Neil.

"Courtesy?" scoffed Del. "And you, do you like them jellyfish too?"

Mari took this opportunity to scurry back to the kitchen just as Nancy came in the back door of the building. She saw the distressed look on Mari's face and wondered why she was pointing toward the dining room in disgust. Puzzled, Nancy went to take a quick look into the dining room in time to hear Del fire back at Neil, "What do you care about the likes of her? You but out!"

"You, sir," returned Neil, "are making sport of her."

"Why are you so interested?" Del fired back. "Hey, I bet you like them jellyfish. I bet they don't have no ears neither!"

"Maybe he's like her and he can't hear too good," said Pete.

"I don't know who you are," threatened Del, "but if you know what's good for you you'll find the door!"

"Hey," cried Kenny. "He's not worth the time. Just run him out of here."

But Del decided to grant Neil some further enlightenment and stood up, saying, "I feel good, I feel like a fight. I could tear you apart right now. I could rearrange that face of yours. You just be glad we ain't outside, you can't never tell what might happen!"

"You can't never tell," echoed Jack.

Back in the kitchen, Mari whispered, "We should get Peg."

Nancy questioned Mari, saying, "What's going on out there anyway?"

"That man stepped in to help me," replied Mari, "and now Del's picking a fight."

"You go out and get Peg," replied Nancy. "I'll go in there and see what I can do."

Del took this opportunity to further indulge the situation by grabbing Neil by the shirt and pulling him close, saying, "Well aren't you something!" Then he gave him a stiff push backward with a pronouncement. "I can run rings around you any time smart man!"

"Rings are my specialty," quipped Neil.

"What's that mean?" replied Del.

Nancy marched up to the men, saying, "What's going on here?"

"Nothing you need to know about, Nancy," snapped Del.

"We're not going to have this kind of stuff in here," lectured Nancy. "You ought to know by now. We'll call the police if we got to."

"Yeah," Del fired back, "and have them haul this guy away."

"Time for everybody to settle down," advised Nancy.

"I can deal with the likes of you, buddy," said Del, firing another volley at Neil. "If we ever cross paths again you just better look out!"

"I cannot wait," replied Neil, stepping up to Del.

"Neither can I!" Del growled back. "You're right, Kenny, he ain't worth the time. Come on we're out of this sty."

"Good move," added Nancy, bristling, "or I'm on the phone."

"I believe you should do as the lady says," added Neil.

"Next time, man, you'll see," cried Del. "Next time!"

The four men swaggered out of tavern, occasionally glancing back at Neil and Nancy in contempt. Del managed to kick a chair across the floor before the door slammed behind him. A round of applause broke out in the room as the men left.

"Thanks for helping out," said Nancy, with some relief. "They're a little rough sometimes. Next time we'll call the police."

"No problem," said Neil, then he quietly returned to his place at the bar.

When Peg returned to the kitchen Nancy filled her in about the incident. After listening to what the two women had to say about the brawl that was averted, she figured she hadn't missed much. Del was nowhere to be seen and things seemed to be back to normal so Peg put her hand on Mari's shoulder, and said, "You'll be okay, Hon, they're gone now. If this kind of thing ever happens again you come and get me right away. I'll deal with them."

Nancy immediately returned to the bar, but Mari remained in the kitchen, trying to repair her shattered pride. Nancy busied herself by cleaning up some spills and clearing away glasses all the while eyeing Neil. After a few minutes she decided to take a tray loaded with things to be washed back to the kitchen and check on Mari. At the same time Mari was just returning to the dining room. As the two women passed one another Nancy gave Mari a quick nod, then made creative motions toward the bar, and mouthed, "You, go over there!"

Mari scowled at Nancy and stopped in her tracks. She self-consciously surveyed the room and toyed with the phone in her apron pocket. After a long moment she slowly found her way behind the bar. Her eyes met Neil's, then in her own quiet way she managed to produce a soft, "Thank you."

Neil put down his paper and addressed the rather meek looking creature behind the counter, saying, "No need to thank me."

"Just some locals," she answered, apologetically.

"They had no right to take advantage of you," replied Neil.

"They come in here from time to time," she admitted.

"Are you okay?"

"I'm okay."

"Are you sure?"

"I can fend for myself."

"Actually, I believe you can."

"Well, most of the time," replied Mari. "Stuff happens, but I'm okay, really."

"That is very good to hear," replied Neil.

Mari impulsively extended her hand to introduce herself, saying, "My name is Mari."

"It is nice to meet you, Mari," he said, completing the gesture. "Neil."

Mari knew someone else by the same name and recognized the word as it formed on his lips, so her response to him was immediate when she said, "Hi, Neil."

Her phone suddenly vibrated. She pulled it from her apron pocket and read a text from Peg that said: "Table 3."

"Thank you again," said Mari, "but you must excuse me."

"Of course," replied the Neil.

Mari waited on an elderly couple, both of which had an unfortunate front row seat to the disturbance. They were gracious to her as she apologized for the misbehavior then she headed back to the kitchen and took a few minutes to nibble on the unfinished sandwich. All the enjoyment was gone, now she was only eating because she needed to. Upon returning to the dining room she saw that Neil had left the tavern so she waited on the small birthday party one final time, apologizing on behalf of the tavern for the incident. They took it in stride and gave her a big tip. It didn't seem to matter. The remainder of her shift did little to sooth her raw and unsettled emotions.

Even after Mari returned home her father seemed distant and unapproachable. Because of this the conversation she hoped for never transpired. Later she managed to speak with her mother about the incident at the tavern and made sure her mother knew she was okay. That evening, instead of pulling out her journal or reading a favorite book she picked up the lonely violin. Meadow jumped on the bed and curled up into a ball as Mari slowly paced the floor to find the right spot by the front window and gently put the bow to the strings. Her hands felt the notes as she worked through them, guiding the bow with melancholy strokes that were at once soft, pleasing, oddly melodic, and uniquely telling.

Chapter Seven: Journey

Someone has captured my thoughts,
Even as my restless heart carries me onward.
At times the days seem long on this journey called life,
Even as I explore the hills and hollows of the land.
Mari

By 7 o'clock in the morning Mari had finished jotting down some ideas in her journal. Now on August 26, she was moving on with the rest of her day. Most of the time her morning routine remained the same, but today she planned to take her car to Al's service station for some minor repair before going to work. She called to schedule an appointment but was told she might have to leave the car overnight. This was acceptable because she could walk the short distance from the repair shop to the tavern for her 10 a.m. to 2 p.m. shift. Nancy had readily agreed to give her a ride when her day ended at 3 p.m. so the minor inconvenience of another half hour at work was acceptable.

The modest three story Stone River Hotel near the Midway Tavern afforded a view of people coming and going in the central part of town. Frank had a room there, and now he intended to check out early because he was trying to get a head start on the heat but somehow he was still running late. Today he would head for Thunder Peak. He included a handgun among all the other things he thought he would need for his hike up the mountain. He knew the slope would be difficult and he intended to spend at least one night on the slopes if need be.

Dan had encountered Frank in the lobby of the hotel. The two men talked briefly, though Dan still didn't get the information he wanted. Frank, on the other hand, found he had been given a new lead, so armed with the new information he figured he might be able to catch the young woman in question at the tavern.

Mari was there when Frank walked through the front door of the Midway, and he approached her aggressively, saying, "Miss, I need to have a word with you."

"What do you mean?" returned Mari, surprised at being accosted by a perfect stranger.

"About your father," said Frank.

"My father?" asked Mari.

"Yes, it's important," demanded Frank.

Although aghast that a stranger would know about the incident, she tried to dodge the questions, saying, "I can't talk now."

But Frank wouldn't let it lay, saying, "It would be in your best interest to change your mind." Mari pointed to her hearing aid. Frank rephrased the statement and spoke a little louder. "You need to tell me what you know."

"I don't know anything," she replied flatly.

"Then I'll talk to your father myself," snapped Frank.

"He won't talk to you," replied Mari.

Failing to get what he wanted, he said, "You're only hurting yourself young lady. I suggest you reconsider."

Mari didn't wait around for any more of the conversation and headed for the kitchen.

"I'll be back," called Frank, watching her disappear.

A frustrated Frank Niverson left the tavern. Mari leaned against the kitchen wall with her eyes closed. She didn't relish any kind of conflict and wanted all of it to go away. Again she forced herself out into the dining area to make the rounds. Then she saw Neil. He had arrived shortly after Frank made his exit and had taken a seat at an empty table in the corner of the room by the front and side windows. His leather hat was hanging on the spindle of one of four chairs and as was his custom he was scanning a newspaper.

Mari's curiosity was kindled and went over to the table, saying, "Hi, may I help you?"

He removed his reading glasses, looked up to greet her, and said, "Hi, Mari, how are you today!"

"I'm doing fine," she replied. "How about you?"

"Very well, thank you," he returned.

She pointed to the paper, smiled, and asked, "Anything interesting in there?"

"Not really," said Neil, "just a rehash of old agendas."

"What would you like?" asked Mari, at the ready.

"Coffee," was his only reply.

"On such a hot day?" returned Mari.

"Yes," said Neil, "that will be all, thank you."

"I'll be right back," she replied.

Although Mari reminded him of his sister in many ways, there were other enchanting things he noticed about her. He saw a quiet kind of sophistication, an elegance transcending the pony tail, simple white blouse, black skirt, and small red apron. Was it her deliberate yet prepossessing spirit that made her so appealing? What kind of eyes were looking out at the world from behind those glasses? For the moment he would draw no conclusions.

Very soon his server returned with the coffee, and asked, "Is there anything else I can get for you?"

"No, this will be fine, thank you once again," answered Neil, making it sound almost like an apology.

Mari wondered what to think about the man, or perhaps she shouldn't think about him at all, but she studied his face, then asked, "If you don't mind my asking, are you new in town?"

"I do not mind at all," said Neil, "and, yes, I am new to the area. I bought a place about six months ago, but I have only been knocking around the house for a few weeks."

"It's usually very quiet around here," she replied. "We don't get too many new people out this way. I may not be the first to say it, but welcome to Stone River!"

"Thank you," returned Neil. "Actually, you are the first."

She smiled amiably, saying, "Well, I hope you like it. I'll be right back in a few minutes." Neil smiled politely as she left to wait on a man and woman with two small children. She interacted with each child in a quiet manner, treating them with respect and with genuine interest, and eventually she returned to Neil with a fresh pot of coffee.

He thanked her for her service and, when she was about to be on her way again, he asked, "May I speak with you later?"

"I'm sorry, what?" she asked, not readily catching his words.

"May I speak with you," he begged, "after your shift is over?"

A little surprised by the personal request, she asked, "What do you want to talk to me about?"

"Stone River," replied Neil. Mari just glared at him a moment, but he continued. "And, about some of the things going on here as well. That is, if you don't mind?"

"Oh," she replied defensively, "I should have known!"

"Please?" he insisted, "if you would be so kind."

"Well, I don't know," she replied, still defensive.

"If you don't want to do so I will understand completely," said Neil. "I just thought you might like someone to talk to. Perhaps you would like to have an intelligent conversation. I will listen to whatever you have to say."

She glanced at the clock over the kitchen doors, then looked at the time on her phone, then eyed Neil. He almost looked as though he might be the one in need of someone to listen. But, then she thought she might have only imagined such a need. She glanced back at the clock, and said, "Well, actually, I'm off work at two. I might be able to give you a minute."

"That would be perfect. I will keep it short," said Neil. "We can talk right here."

"All right," said Mari, going along with the offer, "when my shift is over."

"Thank you," replied Neil. "No hurry, I will wait for you."

She walked away still unsure about sitting down with someone she had only just met. Somehow the man seemed safe enough. She was more curious than afraid and felt she might at least owe him some time after their previous encounter. It was a few minutes after 2 p.m. when Mari walked back into the dining room. Neil was still sitting in the bright corner reading the newspaper.

Mari greeted the man pleasantly, saying, "I can speak with you now if you like."

"Thank you for taking the time," said Neil, as he got up to make sure she was comfortable in the chair across from him. "How was your day?"

"Not too bad," replied Mari, "it keeps me busy."

"The coffee is always excellent here," added Neil, returning to his seat.

"Thank you," she said, with a smile.

"Are you surviving this heat?" he asked.

"Yes, just barely," she said, casting her eyes on the blades whirling overhead. "The air conditioners can't keep up and these fans don't help much."

"I must agree," he said.

"A heat wave," she acknowledged, "they say it will end soon."

"I expect it will," added Neil. "So, have you worked here a long time?"

It took a second for her to pick up on what he had just said, but she answered, "Five years I guess, off and on."

"You must put in some long hours then."

"Yes, or it feels like it sometimes."

"Of course."

"I think Peg keeps adding to my hours."

"I see. I don't know if I ever got your last name."

"My name?"

"Yes," replied Neil, acknowledging with a gentle nod.

"Cygnet," she answered, "you know, like the swan, Mari Abigail Cygnet."

"A very beautiful name indeed," replied Neil.

"And you?" she asked.

"My name is Neil," he returned, "Neil Clayborn."

Not exactly understanding any of the words beyond his first name she replied by trying to sound it out, saying, "Clay—"

He tore a small piece from the newspaper and wrote his name on it. Having read the name, she reached over the table to formally shake his hand, saying, "It's very nice to meet you again, Mr. Clayborn."

"Likewise, Miss Cygnet," he replied.

"Again," returned Mari, "I want to express my thanks for what you did."

"Please," insisted Neil, "just forget it."

"Those things usually don't throw me," she added. "I guess it was just a bad day."

"We all have a bad day now and then," he said.

"What's this all about?" she added, with a desire to get on to the point.

"Have you been approached by anyone else about the sightings?"

"Yes," said Mari, "actually, it's been real strange around here."

"How are you doing with all of this?" returned Neil.

"Don't worry about me, I'm okay," said Mari, as she relaxed a little and took the elastic band out of her pony tail. This let her hair fall easily on her shoulders, where it now discretely covered the hearing aid. It also delicately framed her expressive eyes, eyes that danced under seriously straight brows.

"I will not worry about you then," replied Neil.

"What do you want to talk to me about exactly?" asked Mari. Neil hesitated regarding an answer, his eyes spoke of something yet to be revealed, and he found himself searching for the right words. Mari, who was very observant and pensive, responded, saying, "I may be deaf but I can read lips very well."

"Of course, I don't doubt your abilities," replied Neil, then he seemed to refocus. "I am aware you have been receiving better than your share of rude treatment but I would like to get more specific regarding some of the issues."

Mari sat back in the chair and defensively folded her arms. She knew he might ask some penetrating questions, but she wasn't ready, mostly she wanted to know why he was at the tavern, she wanted answers of her own, so she had to ask, "Are you one of those special investigators or something?"

"No, I am not. Well, actually, I have a personal interest in what is going on here."

"In Stone River?"

48

"Not only Stone River but some other things as well."

"Why?"

"My own curiosity, for I entertain many interests."

"Like what?"

"Science, astronomy, the oceans, tall ships, well, you see...I enjoy sailing."

"Whoa! Sailing? Aren't you a little far from the ocean for that?"

"Hmm, sailing? That indulgence does sound rather odd does it not? I can explain."

"Please do!"

"I have been working with geologists and physicists from out east. We are looking into natural resources as it relates to new energy sources. Sailing is just a hobby."

"So why this place?"

"We find the geology out here to be unique, and it suits our interests. I also find there is a certain freedom here, there is a smaller population and there are lots of open spaces."

"Open spaces we have," replied Mari, confirming the obvious.

"It seems to fit our needs," said Neil.

"What kind of company do you work for?" she questioned.

"I am from New York," answered Neil, "but presently we are in the process of starting our own company. Essentially, that's what brings me out this way."

"That's a big step," replied Mari, "I hope it all works out for you."

"I am confidant, and the future looks good," answered Neil.

Mari soon became aware of something about the person with whom she was speaking, for he carefully chose his words and used hands at times, which made it easy for her to follow the conversation. Yet she still had her own questions to ask, saying, "What do you want from me?"

"The military is in defensive mode," replied Neil. "The government is sending out agents to gather intelligence. No one person seems to have an answer. The average citizen is going about his or her life minding their own business yet they are the ones who seeing the anomalies. Unusual events are occurring in the lives of ordinary people. I understand this, so I want to talk to those people. So I will respect whatever you have to say because want to understand things from your perspective."

"Thanks, for your concern," said Mari, "but I'm afraid I may not be of much help."

"Perhaps," replied Neil, "but I will still listen to what you have to say."

"So, what have you seen?" asked Mari, now turning the questioning back on her interrogator. "Have you seen any of those UFOs?"

"I thought you might ask," replied Neil. "When I was very young I saw some objects in the sky. No satisfactory explanation could ever be found. Then, recently, as so many others have reported, I witnessed certain unexplainable phenomenon on the land and over the ocean as well. I have received very few answers. It's a complex issue, so I took it upon myself to do some investigating. I decided it was time to look into these things. Therefore, please forgive me, for now I must ask you about what you father saw?"

Mari recoiled at the boldness of the question, and exclaimed, "Of course, everybody knows about it now!"

"I am sorry," said Neil, aware of her concern, "but do not worry, I do not take this lightly, nor will I make the information public."

"Maybe so," replied Mari, "but it's just—"

"Did you see anything yourself that night?" urged Neil.

"No, not at that time," replied Mari, giving in somewhat. "but it was on the Sunday before. I saw a light over the mountains." Then she folded her hands and sat back in her chair in silent expectation.

"Was that all?" asked Neil?"

"Yes," returned Mari. "That was it. Other people have seen those lights too."

Neil noticed how the clear polish had worn off her finely manicured nails and he noted the ornate bracelet on her wrist, one which included a small cameo. But, he could also tell she was becoming uneasy, yet he probed further by asking, "Is there anything else you might like to add?"

"No," she replied, emphatically.

"I must return to the question of your father," he pressed. Mari immediately grew tense and she turned to see if anyone else in the room might be watching or listening. When she turned back to Neil his next question felt like an invasion. "He did get a close look at something did he not?"

The young woman nervously picked up one of the shiny spoons from the table setting and toyed with it. She shifted in her chair slightly, and as she did the casually open collar of her blouse revealed the Mariner's Cross. She was just about to answer the question when a loud truck rumbled into the parking lot on the south side of the building. As it rolled to a stop, the afternoon sun blazed off the windshield and the brilliance traveled through the partially open blinds of the window. The light was broken into narrow bands as it spread across the two people sitting at the table. It also struck the necklace. When Mari turned to avoid the glare the reflection disappeared, but it caught Neil's attention and he became entranced by it. He didn't wish to stare at the pendant so he immediately redirected his gaze back into her expressive and unblinking eyes, saying, "If you don't want to talk about this now, I will understand completely. Perhaps some other time then?"

Mari saw Nancy gawking at them from behind the bar so she leaned toward Neil and lowered her voice, saying, "I don't know what my father saw exactly. I wasn't there and my father won't tell anyone about what happened. He says people should mind their own business. I suppose I agree. I wish all this would go away. Actually, I really don't like the thought of aliens from outer space."

"I understand completely," replied Neil. "That is not something most people go looking for. So it seems as though he is determined not to discuss it. Am I right?"

"Yes," she replied, sitting back in the chair, "he is quite determined, especially with somebody he doesn't know."

"I see," said Neil. "Is there anything more you might like to say?"

Mari hesitated, she bit her bottom lip for a moment, then said, "I have been going out of my mind trying to figure it out. I probably shouldn't mention this but my father did say it was like some sort of huge creature." She drew a breath and continued. "He said it looked like 'a jellyfish' or something and there was a silver man out there with it. He saw it and it saw him."

"Hmm," replied Neil, appearing a little surprised but aware of her distress. "I can't begin to know what that must be like. It must be very difficult for your parents and you for that matter. I don't blame you for your fears."

"It sounds awfully strange doesn't it?" added Mari.

"I must agree," said Neil. "Is there anything more?"

"No, I can't think of anything else," said Mari, showing resolve. "People don't like to be ridiculed or have their lives shattered by things they don't understand."

"Yes, of course," said Neil, "yet, I must ask a few more questions. Did he ever find anything missing, broken, or were there any animals adversely affected? Was your father injured during the encounter?"

"Why do you ask?" she questioned.

"I have heard about certain manifestations," replied Neil. "At times there is a pattern with these things."

"There wasn't any damage that I know of," she continued, "and no one was hurt. Although the animals seemed a little spooked. That was a while back, even before my father saw what ever he saw."

"Was there some previous encounter?"

"I don't know, no one saw anything. Its just that the animals were acting funny."

"But you say you found nothing unusual anywhere on the property?"

"No, we didn't come across anything at all."

"I see."

"So what can you tell me about all this?" asked Mari.

"Well, I am afraid I do not have the answers yet," replied Neil, "the search goes on, and oddly, I have no more information than you do."

"Someone must know what's going on!" insisted Mari.

"Perhaps," said Neil, "I wish I could say more."

"Well, I have told you all I know," volunteered Mari.

"I think our discussion here has been sufficient," replied Neil. "You have been most accommodating in all of this. I will continue my quest. Things are what they are, but I want to express my thanks to you again, Mari, for your openness with me. If an opportunity presents itself, I may be able to give you an update. Please, let me know if I can be of any other assistance."

"No, not at this time, but I really didn't know what to do," replied Mari. "I guess I needed to talk to someone, even if it's just to know we're not all going out of our minds."

"You are not, I assure you," said Neil. "You have been very courageous and helpful, more than you know."

"Thank you," she replied, feeling somewhat unburdened.

"Therefore," said Neil. "I will not keep you any longer. I'm sure you need to be on your way."

They pushed the big wooden chairs back to the table, and then before she realized it, more words were tumbling out of her mouth, when she said, "I'm waiting for Nancy to give me a ride home. She'll be off work soon."

"I could take you home if you like?"

"No, you don't have to, thank you, Nancy can do it."

"I would be glad to help."

"Thank you for offering, really, but I'll wait for Nancy."

"I have the time," assured Neil. Mari looked for Nancy, but she had stepped away from the bar. Neil insisted, "It would be no problem."

"Are you sure?"

"I am quite sure."

Mari found herself giving in, but said, "Please, give me a minute." She headed back to the kitchen as Neil waited patiently by the table for what seemed an uncomfortably long time. Finally, she returned. Nancy was back at the bar staring at the two of them as Mari said, "Okay Mr. Clayborn, I accept!"

"Very well then," replied Neil, "it would be my pleasure."

Within minutes he was assisting her into his Jeep. The drive from Stone River was relatively short so their conversation was limited mostly to the heat and directions home. The hot afternoon air churned through the open windows of the moving vehicle, wistfully tossing Mari's hair around her face. It wasn't long before the passenger informed her chauffeur regarding the house coming up on the right side of the road.

A cloud of dust billowed from the Jeep as they entered the driveway and soon rolled to a stop under one of the huge trees along the driveway near the house. Neil noticed that the yard was replete with a bright display of late August flowers in the fullness of bloom. The house, the barn, and adjacent buildings were almost glowing in the mid afternoon light. A patch of tall sunflowers were radiating yellow and green by the windmill, effectively enhanced by the deep red paint on the well house behind them. The scene shimmered like a folk painting imbued with three dimensional energy. All this was incredibly inviting, an almost iconic image of country living that appealed to the past, yet the man suddenly began to have second thoughts. It was too late, though, because here he was and the young woman was asking more questions.

"Tell me, Mr. Clayborn," said Mari, "what's really going on? Please, if you any information at all I would love to hear it."

"I wish I could provide the answers you seek," replied Neil, earnestly. A moment passed where neither of them were quite sure of the other, but he had to ask, "How did you end up at the Midway anyhow?"

"Maybe I should ask you the same question!" exclaimed Mari. They both laughed nervously, but she said, "Well, I'm 25, and just out of college. I started at the tavern when I was in high school and now here I am. That's it I guess!"

"What did you study?"

"Architectural design. I have some interesting prospects, but I haven't found anything yet."

"I hope it works out for you."

"Yes, and for you as well."

"Things are progressing rather nicely."

"Thanks for the ride," said Mari, opening her door.

"My pleasure," said Neil, now feeling strangely shy.

Once she was out of the vehicle she ducked her head in the window, and said, "Why don't you come in and meet my parents? I'd like to introduce them to you."

"You would?" returned Neil, rather shocked at the offer.

"Yes," replied Mari, "I would. They won't bite."

"Possibly," admitted Neil, "I might be able to spare a few minutes."

"Okay!" declared Mari.

After Neil stepped out of the vehicle he spied the open sided structure within the circle of trees in the side yard, and remarked, "I must say this is a very beautiful place."

"I really love it here, I always have, its like a little part of heaven," she replied. "Come on, let me show it to you."

Mari led the way as they strolled across the front yard, then stepped through the gate in the arbor. Thoroughly taken by the atmosphere, Neil remarked again, saying, "I can see why you love it so much here."

When they stopped to look up through the mature leafy branches of the pear trees, she said, "I used to spend a lot of time here when I was young."

"You must have a lot of good memories," returned Neil, visualizing a little girl running around the big yard all by herself with only her imagination guiding her. "Any brothers or sisters?"

"No, I'm an only child," offered Mari.

Soon they found themselves at the very center of the gazebo, which provided a much welcomed shelter from the sun.

"This is quite charming," remarked Neil.

"It's my favorite place to be in all the world," she added, "especially in the summer."

"Your parents must be very proud of their home," he replied.

"Let's go in now," replied Mari. "I can't wait for you to meet them."

Neil was quickly brought back to reality as they walked around to the small porch on the side of the house. Mari let the screen door close gently behind them as they entered the kitchen, and called out, "Mom, we have company!"

Her mother appeared almost instantly from the dining room. She was more than surprised to see a man standing next to her daughter.

"Mom," voiced Mari, "this is Neil!"

"I'm very pleased to meet you, Neil," replied her mother, not hiding a certain sparkle in her eyes. "Mari has told us so much about you. She told us all about what happened at the tavern and she's been going on and on about it."

"Mom!" countered Mari, with a blush and trying to move on. "He offered to bring me home."

"Oh, well," answered her mother, smiling back, "and thank you for what you did."

"You have a fine daughter, Mrs. Cygnet," replied Neil, "anyone else would have done the same."

"No one else did," added her mother soberly. "So, Neil, where are you from?"

"New York, actually," replied Neil. "I bought a place out on Coverton Road about six months ago."

"Well, I must say, we all welcome you to Wyoming," said Jennifer. "I'm sure you'll like it out this way."

"Thank you," replied Neil. "It's certainly beautiful country."

Mari's face was beaming as her mother said, "You're welcome to stay for supper if you like! We are going to eat early today."

"Thank you, I appreciate the invitation," replied Neil, "and I would love to accept, but I am sorry, I cannot stay."

"Are you sure?" quizzed Mari, with the disappointment spilling into her voice.

"I am afraid so," said Neil, "I have business that I must attend to."

"Your work, I suppose?" questioned her mother.

"Yes," added Neil, "it is hard to get away sometimes."

"It's always hot in this kitchen," remarked Mari, "let's go in the living room, it will be cooler in there."

Jennifer trailed behind as Mari led Neil through the dining area to the living room. Neil continued to display an unusually keen interest in the house, and remarked, "You have a very beautiful home, Mrs. Cygnet. I have been admiring this fine example of Victorian architecture from the moment I arrived. It has just the right touch."

"Thank you," replied Jennifer proudly.

"My grandfather built the house after the original one burned," added Mari.

"I am sorry to hear that," said Neil, "I am sure it must have been wonderful as well."

"It was quite some time ago now," said Jennifer, "but we've worked hard to keep this one up."

"Very impressive," replied Neil.

"Well, you two," replied Jennifer, pointing toward the kitchen, "you'll have to excuse me a minute."

Neil began to feel somewhat more at ease as he was immersed in the inviting atmosphere of the large sunlit room, reminiscent of the beginning of the twentieth century, yet not suffering from the weight of the heavy trappings so evident of the era. Among the things of interest within the room were several early American style paintings, one of which was an excellent example of a sailing ship within an antique gold frame. It hung by the stairway leading to the second floor, and he would have asked Mari about it but, suddenly a deep voice boomed from the kitchen. The patriarch of the house demanded information, saying, "Whose Jeep is that out there?"

A stocky well built man suddenly appeared with Mari's mother in the archway of the dining room. Mari cheerfully greeted her father but there was no immediate response, so Mari excitedly said, "I'd like you to meet a friend of mine. This is Neil Clayborn!"

"Yes," replied her mother, echoing her daughter. "This is Neil."

Although Neil was over taken by a great deal of curiosity he was again made aware he was the stranger in the house. The confrontational nature of the young woman's father soon took the edge off the welcome, even so, he cordially extended his hand and greeted the man of the house.

Her father acknowledged Neil, by saying, "Mr. Clayborn, I've heard about you! I've also told Mari she shouldn't be working at that tavern."

Mari caught the drift of the conversation, and countered, "Let's not get into that now, Dad."

"Just so your friend here knows where we stand," returned her father, without taking his eyes off Neil.

"Now William," scolded Jennifer.

"He just moved out here," added Mari, trying to move things along.

"All right," pressed William, "what kind of work do you do, Mr. Clayborn?"

"Research," answered Neil, smoothly, "scientific research, mostly."

"Neil is a physicist," informed Mari. "He's also investigating some of the recent sightings around here."

"Oh, is he?" said William. "And, a big paperwork job in the city too I suppose? Well, when you're away from your desk you're not going to go snooping around here!"

"No, sir," answered Neil, contritely.

"I have heard that one before," contended William. "I've been approached about ten times already by nosey people just prying into other peoples affairs. Now if they would mind their own business maybe things would settle down some."

"I can understand completely," replied Neil, trying to be accommodating.

"Some things are better left well enough alone," informed William.

"Everyone needs their space," replied Neil.

"Good," stated William, "I'm glad you see it my way."

"Neil, would you like some ice tea or cold lemon aid?" asked Jennifer, hoping to learn more about Mari's new acquaintance.

"Thank you so much," replied Neil, "but I really must be going."

"The lemon aid is fresh squeezed!" returned Jennifer.

"It would be no trouble," added Mari.

"That sounds wonderful and I wish I could stay," returned Neil, observing the disappointment in Mari's eyes, "but I am on a tight schedule. It has been nice meeting all of you."

Mari's father grumbled under his breath, but Jennifer offered, "I'm glad we had a chance to meet you Neil, maybe you can visit with us some other time then?"

"Yes," said Neil, "of course, I will see what I can do."

"Must you go so soon?" said Mari.

"I am afraid so," returned Neil, earnestly.

"Well, then," said Mari, "let's go out on the front porch."

Mari directed Neil to the door. Her father had plunked down in his favorite chair and was holding a newspaper up to his nose and glanced over the top just long enough to see Neil and his daughter disappear into the yard.

"Thank you again for the ride," said Mari. "I apologize, my Dad can be rough at times, especially with all that's been going on. He is nice once you get to know him."

"It is quite all right, Mari, I understand."

"I do want you to like them. Things are upset now that's all."

"I find they really care about you, Mari," said Neil. "You should listen to them, you are lucky to have them."

"Yes, I know," she replied, as they walked to the Jeep, "they're concerned about what goes on around here. I'm sure they'll be okay, this will all work out, just give them some time."

"Of course," agreed Neil.

"You can come to see me at the tavern anytime you like," added Mari.

"Thank you, I believe I should like to do that," replied Neil.

Mari watched the Jeep as it left the driveway and headed in the direction of Stone River. She stayed in the yard gazing out at the road until the churning cloud of dust had completely rolled away.

By this time Frank was following a narrow trail up the mountain on foot. The terrain was rugged and forested, replete with breath taking views of an inviting green valley as well as the impressive mountain peak that marked his destination. The summer heat and lack of rain had allowed much of the surface vegetation to become dry and brittle under foot. And, although Frank was not seasoned hiker he was determined to find evidence of anything that would shed light on what might be transpiring on and around the mountain.

Del and his friends had not entertained pleasant thoughts of their last visit to the Midway Tavern and they were still trying to forget. The tense encounter had struck a chord of humiliation and it lingered in Del's brain. He vowed to get even, but for now he would turn to other appetites, like roaming the back roads looking for any kind of excitement. The men would linger in some small town until they became unwelcome or until the authorities would catch up with them, at which time their animal sense would kick in, forcing them to move on in an ever restless pursuit of adventure. The dominating personality of Del Toller was suffused with a predatory instinct for discovering the pulse of an event. He also had a more than a casual interest in Mari, but at the same time he was suspicious of her and was determined to find a way to make her comply with his wishes.

As the evening progressed Del would eventually cruise a certain road to the southwest of Stone River called Dovetail. The men were familiar with the many rutted trails that branched off to the north and to the south, all of which disappeared into the very recesses of the wilderness. At this time Del had no intention of taking any of the lonely trails. The sun had ducked behind the mountains and the late summer woods flew by the windows of the truck creating an almost hypnotic effect. Suddenly, Pete, who was sitting in the back seat casually looking to the south, saw something through the trees deep in the woods. He blurted out, "Hey man, I think I just saw a green light!"

"I think you've got a big imagination," chided Del.

"No, man," said Pete, "I mean it! Like one of them strange lights or something. It was a green flash!"

"What did you have for lunch?" quipped Jack.

"I mean it, I saw one of them green lights, I swear!" returned Pete, with true excitement beginning to surface.

"Green?" laughed Del. "I know what's green! What you been smokin' boy."

"Hey, I think I saw it too," exclaimed Jack, "back there, in them trees."

"Told you," declared Pete, "back there, over in that direction."

"All right man we'll have a look see, but this better be good," replied Del.

Kenny shook his head in disbelief as the other two men tried to convince Del they really did see something. Del was not interested in the wilderness if there was no immediate pay off, his habit was to slip through the country side as a means of acquiring a different form of wildlife, but this time his curiosity was getting the better of him. Reluctantly he turned the truck around and caught the first trail going south. Now, against his usually strong, self absorbed and unbending will, he drove his truck down the two-track road.

"You better be right," advised Del, losing his humor. "If we don't see somethin', you owe me, I ain't going after this for nothin'."

Once on the trail Pete and Jack lost sight of the illusive glow, nevertheless, Del drove deeper into the forest hoping to see something, anything that would make for a good story at the next bar. Like many trails of its type it was made up of two parallel dirt paths with deep ruts, rocks, and unexpected hairpin turns.

"This is swell, we better not be breaking somethin' on this truck," warned Del, as they banged and bounced, ever deeper on the trail.

"I know I saw it," added Pete.

"You and Jack is always seein' somethin'," scoffed Kenny.

"I don't know about them flying saucers," said Del, "but I'd like to see them little green men. Pete, you're all fired up, where did you say you saw them lights again?"

Pete pointed to the west of the trail, and said, "Over there, out that way."

"This trail is getting worse," said Del, still in command. "Looks like we'll have to park it. We got to get our feet out and we're going to be doing some hikin' in the dark."

"You know, Del," added Jack. "We're gettin' close to that Cygnet property out here."

"Hey," returned Del, with new interest, then scoffing at the realization. "At least now we got a good reason to explore."

Del wedged the truck into a naturally open spot next to the trail and cut the engine. The doors flew open and Del grabbed a pistol from under the front seat. They were primed and ready for the hunt, but now they needed a plan so they all clustered around the truck in the dark to argue about the direction of the mysterious glow.

Sometime earlier, the Cygnet family had their evening meal. Now Mari's parents were bound for the nearest shopping center on a weekly trip for household necessities. In the remaining daylight, and having some quiet time for herself, Mari strolled through the yard to admire the flowers and contemplate the events of the day. She was outwardly satisfied, though inside there were many things still unsettled. The westerly winds had increased significantly as warm bursts of air provoked spontaneous dust devils in the open places, even playing tag on Landings Road that traced by the Cygnet ranch. Mari recalled her father's admonition about her lonesome excursions, yet something tugged at her heart and it would not let go. She was convinced a short ride would free her soul so she left a note concerning her whereabouts on the kitchen table, though, ultimately she knew she would have to answer for it later. Besides, she had her phone just in case anything happened.

Evening was well under way when she entered the barn to get her horse. All but one of the horses on the Cygnet ranch had been on edge, skittish, and loosing connection with their keepers, seemingly affected by something intangible. This had occurred some time before the incident in the corral and they now appeared to be doing better, yet her ten year old draft horse had not been affected in any way. King was a beautiful animal and Mari knew his habits and trusted his muscular frame, so it was without any hesitation that she brought him out of his stall. She took a few minutes to speak softly to him and brush down his chestnut brown coat. Now, with the saddle securely in place the gentle animal willingly followed her out of the barn. They went through the corral to the gate on the opposite side. From there the lane would take them out into the open fields and the beckoning wilderness.

Their property was extensive and Mari could stay in familiar territory while still managing to get away from things. Riding gave her new vigor, she loved the rugged and rolling landscape, sculptured rocks, and twisted pines. The air was still warm but fresh and full of life, instilling a great sense of release. She felt she could ride forever. Somehow it was the place itself, the solitary reality of it, and the vision she took with her when it was over that she loved. But, she wasn't truly alone—she had King.

She left her burdens behind her. Now veering off into an open field of wild grass she let the horse run. She could feel the wind in her hair as the hooves of the great animal pushed them speedily over the ground. The Mariner's Cross bounced on the chain around her neck with the rhythm and motion of the horse as she let the animal find its stride. The beauty of the land existed in a setting of contrasts which caused a visceral reaction within the soul. When the time seemed right Mari nudged the horse back to the trail and she followed it until they arrived at the northern perimeter of the property. The evening sun had long disappeared as they reached the narrow ridge separating the Cygnet property from state land. It was about a quarter mile long and wooded, and ran from east to west, where it obscured any clear view of a large clearing located to the north. Mari decided to take a few minutes to rest before returning home so she jumped down and led King to a place where she could secure him.

Del, Pete, Kenny, and Jack were all on foot in the darkness heading into the deep underbrush in search of the odd lights. They were approaching the north side of the same ridge where Mari had stopped. The men decided to mount the ridge to see what was on the other side so they crept quietly through the trees to the top. From their position they could see down on both sides of the elevation. Until now, all they saw were the normal things one would find in a dark wooded area but, it would be on the north side of the ridge in the adjacent clearing, where they would finally catch sight of the elusive green glow. It appeared much dimmer and smaller than the one Pete had seen and was pulsating at regular intervals. As the men crouched in the brush they saw a large spherical shape that was much darker than its immediate surroundings and the mysterious blinking light was on the top.

"What's that thing over there?" sputtered Jack.

"I don't know," whispered Del, "but that must be Pete's green light."

Looking down the south side of the ridge the men suddenly caught sight of the small white beam of a flashlight nearly the same distance from them as the green light.

"Now I see a light down there on that other side!" cried Pete.

"Quiet!" whispered Del. "We got to set here and see what goes."

"What is that big black thing anyhow?" whispered Pete.

"Looks like a huge ball or something," remarked Del.

"This is too weird," added Kenny.

"Shut up!" admonished Del, in a gritty whisper.

Mari knew exactly where she was and how to get home. She could trust the horse on the trails even after the light of evening had departed but she also knew she must soon be on her way. After a few more minutes she turned off the flashlight and climbed into the saddle. This was when she caught sight of the mysterious green light on the other side of the ridge, the same light seen by the men crouching in the woods up on the ridge. She decided to dismount the horse and find something to hitch the animal to. As she tied King to the branch of a tree a series of muffled hissing sounds came from among the trees a short distance away. This took place between the men and Mari's present location, which she could not hear, and because of this she didn't notice anything out of the ordinary. If she had, she would have seen a series of dark shapes on the move over the ridge.

"I think I just saw something," said Pete.

"Yeah, somethin's movin' fast." croaked Del.

"Yeah, but what's that white light flickering down there," said Jack, peering around a tree trunk.

"I just heard some strange noises," whispered Pete.

"This is nuts," said Jack.

"Don't you know nothing city boy?" whispered Del. "That's a horse down there."

"So much for little green men," said Kenny, rather boldly.

"Keep it down," rasped Del.

"Something else is down there," whispered Jack.

"That sort of looks like a girl," added Del. "Hey, what if that's Mari!"

"Can't be," said Pete. "What's she doin' out here?"

"It's her property and she's always riding," whispered Del.

The dense stand of trees on the ridge provided limited cover as Mari slowly crept up the hill in search of the green light. She crossed over the flat top but when she reached the northern edge her heart skipped a beat, for now she had a full view of a large dark object. It was approximately thirty feet in diameter without any discernible features. She crept half way down to get a closer look and saw an object that tapered back like a cone. This was all she could see for the feeble flashlight could not penetrate very far into the darkness. The thing seemed to be like a stationary globe with a cone on one side and it was sitting on a low pedestal. Mari wondered if this was the object her father had seen, but by now her curiosity was more than satisfied, so she scrambled back up the ridge and back down the other side.

"What's that?" cried Jack, seeing some dark shapes moving among the trees.

"Heck if I know," answered Del.

"What kind of a creep show is this?" declared Pete.

"Keep it down!" admonished Del.

"I don't know what that thing is but I'm sure that's Mari down there," said Jack.

"Has to be," said Del, "what's she doing out here anyhow?"

"Them dark things by that globe don't look like no people," cried Pete.

Suddenly the object became covered with an eerie green luminescence. The ghostly light bathed the entire area as Mari dodged trees and logs on her run back to the horse.

"Look at that!" cried Del.

"That thing is moving!" cried Pete.

The object lifted up from the ground and stopped just above the trees. Mari untied King, and once she was in the saddle she gingerly nudged the animal back on the trail toward the ranch but the horse seemed sluggish and slow to respond. This behavior wasn't like the strong dependable animal she knew. The horse pranced and stomped at the ground. No amount of coaxing would get him to move from the spot where he stood. Within moments the object left the clearing and hovered directly overhead and an intense hissing sound filled the air. King reacted by rearing up and Mari fought for control. The object began to strobe, which further disoriented the animal, and it bolted into a gallop. Mari slid from the saddle and plummeted to the ground, landing in a patch of tall grass by the trail. When she hit the hard rocky soil her glasses flew off and her phone tumbled out of her pocket. King ran down the trail as fast as a horse of his breed could go while his rider lay unresponsive. The object hovered over the spot were Mari had fallen and descended to within twenty feet of her body. An instant later it shot into the high clouds leaving Mari unconscious and alone. Del and the others looked on in disbelief, straining to see what was happening.

While the men were considering whether to help, run, or stay put, having seen more than they bargained for, another object appeared above the clearing on the north side of the ridge. The new arrival was saucer shaped and covered in amber light. This visitor, which was roughly the same size as the green object which preceded it, entered the clearing and hovered. It did not land, and after a few moments it darted above the trees, then swooped down to hover about fifteen feet above the woman on the ground. The men watched in awe as it changed its relative position several times. After a few minutes it retreated upward and was gone.

But the drama was not over, a third object appeared. It had a more strident sound that reverberated through the trees, and lit up the entire area as it hovered over the spot where Mari lay, casting much more light than the other two objects combined. Three long silvery tendrils came down from the bottom of the object. Each had a small bulb-like end that flexed back and forth. Mari became semi-conscious as the flexing probes nearly touched her face. Again she blacked out. The tendrils withdrew and the object traveled back over the trees to settle in the clearing on the other side of the ridge. Once there, it transformed into something that resembled a glowing Solmissus with its many tentacles. A humanoid form emerged from the monstrous display and headed over the ridge.

"Let's get out of here!" cried Pete.

"Yeah," cried Jack, "I'm for that."

"No, not yet," cried Del. "I want to see this."

A being clothed in glistening silver walked over the ridge and down the southern slope to the place where Mari lay. It knelt down and made a quick examination of her body with a small device. A gloved hand touched Mari's head as if to examine her, then it retrieved her glasses and her phone. The air was pierced by a sharp howl, that was followed by a loud snap, accompanied by a low pitched throb and a circular wall of glowing sapphire instantly spread out from the perimeter of the Solmissus. It extended upward forty feet above the ground and spread out in all directions, traveling over the hill and through the trees, where it engulfed Mari and the silver being kneeling beside her. It also reached the men hiding in the brush. A paralysis overtook them and though they were unable to move they were very much aware of what was taking place. Mari's limp body surrendered to the being as it picked her up and carried her over the hill toward the creature where they were swallowed up by it. The creature dissolved into a mass of fluttering sails and entered the sky. The green object came out of nowhere and made a rendezvous but kept a respectable distance from it. The amber light also reappeared and trailed behind the other two objects as they disappeared into the night. The men in the woods now began to regain their ambulatory capabilities.

Del cried, "We're out of here, now!" None of the other men disagreed as they ran wildly through the woods back to the truck. The pickup started without difficulty and they wasted no time making an exit from the wilderness trail. The tires screeched when the rubber grabbed the paved road and Del kept driving, taking road after road, speeding aimlessly into the night.

King stopped along the trail approximately a half mile away from where Mari fell, he lingered there for a while, but something finally nudged him homeward. Eventually he returned to the corral and waited patiently for someone to open the gate.

Earlier that day, Frank had not progressed as far as he hoped. It soon would be dark and he felt he was no closer to finding the evidence that he was looking for. The trail on Thunder Peak continued to grow ever steeper until he was confronted by some extraordinarily thick underbrush. He was able to pull himself along on his stomach until he reached an open area. Grumbling, he suffered scratches and scrapes, and tears in his clothes but he was on his feet once again. It was disappointing to see that the terrain had now become nearly vertical in some places. Yet this was a far easier climb than scaling the eastern slope where the entire side of the mountain had crumbled down. He took a few minutes to examine his surroundings and spotted a narrow but prominent formation jutting out from the rest of the rock face like a high garden wall. After slipping between the rocks and a tangle of branches he saw what looked to be a natural opening in the rock. He believed this would be a good time to get the flashlight and the pistol out of his pack.

Cautiously, Frank entered the dark opening and discovered a small cave. He also found that he wasn't the first person to experience the confines of its rugged walls, for ground was littered with beer cans, sticks, paper, and there was a pile of charred wood which still smelled of smoke. The interior was about thirty feet in length, fifteen feet wide, and measured about ten feet from the ground to its jagged ceiling. The back wall, being relatively flat, had been emblazoned with graffiti. A short time into his search he heard a rustling sound on the outside of the cave and wheeled around to see what might be there. In the process he accidentally struck the flashlight on a sharp rock protruding from the wall. The light flew out of his hand and went out when it hit the ground. A vigorous flapping of wings and the hoot of an owl could be heard as Frank groped around in the dark.

He recovered the flashlight, but it would not work. Then he remembered another tiny flashlight he carried as a spare, but found it wasn't working either. After twisting, tapping, and fumbling, he was still left in the dark, and cried out, "Cheap junk!" He decided to try the larger flashlight again and continued to fumble with it. Persistence payed off and a beam blazed forth so he resumed his search. His attention was immediately was drawn to the back wall where the prolific use of spray paint was evident. As Frank observed the wall he mumbled, "Smart, real smart. They did a better job of it 6,000 years ago and those guys didn't have florescent orange!"

Falling back on his habit he pulled the pack of cigarettes out of his backpack and put one of the sticks between his lips as he examined the cave. He was hoping his trusted sources might have some ideas and tried to make a call but the phone wouldn't work. Returning his attention to the back wall of the cave he found it to be somewhat smoother than the rest of the interior. As he examined the surface he noticed a rather peculiar eight inch circle. He thought nothing of its irregular shape until he discovered what seemed to be another faint though perfect six inch circle cut within it. This was unlike the rest of the graffiti, because there was a variance in the texture of the rock. There was also a small ledge at the bottom of the circle, which was masked by the images created with the spray paint. He also noticed the inner portion of the circle seemed to be composed of a separate piece of stone defined only by a hairline crack. He dropped the cigarette and on a whim he used a pocket knife to dig around the edge of the odd stone. Frank worked at it until he was able to remove the stone. Now there was a shallow cavity with a small perfectly formed disk at the back. The disc had the appearance of a gemstone and was blue in color and smooth to the touch. Frank chiseled around it with the knife but it wouldn't yield to his efforts as did the larger piece.

Now he felt he was onto something but at this moment the flashlight decided to fail. He was left groping in the dark once again, this time for the cigarette lighter. It lit up with one flick of the lever. He found a short piece of rusty wire by the charred wood and wound it around the lighter to hold the button down. This kept the flame going like a miniature torch. Next, he looked for a place to set it down and found that the small ledge at the bottom of the cavity in the wall was just large enough to hold the lighter. By the light of the meager flame he finally managed to get the flashlight working again. The cave brightened. Meanwhile, the lighter had fallen against the small blue stone at the back of the cavity. He retrieved the lighter, but quickly let it fall to the ground because it was extremely hot. The flame went out. Then there was a clicking sound behind him. To Frank's amazement, a section of the back wall, which was slightly smaller than a domestic entry door swung open into the cave. He managed to control his astonishment and cautiously poked his light into the opening and saw a platform with a narrow staircase descending into the depths of the rock. It was dark and a damp earthy smell welled up from the opening. After retrieving the lighter and taking one last look around he headed for the open door. With the flashlight in one hand and gun in the other he started down the stairs. He had descended only a few steps when the door of the cave slammed shut with an echoing thud. Leaping back up to the platform he found the opening had become like a solid wall again with no visible latches, circles, or blue stones in sight.

Realizing he was now trapped he considered his options, which were few, so with a new rush of adrenalin he followed the narrow steps downward. An increasing amount of condensation appeared on the walls as he made his way down. Small landings were located at approximately every one hundred feet in the decent, so when he reached the final landing he estimated he had gone down to a depth of about a thousand feet. At this terminal he found a three by seven foot door with a very obvious disk set into the wall next to it. He put the flame of the lighter to the disk and the door snapped open! Here was a perfectly formed cubical with smooth walls and another door on the opposite wall but this time there was a mechanism next to it. By putting his ear against the polished metal surface he could hear mechanical activity so he pulled the lever on the wall. The door disappeared and he was presented with a long gray hallway where he discovered a series of panels to his right that looked like doors but with no visible means of entry. Abreast of one of the panels he heard an odd sound. It snapped open. Two silver beings stood before him and each had a weapon. A burst of energy from one of the weapons rendered Frank unconscious.

Towards morning William Cygnet discovered King waiting silently at the gate of the corral unharmed and cooperative, quite ready to return to his stall for the night. The police had been notified about the disappearance of his daughter and they eventually arrived in the predawn hours to help search the wilderness and trails.

Chapter Eight: Discovery

I have traveled through the night.
I was taken,
Yet each new day carries the essence of discovery.
Mari

The fog of sleep was lifting and a cool breeze gently brushed against Mari's cheek. It was just after midnight and thoughts of home, horseback riding, and strange lights had begun to collect within her mind. Her eyes turned to the host of stars twinkling in the dark expanse above her head. The stars were captivating and she was enjoying the wonder of it all, so much so, that disappointment set in when the stars began to fade. Soon she realized there were no trees anywhere within her field of vision and she was not on the ground but lying on a soft comfortable bed with a pink blanket tucked around her. A woman dressed in a simple pink hospital uniform was sitting in a chair next to the bed.

Although still feeling drowsy, Mari questioned the woman, saying, "Where am I?"

The woman answered with a pleasant voice, and said, "Everything will be fine but you must rest for a while."

Mari responded by saying, "I fell off my horse. I was trying to get home—" Her eyes grew heavy and she yielded to a few more minutes of sleep. When her awareness returned she realized the sky above her was a now a wonderful shade of pink and the woman was still sitting in the chair as before.

Mari asked the woman who she might be and the woman got up from the chair to adjust the blanket on the bed and answered, saying, "I'm Dr. Canton, but you may call me Candice."

Mari remembered hitting her head, but it seemed like a dream, and though she was not in any pain she put her hand to her temple as if to feel for an injury, then she insisted on getting up, saying, "I need to go home."

The doctor said, "No, not yet," and rotated her hands with the index fingers pointing toward each other emphasizing her speech as she said, "You are now recovering from a severe head injury and you must rest."

"I feel okay," Mari replied firmly.

Candice saw the determination of her patient so she reluctantly let her sit up and returned her glasses to her. Something about the room seemed unusual. There was a gentle light and everything was the same color of pink. Looking down at the floor she found it to be transparent allowing her to see down into the space below. This made her feel a bit queasy, still, she was determined to get out of the bed so the doctor helped her rise to her feet. Now she became aware that she was inside a perfect sphere measuring about twenty-five feet in diameter. The medical equipment next to her bed and even the strange equipment below the transparent floor gleamed with the same shade of pink. There came a soft beeping sound, which Mari couldn't hear, but Candice was prompted to approach one side of the sphere. She opened a small hatch and stepped out of view to held a conversation with someone outside.

Moments later the doctor returned with the other person.

"Neil!" cried Mari.

"Hello, Mari, how are you?"

"I'm okay, but—"

"I am glad to see you are up and about."

"Yes, but where am I?"

"You are in a special place where you can recover your strength," assured Neil.

"You have received the best possible care in this facility," affirmed Candice.

"Everything will be fine," said Neil, now using clear American sign language for emphasis. "You should make a complete recovery."

"I fell off my horse...I don't know what happened...there was this light and—" she rambled.

"You received quite a serious injury to the right side of your head," remarked Neil.

Mari put her hand to her temple again and felt for a welt but there was no swelling or pain. Still confused, she said, "I don't remember much, I'm having trouble recalling everything."

"That is quite understandable," said Neil, "you experienced severe head trauma, but I assure you, you will be fine in no time at all."

"I'll return to check on you in a few minutes," assured Candice, "I believe you are in good hands now."

"Thank you so much for your help, Candice," replied Neil.

"I'll be around," said the doctor, displaying a small but strained smile. "I'm here to help as always."

As soon as the doctor left the chamber, Mari asked, "What hospital is this?"

Neil ignored her immediate question and now communicated using sign language only, to say, "You were unconscious for a number of hours but you are going to be just fine."

"Neil, you're using sign language?" observed Mari.

"Something I picked up along the way," answered Neil.

"But you—"

"I can explain, but we want you to know that we were determined to give you the very best medical attention possible."

"Was it that serious?"

"Yes, Mari, I am afraid it was."

"Do my parents know?"

"They do not, but we have arranged for you to contact them shortly."

"They must be so worried!"

"We could not leave you unattended out there in the woods."

"What is this place?"

"I will explain—"

"Are you a doctor?"

"Not in the way you are thinking, but I did make sure you got the necessary assistance."

The door to the chamber opened again and Candice stepped back in. Neil said to Mari, "The answers will come soon enough, but for now, I have asked Candice to assist you. She will provide everything you need and see that you rest a little while longer."

"But I'm feeling so much better now!"

Neil saw the anxiety begin to well up within her, and said, "I will return in a few hours, Mari. Candice will make it possible for you to call home. Now, please, you must go with her. I assure you, everything will be fine."

"Where are you going?" asked Mari.

"We have a special quarters for you to stay in," said Neil, not answering her question.

"But, Neil," she pleaded, "can't you stay with me?"

"Please," he insisted, "please go with Candice."

Neil disappeared through the hatch and left the two women alone in the spherical room. Mari felt disoriented again and found it difficult to accept the new demands in an unfamiliar place. She could do no more at this time than to reluctantly follow Candice out into a long corridor that had the appearance of a medical facility. This led to another, then another, and finally another hallway that looked as if it were part of some magnificent hotel with heavy woodwork and papered walls. They walked past many beautifully carved wooden doors with different symmetrical leaf and flower patterns. When they came to a door carved with a delicate rose pattern, Candice opened it and Mari followed her inside. The doctor was still not forthcoming about the whereabouts of Neil when asked, but she said that Neil would explain everything when he returned. Then Mari insisted on calling home and pulled her phone out of her pocket.

"Your phone will not work here," replied Candice, curtly. "We will provide a secure line for you to call out."

"Why not?" asked Mari, resisting the restrictions put on her.

"I'm not at liberty to discuss that with you now," said Candice, "but you are free to use our communications." She did honor Mari's request by bringing her over to a desk with a small communication device on it and let her make a call. The device translated incoming speech into text so Mari could communicate in her own way. She was heartened to communicate with her parents, who were relieved beyond measure at the sound of their daughter's voice, but the lack of detail on the part of their daughter was not comforting. Mari assured them she was indeed alive and well and she would be home soon but she couldn't even begin to tell them where she was. Once the call ended the device no longer allowed the reception or the transmission of calls.

Everything had been done to make sure their newcomer was comfortable in her new quarters, so Candice excused herself from the room. Now that she was alone, Mari began to look around the living space, all of which resembled an old fashioned hotel with everything a person would want or need. There was a small kitchen, the bed was soft, the chairs were comfortable, and there was an ample quantity of fresh food in the refrigerator. She also discovered two sets of green velvet curtains on the wall of the large living room. Pulling the draw-string on one of the sets revealed a large mirror. She went to the other set and found a painting of an obscure mountain scene. This was somewhat disconcerting and it only left her more confused. Feeling tired, she thought a short rest on the large comfortable bed seemed to be in order. Fatigue was setting in and it wasn't long before the elixir of sleep took over.

Several hours had passed, after which Candice let herself into Mari's room. She gently touched the sleeping woman on the shoulder and spoke her name. Startled, Mari's eyes popped open, but in a soft and coaxing voice, Candice said, "It is time."

"Time for what?" questioned Mari.

"For Neil to return," replied Candice.

"How long was I asleep?" asked Mari.

"Not long, but you have rested well," was the doctor's reply, "and I should think Neil will be here very shortly."

"Will I be going home?" asked Mari, beginning to hope.

"It will be as soon as it is feasible," replied Candice, with a pleasant smile. "Neil will take care of how and when that will take place. Don't worry, everything is going very well at this point." The woman then left the room and closed the door quietly behind her.

Mari felt as though time was standing still but just as she began to feel anxiety creep back into her soul she heard a soft knock on the door. Neil was there to greet her and as always he was extremely neat in appearance. He asked her how she was feeling, to which she replied, "I'm okay I guess, I'm just feeling a little foggy."

"Quite normal," said Neil, "you had us all very concerned for a while, though you are recovering rapidly. I am sorry for any distress we may have caused. I shall now provide some pertinent answers, so I would be pleased if you would take a walk with me. Now that you are here, things must no longer remain hidden."

"What do you mean?" replied Mari, anxiously. "Where are we going?"

"Listen, Mari," said Neil, "I want you to know that your well being was our first priority. We were successful. We came to your aid because it was necessary."

"I believe you've already told me that."

"Yes," replied Neil, appearing to regather his thoughts.

"What are you saying?" asked Mari, nervously.

"I take complete responsibility for bringing you here," answered Neil. Mari grew silent and Neil recognized that she was having difficulty when she backed away from him. "Things have become extremely complicated, but there are still some things I must reveal."

"Neil, what things?" she pleaded.

"Trust me," was all he said, then he took her by the hand. Mari's apprehension only increased as they walked down passageway after passageway. It was impossible to get any sense of direction because all of the corridors were of similar dimensions. The wall surfaces were imprinted with stylized versions of many kinds of mountain flora, exhibiting vines and leaves that intertwined each other, and upon closer observation the designs were imperceptibly changing from one to another.

Neil easily communicated with her in sign language, saying, "I mentioned our work when we spoke at the tavern. Actually, we began something called the Mechanics Project, this in turn led to the construction of a safe shelter for our ongoing research and what you are about to see."

It wasn't long before the leisurely walk took them to a large elevator. Although it was spacious inside Mari was not at ease when the doors closed them in and it traveled upward. A slight vibration came from within the walls, one that could be felt, and soon it began to increase. Mari eyed Neil suspiciously as he took what looked like a cell phone from his belt, saying, "This is what we call the Remote." He tapped an icon on screen then put it to his ear. "Yes, Marcus, Mari and I are coming up. I have had some delays but we will be there shortly."

When the elevator opened, the two of them stepped into a great circular hallway of pure white. It curved away to the left and to the right and was illuminated by a narrow band of light embedded at the peak of the arched ceiling twenty feet above the floor. Directly in front of them were two silver panels which formed a ten foot square. These began to part as they walked toward them and a symphony, no, a storm consisting of light, water, and sound thrashed behind a transparent barrier at the opposite end of a twenty-five foot long tunnel.

Mari became frightened when she saw it, even so, he led her ever closer to the frenzy, and she exclaimed, "Neil, that's what I saw in the woods!"

"Do not be afraid," said Neil.

Vivid memories returned to her mind with a vengeance, and she turned away, saying, "I want to go back now, please!"

"No harm will come to you," assured Neil. "What you are seeing will not harm you."

Although it was terrifying, the violence soon abated, quite simply dissolving away, leaving the transparent barrier dark and silent.

"This is crazy!" cried Neil's reluctant guest, as she tried desperately to hold on to some form of reality.

"There is no danger," he said to her. "I am not an alien, Mari. I am human like you. I live in Wyoming just as you do."

"I'm not ready for this!" she cried.

Mari felt trapped when she looked back and saw the panels to the outer corridor close behind them. The transparent barrier that now faced them was like a type of circular shutter composed of multiple leaves. It began to open. Leaf slid over leaf in quiet motion expanding from the center to the outer edge to create an opening. When the process was complete they were greeted by a moisture laden haze and a very wet black marble floor. The air within the huge chamber smelled fresh, like after a thunderstorm on a warm summer's evening.

"I assure you," said Neil, "there will be no monsters."

"No monsters?" she whispered.

"None at all," he replied.

The haze was beginning clear and Neil bid her to step in. Something luminous began to take shape within the fog of the chamber, and though Mari couldn't hear the trickle of water flowing into multiple drains, she could watch the haze disappear as it was drawn away by an aggressive ventilation system. As the air cleared, he said to her, "Of all the eyes from the outside world, yours are the first to fully gaze upon the final result of our work."

Not sure of what she was seeing, Mari asked, "What is this?"

"A vessel," he replied.

She recalled all the reports of alien objects, yet nothing she would apply to what filled her eyes at that moment. "Its like a jewel!" she exclaimed.

"An excellent observation," replied Neil. "This is the culmination of an intense manufacturing process. In so doing we have incorporated many synthetic materials, the forms of which replicate such known substances as sapphire, amethyst, zircon and beryl."

"But my father saw—"

"A jellyfish?

"Yes, that's all he would tell us."

"The Solmissus is not alive I assure you."

"Not alive?"

"It is not," promised Neil. "I must admit we take advantage of a bit of theater at times. You might say it is something of a diversion."

The object before them measured one hundred and fifty feet from hull edge to hull edge. Its upper and lower surfaces were identical, in a shape that was indeed circular, and it shimmered with a lustrous inner light. Four self leveling struts elevated it seven feet above its own reflection so that the entire vessel reached a total height of forty feet. The larger center portion of the hull diminished to a narrow outer rim. Eight external sapphire ribs divided it into sections, which merged with the outer rim, then extended beyond it in a sword like fashion. Each extension featured a mild delta wing shape and terminated ten feet from the hull and all were capped with a small transparent sphere which glowed with white light. Sixteen silver spars protruded from the vessel horizontally, stemming from a point on each rib about one-third the distance from the center. These began to retract back into their nests as the two people advanced on the vessel.

By this time, though, Mari's attention was drawn to yet another feature of the vessel. For within each of the sections between the ribs there was a single large convex oval surface that resembled an engraved cameo of ivory and sardonyx. These were fifteen feet in length and eight feet wide and oriented lengthwise between the inner hub and close to the outer rim. A frame of amber beryl surrounded a continuous flow of images on each of the ovals, which consisted of landscapes, seascapes, people, and things. On the upper surface of the vessel the head of the image was oriented toward the hub, whereas, on the under-side the top of the image favored the outer rim. Between each oval and the outer rim of the vessel there was a scrolling ornate flourish of amber beryl.

Eight individual ports or windows were assembled near the central portion of the vessel. These were rectangular, silvered on the outside, and oriented horizontally around the circumference. A single six foot diameter star sapphire covered the central hub both top and bottom, which had a separate outer ring to increase the diameter by another two feet. The three inch wide outer rim of the hub was capped with amethyst and perforated by thirty-two oval openings. All of this shimmered off the black marble floor in an interplay of color and form.

"Did you bring me here in this?" asked Mari.

"Yes," confessed Neil, "you were unconscious at the time."

"I feel as though I would like to reach out and touch it," she voiced, "just to see if it might be real."

"You shall do so," answered Neil. Then he gave a voice command to the ship, saying, "Companion-module."

The inner portion of the sapphire disk on the underside of the vessel began to descend and with it came a gleaming white cylinder struck by lines that appeared to divide it into multiple sections. It abruptly stopped when it reached the floor, after which two large sections opened. Neil motioned for Mari to join him in the small yet plush compartment within. It was illuminated at the ceiling and the floor, and the inner surface was covered with a deep red tufted fabric with trim that resembled dark cherry wood. Neil's guest resisted the impulse to actually touch her surroundings as she tried to deal with the place in which she found herself. As the cylinder traveled back up within the vessel, Neil, now speaking and signing, said, "In short, we have resolved some of the difficulties which have persisted regarding the theories of relativity and quantum physics. By the use of several uniquely dissimilar processes we have subsequently been able to control a vast amount of energy. Nevertheless, you could say it is all about the light."

"Light is a good thing," replied Mari, trying to sound positive.

"This is not an alien vessel," continued Neil. "You will find no magic, only mechanics, this is not mysticism, only mechanism. It was constructed here by the mere application of physics out of the materials needed for its specific function. An innovation of the human mind. Perhaps it was good timing on our part, perhaps it was the chance assembly of certain talent, however conceived, it is at our disposal."

The doors of the companion-module opened to the upper-most deck. Here, on the A Deck or what could be called the bridge, was a circular enclosure with eight horizontal viewports. All slanted toward the ceiling as they wrapped around the hull and conformed with the design of the vessel. The companion-module was then at the epicenter of a compartment that received a 360 degree fusillade of illuminated data. The ports functioned as both windows and display screens for text and pictorials. The data flowed in a continuous upward cascade with small frames of information intermittently highlighted at brief intervals, effectively displaying magnified texts or holographic enlargements for closer scrutiny by the viewer. Six seats were strategically placed at specific locations, which incorporated devices and appointments to comfortably accommodate each user. Each one also possessed a slightly different contour and its own array of controls. More available seating was stowed underneath a deck of dark blue carpet-like material that was replete with an interwoven three rope design in gold.

Also set within the control consoles were two fourteen inch oval paintings. Each directly opposing the other, obstructed only by the companion-module in a straight line of sight. These were rendered in a nineteenth century American style and each possessed a miniature clipper ship in a bottle at the bottom portion of the frame. One was titled Search, and it depicted a ship of sail at rest in a peaceful harbor. The other was named Discover, and portrayed a violent sea striking the rocks of a jagged shoreline.

Neil spoke out loud now, saying, "We have a special guest with us today."

The ship immediately responded to his statement with one word: "Acknowledged."

Neil turned to Mari, and using sign language only, he said, "Please, speak your name."

She complied with her finest voice, and said, "Mari."

The system generated soft musical tones, then silently displayed: "Mari Abigail Cygnet," on all the screens.

"It knows me?" she questioned.

"Acknowledged and confirmed," came another script.

"Oh," she replied, "of course it does!"

Neil began speaking and signing, when he said, "The computer anticipates thought patterns as it interacts with the user, then responds visually, and or audibly. Thus it assists the crew by indicating what we need before we know we need it. You might say it gets into our heads, but this helps us sort through the deluge of information we must receive. All governed by a triplex computer, where each component is fully independent, yet completely unified. Together they form a singular device."

Just as Neil finished speaking, one of the port screens became transparent and for the first time Mari could see out. The view revealed a row of large windows in the cavernous dome about thirty feet above the floor just to the right of the circular entrance. Now she could observe people moving about freely within the bright enclosure.

Yet, it was where she now stood that she finally felt she could touch a part of such an atypical world. One that was an amalgam of old and new technology, and ergonomics under the influence of 19th century design. She ran her fingers along polished wood and shining crystal, then felt the synthetic fabric of the seats and observed the display screens alive with data; hoping for something to assuage her questioning mind, something, anything that might reveal the true reason for the technology that seemed to be swallowing her up.

"I must say, this is all very beautiful," concluded Mari, "but why, Neil, why all this?"

"From here we can search the cosmos," he replied, "the sky, and even the sea. But most of all, it is our intent to seek the mysteries of space. This is the commencement."

"Are you the captain?"

"Some would say that I am," he replied, "but you could say we have all come together to lend a collective hand to this project. So, Mari, we are now finished here. Now please come with me, there is much more."

They explored the other decks of the ship and inner cabins which housed the crew quarters and even the medical unit where she was first treated for her injuries. The lowest deck of the ship proved to be of a similar structure as related to the uppermost deck, only inverted, where a set of viewports similar to the ones on the bridge traced around the bottom edge of the enclosure flush with the deck. Here he explained the power systems and engine components. The two of them entered the companion-module for the last time to exit the ship.

Once their feet touched the marble floor of the dome the Remote on Neil's belt chimed, he then asked Mari for a few minutes to speak with the caller. She acquiesced, and it was at this time that she took it upon herself to walk around the vessel on her own. Her immediate attention became focused on the cameos, especially the one directly above them as it displayed a picture of twelve people. She studied their faces and read their names: Marcus Zaire, Christopher Cain, Dr. Candice Canton, Thomas Kenner, Dr. Isaac Wells, Brad Combs, and Gena Porter. Then the image disappeared. An intriguing landscape of the Bighorn Mountains instantly took its place. The cameo on her left caught her eye as it rapidly displayed the state flags of the US. Then, just as abruptly, the image of the twelve people appeared once again within the frame. Now she could read the rest of the names: George Henderson, Wilmer Tack, Dennis Coleman, Gordon Bradford, and Neil Clayborn. The next cameo presented a stunning view of the Statue of Liberty, then it displayed other such landmarks and monuments. And the next one also displayed various scenes of American history.

Neil's guest was now enjoying what seemed to be a strange museum tour, one that certainly must be part of a dream; one she expected to wake up from at any moment. Mari's solitary walk was now almost complete as she gazed up at the eighth and final cameo. But suddenly she had a reason to pause, because for an instant she thought it was her own portrait framed above her. The resemblance was uncanny. The three quarter view of a woman standing barefoot on a large rock jutting out over the sea riveted her attention. The young woman was dressed like a maiden from antiquity in a simple white robe and was gazing down contemplation. Her hair was flowing around her shoulders and she carried a book in her arms. The word 'Celestial' was plainly inscribed at her feet. Then, all too soon the image was replaced by a diagram of the solar system. So continuous and unending was the pictorial flow that it made the ship seem alive.

Neil finished his conversation, but Mari couldn't resist remarking about the cameos, exclaiming, "These are lovely!"

"Thank you," he replied, accepting the complement.

"Whatever are they for?" she asked, puzzled.

Neil answered in his typically factual way, saying, "Actually, they cover the elliptical modulation rings and corresponding induction coils, which facilitate control of the ship. They are quite essential, and function much like the rudder of a ship."

"But, why the pictures?" she further inquired.

"We find them analogous to the figureheads found on the bows of the great sailing ships of old," he answered.

Then, as if Mari had wished it, the image of the young maiden returned through the clouds on the cameo above them. It flickered with life and Mari asked Neil about it, saying, "Who is that?"

"Celestial," answered Neil, "my sister."

"What a pretty name!"

"I think so."

"It's a wonderful portrait."

"Thank you, Mari, I am particularly fond of it."

"Who is the artist?"

"It was a collaboration of sorts."

"These are all so beautiful."

"I am glad you find them pleasing."

Then, as quickly as the portrait had appeared it disappeared, only to be replaced by a schooner gently plying the waves on some distant ocean. Mari's curiosity was getting the better of her, so she asked, "Is your sister here with you?"

"No, Mari, she passed away when she was just seventeen."

"Neil, I'm sorry. I can tell you must have loved her very much."

"Yes, I did."

Something more welled up in her, so Mari gently pressed, "If you don't mind, may I ask how she died?"

Neil's eyes searched the entryway to the dome, and said, "You may ask." His gaze remained distant and searching before he spoke again. "She was abducted, murdered, and left alone to die of a gunshot wound in a field of stones."

"Oh," cried Mari, observing his pain. "I can't even imagine such a thing. I didn't mean to pry."

"It was some time ago," said Neil, then he gently put his arm around the young woman at his side, "yet, I must say there times when it does not seem to be so."

"Did they ever...?"

"Catch the perpetrator?" answered Neil. "No, he or they are still out there somewhere." The mind of Mari's host and guide seemed to flee into the past. It was as though he expected his sister to walk in through the corridor at any time. However, a new image hovered above them and Mari hoped Neil would explain it to her, but he broke the uncomfortable silence, and said, "Come with me, there are some people I want you to meet."

"Oh, of course," sputtered his guest, somewhat relieved at the change of subject.

Without further explanation he swept her across the floor and through a small doorway by the circular tunnel where they began to climb a six foot wide spiral staircase. This took them up several levels to a brightly lit room, which proved to include the row of large windows she had seen from the ship. Two men and a woman were sitting near a vivid display screen and Neil began with an introduction, saying, "Mari, these are some of my colleagues, I would like you to meet Marcus, Chris, and Gena."

Marcus was the first to respond, "So, Neil, now we know why you have been spending so much time at that tavern!"

"We have heard so much about you, Mari," added Gena.

"Oh, my!" blushed Mari, now sporting a sheepish grin.

"All good of course," replied Chris. "We certainly would have chosen better circumstances, but you are welcome here. If there is anything you need, please let us know."

"Thank you so much," said Mari, "but I look forward to returning home."

"I assure you," said Marcus, "we are working as diligently as possible to accomplish that end."

"Did you enjoy the tour of our facilities?" asked Chris.

"Oh yes," she replied. "You have a wonderful ship."

"We are in complete agreement then," returned Chris.

"By the way, Neil," said Marcus, with immediacy and concern, "we have uncovered a few things I think you should be brought up to speed on if you have a moment."

"Yes, of course," replied Neil, then he turned to Mari. "If you don't mind, I need a few more minutes. You may have a seat here if you like. It should not take long."

"Go ahead, I'll be fine," replied Mari, sitting down on a bench by the windows. She fixed her eyes on the imposing vessel below, and even though Neil and the others were only a few feet away, a lonely feeling crept over her. Her thoughts began to return home to her family. She wondered if they were well and what they must be thinking or feeling at that very moment, but she also wished they could know about all that was transpiring.

The cold serenity of the observation room made the ship seem all the more inviting. She was drawn once again to the ever changing cameos and couldn't help but review the tragic events that surrounded Neil's sister, because there she was again, right below her window, larger than life and very animated within the pulse of the image. But it wasn't long before a new image flickered on the oval, this was the one she wanted to inquire about earlier. The amber frame contained the image of an ancient coat of arms featuring a shield of armor with two lions aggressively attending each side. The sun's spreading rays were emblazoned on the center of the shield between the lions along with three arrows chasing one another in the center. There were three stars above the shield and above the stars a single dove held an olive branch in its beak. On the lower part of the image a banner displayed the word: *AURORA.*

Neil suddenly broke Mari's trance, and before she knew it she was whisked back to her quarters. Now she could only think of one more important question to ask, "When can I go home?"

"We are working on it," replied Neil, once again. "There are many reasons for the delay and you must find your quarters sufficient a little while longer. I want you to be as comfortable as possible in your residence with us. I will have dinner brought to your room."

"Can't you stay with me for just a little while longer?" she begged.

"I will return for you early tomorrow morning," said Neil. "Everything will be fine, I promise." He gave her a hug. "Goodnight, Mari, I will see you tomorrow."

Feeling disappointed by the further delay, Mari distracted herself by browsing through the ample supply of books in the large bookcase covering one wall of her room. Before long, Candice arrived with a cart of hot food. She made sure her guest was comfortable then left her alone once again. Mari wondered if it might be possible for her to leave the comfortable lodging if she attempted it on her own. It was some relief to find her room unlocked with nothing to prohibit the free swing of the door. However, with no idea of where to go or what to do she sat down to dine. The food was much better than expected, then once she was satisfied and felt rested she began to feel more hopeful. Reclining on the bed to contemplate what was sure to be an awkward and uneasy return to her own world, she let the extraordinarily comfort of the bed have its way.

As Mari slept in an unknown bed, within an unknown room, inside an unknown edifice, at an unknown location, the authorities in Stone River were desperately trying to piece together scant information. They were pursuing all possible leads regarding a missing person report with no appreciable results. Those who knew Mari offered up earnest petitions on her behalf, but most of the population of Wyoming who prayed, prayed for rain.

Chapter Nine: Disabled

Things are not as they appear,
For what is this strange place I have come to know?
Sometimes I feel small and disabled,
But my spirit is not quenched.

Mari

By eight o'clock in the morning on August 28, Mari was wide awake, and much to her amazement, feeling much better than before her uninterrupted sleep. After rising she devoted some time to prepare for the day, but yearned for her journal, for there was so much to write about. Before long, Neil was knocking on her door and making his now familiar announcement, "Mari, please, come with me."

The woman was more than ready, although she still had no idea of what the next minute would bring. Ever persistent, she pointedly asked, "Are you going to take me home now?"

Neil, along with signs and careful words, said, "Not quite yet I am afraid, the schedule is being reworked. In the mean time, please grant me a little more time with you."

She was uncomfortable with the continual delays, but she replied, "Sure, of course. Though, I must say, I'm feeling quite hungry."

"I believe we shall do something about that," he replied.

Their walk took them to a rather narrow pale green hallway, where a large dark opening greeted them at the end. Complete darkness met their eyes, but soon the outline of trees could be seen with a host of stars twinkling above.

"Are we outside?" she asked in surprise. "Why is it so dark? I thought it was morning!"

"This is the park," he answered, "and no, we are not outside. Daylight abides high above this mountain at this time, but down here we have created our own world."

At first it seemed to be like midnight, yet, the stars gave way to twilight and the twilight became daylight. Puffy white clouds slowly rolled overhead in what was now a pure blue canopy even larger than the hemisphere that housed the ship. It was as if they were standing at the doorway to an enchanted garden, but one which was slowly rotating clockwise. Neil encouraged Mari to step onto the eight foot wide oak promenade encircling the entire enclosure. From there they took one of three marble footpaths lined with lamp posts and wooden benches. Each path meandered through tall oaks and maples. A circular pool of water occupied the center of the park complete with a trickling fountain. A statue of maiden warrior with an outstretched sword stood on a pedestal above the flow of water. Her sword pointed down toward twenty-four incremental marks and numbers on a ring at the base of the pool. By means of these marks and numbers the figure with the sword indicated the hour of the day, which now pointed to 0821. A large gazebo stood a short distance from the fountain and a patio of translucent material resembling ice extended out from the shelter into the surrounding garden. Neil then insisted that

Mari join him inside the structure where a grand piano pleasantly filled the air with perfectly tuned notes struck by automated keys. Mari was unable to hear any of the notes generated by the instrument, but her eyes quickly found the violin that appeared so lonely on the empty piano stool.

"Do you play the piano?" she asked.

"I make the attempt on occasion," he admitted, "but not as often as I would like."

"The violin too?" she added.

"I have found little time for it as well I'm afraid," he replied.

"I have always been fascinated by music," she said, whimsically.

"Impressive," he replied.

"I have a violin," she remarked.

"Are you a musician?" he asked, with astonishment.

"Most people would say no," she answered, with a mischievous giggle.

"You continue to amaze me!" he admitted.

"It is more of a feeling than anything else," she answered.

"I am sure it must be a good feeling," replied Neil, as he directed her to a table set for two. He drew various hot dishes from a warmer, and after serving his guest he joined her at the table. "All of us seek a time out now and then, that is, when we feel the need to get away. May I ask if this is to your satisfaction?"

"This is marvelous!" exclaimed Mari, with delight and surprise.

"Then, let us eat," replied Neil.

"I am hungry," she confessed, eyeing all that was on the table.

"Good," he added.

"This looks so wonderful!" she returned.

With sincerity Neil carefully and silently formed the words on his lips, saying, "Thank you." He was about to offer her some fruit when she politely asked if she might say a short blessing over the food. Fascinated by her request, he responded by saying, "Yes, of course you may, by all means."

The man followed the cues of the woman, but this small act on her part evoked even more curiosity concerning her. He was eagerly attentive to the words of the one gracing him with her presence, words which were not so much a supplication as they were a communion, a conversation in a personal and adoring manner made on intimate terms. Arising from an awareness of the continuous presence of the One she knew to be watching over all of life. The expression was not selfish, nor vain, but something rooted in a perception on her part now much more comprehensive than he had previously imagined.

Neil thanked her when she finished, but Mari replied, "You're welcome, but don't thank me, I would rather have you thank Him."

"So much like Celeste," he said quietly, humbled by her gesture.

"I'm sorry, what did you say?" she asked.

"Oh, nothing," he replied.

This rather traditional breakfast of buttermilk pan cakes, bacon, eggs, and dishes of fruit, which happened to include her favorite combination of blueberries and black cherries, seemed to be a delight for the one being served.

It wasn't long before Neil made his thoughts known, saying, "I believe you must have a thousand questions. You may ask about anything you wish."

Mari then made known her delight in the food, saying, "Oh, my, this is very good. Who does the cooking?"

"It was my hand this time."

"You have a very good hand."

"Sometimes I get it right, but seriously, as I was saying, you may ask of me anything you wish. There are no restrictions."

"I might ask a lot of questions," stated Mari.

"Please, if you are so inclined," replied Neil, now with an earnest look she had not yet observed.

As the piano continued to play soft chords, she finally spoke, "Who are you, Neil? What brought you to this place?"

As the man on the other side of the table put down his cup of coffee, he replied, "Like many things in life there usually is a multifaceted answer, but where to begin?" She studied his face closely as he continued. "I have always been fascinated by the properties of light. Our research took us—" Then realizing he was beginning to stray into territory leading away from her question he returned. "Oh, yes, who might I be?"

She raised an eyebrow and flashed her wide inquiring eyes at him. He signed as he spoke, saying, "I will do my best to keep to the essentials. To begin with, my parents were originally from a small town in New York. My father's career in industry took our family to England shortly after I was born. We lived over-seas until I was about to attend college, at which time we moved back to New York. Physical issues kept me sheltered for most of my childhood. I endured much in the way of speech therapy and tutoring. My teachers were British, perhaps that is how I come by the accent. Anyhow, I was encouraged to read and developed a ravenous appetite for books. I was fortunate enough to attend a somewhat prestigious university where I obtained several degrees. I worked at various research facilities as an assistant and occasionally contributed to specific projects. I had many ideas, but you could say they fell on deaf ears. No disrespect to you, Mari, for some of those ears were more deaf than you could ever be to the world of sound."

Mari signed back, "There are many kinds of deafness."

"How true," he replied, "and this brings me to the point where I now must say a few words about my sister." Mari stopped eating to primp, but ardently observed his every gesture as he continued. "My sister, Celestial, yes that is her real name, I guess my parents just liked the sound of it but we all called her Celeste. She loved science and astronomy and had an enthusiasm that was most contagious. And, it was because of her that I started thinking about science in a new and different way. For example, she became transfixed by the aurora borealis or what we call Northern Lights, she was always seeking the opportunity to see them. We were alike in many ways, and we shared something beyond mere words."

"I see how she was a major part of your life," said Mari, "and I'm sorry she is not here to share it with you."

"There is another person as well," remarked Neil.

"Who might that be?" injected Mari, quite before he had a chance to say another word. For she could see his thoughts had gone somewhere else for the moment.

"His name is Jacob Smithson," replied Neil. "Actually, we independently hatched many similar theories, a kind of parallel discovery and, he was kind enough to let me run with some of his ideas, although at times he thought my concepts were somewhat convoluted."

"Where is he now?"

"We went our separate ways."

"So, your sister must have been the closest one to you?"

"Yes, she was, always."

"I think I understand, but as you know, I've never had any brothers or sisters."

"Perhaps you are referring to other female companions then?"

Mari said nothing in return and only produced the slightest hint of a smile, to which Neil answered definitively, "No, every moment was taken up by my studies or research. I did not have very many friends. I had aspirations of being an artist but science took precedence and I found it difficult to get close to anyone. My life would not have appealed to very many people, especially women. "

Mari took another sip of tea, her sparkling blue eyes looked as large as the saucers on the table as they peered at him over her cup. Her voice was soft and lilting when she replied, "You seem fine now!"

Neil gazed into her eyes and replied using sign language only. "And, you are all the more so."

She was demure as she put down her cup and meekly looked away.

"Particle physics and aestheticism," he returned, "they are an intriguing mix are they not?"

But she grasp the thought completely, exclaiming, "Oh, I believe the universe is a beautiful place!"

"You have found my heart," replied Neil. "There is beauty to be uncovered, certainly, startling beauty, which leads me back a number of years to when I was assigned to work with Marcus and Chris. We became close friends. They expanded my world, then as others joined us we pushed onward. Each of us came from a different background and ethnicity. For example, Marcus has surmounted many obstacles, overcoming prejudicial barriers. What I am saying is, we all gave up something to be fully dedicated to this project and its operation."

"But why this place?"

"An abandoned gold mine provided the perfect cover, so we began working under the guise of a fledgling mining operation. It offered plenty of working space within the depths of this mountain. Do you remember the news about the Thunder Peak disaster some years back?"

"Yes, I was very young at the time but I do remember everyone talking about it."

"There was no actual disaster, only a calculated move to conceal this enterprise.

The plan succeeded. After the so called incident we were believed to have perished. Our former selves no longer existed, we could start anew, unhindered by any outside concerns. But this brings me to something else I must say. Our family name is Shepherd, my name is John Paul Shepherd." Mari just stared at her host as he sat back in his chair. "That man was declared dead by the outside world along with all of the others working within this mountain. Then, I was the first to venture out, seeking to discover the public mind, and in so doing I found it necessary to take on a new persona."

"John Shepherd?" she returned, as if to be sure she got the name right.

"Yes," he replied. "Neil, was my nick name from the time I was very young. It had to do with the fact that I had such an avid interest in space travel."

"So, have you ever been anyone else?" she asked, half jesting, yet quite serious regarding her thoughts about him.

"Never," said Neil, with a nervous chuckle. "Please, forgive me, I don't mean to be something I am not, but it seemed necessary at the time."

"I want to believe you, I really do, but it's just that I need to find something I can hold on to. My world has literally changed over night."

"I am aware of that and I want you to know things are changing for us as well. However, that may not be of much consolation at this time."

"I don't know what to think."

"I am still the man you have come to know. That will not change."

"How have you remained so hidden down here?"

"This entire complex has been actively shielded regarding electromagnetic energy and mechanical vibration. Our new technology demanded secrecy, yet the potential for something positive propelled us forward. We had discovered entirely new ways to produce, store, transform, and control massive amounts of energy. Once we were committed to producing a vessel, and as it became operational, things transpired rather quickly. So you see, our work has opened a gateway through which we are still passing. When the time is right we will make it known."

"Do you have other ships?" asked Mari.

"No, no," said Neil, "one is quite sufficient for now."

"What about all those other lights people have been seeing?" questioned Mari. "What are they?"

"Not having access to secret government files or classified information we had to learn what we could by conducting our own investigation," replied Neil. "We had not anticipated the fact that once we emerged from the confines of this shelter that we would immediately be shadowed by unknowns. The investigative activity on the part of United States and other governments and their respective agencies have also increased from the time of our emergence into the world. All this only added to the challenges we faced."

He continued, "All of the unknowns, call them UFOs if you will, have been under suspicion but for us all the more so. We responded to all of this with the hope of making contact with the unknowns but without success. For the time being however, we watch them and they watch us. And, we are keenly aware we have become yet another UFO, thus adding to the confusion but, once we learn our ABCs..." He winced at the sound of it. "Something we call the Atmospheric Bridging Capability...at such a time when it does becomes operational, it will increase our speed and maneuverability in planetary atmospheres. In other words, we shall appear even more like the fleeting unknowns in the not so tranquil skies above our world."

"What do they want from us?" replied Mari.

"Your property, or portions of it," replied Neil, "have been the subject of three separate visitations by certain alien craft. The last time occurred during your fateful ride into the back country. Before that time we were following them to determine what they were up to. Now regarding the time when your father had his encounter with us, we had planned to get in and out before anyone discovered what we were doing. Unfortunately, things did not work out that way."

"Could they cause us harm?" asked Mari, now worried about her family.

"As far as we know only animals have been the target, yet we cannot completely rule out human contact or abductions. We happened to detect an unknown presence on your property then it immediately departed as we approached. We then thought it necessary to determine why they were there. In doing so we discovered a foreign device implanted under your soil. Removal was imperative. We did so and disabled it, then we brought it back to our lab for examination. It was during the removal operation when your father had his encounter with us."

The things of which Neil spoke were frightening, but with notable skepticism, she said, "I find it odd that these UFOs always seem to seek out farms and ranches when they have our entire world of technology to explore. What could we possibly have that interests them?"

"It's apparent their technology is well in advance of our own world," said Neil. "They seem to frequent the hidden parts of the globe with interests that may include our planetary geology. We have conducted periodic sweeps of the area to locate other probes but none have been found." Then, Neil appeared to completely change the subject, saying, "I think your necklace looks very nice on you."

"Thank you," returned Mari, "it was a gift from my grandmother. I lost it a few years ago."

"That is quite interesting," said Neil. "I say this because your property was subjected to visitation on three different occasions. I will now address the first. We were tracking them, only to discover they may have an interest in your property. We may have scared them off, so when we investigated the landing site after the fact we found nothing. Yet, it was on that first visit when I found your necklace."

Mari was stunned at the revelation, and said, "My mother found it hanging on the barn!"

To which he replied, "I saw it on the ground when we were there looking for evidence of alien activity and I picked it up. I knew it might be of special value to someone so I hung it on a hook outside the door of your barn."

Mari nervously fingered the pendant, saying, "I've been wearing it ever since my mother put it in my hands."

Neil explained, "As you may remember, I started coming to the tavern long before any of this. Things just got ever more complicated. Your necklace is a reminder of something which identifies the heart in the midst of all this chaos."

"When you were following them at the time I was out riding," said Mari, "did you know I would be there?"

He answered her again by signing and speaking, "On our approach to the area just before our third encounter we were unaware of your presence in the vicinity, however, our paths crossed once again. Regarding your accident, we detected your presence as you lay on the ground and realized we could not leave you unattended. Then, because of your injuries, we could not risk taking you home or anywhere else for that matter. You needed immediate and specialized treatment and we had the means to provide it. Another reason also existed, there was a considerable amount of activity in that location, and if any of the purported instances of human abductions were to be proved true, then we felt we had no choice but to intervene. We brought you here for medical reasons, but also to protect you...from them."

The alarm on Mari's face was evident, and she replied, "Is my family in any danger?"

"I now believe you and your family members are not part of their immediate focus at this time. Their probes may be intended for other reasons. I also believe you should return home, but I would advise caution on your part."

"I saw some sort of light hovering over me just before I fell. Do you know what that was?"

"It was green was it not?"

"Yes, and there was a dark object in the woods. I saw it and I was frightened, then it was above me, but I don't remember what happened after that."

"I'm apt to believe your encounter was a coincidence."

"I guess my father was right about not riding out there!"

"This time I must agree, still in all, I find that you have a very intrepid spirit!"

"How could I have been so foolish?"

"Mari, I now must say something of utmost importance. Please keep what you know about this place secret. Do not reveal what you know to anyone, not just yet, not even to your family. We need a little more time to deal with these new developments."

"What's going to happen now? I don't know what to do!"

"All this leads me to another point which concerns the fact that you are here. I will now take this opportunity to make known my wishes as well as to speak on behalf of everyone here. I am hoping...that is, we are all hoping you might consider becoming a part of this project."

Mari was caught off guard once again, but answered, saying, "How could I ever be of any assistance to you?"

"I assure you," said Neil, "you will indeed be returned safely to your home, but you must know it is my sincere desire for you to join us. The secret is slipping out of the confines of this mountain and we can't keep ourselves hidden forever. Things are changing and I see great potential in you Mari, I think you would be a valuable asset to this endeavor. Here you would more than satisfy any adventurous notions you might entertain." The piano suddenly stopped playing and all was quiet except the trickle of water in the fountain. "Know this, that I will certainly abide by any decision you make, but please, consider what I have said."

Home was all Mari could think about at the moment, so she said, "Thank you, but I can't decide now, this is all so much more than I can get through."

"I think I understand," said Neil, "I really do, but please think on these things, as my greatest wish is for you to remain with us."

"I need some time."

"I would have it no other way."

Mari thought for a moment, then said with new boldness, "May I ask a personal question?"

"Yes, of course you may."

"What do you believe in?"

"A thoughtful question indeed!"

"What do you really believe, I mean in your heart of hearts?"

He picked up the teapot to add more of the brew to her cup, for which she thanked him, then he said, "What I believe?"

She affirmed her question, by simply saying, "Yes."

"I believe there is something that motivates humanity to journey outward," said Neil, "to search the world and the universe, to fully explore all there is to explore. Collectively we have pooled our resources in what you might say is a search for the truth."

"Is it the truth of the universe?" she queried.

"Truth in its purist form," he said.

"Might that be a search for God?" she replied.

"I must say, I believe certain things shape us and set our direction," replied the scientist, brooding for a moment before he proceeded. "As for me personally, my mother was Jewish and my father was Protestant. And I, well, I grew up between the two. My sister's death was unimaginably difficult. It haunted them, it haunted me, it haunts me still. It took me years to assimilate that day. Celeste was given to a certain joy and often spoke of her Bright and Morning Star, she searched the scriptures as I search the heavens. She had a unique logic and understood the purpose of things not seen. I cannot express her loss, but I have retained her spoken words in my mind She did not deserve such a senseless evil. It left an emptiness in the soul. Therefore, I seek evidence as wrought by pure scientific investigation. This is what drives me onward. We finally have the means to discover real answers. Yet I must confess, the more we discover, the more the evidence points to some grand design. Regardless, I believe the answers await in the heavens. That, Mari, is how I seek the truth."

"Your sister's life had a purpose, even if you don't see it," said Mari. "She found the Truth and you loved her for it. You cared for one another and her love will forever be with you."

"You are very astute," replied Neil. "Now I would like to ask you a question. What interests you, what is it that you seek?"

"What I have to say may not be very interesting from your perspective," she replied, "but I do appreciate the truth when it is spoken."

"We all have a journey of some sort," he replied. "So tell me, I am still very intrigued, I want to hear what you have to say."

Mari stirred a little more sugar into her tea, and said, "Well, to start with, I was born on the twentieth of July—"

"A very fine day indeed," added Neil.

"I was adopted at the age of two," she continued, "so my early years were kind of mixed up. I was a skinny kid, kind of awkward, and I was even accused of having an eating disorder. I was teased and bullied over my hearing difficulties, hearing aids, and use of sign language. I even had braces for a while. I was no beauty queen."

"I beg to disagree," replied Neil.

"I went to school for the deaf and blind," she said. "I also attended a regular high school like anyone else. After that I was off to college."

"I would say you have done very well," added Neil, paying a compliment.

"I did all the things the other kids did," she said proudly. "I had a few close friends, I did my homework, I was in track for a while and I even won a few sprints. For a brief time I even studied ballet but I longed to hear the music. Anyhow, it was all a good experience for me."

Neil was signing only, when he said, "If you don't mind my asking, how did your hearing loss occur?"

"I don't mind at all," she said. "I get that all the time. Early in my life I had severe ear infections. The damage was done."

"I see," acknowledged Neil, quietly.

"I have extremely limited hearing in my right ear even though I have a hearing aid."

"So nothing could be done?"

"There were some questionable procedures available, my parents looked into the possibility of implants and the like, there were risks but no guarantees. I accepted it as a part of my life, it's who I am."

"You must have had some difficult times," injected Neil, "yet, I find you speak very well."

She informed him, saying, "If you mean I speak very well for a deaf person, then thank you, but I can do anything anyone else can do."

"I'm sorry," he signed, "I did not mean to offend—"

"No offense taken," she returned, with her infectious smile. "I'm just like everyone else in many ways. It's my kind of normal, yet I must admit it would be fun to experience the world of sound if only for a day. But I accept who I am. I don't think of myself as disabled."

"I am glad you have moved forward," offered her host.

"My parents have been truly supportive," she added.

"That is a wonderful thing," added Neil. "It is evident you are very proud of your family, your up-bringing and the ranch."

"Oh, yes," said Mari, "William and Jennifer are the only parents I know. I've had a good life, but I know they must be very worried about me now."

"I would not have chosen this course of events," admitted Neil. "We are work-ing hard to fix it."

Mari paused a moment, but said, "I think of William and Jennifer as my true par-ents, but someday I would like to find out who my biological parents are, just to un-derstand my roots, regardless of what I might find."

"Yes, I understand."

"Perhaps, when the time seems right. I will use discretion."

"What, may I ask, is the thing you want the most?"

"That the clay would remain soft in the hands of the Potter and that my heart would remain open."

Neil was sure of what her next answer would be, when he asked, "And, who would this potter be?"

She gazed in her own kind of silence at the gently rippling pool under the foun-tain of water flowing so freely with sparkle and life. Then she turned to him, and said, "The Bright and Morning Star." Neil understood the connection, yet it was in his very nature as a scientist that he would crave the knowledge of how things worked, so in this way he was quite sincere when he asked her how she arrived at such a conclusion. She then replied, "Like you, I was searching for some kind of truth."

"And?" he replied.

"The Truth found me," she said, emphatically.

"How can that be?" asked the scientist.

"It was the Lord," she said.

"Hm," he muttered, now apprehending her meaning, but still questioning. "Do you know Him as the Christ?"

"Shiloh," was her answer.

"Ah," he said, discerning her reply, "and you needed salvation?"

"I found atonement and grace," she said.

"Some might call that dependency," he countered.

"My strength is in Him," she answered, resting in her conviction.

"So, you gave up your freedom?" he returned, still trying to understand.

"I found liberty," she replied.

"Do you not have your own mind in the matter?" he wondered. "Is there any-thing you still seek?"

"That His grace would abound," she said, with confidence.

"Is that all?" he replied, wondering about such an answer.

"Actually, you may find my innermost thoughts in the third chapter of Proverbs," she added, "where, it speaks of trust. (6)

"What then remains of your aspiration?" he asked.

She thought it over, and replied, "I still dream."

"My sister had dreams," stated the scientist, with an air of cynicism.

"Yes," replied Mari, "she did, and from what you've said she shared those dreams with you. Certainly her love for God was deep. We don't always understand sovereignty, but your sister is now in His arms."

"Perhaps," replied Neil, "but, Celeste never had the chance to see the fruition of her labor. Therefore, I endeavor to find the greater meaning. I trust the future to ultimately provide the answers."

She replied, "We must be careful where we put our trust."

To which he replied, "My intention is discovery."

She answered, "What you earnestly seek, you will surely find. If you seek the truth behind all things, I believe you will certainly find it. I have come to know that things are wrought in the dark places or in the light, yet many times our own vision fails us and we see only in twilight. We must walk by faith."

He considered her words, and replied, "Light and dark. Atonement and grace. Yes, Mari, you intrigue me. There is more to you than one might surmise."

"And," said Mari, "there is more to you than meets the eye."

"Your eyes see very clearly I might add," returned Neil.

"I only seek the Wisdom that comes from above," she affirmed.

"Wisdom?" he replied. "Yes, we shall talk more about these things later. Now, would you like to dance?"

Mari was taken aback, and stammered, "I don't know...I'm a bit clumsy...I'm really not very good at it...and besides I can't hear the music."

Neil casually walked over to the piano and touched several buttons on a small key pad. The music started to play once more, this time with more sensuous chords entering into a melody accompanied by an ambient background arrangement. It was soft at first, but sprang to life with ardent fidelity. He then bid her to accompany him to the translucent surface by the gazebo. When they stepped onto what would be their private dance floor the outer edge began to glow, then, dancing in perfect harmony, a three dimensional image of themselves appeared only a few feet away.

"They will show us," said Neil.

"They are you and me!" exclaimed Mari. "And I can feel the music!".

"A waltz," replied Neil, who proved to be an able dancer, though his right leg always seemed prone to give him some trouble, "just follow them and go with the flow, we shall both learn together."

Mari was awkward at first, but soon a connection was made as she was spirited along by her own dancing image. She became lighter in step and Neil sensed she was having fun with it. In time, the dancing doubles left them alone with only the floor and the music to guide them.

Neil asked, "How are you doing?"

"I love this," she said, as her steps seemed to float across the floor. "I think I'm getting it, although I think they are better dancers than we are!"

"I believe you are getting it."

"This place is magical!"

"There are good people here."

"You have wonderful friends."

"They have welcomed you in," assured Neil.

After a while their rhythm developed a unique synchrony, and they seemed to loose track of time. Ultimately the music died away and Neil insisted they to return to the gazebo, but even after Mari was seated quite comfortably, her mind was still on the dance floor rehearsing with the dancing images.

"Did you get enough to eat?" asked Neil, jarring his guest out of her trance.

"Oh yes," she replied, "more than enough, it was very good." Mari was still thinking about the dance, but continued, saying, "I have come across paths I never expected to walk. I must thank you for all your care and concern, I won't forget this, you have been very kind."

"You are most welcome," replied Neil. "You have brought a certain light to this place, but very soon we will be leaving, for preparations are being made as we speak, but first—" Her host got up from the table and caused the piano to play yet another melody. This time the notes entered into more delicate and tender chords. Neil drifted in thought as the hammers struck the strings—Mari could see the piano keys moving from where she was seated but could not hear the sound—then, as if returning from a daydream, he drew away from the instrument and approached a small three drawer cabinet. He removed from it a small ornate gold box then returned to the table with it and handed it to Mari.

"What is this?" she asked.

He communicated with sign language only. "Something I want you to have."

She gazed at the box, admiring its beauty. A twinge of impatience overtook him and he could not help but urge her, saying, "Please, open it."

She carefully lifted the hinged cover. Within the box she found a pair of delicate earrings, each of gold and set with a single star sapphire.

"Thank you so much!" she exclaimed. "These are lovely."

Neil watched her closely. She quietly pondered the gift as the piano played even more lustrous tones with a swell of intricate melodies subtly rising behind. He urged her again, saying, "I would love to see how they look on you."

Neil seemed to be excited about the prospect so Mari decided to do as he wished, saying, "I need to take the old ones off first."

As she began to remove the pearls from her ears, he asked if he might be of some assistance, so she let him brush back her dark brown locks, the body of which so fully covered her ears and the obvious hearing aid. Then he guided her hands as she fastened the earrings to her ears, saying, "I think they look splendid!" He sat down again and reached over the table to put his hands in hers. Their eyes stayed on one another as they probed feelings yet unspoken. Her internal barriers were falling. Their thoughts and dreams became woven to a point where she finally felt at peace within this strange and wonderful place.

In some ways Mari didn't want their time together to end and felt a certain delight in this shared moment of care and silence. But then, it was among these most peaceful and intimate feelings that a totally new emotion suddenly swept over her. Her eyes became very wide, her lips parted as if to speak, yet she couldn't find the words. She let go of Neil's hands and drew her fingers up to her ears, crying, "Oh? Neil? What's happening?" Her eyes desperately searched for something she could not see, then she rose to her feet and exclaimed, "Neil! I can hear! I can hear!" She heard every note of the piano. "Music!" She laughed, then cried, then put her hands to her ears again. She sat down and looked frightened, Neil became worried, but she reassured him. "No, no, I'm okay. I'm okay, really!" The fountain was trickling and splashing. "Water, that's water! Oh, my—my voice—I can hear my voice!" She removed the old hearing aid as if to attest to the fact that she no longer needed it. "I can hear...everything!"

"We created them just for you," said Neil.

"How is this possible?" cried Mari, as her eyes glistened with tears of excitement.

"Technology," replied Neil.

"It's a miracle!" she exclaimed.

"Technology, Mari," he said again, "nothing more."

She was filled with a new kind of wonder as he took her by the hand, saying, "Now come with me, soon you shall be home."

Mari could barely contain herself as she listened. Something inside had been awakened and craved affirmation. She felt so incredibly alive and kept touching her ears. She looked around with new eyes, because even the leaves on the trees seemed more intensely green. She immediately became so enthralled by Neil's voice that she could hardly concentrate on what he was saying. No longer did he use sign language.

The port dome was now a hive of activity as five individuals in white lab coats serviced the ship. Some of the cameos had been swung out of position on the hull for the testing of internal components and an array of complex machinery surrounded the vessel. Neil handed Mari a small communication device, and said, "I must stay here for a while to verify the tests. I would like to have you return to your quarters for a little while. You may call me if you need to."

"I don't mind staying here," said Mari, with growing excitement, "this is all so exciting!"

But Neil insisted, saying, "There is a complexity to these operations, so I believe your time would be better suited if you would get some rest before we leave. I will come for you in a little while."

Candice appeared out of nowhere to assist Mari back to her comfortable room where she could wait while Neil would be involved with the operations until five p.m.

Mari was disappointed by the separation but still reveling in her new sensory experience, thrilled by even the slightest of sounds. It was much too difficult to rest. She couldn't help but notice the sound of her fingers leafing through a book or her own voice as she repeatedly talked to herself. She also fell to the enchantment of the music as it subtly filled her room. The experience was intense, sound felt like color in a black and white world. She wanted to share it with someone, she wanted to shout out loud, but most of all she wanted to go home.

From the time of his capture Frank was isolated in his cell. His attempts to communicate proved futile. An attendant responded to his requests for food and drink but little else was allowed. He had to endure confinement in a sparsely furnished room where the bed, table, and seats were molded into the wall like a child's play house made of plastic. The door had a section with bars and a solid panel that could slide to the left or to the right. Frustrated, Frank banged on the door as hard as he could, and cried out, "I'm sick, I'm sick. Hey, you out there, I need help!"

The attendant appeared at the door, saying, "What is it?"

"I need help!" groaned Frank, hunching over, looking as if he might collapse. "I'm ill."

The attendant asked, "What's the matter?"

Frank groaned.

The attendant said, "Wait a moment," then shortly returned with a medical bag and a weapon.

Frank reconsidered his tactics, saying, "Wait, I think I feel better now. It must be indigestion from that food you gave me. Got any antacid?"

The attendant did not answer, but took a package of tablets from the medical bag, then slid them through the bars of the door.

Five p.m. came and went and Neil had not returned for Mari. She tried to call him from the device he had given her but there was no answer. After another hour slipped by she decided to investigate on her own. She slipped out into the corridor and found it empty, except for a precise rhythm churning from somewhere deep below the shiny foor. Her curiosity pulled her further down the corridor and soon she began to hear music again. It was coming from an open door. Walking in, she discovered a very simple apartment, unlike the well appointed quarters she had been given.

Several lamps were still lit in the living room, so Mari called out, "Neil, are you there? Neil? Hello, is anyone there?" There was no answer. The furniture was antique, very plain and well used, but arranged in an orderly fashion. Three seascapes hung on the walls and numerous blank canvases were on the floor. There were several figurative sculptures in bronze clustered in one corner and books were scattered everywhere. She found a simple desk where an adjustable magnifier sat on a thick stack of paper. Photographs in small golden frames lined a modest shelf on the wall above the desk. One of them revealed a man and a woman with a young girl that unmistakably resembled Neil's sister. There were more pictures on a nearby dresser, some were of people, others were of places, still others were images of things she did not recognize.

On her way out of the apartment she noticed an old motorized wheelchair in the corner by the door with about ten books stacked on the seat. Wear marks on the control box indicated it had been well used. She resisted touching anything and decided it was time to continue her search so she entered the corridor again.

Time was passing at an agonizingly slow rate for Frank and he was trying to think of another way to escape his solitary confinement. Suddenly he heard an automatic door open and close. Resisting the temptation to jump up he stayed seated on the bed. He could hear quiet footsteps approaching and saw a young woman walk briskly past his cell.

"Human!" Frank said to himself, as he was relieved by the presence of someone besides himself, but on second thought, she looked familiar. He jumped up and ran to the door and called out from behind the bars, shouting, "Hey, Miss! Hey you from the tavern!" He felt sure he knew who it was. "Hey, Miss, I saw you at that tavern. Hey, you, come back here!"

Mari heard the shouts and only looked at him out of the corner of her eye, but it was unnerving, so she decided not to stop. She thought she recognized him, but felt it might be better to ask Neil about it first, so she continued on and after arriving at a few dead ends she found her way to the familiar elevator then took it up. It opened up to the circular hallway and she found that the tunnel to the port dome was already open. Even the iris at the opposite end was open, but the service equipment no longer surrounded the ship and there was no one in sight. The observation room windows were dark and so was the ship, but faint rhythmic tones still resonated through the floor, which now seemed more like music than noise. Mari became so caught up in the sights and sounds within the dome that she failed to realize that someone was walking behind her.

"Hi, Mari!" called Marcus. "How may I help you?"

"Oh my," cried Mari, instantly wheeling around to see who it was, "you scared me...I didn't even know you were there!"

"I'm sorry," said Marcus, smiling calmly. "I didn't mean to frighten you."

"I...I'm looking for Neil," replied Mari, still recovering.

"You are?" answered Marcus.

"Where can I find him?" asked Mari, now feeling like an intruder.

"I think he may still be working on communications within the ship," replied Marcus, as he pulled something from his lab coat. The device looked like another version of the Remote Neil carried. "Some of the systems have been switched off so that he might run some tests. I'll see if I can contact him."

"Neil was supposed to come to get me more than an hour ago," she explained, "when he didn't come, I thought might find him here."

Marcus placed a call, saying, "Neil, this is Marcus, please reply." There was no answer on the device so he tried again. "Neil, this is Marcus, I have someone here to see you." When there was still no response, he directed his conversation back to Mari. "The communication system must still be down. He gets absorbed in his work and may have lost track of time. I tell you what, I'll have you look in on him. You go ahead, I'm sure everything's okay."

"Thank you so much," said Mari, appreciating the courtesy and relieved she didn't receive a reprimand for her wandering.

Marcus motioned for her to walk toward the ship and as she did so the companion-module assumed its downward position. Mari bravely stepped into the enclosure and the doors closed. For the first time she heard a smooth gentle hum until it stopped and opened to a darkened bridge. This time there were no cascades of data, only one tiny display screen flickered with life just out of sight around the central column. Small overhead lights radiated a faint glow as she confidently entered the bridge and stepped around the companion-module toward the pilot station. Neil was in the pilot's seat, but her eyes gazed upon a stranger, for his body was out of shape somehow.

Mari forced out a whisper, saying, "Neil?"

He turned to her, and with slurred speech, said, "Hi...Mari!"

"What's wrong?" she squeaked, almost choking on her words.

"Nothing...wrong," said Neil, seeming to struggle with the words.

"Can I help you?" asked Mari.

"No...need," insisted Neil. "Forgive...me I got...involved. I thought you might...be Marcus. Please...sit...down."

Mari took the seat next to him and stared. He seemed so helpless and confined by the oddly formed couch. He definitely had her attention. His left hand rested limply near a small lever on the armrest of the seat as his right hand casually reached for a touch screen nearby. His fingers attacked the icons with precise strokes and within moments the ship began to throb with life again. The illumination within the compartment began to increase and at the same time a change transpired within Neil's body. His face and limbs relaxed and gave up their listless modality, the change continued until he was like the man she knew before. He took a deep breath as the seat readjusted itself to an upright position. Then taking a handkerchief from his shirt pocket he wiped his face. He removed the reading glasses from the console at his side and slipped them into his shirt pocket. Then he promptly stood up to address Mari in a voice as precise and articulate as ever, saying, "Cerebral palsy. Please, no pity."

"Marcus said it was okay for me to come to see you, I just—" sputtered Mari.

"Do not worry," said Neil. "Actually, I am glad you came."

"I only wanted to be with you," replied Mari, jumping to her feet.

"Some would say I am quite disabled, even handicapped, would they not? But, then, as you are quite aware, what is a disability? Believe me, I had planned to tell you but the time never seemed right."

"It's okay," replied Mari, "but how—"

"I use a CMR," said Neil, quite casually. "A device called a Cerebral Muscular Response device that works in conjunction with the electrical activity in my brain and compensates for flawed connections to facilitate the appropriate neuromuscular response. I had it switched off along with most of the other systems within the ship for testing. I was attempting to make some design changes. As you know, I am always seeking to improve the performance of things. Thus far, I am my own test subject. Things are not yet complete regarding the device or even the ship for that matter. I am working to create a smoother response time. A little forethought eliminates a lot of afterthought. And, no need to worry. I can control the ship from this seat without the CMR if need be."

"It was only a test?"

"A test."

"You're okay?"

"I am okay. Presently, we have found no permanent solution. You see, Mari, this is the other side of our research, there are many more benefits to come...much more than we ever thought possible."

"You could help a lot of people!"

"Yes, and someday we will. We are still learning. By the way, did Candice come with you?"

"No," she replied, "I came alone."

"Are you okay? You look a little pale."

"I'm fine," she replied. "I...I'm still learning too."

"Then we shall move on," said Neil.

As they entered the companion-module, Mari said, "I saw someone in some kind of jail cell. I think I might know him."

"Yes, you do, the man is Frank," confessed Neil. "He was...uninvited. I am afraid there has been a little breach in our security system due to some of our technical difficulties. We will let him go at the proper time. No harm will come to him. He contacted someone by the name of Jed Mullen who at one time wanted to work with us. We had misgivings concerning Mullen, unfortunately things did not work out. Frank discovered the connection, he also happened to find his own way into our facility. The holding area was actually designed for our own use should any of us be adversely affected by the new technologies we were working on. It proved to be unnecessary."

Neil decided it was time for Mari to see another part of the facility before her trip home and took her from the port to another area that housed a grand laboratory. There he introduced her to a few more of his colleagues and revealed how some of the others also had certain disabilities and how the new technology has assisted them. Next, they entered a tooling area, where he explained how they manufactured and constructed large portions of the ship, then he said, "We have the ability to form and project specific elements for isolated purposes, but we are not yet capable of transmitting such material through the air over any appreciable distance. It is a work in progress, only inorganic material can be materialized and projected. We also have devices similar to medical MRI equipment. We used them to make readings of your inner ears. It was applied to create the earrings." Next he brought her over to a workbench where a four foot long glass bottle was securely held in a cradle. The bottle contained a strange cylindrical object, and Neil reflected, saying, "This is the devise we extracted from your corral. We do not yet understand its purpose."

"What if you had not removed it?" asked Mari.

"I do not know," replied Neil. "We believe the unknowns may be seeking something underground."

"Now I see why you wanted to speak with my father," said Mari. "You were only looking out for us."

"We deemed it necessary to do what we did," replied Neil.

The moment of departure was drawing near. This time Mari would be boarding the ship as a passenger fully aware of what was taking place. Chris and Candice were already on the bridge to welcome Mari aboard when she arrived with Neil and Marcus. Activity increased in the observation room and soon a blue light filled the dome. A rectangular opening appeared in the upper part of the hemisphere and within seconds the vessel traversed the access shaft. There was no sensation of movement or speed whatsoever within the ship, but a blue shooting star would again be part of the night, guided by the whims of people she had only begun to understand.

No sooner had they entered the sky than an alert interrupted the flow of data on the screens with a message: "Unknown craft on approach. 3.25 miles / 5.230225 kilometers."

"Now matching our speed but keeping their distance," said Marcus.

"We have an unknown mimicking our flight path and they are gaining on us," reported Chris.

"As expected," quipped Neil. "We shall change course as needed. I suggest alternate 35."

"Initiating alternate 35," replied Marcus.

Although they hoped otherwise, the appearance of the object was actually no surprise, nor was it a surprise when it began to shadow their every move. A flight plan designed to create a distraction from their own intended destination was now in place. This deviation would make the short trip considerably longer than they planned but a necessary precaution.

"They were waiting for us," said Candice.

"This is no a coincidence," stated Marcus.

"They frequently seem to be aware of our intentions," added Candice, "even more so now."

"If you are referring to this specific mission," replied Neil, "that is possible, but there may be other motives at work here."

Movement on the part of the alien craft soon brought it within three thousand feet of the Earth ship. Marcus tried to open up communications with the craft but received no response.

Neil kept Mari updated, saying, "Our information reveals this to be the same type of craft that appeared at the time of the Pacific eclipse, in your corral, and on the night of your horseback ride. From our recent observations we have determined that they tend to show aggressive behavior at times, provoking us, but then retreat from it. It is our intention to find out what they are up to."

Marcus attempted to open up communications with the craft on multiple frequencies, saying, "This is the *Aurora*. We seek contact. We intend no hostility. Please state your purpose."

When there was again no response from the alien craft, Neil again informed Mari, saying, "We have observed two different types of craft. We simply refer to them as type I, and type II, for lack of a better description. The Type I designation has been assigned to the green objects, which have proven to be aggressive. Type II identifies the amber objects, which have exhibited more passive behavior. There are also differences in the configuration of each, but we have been unable to determine their exact design. The object tailing our ship is of the Type I variety."

They were debating their next course of action, when communications alerted them to a message. It was a script revealing only one word: "Follow."

Everyone, though now rather astonished, retained stern faces as they analyzed the situation. Then Neil said, "I believe this may be our first contact."

"They want us to follow them?" questioned Marcus. "They're following us!"

"We now know they have the ability to communicate," added Neil.

"Look," said Marcus. "They have just made a course change, and are now heading directly away from us. Their speed is increasing."

"I suggest we take them up on the offer," said Neil.

"May I provide a word of caution," advised Candice.

"It's obvious," added Marcus, "that we don't know what is on their mind."

"I would like to get this resolved," added Neil.

"So would I," replied Marcus, "although at this point we know nothing about them."

"Then I believe we should oblige, perhaps to honor their request," suggested Neil.

"If it is indeed a request," countered Marcus.

"One way or another we shall soon find out," replied Neil.

The alien craft maintained its new course and the terrestrial ship followed. Two points of light now raced away from the western landscape of the United States until the speed of the objects increased from hundreds of miles per hour to thousands and then left the atmosphere of the planet. The *Aurora* related differently to the physical environment of space. There were no atmospheric gases to react to fields produced by the vessel so there was no mist to form around it. There was no vapor trail to be seen, only the ethereal blue sails pulsating with power. The alien craft altered its course again to one that would take it to the plant Jupiter. Within only a matter of minutes the mysterious craft was encroaching on the Jovian world, where it entered into an orbit around the planet. The *Aurora* gradually caught up and entered the same orbit. At times the two crafts became hidden from the Earth when on the far side of the planet. It was then on the second revolution when they were on the far side of the planet that the alien craft began to lose its luminescence.

"I really hope they are not going to request that we land on the planet," remarked Candice.

"I find that doubtful," said Neil.

"That is not a test I would like to take at this time," added Chris.

"We will wait for them to show their hand," said Marcus.

"And we are at present conveniently obscured from the rest of humanity," submitted Neil.

"That looks like the object I saw in the woods," added Mari.

"Yes," replied Neil, "I believe it is similar."

Marcus sent a verbal message, saying, "This is *Aurora*, we have responded to your request. Please reply."

The craft, now dark like gray metal, presented itself as a large sphere approximately 300 feet in diameter with an assembly of rods on one side that tapered away from the main body to a single point to form a cone.

"What are they up to?" asked Mari.

"Some form of peaceful communication, I hope," remarked Chris.

The crew of the *Aurora* watched as the rods of the cone began to fan out from the sphere, finally stopping at a 20 degree angle with a single extension at the center. After this was accomplished the entire craft rotated around 180 degrees. Now the spherical part faced the *Aurora*.

"We are now getting an incoming signal," said Candice.

A small screen lit up with information and Candice directed the feed to the port screens where a text message appeared: "We honor this opportunity. We will initiate further contact in exactly twenty-four hours as you mark time. Your ship must return to these exact coordinates. We will engage in dialogue with the one called Clayborn. We will accept no one else. This is the Seruzian Principality. We await your decision."

"What is the Seruzian Principality?" asked Candice.

"Apparently they are," answered Neil, reading the questioning faces of his friends. He would then send out a reply to the message. "We will consider your invitation and will discuss the matter, but we request further information regarding this offer."

A reply came back to the *Aurora*: "We await your final decision."

Candice questioned, "Why would they request contact with only one person?"

Neil responded, saying, "After all we have the United Nations. Their eagerness is evident and human representatives are plenteous."

"I don't like it," stressed Candice, turning to Neil. "Why only one person?"

"Is this not what we came to seek?" replied Neil.

"They seem menacing to me," added Mari.

"You know Mari speaks from recent experience," cautioned Candice. "Look, Neil, they know your name, and they produced text in our language, yet we know nothing about them."

"They 'are' seeking contact," informed Neil.

Chris countered, "They have been watching us, there are many ways they could have obtained such specific information. I think we should make the most of this opportunity but it should be on our terms. They come up short in providing information to us."

Neil added, "If they had intended to do us harm would not they have done so before this? Although we have evidence they have been planting probes, we have been unable to observe any hostile intervention on their part against human subjects. They have had many opportunities to do so yet now they seek to communicate. Perhaps we would do well to honor their request."

"We have not been able to glean much from our sensory data," said Marcus. "Also, I might add, we have had our own data blocking equipment fully operational for only a short time. Who knows what they could have learned about us?"

"What happens if we do not honor their request?" asked Neil, submitting another scenario.

"A conundrum we must unravel," added Chris.

Marcus added, "It's interesting to note that their request specifies only one representative of our entire planetary population."

"I may not be the best choice on their part," returned Neil, "but if we want to build a relationship we must start with simple communication. Whether we like it or not, I believe we must move forward with this. We have the means to defend ourselves if need be. Most likely they do not have a complete knowledge of our technology, largely because part of it was added after we installed all of the blocking devices."

"What if they become aggressive on a planetary scale?" said Candice.

"All the more reason to get personal," answered Neil.

"At least there is time for us to prepare," said Chris, looking for something positive.

"We may be on an irreversible course," replied Neil. "We can only proceed with what we know." After further discussion everyone agreed to send a reply: "This is Neil Clayborn. We hereby accept your offer, though further information about such a meeting between of our worlds would be much appreciated."

A reply was immediately sent to the *Aurora* from the alien ship: "We will expect the one called Clayborn at the appointed time and appointed location. We will accept no other."

The individual ribs began to collapse to form a trailing cone and the surface of the object became shrouded with the characteristic glow. Seconds later it departed from the planet, leaving the solar system and the *Aurora* alone in its track around Jupiter.

"There it stands," said Marcus, with marked cynicism.

"We will proceed with the appropriate caution," replied Neil.

"The *Aurora* has not yet been fully tested, especially the new weapon systems," added Chris. "We have yet to do the final stage trials."

"That is true," replied Marcus, "but even so, I think we possess the ability to hold our own at this time."

Mari felt her own emotions heave like a roller coaster but remained silent as the discussion continued.

"I agree with Marcus," added Neil. "I will not entrust this foreign presence with anything but our desire to establish a dialogue."

"Dialogue is the key," said Marcus. "We will weigh the risks at hand."

"There are always risks," said Neil. "We will discuss this with the others when we return to port."

"But first," reminded Candice, "we have a task to complete."

"Yes," agreed Marcus. "It is now time to take Mari home."

Conversation on the bridge momentarily ceased as the *Aurora* broke away from the massive planet and a new course set for a return to Earth. Neil was now standing in one of the shallow wells of the deck gazing into a viewport displaying a virtual representation of the location of the stars as they appeared in their direction of their travel. Mari came along side, and entertaining some confusion, she said, "I don't know if I can take this all in."

"I do not believe any one of us can completely comprehend what has just happened," replied Neil. "We will proceed one step at a time."

"She is right," said Marcus, "nor can we truly grasp the scope. One way or another, we all must be united in this."

"I would say," replied Neil, "that would be of immeasurable value."

"Your colleagues are wise," said Mari. "I see strength in their approach."

Neil turned to her, and said, "Undiscovered life forms, the far reaches of space, the planet Jupiter? You see, Mari, we are crossing new boundaries every moment."

"Always seeking," added Mari.

"Notice what you see before you," replied Neil, "remember this time, for soon you will be home."

"And, may you remember all the things we spoke of when we were together," replied Mari.

"I surely will," replied Neil.

"We seem to be going so fast!" remarked Mari. "How do you measure the speed?"

"Speed is interpreted in a TLF, or a trans-light factor, which is indicative of velocities many times the given speed of light. At this moment though, we are well below that of light and have only made a small circuit within our own solar system."

"Space is so vast," remarked Mari, thoughtfully, not breaking her gaze into the viewport which provided an enhanced view of space. "The Earth and the stars are truly beautiful in such blackness."

"Space encircles all things," returned Neil.

"It's incomprehensible," returned Mari.

"Majestic infinitude," added Neil, now speaking poetically.

"It magnifies its Creator," said Mari, revealing her innermost thoughts.

"It enlarges the questions," said Neil, never ceasing to probe. "It is our turn to open the door and make the ultimate journey. Such a feat is within our grasp."

"Open that door with care," advised Mari.

"I must say," returned Neil, now gently squeezing her hand, "you have a way of seeing inside, but I am looking out there to other worlds. I am looking to a new dawn."

Mari became mesmerized by what was taking place before her eyes, as if she were in some grand drama out of step with time, but before long the familiar blue planet began to fill up the viewports. A globe that was captivating as well as inviting and full of life, keeping its secrets and turmoil well hidden by the presence of astounding beauty. Continental land masses, the great blue oceans, and the spiral of white clouds grew larger and larger. But soon the ship would enter the atmosphere under the cover of night and tiny points of light would appear to be rising up to greet them. Civilization was emerging from everywhere as the *Aurora* gracefully descended, gliding in stealth to gently land in a clearing edged by thick woods and fields ripe for the harvest.

The crew waited patiently in the darkened ship as Neil and Mari stepped out onto the grassy turf. Their lungs became filled with the fresh air of the Wyoming night and Mari immediately felt at home, even if she didn't know the exact place. Neil led the way as they traveled down a winding path, which eventually ended in the backyard of an old farm house. The next thing she knew she was pushing aside a tangle of grapevines at the edge of an over grown lawn.

Mari whispered to Neil, "Who's place is this?"

"Mine," he replied. "Remember?"

"Of course," she answered, eyeing Neil with the sudden realization that the house he spoke of might actually exist. It made sense and seemed out of place at the same time, but she was too busy thinking about her own home to care.

They entered an enclosed porch which connected the garage to the house then they took three steps up to a locked door. The house had been vacant for a considerable amount of time. In fact, everything about the dwelling was suffering from protracted emptiness. A bare florescent ring on the kitchen ceiling flickered to life as Neil started searching for something in the empty cabinets and drawers. While doing this he removed a table knife, a partially used spool of string, a rusty screwdriver, and an old hammer with a broken handle from the counter and threw them in an empty drawer. At last he opened a small drawer to the left of the sink and found a set of keys.

They left the house and entered the adjacent garage. Minutes later Neil's lone passenger was watching the dark landscape fly by the window of the familiar blue Jeep as they bumped along rough rural roads. The speed of the vehicle was infinitesimally small when compared to the *Aurora* but the sensation was almost overwhelming. Her entire journey had taken place over a number of hours, nevertheless, it seemed as though weeks had gone by. Then as if awakening from a dream she realized she was entering a familiar driveway.

Standing by the parked vehicle, Neil gave Mari a hug, and said, " Remember what I said, but please do what you feel is best. I will accept what ever decision you make."

"I will think about what you said," returned Mari, putting a hand to her ear to feel one of the earrings. "But there's so much to consider."

"You may keep those," replied Neil.

"Thank you," said Mari softly, then she removed her necklace and handed it to Neil. "Here, I want you to have this."

"No, Mari, I cannot. It means too much to you!"

"I want you to have it."

"How can I?"

"Because of what you have given me."

"I regret these circumstances," returned Neil, clutching the small symbol of her thoughts in his hand, "but I am not sorry you have entered my life."

"That's why I want you to have it," insisted Mari. "You are about to do something no one else has done. I want you to remember me and what I believe. I want you to remember what you have right here as a whole new world opens up before you."

He kissed her on the cheek, then said, "Thank you." A long moment transpired before he spoke again. "Mari, I believe I am falling in love with you."

"You have captured my heart," she returned, "and you have my thoughts and my prayers. But, please, be careful. Do not abandon truth."

"That is my intention," said Neil.

After a lingering goodbye she stood on the lawn to watch the vanishing tail lights as they disappeared into the night. When she turned to face the front porch a light came on in the living room, then two people became silhouetted in the frame of the front door. William and Jennifer welcomed their daughter home with a burst of emotion. There was so much for her to say, yet so much she could not, but she assured them that everything was well and that she had suffered no harm.

By the time Mari retired for the night her mind was yet to completely return home. She felt as though she must write it all down while it was still stirring within her, but she only stared out of her window into the night. A warm breeze sifted through the trees and through the open window along with the sounds of the night, sounds Mari heard for the first time. There was a momentary burst of light from high above the house which lit up the night, like lightning without the thunder. This was followed by a subtle blue flash. Afterwards, there was only more silence as another night without rain crept upon the land.

Chapter Ten: Concurrence

Is there a plan or is it just concurrence?
Mari

By the early morning hours of August 29, Frank had been given a sedative, then returned to the very cave he found at the beginning of his fateful adventure. He would remain there to recover from his artificially induced sleep. Soon he found himself stumbling down the mountain trail in much less time than it took to make the upward climb. The truck was still parked at the end of the two-track where he left it. All his gear was with him, even his phone, which was now operating normally and receiving messages, making it possible to call the intelligence unit based at White Lake. Frank would call one person in particular, Gen. David Staffer. This set into motion the men and equipment necessary to investigate the mountain. He headed back to Stone River, now armed with the vivid memory of his experience and filled with conviction and vindication.

Neil met with his colleagues to consider the conditions and weigh the risks of the opportunity before them. Although there were many unanswered questions, all were able to reach an agreement to push forward because they considered the new frontier to be worth the risk. The ship was declared ready for flight and, when the time for departure came, all of the members of Star Harbor assembled in the observation room. Most of his team were perfectly content to remain at the base but Marcus had mixed feelings. Being a man of many abilities and interests, he didn't mind staying behind with the rest of the crew, perfectly happy to work behind the scenes to facilitate orderly operation and direct the missions. Although he was excited about the possibilities, he secretly wished he could be part of the initial contact between humanity and extra terrestrial life.

Before the departure, Neil tapped out a code on his screen. A small drawer opened up on the console near his seat and he removed the leather band that had been ever present on his finger and slipped it inside. Next to it he placed the Mariner's Cross that Mari had given him and closed the drawer. His final words were, "Keep the harbor lights on for me." In an instant the enclosure was empty and the results of their years of labor broke the bonds of Earth in an outbound journey once again. Travel proved uneventful, even as he was only one lone person penetrating the vastness of space. Neil had arrived early for his appointment and specified location as he entered into a high orbit around Jupiter. The *Aurora* was the only vessel there. No alien ships were in sight or on long range sensors. The communication frequencies were silent.

As the appointed time arrived a distant object was detected approaching at great speed and on a collision course. Within seconds a massive object joined the *Aurora* in orbit. A massive green sphere measuring six hundred feet in diameter had settled in at a distance of less than fifteen hundred feet from the *Aurora*. It promptly lost its glow and dark narrow lines defined what appeared to be sections on the surface of the craft. Some were circular and others rectangular, but no windows or ports were evident. Then, the distinctive cone began to unfold from behind it and the communication system on the Aurora started to receive data that identified the alien craft as well as a set of instructions to determine a specific approach sequence, directing the earth ship toward the central portion of the alien craft.

A single rectangular outline on the front portion of the vessel became traced with yellow light and signaled the opening of the four equal sections within it, each parting in opposing directions to create an opening. Neil then received instructions to enter. A small illuminated circle appeared in the center of the opening and remained there. A this point Neil began to have second thoughts but he had made a commitment, so he acknowledged the landing instructions and brought his ship down to minimal power, his communication stated, "I have come as requested."

"The Seruzian Principality receives you," was the reply.

Neil responded, saying, "I will proceed as per instructions."

Prior to the entry process Neil had materialized a small structure on the under side of the ship. The configuration included a platform designed to extend out from the companion-module, which included two four foot high vertical poles on each side to provide light. This would create a surface on which to stand when and if he was to exit the ship to meet with his hosts.

Guidance information steadily appeared on his monitors as the *Aurora* glided toward the alien ship. The landing area was extremely dark and remained so until his ship crossed the threshold from space to the inside of the craft. Soon the *Aurora* touched down on the designated landing surface and shortly thereafter the entire enclosure increased in brightness. Although it remained dim by human standards. After the doors of the receiving area slid together to close off the opening Neil waited for the next communication. He observed that the landing area was pressurizing with a breathable atmosphere. Once this was accomplished five hooded beings near the back of the enclosure began advancing toward the ship. Eventually the five beings came within ten feet of the platform on the *Aurora*. Neil then received instructions to disembark and stepped out of the companion-module to stand at the edge of the platform. Now he would speak his first words in person, saying, "I have accepted your invitation. I come in peace."

A long dark hooded robe concealed each of the beings, which made their movements more difficult to observe. The five remained in a semicircle so that the beings on the ends were as close to Neil as the one in the middle. The close proximity of his alien hosts enabled him to see their physical features more clearly. Their skin appeared dark green in color and randomly marked by irregular brown patches. They also had large eyes covered by a heavy lid and squinted in reaction to the light emitted by the lamps of the platform on which Neil stood. A minimally visible nose appeared just above a wide mouth with barely noticeable lips. Their hands each had five long fingers with an extra claw like digit along side the little finger. Neil observed a slight movement under the skin, which made the skin appear to undulate at regular intervals.

The central figure stepped forward and spoke in a deep, hollow, almost mechanical voice, saying, "We receive the one called Clayborn."

"We thank you for this invitation," replied Neil.

"The Seruzian Principality welcomes you," said the being. "I am Thallor, Chancellor, and Director of Sector 66."

"I welcome this meeting and I come as a representative of my world," explained Neil, trying not to recoil at their appearance.

"We highly desire your cooperation," replied Thallor.

"I am but one man," said Neil, "yet there are many on my planet who would also value such a dialogue."

"That may be so," said Thallor, "but we will receive only you, Clayborn, because we have found you to be someone with whom we might have direct communication. We do not wish to speak with any other."

"I am honored that you desire contact," replied Neil.

Thallor replied, "We have greatly anticipated this moment."

"As have I," replied Neil.

"We have been looking forward to this time," returned Thallor. "Although you refer to others of your world, we do not detect peace among the nations of your planet."

"That is true, many people and nations are in strife," said Neil, "but our planet is making progress toward a better world."

"We find that your world has made minimal progress in that regard," replied Thallor, "but your move into space is unique and we applaud it."

"Exploration, is our goal," said Neil, "for we seek to investigate our own world and the space around it."

"And it is that exploration that interests us," replied Thallor.

"We have noted your interests," replied Neil, "for we have observed your activity during our last solar eclipse and in many other instances. Why such attention to our humble world or an eclipse?"

"We find your planet has a unique relationship with its adjacent star and accompanying moon," returned Thallor. "We also study the flora and fauna of your world and other related phenomena."

"Not long ago we discovered a foreign device in our soil," stated Neil. "Can we also attribute such things to your study and technology?"

"We are aware that you are in possession of one of our probes and we will dismiss such action for now," answered Thallor. "Very soon we will disclose the reasons for such things. We will require its return in due time, but we see something in you Clayborn, something unique, something we do not find anywhere else. What I say now is of utmost importance. We are inviting you into the Principality so that we might reveal to you our quest. Therefore, we welcome you so that we can make plans together, plans to benefit all of Sector 66."

"Tell me of this Sector 66," said Neil, revealing his own quest for more information. "What part of space does that include?"

"We greatly admire your curiosity," replied Thallor, "but we will reveal more in due time. At present, our observations have brought us to the conclusion that an intervention must occur."

"Intervention?" repeated Neil, questioning their bold assertion.

"Do you not want to avoid strife on your world?" purposed Thallor. "Do you not look to the future? Our quest and your quest are much the same. You need not worry about others on your world for we have the means to end such strife."

"How might our conflicts be of interest to you?" asked Neil.

"We deem it necessary to act when your civilization has failed to achieve its goals," said Thallor. "At such a time when any civilization has progressed into chaos we are then able to bring about peace."

"By what means would you do this?" asked Neil, seeking a motive.

"That will be discussed in our further conversation," replied Thallor. "We cannot allow the hostile civilizations on your planet to spread into space. Your world is creating its own path of destruction and we look to facilitate peace by putting in place certain restraints. In this way we will help your species. We can also help you, Clayborn, so you may continue to rise above your own kind and be a part of a new type of universal order and authority. We will let you minister as one of our representatives. Therefore we must plan together. When you join with us you will be allowed to assume the position of a Preceptor, yes, you may even become a supreme ruler over many appointments. We have followed the events of your world and have detected an inevitable march to that place in time where your kind will need assistance."

"I do not believe any type of intervention is necessary at this time," returned Neil.

"Perhaps," replied Thallor, "but I must say again, Clayborn, something unanticipated has occurred. You appeared with your unique technology and with that we were as you might say, surprised. We have found you to be singular. Yet, we suspect the actions of the Ambhuri in this, we believe they may have given you important elements not attainable by your own means. We believe they may have supplemented your technology. But it would not be to your advantage to be working with the Ambhuri."

"Who are the Ambhuri?" returned Neil, surprised at the revelation of a separate or even rival alien presence. "I don't know them. I have made no contact or received assistance from those of whom you speak, nor have I received any significant technical assistance from the powers of my own world."

"We find it difficult to accept that premise," informed Thallor. "The Ambhuri do not have the same interests as the Principality. They obstruct our progress, they interfere, they pose a great danger."

"Our technology is ours alone," said Neil, trying to clarify the issue. "I have come on my own, no one has sent me, and we have never communicated with the ones you call Ambhuri."

Thallor turned to the others of the welcoming party to begin a discussion between themselves in their own tongue. After some minutes he returned to Neil, and said, "We question this because these events puzzle us, but in the present context it does not change our offer. We encourage you to form an alliance with us."

"I can't make such an alliance at this time," replied Neil, "nor can I speak for all the inhabitants of my planet in such matters. I say again, I don't know the ones you call Ambhuri. My technology originates from a small group of individuals of which I am part. Collectively, we come to offer friendship and communication with a desire to begin a dialogue that will benefit all."

"This we are now doing, Clayborn," remarked Thallor. "It is a great opportunity."

"I realize your technology has brought you over the vast expanse of space to our solar system," said Neil, "so I welcome you in hopes of a peaceful coexistence."

"That is what we seek," replied Thallor. "Indeed we posses an advanced technology beyond that of your world, however it is because of your appearance that we have sought you out."

"All of this because of my technology?" said Neil, searching for a connection.

"We had not anticipated that humanity would take such a leap forward, not for another one hundred, possibly two hundred of your years," replied Thallor, now showing irritation with Neil's constant questioning. "We wonder, how it is that you have come this far? Further more, we do not see humanity as capable handlers of such power. You must embrace containment. You must not let the others of your kind come to grasp what you posses."

"Before I can make any decisions," inquired Neil, "I must know more about your origins and your interests."

"No further information can be given until you make a determination," countered Thallor.

"I need to know the entire objective and all of what you propose," answered Neil.

"In time we will be forthcoming," said Thallor, with notable aggravation. "Your eyes have been opened, Clayborn. We have observed that true power cannot properly be controlled by your world. We can facilitate with measures suited to the need. As for you, we can make it possible for you to reign over your world. We will assign you to a high position within our ranks and you will be the recipient of great wealth."

"Who has given you this authority?" questioned Neil.

"We are the final authority in these matters," lectured Chancellor Thallor, "the authority of the Seruzian Principality will determine your course."

"I am sorry," said Neil, "I cannot agree to those terms."

"Again I must say, we offer a great opportunity," said Thallor. "You will learn of us and become one with us. Your technology will operate in league with ours. Why, you will even be seen as a god by your own kind."

"I cannot make decisions for other peoples and nations of my world. It is not my intention to rise above them."

"Do you not yet understand? You have received an invitation to greatness!"

"Again, I say to you, I do not aspire to such things, I am an explorer. I must seek council among the proper authorities of my own nation on my own world."

"We do not see an appropriate response on the part of your nation," countered Thallor, "neither do we find it in any other. No discussion with any other representative from your planet can be permitted. Your decision is singular."

"I must say again, I cannot make a decision at this time."

"Most assuredly, you must comply."

"Please, I need more time."

"Why have you not yet understood? You see, now, you do not have a choice."

"My objective is peaceful but I find, perhaps, that your intentions may not be."

"Our intentions are our affair. Your obligation is to comply."

"My obligation is to my world. I find that your initial invitation may have been misleading."

"You came of your own accord and by your own insatiable curiosity," informed Thallor. "We did not make you seek us out."

"We only desire an equitable exchange of ideas and civility," said Neil.

"We find that interesting," replied Thallor, "but that is for a later discussion. There is nothing you can do to change the course you have chosen. If you comply with our demands you will be allowed to control your technology. If you do not comply then it ultimately must fall into our hands."

"That can never be," announced Neil, with new determination.

"You have much to learn, Clayborn, and you will learn it from us!" demanded Thallor.

"Perhaps in time—," but Neil never got to finish his reply, for by a single motion of his hand, Thallor signaled for the two beings stationed at each end of the semi circle to take hold of him. Unlike the slow methodical movements the creatures evidenced thus far, the action taken against him was like the strike of a serpent, of lightning speed, and so without warning that their visitor had no time to react. The alien agents were able to instantly subdue their human subject, securing him by a tight grip around the neck and arms. They searched him, and removed the CMR device from his person. Without the CMR, Neil was unable to stand on his own and fell to the platform. His captors were amazed at the debilitating condition of the one at their feet. More than pleased, they dragged him out of the receiving area and hauled him down a narrow passageway leading from the receiving area. At the end of the passageway they entered a room composed of gray metallic sections. The claustrophobic chamber was extremely cold, dim, and permeated with the stench of decaying flesh. A black rectangular slab rose up 24 inches from the center of the floor with five slender tethers protruding from around the perimeter. The two hooded beings occasionally jabbed Neil with a probe that inflicted intense pain like the forceful blow of a mallet. Then they stretched his crippled body out on the slab and shackled him to the tethers, one around each of his limbs and his neck. Once this was accomplished the tethers began to withdraw into the slab. Now he was stretched out and held tightly on his back. With only the slightest move on his part the cuffs would cinch and the tethers would pull with greater force to oppose him. These shackles could easily restrain a strong man, so for Neil, it was impossible to resist the tension.

Once their human subject was conveniently out of the way, Thallor and two other beings boarded the *Aurora* by way of the already open companion-module doors. Unhindered, the foreign presence stopped at each deck to perform a thorough search for other occupants or anything of interest. Thallor commanded the others to leave any equipment and small unbound items where they found them until they could be assessed and catalogued. The search of the ship finally led them to the bridge, where they sought to gain immediate control of the vessel. One of them by the name of Dine, was carrying the CMR device they removed from Neil, but the attending guard accidentally bumped into him and it fell to the deck. Dine lashed out at the guard in frustration, striking him across the face. By this he made known the infraction and the guard submitted. Then, before Dine could retrieve the device, an alert rang throughout the bridge. The active display screens faded to black and all of the instrumentation and overhead lighting shutdown leaving the invaders in complete darkness. Thallor shouted, "Fix this blackout! We must gain control of this ship."

They switched on their own lights and searched for clues leading to the restoration of power. While the alien presence went about doing this a faint red glow appeared from ceiling fixtures. Simultaneously, all of the visual screens began to repeatedly flash a message in large red letters in all known languages: "All intruders must leave this vessel immediately."

"Do these beings think we will give up because they politely ask us to leave?" exclaimed Thallor. "Now find a way to override these controls and shut down that noise!"

"Yes, Chancellor!" acknowledged Dine.

They scanned the instrumentation and groped the mechanisms for clues. But through no action of their own the alert abruptly became silent and the message screens became dark again. With the distraction now gone the invaders continued to search for a way to override the locked up controls. They believed taking time to gain the necessary technical information by seizing control of the ship was preferable to a messy dismantling process.

As Dine was examining one of the control panels he came across the oval picture of the harbor titled Search.

"These toys and images of their planet seem to humor this species," said Dine, "they are useless indulgences and an unnecessary diversion."

Thallor added by saying, "Yes, they delight in trivial pursuits, but they can ultimately be controlled by them. How could this species have attained such technology?" Dine was fascinated by the small ship in the bottle and reached out to touch it, but Thallor shouted, "Get to work. We must find answers!"

"Yes, Chancellor!" answered Dine. Although he was a skilled engineer in his own world his efforts did not proceed smoothly. Even with the powerful tools at their disposal the systems of the *Aurora* proved more elusive than they had anticipated.

The table on which Neil was held was as cold as a block of ice and growing colder. As he wrestled with the restraints the lurid green glow on the ceiling began to increase in brightness. Suddenly a sound like the sharp blast of a trumpet hit his ears and the light began to flash. He twisted and pulled, but the restraints fought against him. If he moved his legs the restraints cinched tighter. If he moved his head, the collar squeezed more tightly around his neck, nearly to the point of choking, thus making it impossible for him to evade the light and the noise. Their captive soon grew fatigued.

After an undetermined period of time the blasting trumpet stopped, the brilliant light above him switched off and the cuffs began to relax. The absence of the light and noise was a relief and he slowly began to recover his senses. When a near normal state of rest finally occurred the assault began again. The scenario would repeat itself over and over and he lost track of time. Then suddenly everything changed, now low frequency sound waves washed over his body, accompanied by the sensation of a smothering blanket. He struggled for breath. Horrific images began to insert themselves into his mind and he could not discern if they were real or imagined. All humanity seemed to be fighting against itself as it became lost in an uncontrollable madness. Uncounted souls endured captivity as fires consumed the cities of the Earth. His sanity left him and his mental faculties seemed to break down. Anxiety overtook him as he wrestled with the tenor of his emotions in semi-consciousness. Then, in the midst of a mental fog he heard a single sharp mechanical click and the chatter of alien tongues. The beasts had returned.

Thallor had consulted with those in higher command in the Principality regarding the fate of their human subject. The alien beings had been at a loss to gain control of the captured ship and could not decipher the puzzle, even though they had been admonished by the upper levels of command to exploit all options. Thallor received a new directive: Seize the ship at all costs. Terminate the occupant and do whatever was necessary to obtain control of the newly acquired property.

Thallor was present with the guards when they entered the cell. As they stood by the slab one of the guards touched Neil on the shoulder with a small probe, this time an acute fiery flame ripped through his body. They smote his flesh again and again as if it were an obsession. The grinding voice of Thallor now rang in his ears, demanding, "You will come with us, Clayborn."

Their victim was in a weakened state as they dragged him out of the cell and back to the receiving area where the *Aurora* stood dark and silent. Thallor and the two guards with him were joined by the one called Dine as they took Neil up to the bridge of his own ship and let him fall helplessly onto the deck.

"We know your infirmities," informed Thallor. "You have been deprived of your power. Give us control of your ship or we will deliver you up to those who will amplify and extend your misery."

Neil lay motionless, but Thallor demanded, "Cooperate with us and you will live, or we will dissect every component of this ship just as we will dissect you. All that you have will be ours." Neil only groaned in pain as Thallor delivered his ultimatum. "If you do not cooperate you will be the very cause of the enslavement of your world. Such is your legacy. If you choose to cooperate we may be inclined to spare humanity of its extinction. What shall it be, Clayborn?"

In a labored whispering breath, Neil replied, "I—I can—not."

"You could have been worshiped as a god!" retorted Thallor, with rage. "Now you will be nothing more than the meat of sacrifice. Take him out!"

"Yes, Chancellor," blurted the others.

Strong alien hands grabbed their victim and forced him into the companion-module. Then Thallor gave the command, "Dine, go and get your instruments. Begin the dismantling process. Tear this thing apart piece by piece if you have to. Do what you must do!"

When the module doors opened Thallor and the others stepped out of the en-closure dragging Neil with them. As they reached the platform by the lamp posts, their captive gathering every last ounce of his strength, somehow managed to break free of their grasp and fell to the floor of the platform. His fingers scratched at the surface with what strength he had left in his right hand as if attempting to crawl away but with little progress. The creatures watched the pitiful attempt with self congratulation and triumph. Neil persisted until he found a small hinged tile. It flipped up and he slipped his hand under it, where he gripped on to a crystalline handle. Sharp points drew blood from his fingers.

The systems aboard the *Aurora* read the signature of his blood and the ship burst to life. At the same time discreetly aimed energy beams destroyed the exit doors of the enclosure and the *Aurora* thrust itself through the opening with explosive force. The contents of the receiving area, including Thallor, Dine and the two guards were sucked out of the alien vessel. As the ship shot through space the external platform began to draw inward toward the open doors of the module bringing Neil with it. The surrounding fields of the ship protected him from the vacuum of space until he could reach the threshold. At the same time a select number of small cylinders emerged from the ceiling on all decks and in the companion-module cleansing the ship of all alien contaminants. Neil was able to roll himself across the threshold and the doors whisked shut, after which the remaining elements of the platform dissolved away.

The decontamination cylinders shut down and the companion-module took its passenger up to the bridge. When the doors opened Neil pulled himself out onto the deck. His destination was the pilot couch, although even short distances still pre-sented a considerable challenge. Inch by inch he crawled around the module wall while the *Aurora*, still on auto pilot, continued to accelerate through space.

During his journey within his own vessel another Seruzian ship had been dis-patched after the speeding *Aurora*. The chase continued for some time reaching a transit many times the speed of light. But then the alien craft fell back. Possibly it was not suited for the task at hand, regardless, the *Aurora* continued at its runaway pace. Finally, Neil, with one last agonizing heave, managed to position himself in the reclining seat. Now at the helm, his body began to regain additional control. The small drawer holding the ring popped open, he removed it, and placed it on his fin-ger. Then he took the Mariner's Cross and hung it over a nob on the console. Even-tually he was able to attach another CMR to his person. After checking the time, he was amazed to discover the entire ordeal had only lasted a number of hours and not days. Now he needed to make a return trip to his home planet, still not knowing if it had been subjugated by an alien force.

At about 3 o'clock in the afternoon that same day, Frank Niverson walked into the Midway Tavern hoping to find Mari and seeking to verify the fact that she was the woman he saw during his captivity.

"Can I help you?" asked Nancy. She had approached with a fair amount of suspicion, recalling the last time he was in the tavern.

"I'm looking for someone," demanded Frank, with impatience.

Nancy fired back at him defensively, saying, "Well, aren't we all."

Frank made it plain why he was there, saying, "Where is that woman with the dark hair? Where is she?"

"What do you mean 'that woman,' who are you talking about?" asked Nancy, in defense.

"That dark haired girl, the one who works here," replied Frank. "I need to speak to her."

"You mean Mari? Haven't you heard?"

"Heard what?"

"She never showed up for her shift on Thursday and she went missing."

"Of course!"

"They say she was abducted."

"I knew it!" exclaimed Frank, with his suspicion confirmed.

Nancy further informed Frank, saying, "She went horseback riding in the evening and never returned. They found her horse just wandering around in back of her place."

Peg arrived in the dining room and entered the conversation, saying, "Her folks got a call from her and we heard she's okay. The police were out here yesterday and they got detectives on it but we haven't heard much about it yet."

"Maybe I'll pay those people an official visit," replied Frank.

Peg immediately cautioned him, saying, "They took it hard. They're private folks and you're not making any friends around here, mister."

"Well," replied Frank, "it's not my intention to make friends."

Just then, Peg saw the front door open, she gasp and cried out, "Mari!"

Every head turned at the mention of the name and they all watched in amazement as the woman walked into the tavern.

Nancy immediately ran up to her and gave her a big hug, saying, "We were so worried about you!"

"Where have you been, girl!" cried Peg, also rushing to her side. "You caused quite a stir!"

"I'm fine," replied Mari, seemingly surprised by the exuberant reception. "I'm fine, really!"

Frank was incredulous, as Peg declared, "Honey, it is real good to see you, everyone's been beside themselves."

"I got home last night, but everything's okay," Mari informed them.

"Okay?" exclaimed Nancy. "The whole town has been turned upside down!

You just up and disappeared."

Mari didn't acknowledge Frank, even though she recognized him, but then she said, "I just want everyone to know I'm fine so please don't worry about me."

Frank didn't know what was behind the odd turn of events, but said pointedly, "I need a word with you, Miss."

"Why?" asked Mari, with a defensive glare.

"I have a feeling you know something about what's going on here, " snapped Frank.

Mari pretended not to hear and shook her head, saying, "I don't understand."

"Where have you been?" demanded Frank, "You know about what's going on don't you?"

"What do you mean?" returned Mari, appearing confused.

"She's deaf you know," declared Peg with a scowl, pointing to her own ears. "Anyhow, you leave her alone."

"I saw you there!" blasted Frank, grabbing Mari by the arm.

"What?" cried Mari, immediately pulling away from his grip.

"Hey, you keep your hands off her!" cried Peg.

"Don't get smart with me young lady," Frank whipped back, but letting go of her.

"What are you talking about?" demanded Peg.

"It's now or later," declared Frank. "Time is running out!"

"Hay, Mack, cool it!" cried Peg. "Leave her be! I don't care what you want. I'll be calling the police." Frank backed down as Peg turned to Mari. "Girl, you get into that kitchen. I'll see him out of here!"

Frank would have followed her but Peg blocked his way and pinned him down with a stare. A momentary standoff took place, then Peg pointed to the door and Frank gave in to her demands. He left the tavern determined to take advantage of the propitious turn of events.

Nancy followed Mari into the kitchen, and said, "I'm so glad to see you, you look good, somehow you even talk better than before!"

Peg soon joined them saying, "I don't know what's going on around here, Honey, but everyone was real worried about you."

"Believe me," said Mari, confidently, "I'm fine." She was doing her best not to let on she could hear, even though changes in her own voice were unconsciously taking place. She was also the closest one to the doors leading to the dining room, and though no one else was aware of it, she could hear the stray conversations drifting around the dining room concerning her. Now she was saying again, "I'm not going to talk to that guy out there."

"You don't have to," said Peg, "but we would sure like to know what happened to you!"

"I will tell you about all this some time," said Mari, "but now I really need to get back home."

"Well, I'm glad you came," encouraged Peg. "And don't worry about anything, you just rest."

"Thank you," replied Mari.

"You can go out the back door," added Peg, "we'll see to that guy. You take care and return when things settle down."

"I'll be back when I can," assured Mari, slipping out as Peg suggested.

When Frank made his exit Del and Pete came striding up to him on the sidewalk. Del, with a trace of respect he didn't usually posses, said to Frank, "We've been lookin' to talk to you."

"Who are you?" countered Frank.

"The name is Del and this here is Pete."

"What do you want?" questioned Frank, ready to dismiss what he thought to be just another inconvenience.

"We saw them lights," answered Del.

"Yeah, so has everyone else, I need more than that," replied Frank, annoyed by the tough looking men.

"We saw that girl out there with them lights!" said Pete.

"Girl?" replied Frank, his ears perking up. "What girl?"

"Yeah, that girl Mari, who works here," said Del.

"Where did you see her?" asked Frank.

"We was drivin' out in the back country," said Del, ready to enlighten Frank with all the information at his disposal. "We was near her place and we saw them lights. We drove a trail near the back of Cygnet's property. We drove in on them trails, then we got out, and we went on foot so we got close enough to see."

"Yeah, that's when we saw those weird things in them woods," added Pete, "and we saw her out there."

"Tell me," returned Frank, "what things?"

"Some pretty weird stuff," said Del. "She was out there in them woods with 'em."

By now the men had Franks complete attention, so he urged Del to elaborate, saying, "Tell me exactly what you saw."

"Them UFOs was flying all over the place," exclaimed Del, "and she was like out there waitin' for 'em."

"You say she was waiting for them?" returned Frank.

"Yeah, but her horse got spooked," said Pete.

"It threw her," said Del, "and she was just laying there. Then there was them UFOs and that blue thing came and landed like some sort of monster, then it paralyzed us and we couldn't move. Then there was like a silver man out there and it came to get her. And the whole thing just took off and we was let go."

Frank was stunned by the account, and asked, "Is that exactly the what happened?"

"Yeah," said Del, convincingly. "We saw it, I swear."

"You were paralyzed you say?" Frank asked.

"Yeah, couldn't move an inch," affirmed Del.

"But we could see real good," added Pete.

"Have you told anyone else about this?" asked Frank.

"No," replied Del. "What do you think, man, who'd believe us anyhow?"

"Well, I believe you!" attested Frank as he patted Del on the shoulder. "You've confirmed my suspicions."

"We just thought you'd like to know," returned Del, with an ear to ear grin.

"Are you sure you're telling me everything?" asked Frank, thankful for the information but still skeptical about some of the details, for he didn't trust the men.

"We told you all we know," replied Del.

"Listen," said Frank, "I want you to tell some important people about what you saw later on this evening. I'll arrange for some officials to come right here to the tavern."

It just seemed natural for the tavern to become the informal meeting place concerning the sightings because it had been the town gathering place for years. But, with the recent talk of UFOs, aliens, and creatures, a slightly different clientele began to show up.

Peg arrived back in the dining room just as Frank reentered the tavern with the men and said to anyone within earshot, "Everyone, can I have your attention? Listen to me!" Peg put her hands on her hips and glared, but Frank kept talking. "Listen, maybe you have been like everyone else around here, afraid to speak up, well, we've got some people who will listen. There are some top agents working in the area. I'll make sure someone will be here at 9 o'clock this evening to hear you out."

Hearing that, Peg called out, "Hey, Mack, who said you could come back in here and hold a meeting? I'm going to have to tell you once again to leave the premises!"

Frank insisted, saying, "This is important, time is running out, there's no time for formalities. You want answers don't you?"

"Well, maybe so," agreed Peg.

"I was up in those mountains myself," said Frank, "and I saw more than just lights."

"Why don't you tell us all about it now?" returned Peg,

"We have high ranking people are on this thing and believe me there will be a followup," replied Frank. "I can have one of them here tonight to answer any questions you have. Everyone can speak their mind."

"Well," replied Peg, "if it clears up some of this stuff then I guess it's okay."

"It will, believe me," said Frank.

"This better be good," groaned Peg, "I'm not having all the crazies in town coming down on my place and I'm not having you pushing people around."

"You'll get those answers this evening," replied Frank. "You can help us put an end to all the false rumors once and for all."

Frank left the tavern as Nancy and Peg just looked at one another and shook their heads. Word spread rapidly and many of the people at the tavern agreed to return to hear what the authorities had to say. Frank's immediate destination was White Lake, where he would meet with Gen. Staffer and other authorities and try to pull some strings to arrange for someone to come out to quell the distrust and draw out more information from the public. Frank eventually spoke to Gen. Staffer about the meeting at the tavern and there was an initial agreement to send someone out but, as the day progressed, plans had changed and Frank was never told that the meeting was called off. Security was tightening up on all fronts with all available re-sources requisitioned for Thunder Peak.

By 8 o'clock a slightly cooler breeze had arrived across the arid land. The rain that had been forecasted on the previous day never came, but unstable weather was developing in the southwest and dark clouds were moving towards Wyoming. Several military units had been mobilizing near Thunder Peak in the latter part of the afternoon and assembled themselves at the base of the mountain and were prepared to send troops up the treacherous slopes if need be. First, they would wait for Frank and his men to penetrate the facility, then send in backup if needed.

Within Star Harbor, Marcus, and the others were rightly concerned that the forces assembling at the base of the mountain might eventually find a way to penetrate the complex. The security systems were still not working properly and they could not forestall a full scale invasion without the help of Neil and the ship. Marcus sent out a series of coded messages to the *Aurora* but received no response. He knew this meant the ship was too far distant to receive the signals in a timely fashion or that something untoward had happened to Neil. Because of the nature of the technology in their possession they had reached a mutual agreement that if the security of Star Harbor was ever compromised the facility would be evacuated so that the underground complex and its secrets could be rendered useless. All personnel would then mix with the general population and essentially disappear.

Christopher Cain was part of the six person team that would be the first to leave, this included Dr. Isaac Wells, Brian Combs, Gena Porter, Wilmer Tack, and Dennis Coleman. Marcus would remain to supervise the termination process involving the internal status of Star Harbor. The thought of bloodshed was abhorrent to everyone, finding it more palatable to prevent an invasion from occurring in the first place. So, late in the day six individuals were climbing the stairway up to the same cave where Frank originally had made his forced entry. Cain was carrying the small metal case containing all the technical information regarding the Mechanics Project so they might retain the vital information concerning the technology.

As daylight waned an Air Force helicopter dropped off Frank, five soldiers, and two special agents on the mountain. In the early stages of their climb a pulsating amber object appeared above them and descended like an agitated mother bird. Eventually the object headed toward the mountain peak where it was joined by two other amber objects then all eventually disappeared. The men continued on in haste, nervously looking over their shoulders expecting an attack by one of the amber objects. As they neared their destination the group stopped just short of a large clearing, remaining under the cover of the trees, there Frank intended to brief them with further information about what they might encounter. Suddenly someone heard a noise coming from the other side of the clearing and everyone held their position in readiness.

Chris and the others with him emerged from the upper portion of the slope into the clearing. Both groups were caught off guard at the sight of the other in the near darkness. The soldiers immediately cried, "Halt. US Army. Drop any weapons you might have!"

The team from Star Harbor, now caught out in the open immediately stood still and obeyed the command. Chris and Isaac slowly pulled out their conventional weapons and dropped them to the ground. Chris had not relinquished the metal case and Frank ordered him to put it down. Reluctantly, he did as instructed. The soldiers also made demands for Chris to relinquish the small device he had clipped to his belt. He would have done so but it failed to release properly and as he attempted to pull it out of the clip his arm jerked away from his body. The edgy soldiers responded by firing several shots and Chris was killed instantly. The rest of the Star Harbor group scattered into the woods and more gunfire broke out. Within a short time all the individuals escaping from the mountain were tracked down and shot.

Frank was not happy with the fact that no one was left alive to capture or interrogate. He hoped the contents of the case would provide the answers they needed, but the information within it had dissolved into a pile of ash the moment Chris was killed. When it became feasible, all of the bodies would be taken away for identification and autopsy.

The three amber objects had returned to circle menacingly above the lofty slopes of Thunder Peak and two armed military drones arrived to confront them. Of the three objects, two departed, leading away one of the drones. The remaining drone followed the strange object still circling around the jagged mountain peak and fired on its target. The object lost altitude as a result of a direct hit and fell to earth near the military units stationed at the foot of the mountain, where it was immediately surrounded by troops.

When Frank and his men reached the cave they used a torch to heat up the button that had previously activated the door to the staircase. The attempt failed so explosives were strategically placed to destroy the rock barrier. The blast opened the way for Frank's men to descend into the depths. They also used the same technique on the locked doors at the bottom and the search for alien life began in earnest.

The men raced freely along silent corridors and into empty rooms. They found the cell where Frank had been held and entered the apartment Mari had once occupied. They even entered the austere rooms of Neil's apartment but up to this point they found no one. Their search took them to the port dome, but there was neither a ship nor alien creatures, however, they did find human activity behind the glass in the observation room.

The members of Marcus's group, Gordon Bradford, Thomas Kenner, George Henderson, and Dr. Canton had begun to make the final preparation to leave the complex. Candice had been chosen as the second person after Marcus to leave the upper level and so she was sent through an escape tube that led from the observation room to the lowest parts of the complex. Once she reached the lower level she accompanied Marcus in the final preparations for the first stage of the destruction sequence. The rest of the personnel within Star Harbor were about to enter the escape tube when two shadows appeared just outside the door to the adjacent hall. The shadows became soldiers that burst into the room. Gordon attempted to conceal his reach for the intercom to alert Marcus and Candice, but as he struck the button one of the soldiers wrestled him down. Marcus and Candice received the warning signal just as they were finishing their work. The two of them would soon enter another escape tunnel that would lead outside. As the assault on the control room continued, Gordon managed to pin his opponent down but in the process the soldier's gun discharged. George Henderson, who was being held by the soldier poised a short distance away was struck by the errant shot. Henderson collapsed, and Thomas Kenner saw an opportunity to get a weapon stowed in a nearby compartment. But quick action on the part of another one of Frank's team just entering the room from the hallway changed the outcome. He fired at Kenner and the man dropped. Finally, all guns were trained on Gordon as he continued to wrestle with the man on the floor. Gordon managed to pin the man down a second time and attempted to get the gun away from him, but the man pulled the trigger and Gordon succumbed to the shot. When Frank arrived he found three people dead on the floor of the observation room.

A larger group than expected had assembled in the dining room of the Midway Tavern, and it wasn't long before tempers flared. Because the promise of knowledgeable military officials had never materialized, more than one person, including Peg, felt they had been fed yet another lie and they were sorely miffed by the no show.

Dan, who had been drinking at the bar for several hours, was getting impatient. He shouted to the group, "Hey, you know I heard someone say that Cygnet girl might be one of them. You know what? I think they're right!"

"How can you say that!" cried Nancy, in shock and dismay. "What do you mean, 'that Cygnet girl?' Come on, you know Mari!"

"Looks like they might know something we don't," came a voice from a nearby table.

Dan jumped off he stool and stood before the crowd, saying, "The Cygnets won't talk to anyone. Don't you wonder why? I say, let's go over there and find out for ourselves!"

"No!" cried Nancy. "Don't you go over there, you know she's not one of them!"

A man at the table nearest the door shouted, "He's right, let's make them talk!"

Del, Pete, Jack, and Kenny were also there, huddled quietly at a table at the back of the room, in a mood to stir things up. Del rose to his feet, and affirmed, "That Niverson guy said he saw Mari with them aliens in the mountain. And, I saw that thing land on old man Cygnet's property out there. I saw one of them creatures come and get her. Yeah, it was like she was waitin' for 'em and it took her with 'em!"

"Do you think she's one of them?" asked another.

"I don't know, but I think she went out for a meet-up," added Del.

"Then we got to find out!" called another.

"Wait!" cried a man sitting near Del's table, now having second thoughts. "We don't know all the facts yet. We don't know who those people are."

"You mean, we don't know 'what' they are!" injected Dan. "We got to find out for sure. We got to stop this thing right here and now. I don't know about you but I'm tired of being lied to."

Nancy confronted Dan again, and cried, "Don't you go. It's not true what they say!"

With mounting determination, Dan replied, "My father lost a prize horse and some of his best livestock because of those things. This time it was the animals, what if they come after us next? Something is going on right here and I'm going to find out for my self!"

"That's not going to help anything!" cried Nancy.

A young woman was sitting with her boyfriend and whispered in his ear. The young man nodded in affirmation, then said to the group, "Does anyone really know where that girl is from? I just heard she's adopted."

"Who knows where she's really from?" said the young woman, now speaking up.

"Yeah, Nancy here keeps saying she's from space just like them aliens," affirmed Dan, "and they'll be coming after us!"

"Dan, no, that's not what I said!" cried Nancy, now horrified. "How can you fall for that stuff? She's our friend!"

Dan pushed Nancy away, saying, "I'm going over there and you're not stopping me!"

"Come on you guys knock it off, you'll just make things worse," cried Peg, who, up to this point had been in and out of the dining room and keeping a casual eye on the crowd. Now she would witness seventeen people as they got out of their seats and head for the door. She tried to stop them. "Hey, come on folks, this isn't the way!"

Del, Pete, Jack, and Kenny were the last ones to leave, but before they did, Peg pulled Del aside, saying, "You don't really believe all this do you? You get those folks to cool down out there."

Del only returned a scowl and continued on his way out with the boys. The four men piled into the truck and became the last vehicle among a steady stream of cars and trucks to leave the parking lot. Defeated, Peg finally called the police but was told all available officers were not immediately available and she would have to wait.

William and Jennifer were sitting in the living room reading and taking full advantage of the unexpected coolness in the air. The sun had set, the television was off and the house was quiet. William happened to look up from his paper to see several pairs of headlights shining through the front windows. Car doors slammed shut, followed by the rise of angry voices. By the time William reached the front door he saw a throng people marching up to the house with more cars still entering the driveway. Four men came treading boldly across the front lawn as others came stomping through the flower beds.

Mari had been up in her room and totally unaware of what was happening. She had taken the earrings off so she might rest in silence, partly as a matter of habit, for it was something she had always done with her old hearing aid. The earrings were now carefully stored in their gold case, which she put in her night stand for safe keeping. Normally at this hour she might already have been asleep, but tonight she was awake in bed with her eyes closed. Meadow, now startled, jumped off the bed and scampered under her bed as if running from something. Mari got down on the floor and tried to coax the cat out but it just stayed there crouching in the dark. When she stood up she could see lights through the front window and went over to see what was going on. Alarmed, she ran downstairs where she saw the worried look on her parents faces.

A muffled shout erupted again from the yard, saying, "Hey, Cygnet, you come out here!"

Then Dan hollered out of the darkness, "Where's that daughter of yours!"

William opened the door and stepped out onto the porch, shouting, "What in the name of all creation is this about?"

"We heard about you!" yelled a man wielding a shiny new ax handle as he approached the house.

"What did you hear?" William yelled back.

"That Mari's one of them," cried Dan.

"Yeah, get your daughter out here," shouted another. "We know about her and them UFOs."

"Come on," came another cry. "Where is she?"

"This is nonsense!" cried William. "Who do you think you are!"

"We know about your daughter," shouted another.

"Rubbish!" countered William.

"We got people that say otherwise," cried another voice out of the darkness.

"You're on private property," shouted William, defiantly. "Get off my land!"

"You listen here, Cygnet," said the man, waving the ax handle in the air. "We got information on your daughter, send her out here so she can tell us her self!"

"I'm not sending her out to the likes of you!" cried William. "Clear off this property before I call the police."

"Bring her out or we'll come in there and get her," came a cry.

William stepped back into the doorway to tell Jennifer to call the police and to get his gun. Jennifer signed to Mari to get the gun then she raced for the phone in the kitchen. Mari ran to get the shotgun from her parents bedroom as Jennifer began dialing the phone but the line was dead because someone outside had severed the land line. Mari returned to the kitchen from the bedroom by way of the back stairs and heard someone banging on the back door so she stopped to lock the inner door. Jennifer pulled her cell phone from her purse on the counter and made another call. The woman receiving the 911 call began asking a series of lengthy and detailed questions after she heard Jennifer say something about 'UFOs' and 'outer space.' Jennifer pleaded with the woman, franticly trying to convince her she was telling the truth. Finally, Jennifer was assured that someone would be out as soon as possible.

Mari peeked through the curtains of the front door just in time to see the angry crowd as they chanted in unison, "Aliens! Aliens! Aliens!"

When William attempted to go back into the house two men jumped on the porch and grabbed him, pulling him down, beating him with their fists, and striking him with the ax handle. He valiantly fought back but the assault continued until he found himself flat on the sidewalk. Mari stepped out of the open doorway with the gun and expertly pointed it at the intruders. More shouts came from the crowd, saying, "That's her! She's the one!"

Jennifer raced to the porch and took the gun from her daughter and shouted to the crowd, "You leave us be! You stop or I'll shoot!"

The mob hushed, this gave William a chance to break free and stumble back up the steps. Two men advanced on the porch and Jennifer fired a single shot over their heads. Silence reigned for a few seconds, then the mob erupted with even more intensity.

"What are you hiding Cygnet!" shouted Dan, tauntingly.

A large but carefully aimed stone flew out of the darkness and hit Jennifer's forehead and she dropped the gun. Mari immediately retrieved it and pointed it at the men, and yelled, "Stay back!"

Another stone narrowly missed Mari as a man cried out, "We can take her!"

Bricks and stones continued to fly, torn from the flower beds in the lawn as the family retreated into the house. No one quite knew for sure how or where it came from, but a box of home made incendiaries magically appeared by the side of the road near the mouth of the driveway. Soon a flaming bottle landed on the porch, the glass shattered on impact to cast its fiery liquid across the wooden planks.

Jennifer wanted to put it out but was prevented from the attempt by the barrage of rocks and bricks. A can of gas was emptied on the east side of the house and a match was tossed. A column of flames exploded up the light blue clapboard siding. Moments later another fiery missile flew through the already shattered front window and smashed on the living room rug. Mother and daughter beat the flames with a small rug and managed to put out the fire. But another bottle struck with a fiery streak racing across the floor. The house was now filling with smoke. William knew they needed to get out and told Jennifer and Mari to head for the west side hallway. There was a window above an outside planter at that location, which was well hidden by thick shrubs and prevented a clear view from the front yard. The planter offered a sturdy platform to stand on before they reached the ground.

Mari realized that her journal, the earrings, and Meadow were still up in her room and against her mother's anxious protest she ran up to the second floor. She found flames engulfing her night stand and bed as a result of someone's careful aim, so she couldn't retrieve the earrings, but she was able to snatch the journal. She called for Meadow and the terrified animal came dashing out of the closet across the hall. Mari grabbed the cat and raced downstairs. She arrived in the hall just as her mother was making an exit through the open window. William was already outside and helping his wife reach the planter. But, her foot slipped on the smooth cap and she fell to the ground severely twisting her ankle in the process. It was now Mari's turn to climb down. She let the cat jump out then made the successful drop down to the planter and to the ground. She assisted her father and mother, but took a moment to slip the journal into the mail box on the gazebo. Hurriedly she rejoined her father and mother at the edge of the woods.

As the fire consumed Mari's room, it took the desk, the bookcase with all the old instruments, the violin, the clothes and umbrellas. On the first floor the fire engulfed everything it touched and one by one all of the family's intimate possessions succumbed to the fast moving blaze.

At that moment Dan noticed three people running toward the woods. He and two other men caught up with them and tried to pull Mari away. They would have been successful had two police officers from Stone River not arrived on the scene. Four soldiers from the military encampment at White Lake also arrived shortly thereafter. The officers immediately dispersed the crowd and rescued the family by apprehending Dan and the men. Four others were also arrested by police.

Prior to this time Del and his boys were among the rabble who managed to escape the melee. From the beginning Del and his friends had remained in the background, staying just long enough to enjoy the developing chaos. They fled the scene just before the police and the military arrived. Army Lt. Henry Calahan was among them, he had orders to pick up Mari and take her to the Army's installation at White Lake. This was deemed necessary for her safety and detailed questioning.

Jennifer bemoaned this action, saying, "Why do you want to take her? She hasn't done anything."

"I have my orders ma'am, it's just routine," said the lieutenant. "She will only be retained for a short while."

"What can she tell you?" questioned William. "I'm the one who saw the thing so why don't you take me instead?"

"It's for her own protection," said the lieutenant. "She will be released after it is safe to do so."

Mari didn't resist as soldiers led her away, but signed to her parents, saying, "Don't worry."

She was brought to a waiting military vehicle and instructed to get in, where she sat uncomfortably among the troops like a prisoner as they got underway for White Lake. The local fire department soon arrived and William and Jennifer were encouraged to spend the night with friends or get a room somewhere while things were brought under control. The couple refused, even after being warned about the danger of unruly individuals seeking to return. Although the firemen did their best under the circumstances, it was too late to save the house. The ash trees along the driveway suffered some damage but the barn, small out buildings, the gazebo, and the woods beyond the yard were spared. After the last of the fire fighting equipment and the last police cruiser left the property William and Jennifer sat down in the gazebo to figure out what to do next.

Mari was escorted to a small trailer on the White Lake compound. Here Lt. Calahan, and Sgt. Hedgeworth proceeded to question her about her connection with the sightings in and around the mountain. The cross examination continued for more than two hours but with little progress. Frustration was building. They thought the young woman seemed rather confused and her interrogators were not sure if they were getting through. They felt as though she couldn't understand most of the questions posed to her because of her hearing impairment or that she was being deliberately evasive.

Lt. Calahan began raising his voice as he said, "Now, Miss, we have a credible witness who claims you have involvement with what we believe to be an alien force. You must reveal any information you have. You know it will only work against you if you don't cooperate."

The young woman sat stiffly in the hard metal chair as the men paced the floor in front of her and seemed to hover as they tried to intimidate her with their loud voices and aggressive body language. She protested, saying she didn't know anything about the events they were describing. The lieutenant continued his questioning by saying, "According to official sources, very little reason exists to cast doubt on the fact that you have some connection with installation at Thunder Peak."

Mari, who by now was feeling the effects of the interrogation, replied, "I don't have any information. I wish everyone would just leave me alone."

"It's our business to get answers, young lady," threatened the lieutenant. "I can have you detained until you decide to talk. I would rather it be sooner than later. There are dire consequences if you lie to us. And, if you are inclined to partake in these subversive activities you could see considerable prison time as a result. You don't want to be locked up do you? A young girl like you would not do well under those circumstances."

Mari caught most of what was being said and became frightened, but replied, "I don't understand, what have I done that's so wrong?"

The lieutenant crossed his arms and turned to the sergeant, saying, "We're going nowhere with this. Is the doctor still around?"

"Yes, sir, he's in the communications trailer," replied the sergeant.

"I want you to get him in here," growled the lieutenant.

Within a few minutes the sergeant came back with the doctor. The lieutenant turned to him, and said, "Take a good look at her. See if she is, you know, normal. Do something simple, see if she has a heartbeat or whatever. I want answers." Then he barked orders to the sergeant. "We don't know what we are dealing with here and we don't have time to play games. I'll be back to wrap this up later. And, find me someone who can communicate with the deaf and get them over here fast!"

The doctor entered the trailer as the other men stood outside and waited. After about ten minutes or so the man came out to speak with the two officers, and said, "As far as I can tell she's totally human, she actually appears to be in excellent health, just hearing impaired. I'd say she's completely deaf or close to it. Other than that, her physical health seems quite good."

"Deaf?" complained the lieutenant, "Well, that we know. It's just all this other stuff. I say it is time we move on."

The men decided to let their subject stew for a while, perhaps if she realized the consequences of withholding information she might reconsider. The officers posted a guard outside the trailer and left the makeshift compound for Thunder Peak. Mari on the other hand was determined not to betray Neil, but she wondered how long it would be before something might accidentally slip out. The weight of all that was happening began to settle on her and she broke down, quietly sobbing, hoping the guard would not hear.

In the beauty and vacuum of space things were in a state of flux. On the return trip to Earth a collection of messages from Marcus spilled in through the communication system. There was notable tension in his voice when he said, "Star Harbor is under attack. There is penetration by US ground forces. Neil, if you are out there, please respond." Then another, saying, "Invading troops are now within the harbor and we desperately need the ship. Unknowns have also been detected over the mountain and we are evacuating the Harbor."

Neil was dismayed by the advance on Star Harbor so he pushed the *Aurora* to expedite his return. In his final approach to the planet he detected the activity taking place around Thunder Peak. He also got no response from any of his team. Then to his amazement, he began receiving a message from a single alien craft now returning to the vicinity of the Bighorn Mountains: "We are Ambhuri. We request immediate destruction of our drone unit at the foot of your mountain. We will provide information on all the troop movement and action in vicinity." Detailed information came pouring in concerning the temporary military compound at White Lake, including their fire power, the number of personnel on the scene, the technology used by the forces, as well as the identity of the person detained for interrogation at White Lake, which happened to be Mari. Neil was more than alarmed by the situation and by the vast amount of detail provided by the alien presence, because he had never received any kind of communication or had any contact with this type of craft before. When he attempted to reply no further communication could be induced from the alien craft. This became his first encounter with the Ambhuri, the very ones detested by the Seruzian Principality.

An intense blue light filled Star Harbor as the landing gear of the *Aurora* made contact with the back marble floor. A narrow crystalline tube formed at the top of the vessel and projected outward until it aggressively penetrated the bullet ridden glass of the observation room. Seconds later a ring of sapphire burst from the ship and the lone soldier in the doorway of the observation room became immobile. Now helpless, all he could do was look on as Neil stepped out of the tunnel. He was grieved by what he saw and checked for signs of life as he examined the bodies on the floor but it was too late. He saw that the chronometer registering the time for the destruct sequence and attempted to communicate with any personnel who might still be alive within the complex but there was no reply. He wanted to linger with those who perished but there was no time. Previously, all had agreed that if they should die while in residence at Star Harbor they were to be buried there. He would honor their wishes, so he found some lab coats hanging nearby and covered them, then he took a moment for a silent remembrance. After glaring at the restrained onlooker he returned to the ship. Once on the bridge he gave an order that resounded through the entire complex, "All intruders are to evacuate this facility immediately!

There are now fifty-one minutes remaining. I repeat, you have fifty-one minutes to evacuate this facility before it is destroyed. This will be the only warning."

As the ship left the mountain the man by the observation room door was released from the effect of the ring, thus giving him sufficient time to exit Star Harbor if he would be quick about it. Frank and the rest of his party, still wandering around in the various corridors and rooms also heard the warning and decided to make a hasty retreat. Each headed for the same staircase they used to make their forced entry.

It took the entire fifty-one minutes for all the invaders to leave the inner confines of the mountain. Just before the last of the men were to reach the cave they began to experience a ringing in their ears and found their footsteps to be strangely unsteady. All of the hard surfaces, including the steps beneath their feet, began to feel soft like foam rubber or wet cement. Three of Frank's men were still within the confines of the staircase to the cave when the clock hit zero. Two of them made it out successfully, after which all of the air space within the mountain began to fill with a gray mist engulfing every empty void. It then became dense and began to harden. The last man attempting to leap back into the cave didn't quite get his left leg out in time and the material congealed around his boot. He struggled but was now trapped by the hardened material and the man ahead of him turned back to help his comrade. In the process the unfortunate soldier had to leave his boot and part of his pant leg behind. By now the entire space within Star Harbor had become solid like the geological rock form which it was hewn.

A set of misty sails journeyed down from the mountain top until it hovered just above the ground near the military encampment. All the troops held their ground and called for more fire power, waiting for hostile action on the part of the strange object. Neil's voice entered every loud speaker on the communications equipment in the camp. Without identifying himself, he said, "Why do you seek to destroy us?"

Gen. Staffer was there and hurriedly found a communication device, then announced, "Our troops encountered hostility and responded. We will resist any invasion."

"Why did you attack the alien craft?" asked the voice.

"It did not heed our warnings," replied the general. "We took the necessary action."

"You must not retain it," Neil replied. "Please stand clear." A moment later a narrow red beam burst from the hovering mist and struck the alien object causing it to burn until only a layer of white fragments remained on the ground.

The nervous troops nearly unloaded all their ordnance on the churning mist, but Gen. Staffer commanded them to hold their position and not return fire, then he said, "What do you want from us?"

"We are leaving this mountain," informed the voice.

"We don't know who or what you are," said Staffer, "but we will defend ourselves and this nation with all available forces. We will do what we must do."

Neil spoke one final time, "Rightly so, but we mean you no harm. Now we must do what we must do."

The *Aurora* returned to the sky.

Chapter Eleven: Midnight

Some may wonder what is on the other side of midnight,
Or what tomorrow will bring.
But that does not matter,
For I will trust in the One beyond all tomorrows.
Mari

It was sometime after midnight, on August 30, and Kenny, Pete, and Jack were armed and on a mission to see what was transpiring at White Lake. The three men had evaded the watchful eye of strategically placed armed men and found a lonely foot path from a nearby road. All was quiet, for nearly all the forces had moved on to Thunder Peak.

Pete brushed aside the branches of a small pine, and whispered, "I told you we didn't need Del."

"I don't know if this was such a good idea, man," said Jack, bending down to get a good look with his own eyes. "You know what happened the last time we was out in the woods. Del said he's got a plan and he'd tell us about it after he gets back from doin' whatever he's doin'."

"We'll find out about Mari for sure this way," countered Kenny, tightly gripping a small pistol.

"I don't see anything going on here," added Jack. "Where is everybody?"

"It's too quiet," informed Kenny.

The men crept closer, working their way through the extra thick underbrush, their efforts allowed them to reach the vicinity of the trailers, where more careful steps brought them close enough to observe the movements of the guard keeping watch outside.

"I don't see no aliens," whispered Pete. "Maybe they didn't bring her out here after all. It's just too quiet."

"Shut up," scolded Kenny, "we got to get closer, they might have her and some of them aliens in them trailers."

"What if there ain't no aliens here?" asked Jack, nervously. "Or what if that blue thing comes back?"

"We're going to find out for sure one way or another," said Kenny, "but it looks like a cover up. If there are aliens, well, someone's got to stop 'em. This time we'll be ready for 'em."

"Quiet!" whispered Jack, forcefully. "That guard's looking around."

It had been more than three hours since Mari had been brought to White Lake, she was tired and anxious, thinking about Neil, and very worried about her family. She prayed she might be released, not only because of her captivity but because the trailer was stifling hot and none of the windows would open. The only good thing about the periodic checks by the guard was the fresh air that came into the small room when the door was opened. Her view was obstructed in every direction, either by the trees, or the communications trailer next door. She was miserable and wanted to complain to the guard in hopes she might be freed from the makeshift prison.

A light fog had settled over the region and the air was moist. The guard fidgeted, completely trampling the patch of weeds on which he stood. He didn't relish being stuck at this lonely outpost while the other troops were securing the mountain. Yet, he wondered about the woman in his custody. To him, she seemed quite normal, even attractive, not at all like an extraterrestrial. He felt sorry for her plight but there was little he could do about it, so now he was resigning himself to a long uneventful night. But then, he thought he heard some twigs snap in the underbrush a short distance away. The ever present sounds of the night stopped and he strained to listen.

The snapping sound had occurred when Pete stepped on large dry branch. Then the soldier heard what he thought were hushed voices and a faint rustling so he radioed the man in the communications trailer for backup. The communications officer came out to join the guard and both troops cautiously worked their way into the woods to investigate. They moved in stealth, trying to pierce the darkness. Then there was another rustling noise and the men stopped to listen. In a single burst of speed, three men bolted from their unsatisfactory hiding place. The soldiers ran in pursuit with the fleeing men keeping well ahead of them.

"Halt!" shouted the guard. "United States Army. Halt now!" But the men did not heed the warning and found another hiding place. It was quiet again and the soldiers continued their search.

By looking through the small window in the trailer door Mari was surprised to find that the guard was no longer there. Hoping this might be an opportunity to at least get some fresh air she tried the door and discovered it was unlocked. Slowly she opened it, and when she saw no one around she stepped down the two metal steps to the ground. This was not the first time Mari had been to White Lake, she had been there many times as a child on fishing trips with her father so she was somewhat familiar with the geography. After gently closing the door, and seeing no one around, she inched away from the trailer toward the edge of the lake. The water was perhaps only 50 feet from where the trailers were located and by following the lake shore she hoped to find a trail that would lead out to the road. She was confident she could find her way around, even in the dark with patches of fog hanging in the air.

The soldiers decided to split up in an effort to find the trespassers. The guard headed farther out as the communications officer doubled back toward the position of the trailers. Unknowingly, the guard overshot the distance the men had run. Pete, Jack, and Kenny suddenly came running out of the woods toward the edge of the lake and saw the soldier so they turned to run along the beach, heading back in the direction of the trailers. Jack tripped over a submerged log and fell head long into the shallow water. This allowed the soldier to overtake him as his friends ran on ahead. When Jack attempted to get up and run, he heard the soldier say, "Stop! Drop your weapon and put your hands up!" Jack dropped the gun and stood still.

Pete and Kenny, continued to run along the shore and became alarmed when they saw someone coming toward them. They stopped, and pointed their guns at the oncoming stranger. Startled by the appearance of the two men in the fog directly ahead of her, Mari instinctively wheeled around and began running back toward trailers. At the same time the communications officer, who had returned to vicinity of the trailers, saw three people running by the water.

The officer took a stable position by some trees, and shouted, "Halt!" The Pete and Kenny stopped, but Pete impulsively fired two rounds at the voice. The shots missed their mark and the officer fired back. Mari was still heading toward the trailers, and the officer shouted to her, "Halt, or I'll shoot," but Mari couldn't hear the order. He cried out again. "Stop, or I'll shoot." The runner still ignored the command so soldier fired and Mari was struck on her right side and fell on the beach.

Pete and Kenny, fearing they might be next, called out in unison, "Don't shoot! Don't shoot!"

"Drop your weapons," shouted the officer. "Now!"

The guns fell into the wet sand and the officer retrieved them. He then escorted the men over to the place where Mari had fallen. As the guard kept his gun trained on the men, the communications officer came up and kneeled down to examine the woman laying on the ground, and said, "It's that girl you had in detention."

"I thought I locked the door!" cried the guard. "What's she doing out here?"

"She's alive," reported the communications officer, "but it looks pretty bad. We'll have to get the doctor back here."

Things were barely under control when the air over White Lake became filled with amber light. Two saucer shaped objects began to circle overhead. Although the objects swooped like bats, the soldiers kept their guns trained on the captured men. One of the objects sped upward and disappeared, the other stopped and hovered motionless about thirty feet overhead. After about forty-five seconds of bathing the beach in a yellowish glow the strange object disappeared.

The breeze was rapidly cooling for the first time in a long while. The fog had begun to move out and clouds, dark with moisture, began to march high across the mountains. A singular blue light appeared over the trees and crossed the lake. Before any of the men on the ground realized what was happening the object was landing near the lake in the only open space available. Kenny, Pete, and Jack decided now would be a good time to make a run for it, they headed for the woods but they didn't get far. A surging ring of energy instantly expanded out from the fading blue light and the men were stopped in their tracks. The companion-module descended and Neil came running to Mari's side. He called her name and brushed the sand from her face. When there was no response he felt for a pulse, he could find none. He knew he must act quickly if there was any possibility of reviving her so he carried her to the ship and brought her into the medical unit where he used all of the technology at his disposal.

A cold synthesized voice stated, "Internal tissue damage. Registering significant blood loss." Neil then initiated an anabiosis field around her that pulsed through her body but she still remained unresponsive. Finally, the automated systems of the medical unit shut down and the computer reported the results, "Patient status—deceased."

Neil brushed back her hair and held her hand, saying, "It should never have come to this. I should have died, not you, Mari, not you!" Again Neil initiated the anabiosis field around her and watched as the aura gently encompassed her body still hoping life would return. He left the medical bay and went to the bridge and his voice broke into the ears of the men on the beach, saying, "What has happened here?"

The troops as well as the soldiers were unable to move, and the guard answered, "We returned fire after we heard shots. The woman didn't heed our warnings and we thought she was armed."

"Why was she brought here?" returned Neil.

"For questioning," replied the officer.

"She is not of your concern," said Neil.

"Who are you?" shouted the guard.

"Innocent blood has been shed," replied Neil.

In the next instant all of the men were released from their paralysis and the ship departed. Neil engaged the auto pilot on an outbound course from the Earth and returned to the medical unit. Putting his arms around Mari's lifeless body he pleaded, saying, "Please, God, if you are there, restore her life. Heal her body and return her to me. Return her to all those who love her." He stayed with her for a long while but there was no change in her condition. Then, reluctantly he let go of her and sank to the deck with uncontrollable sobs.

William and Jennifer were salvaging what they could from the ruins in the pre dawn hours and only managed to recover a few small personal items. Only a few glowing embers remained of what once was a home. William and Jennifer were alone, distraught, and worried about their daughter.

Thick cloud cover had arrived over the land. Gusts of wind blew across the open areas and shook the tops of the trees in the yard, Jennifer grabbed William and began to cry, saying, "What has happened to us? William, what will we do now? What will we do?"

Her husband replied, "I just can't believe those people would turn on us."

"Why did they take Mari?" cried Jennifer. "When will they let her go?"

"I don't understand any of this," was all he could say.

They were still in a state of shock but something was coming their way. William was the first to see it. It became brighter and grew larger. He recognized it immediately as it hovered momentarily near the driveway and landed firmly in the front yard. This time when the mist dissipated it revealed a dimly lit object, there were no creatures, there was no grand display, then a confusing shape appeared at the opening of the companion-module.

Neil stepped out of the ship with Mari's lifeless body cradled in his arms. An almost living image of Celeste faintly shimmered above them as Neil stopped at the edge of the ship's looming hull. He wanted to turn back but he knew he must complete what he had started. Small streams of condensation trickled off the ship's polished edges and struck the man and the body of the woman in his arms. William recognized the approaching man as the same one who had visited their home not so long ago. Without exchanging any words William took his daughter into his arms and laid her on the grass.

"I brought her back from White Lake," said Neil.

"She's dead isn't she?" declared William.

"I was too late," said Neil, "I could not help her."

"This is all because of you," returned William.

"She was shot by the soldiers there," replied Neil. "I did all I could, but I could not bring back her life."

"No!" uttered Jennifer, hunching over the body.

"She had wisdom beyond her years," said Neil.

"Mari," sobbed her mother.

"I am so sorry," replied Neil.

Anger was in William's voice when he said, "We don't know who you are or even what you are, but we want you to leave us. We want you to leave this place."

"I loved her, Mr. Cygnet," said Neil, "more than I can ever say."

"What kind of love is this?" cried William. "We never want to see your face again."

As Neil, stood before them overwhelmed by his own grief, William, his voice quivering, said, "You are not welcome here."

"As you wish," replied Neil, and he returned to the ship. It assumed artificial life once again and departed into the night. The Mariner's Cross still hung from the knob on the control console where Neil had placed it on his return trip to Earth. He was now confronting a finality he was powerless to undo.

Restless winds were on the increase as intermittent drops of rain began to fall to earth. Lightning struck through the clouds in a glorious display. Thunder rolled across the mountains and over the low lands. Three rain soaked figures remained in the place they called home; one standing, one kneeling, and one in quiet repose. Time was set adrift for William and Jennifer; the thing was gone, their home was gone, and their daughter was gone.

Chapter Twelve: Memorial

The Lily of the Valley blooming by the lonesome bridge of twilight
shall be my memorial.
Mari

Moisture seeped ever deeper into the parched soil of Wyoming. People stood outside to be a part of the life giving drops which had come from heaven to saturate the ever thankful ground. It was a revival, it was hope, an agent of new life, it was something everyone longed for. And as lighting struck through the sky another light became visible over the Cygnet property. Soon it would occupy the exact spot where the *Aurora* once stood. This time it was an amber glow that grew dimmer and dimmer until a silver disk appeared. The entire object was not as big as the previous one but the fearful couple still expected to see Neil appear. Instead, they watched in semi dread as two small creatures emerged from the opening in the side of the object. The creatures were dressed in white with a loose hood covering their heads. The humanoids appeared somewhat comical, but the comedy was lost on the horrified onlookers. Each being appeared to have a weapon and signaled for William and Jennifer to step back as they came close to where Mari lay.

One of the intruders kept a hand held device pointed at William and Jennifer as the other re-entered the craft and reemerged with a rectangular box, which automatically unfolded and became a small platform. The creatures placed Mari's body on it and a white covering instantly formed over her. The beings then pulled the curious gurney into the silent craft. The opening closed, the amber glow appeared again, and the craft took to the air with great speed. Jennifer ran to the spot where the craft had been and collapsed on the ground. William stood helplessly gazing into the dark.

The envelope around Mari's body dissolved. The two individuals now present within the enclosure talked among themselves in an alien dialog as they started their procedures.

The one called Zarkis expressed his thoughts to the other, saying, "This human subject has specific tissue damage from a single solid projectile, otherwise, the condition is exceptional."

"Yes, there is significant damage here, though I did not expect sustainment," said Arka, now taking charge of the procedure. "Their technical capabilities have advanced greatly."

"I find their violence objectionable," offered Zarkis, "yet these new developments puzzle me."

"Fortunately this body reveals evidence of their technical capability," replied Arka, "yet they have limitations. It is as Tallis has said."

"They have not yet fully realized all of their technical capacities," said Zarkis. "If more time had elapsed we might not have accomplished our goal."

"Now," said Arka, "give me that micro probe."

Zarkis handed him the instrument, then he thought to enlighten Arka, saying, "These recent developments have caused me to reassess our recent information. I must say, Tallis has seized the moment, but he may have reacted too quickly. For this reason I question his judgment."

"His judgment is usually true," returned Arka, as he picked up another instrument, "he has affirmed this."

"That may be correct," replied Zarkis, "but as you are probably aware, this could be our undoing."

"That may be," sighed Arka. "That may be."

In time Mari was transferred to a transparent cylinder where electrical charges jumped from the inner surface of the cylinder to the surface of her body. The electrical activity eventually ceased and her body remained immobile, her eyes opened, blinked, and stared.

The rains had come to an end just before dawn on August 31. But, regardless of the weather conditions the *Aurora* was able to travel through the planetary atmosphere just as a sea going ship would sail the ocean to bring its pilot to far and distant ports. However, the sole occupant of this ship could not savor any such freedom nor could he find refuge in any harbor. He was still on the run, sailing from horizon to horizon, only to find that his attempts to forge a new frontier had churned up catastrophe. Comfortless, his mind raced to and fro. He conceded to the fact that his own arrogance and pride may have long ago corrupted his soul and because of this he may have opened the flood gates for hideous new predators to unleash a malignant evil.

He considered his own destruction, where he would permit an all consuming fireball to terminate all his efforts, and thus devour the dreams of a thousand nights. But he hesitated. Instead, he chose to drop the ship through the atmosphere in a controlled reentry. At last the *Aurora* came to rest in a forest valley at the base of another mountain called Cloud Peak in the Bighorn Mountain range. The ship's pilot switched off all major power systems and remained cloistered on the bridge. Sitting in the dark he was unable to decide if this thing wrought by collective passion should survive or simply cease to exist.

Neil had lost his sense of place, yet it may have been for that very reason he chose this one location. He forced himself out of the ship to wander across a knoll of tall wet grass and native flowers where he found a large flat stone. This created a platform about seven feet across and it was this spot where he and Marcus once discussed the future. He would now contemplate it once more, lamenting over those he once knew, though each one of them had been aware of the risks. He ran the delicate gold chain of the Mariner's Cross through his fingers, this was all he had left of Mari. She too, had become part of him, a wonderful mystery, and a light shining into his heart. He could not let go of her in this meditation without solace.

Eventually he returned to the ship, thinking that perhaps the world might continue on in peace if he were to depart from it. However flawed the strategy might be, he also considered taunting his foe and letting the dark forces chase him to the ends of space. Although his mind was still clouded with emotion he finally decided he must leave the mountains and leave his old life behind no matter what the outcome.

It did not matter where he would go, he was determined to leave the planet he called home.

On the bridge, in the midst of his preparation to leave he was interrupted by an alert, and it rang clearly throughout the ship. His instruments were picking up signals of alien origin. One lone screen by the pilot station read: "Ambhuri seeking contact."

Neil wasn't ready to talk, he was ready to do battle! He wondered if he had misread their intentions concerning the alien drone he was asked to destroy. Now they might be seeking retribution. The other possibility would be a Seruzian deception. He entertained the ramifications of an Ambhuri partnership with the Seruzian Principality where the two would secretly be in league to wrought destruction on the Earth. Although he had misgivings, he responded by sending a short message: "This is the *Aurora*. I have received your communication. Please state your intent."

In return they stated: "We are the Ambhuri. We seek contact."

Neil replied: "I respectfully request the exact nature of this contact. Please specify."

Again came the words: "We are the Ambhuri. We seek contact."

Neil paused, then typed his response: "Please reveal the exact time and location of this contact."

The Ambhuri, stated: "Contact immediate. Present location."

Neil's response was: "State your purpose."

He got a simple and immediate answer: "Contact." Then Neil, not knowing what to think, he reluctantly granted permission, to which he received a final responce: "Seven minutes."

There was no time to think it over, alien life had found Neil Clayborn once again and the seconds were ticking by. In exactly seven minutes an Ambhuri craft was landing in the clearing within proximity of his ship. The object produced an amber glow much like those he had seen before but this time it was brighter and larger and was only separated from his own ship by a moderate expanse of wild flowers waving in slight breeze of a dark night. All systems on the *Aurora* were set for immediate retaliation if need be.

Neil would need proof of their designs so he deployed the emergency platform, and he made an exit from his ship in no way as innocent as before. Now he stood with a weapon at his side. The silver object across the field was appointed with several ominous projections, which resembled a foreign kind of weaponry around the perimeter, some of which were aimed directly at the *Aurora*. As he waited, a row of white lights snapped on and lit up what appeared to be a closed hatch in the side of the ship. The hatch opened and two small humanoid beings in flight suits emerged. They did not speak, but immediately motioned for Neil to approach. Neil remained riveted the platform, he had lost his trust, now he would wait for them to outline their purpose.

Each of the creatures raised one of their long slender arms, once more beckoning him to approach. There were no visible weapons in their small hands but they seemed impatient for him to come toward the opening of the craft. Neil was quite determined to wait for them to make known the reason they had come. Soon the opening of the craft became occupied by a larger being in a full length robe, hooded and dark, not unlike the Seruzian cloaks. The brilliant lights on the alien craft made it impossible for him to distinguish any features as it stood with the two smaller beings. Remembering Thallor and the deception, he was repulsed and put his hand to the weapon at his side, ready for the nightmare to begin again.

The hooded form began its approach and moved steadily across the field until the figure stood only few feet away from him. Then came the declaration, when a voice said, "Neil, it's me, Mari!"

She removed the hood and he clearly saw a woman's face, it looked like the woman he knew, but how could this be?

She spoke again softly, saying, "Neil, don't you know me?"

Overwhelmed by her presence, he signed, "I thought you were—"

"Dead?" she answered. "They saved my life. The Ambhuri brought me back to you."

"How?" he questioned, at a complete loss for words.

She reached out and touched his hand and repeated the words he once proclaimed to her, "I am not an alien, Neil, I am human like you. I live in Wyoming just as you do."

The two creatures by the open hatch raised their hands in farewell as they stepped inside the craft. When the hatch closed the alien craft became covered by an amber glow and the Remote at Neil's side sounded a muffled tone. A text read: "Future contact." The craft entered the sky, leaving the man and the woman alone face to face. With only the *Aurora* casting its light on them, Mari reached out to Neil again, this time he responded with an embrace. Her body felt soft and warm and so very much alive.

"I thought I would never ever see you again," confessed Neil. "I was lost without you."

"I could only think of you and of home," replied Mari.

"I longed for you," said Neil.

"I wanted to be with you," replied Mari.

"I was in unquenchable pain," he admitted.

"For a time," she lamented, "I thought everything was lost."

Neil was in a state of apprehension, unbridled excitement, acute curiosity, and profound appreciation. He knew or at least hoped this must in fact be Mari, but could she be the same woman he knew before? But in the soft and lilting voice that was hers alone, she said, "Somehow I felt protected by the One I know, yet I wanted to see you again, more than I can ever say."

"I thought of nothing but you," he replied.

"There is a chill in this night air," said the woman in his arms.

"We must get you on board the ship," returned the man.

For Neil, the questions could not be avoided. He desired to know everything possible about her experience. Such as, how was the miraculous healing process accomplished? He took her to the medical unit where he made various scans, searching for foreign implants, devices, or anything else that might be amiss. He found evidence of scarring at the site of the wound but otherwise she had been completely healed. As far as he could ascertain by the accumulation of information provided by his own technology, this was in fact Mari Abigail Cygnet, not some impostor, nor a clone, and surely not a machine. In every way she seemed to be the same soul he had known before.

"Who are they?" he asked.

"They call themselves Ambhuri," she answered. "They have unusual instruments and strange machines and technology that is different from what we know."

In the process of her physical assessment Neil noted the absence of her earrings, and the fact that she was still deaf, so he removed a silver case from a nearby drawer and handed it to her, saying, "These are for you."

Inside, Mari found an identical set of earrings, and exclaimed, "I believe the others were lost in the fire. Thank you so much!"

"I must ask," said Neil, "did they ever make known their future intentions?"

She answered him, saying, "I remember very little. I didn't see much and they didn't communicate with me very often, yet I felt no harm in their presence, and they were kind and treated me very well."

"Do you know what they want from us?" asked Neil.

"I don't know the answer to that."

"Do they ascribe to a deity of any kind?"

"I don't know that either, I did not put my faith in them. I could only cling to the One I already know."

"How about their alliances with other life forms beyond our own planet?"

"All those things are unknown to me. Yet, all this has not shaken my faith, for I have accepted what has happened to me. All I know at this time, Neil, is that I am here with you."

"And that is all that matters, Mari. I find your vital signs to be within the prescribed range and I proclaim you to be in excellent health. I will say again, I am grateful to have you back...under any circumstance."

"They made it known to me that your technology was responsible for sustaining my body until the time of their intervention, but you were unable to complete the necessary processes to revive me. They said they initiated something they called cellular reconstruction."

"We had entertained such possibilities," said Neil, "but we were unable to pick up the clues for the next step. They may have more knowledge about our technical applications than we do. There is so much I do not know and so much more to discover. We were not finished with our experiments. I only felt that I should somehow return you to your home. I could do no more."

Mari jumped off the examination table and threw herself into his arms, saying, "You did what you could and I'm blessed to have my life back."

"It's wonderful to hold you," replied Neil, with unusual affection welling up within his being. "I cannot entertain the thought of life without you. I don't know what will happen now, I can't predict the direction our lives may take. Still, my hopes and dreams for you have not changed, but Mari, you must know I will not hold you captive."

"I respect that," she replied.

"Always remember," said Neil, "you are no one's captive."

Then she said something he knew she must say, "Neil, take me home."

He was certain Mari was strong, and each time he looked into her eyes he tried to understand who she was. He could see that she was the same woman he had come to know before she was so violently taken away. Only now the enigma of her being was even greater. Their lives had been transformed into a fragmented puzzle of multiple dimensions.

It was the first light of morning on the Cygnet ranch. William and Jennifer had returned to the property to tend the animals and pick through the rubble hoping to salvage what they could. The questioning and cross examinations had ceased and Jennifer was still in a state of shock. It was with a deep feeling of resignation that William put the single suitcase in the truck bed, then taking one last look around he climbed into the drivers seat next to his wife. Suddenly a blue light caught his eye. William and Jennifer were weary and wanted no part of the invasion that had torn their world in two, but there was no choice, the thing was returning just as it did on that dreadful night.

Mari was feeling unusually anxious, more than in all of her experience thus far, and she expressed it to Neil, saying, "I want to go to home so badly but I'm afraid."

"Go to them, Mari," affirmed Neil. "Everything will be okay, I'm sure. I will depart and return again only if you so desire."

"Please, don't leave right away," replied Mari, "not just yet, I want to see you after I have returned to them."

The companion-module opened, and before William and Jennifer could even grasp what was happening, their daughter came running to them and fell into their arms. Any fear between parent and child had melted away. They would talk at length about the intervening dark hours after she had been taken away. At last, they gathered in the gazebo to discuss the impending future. It felt good to be home, such as it was, yet there was still one other thing on Mari's mind, so she got up from the bench and went to the mailbox by the steps to bravely look inside. "It's not here," she moaned, with obvious disappointment.

"Allow me," said her father, then he led her back to the truck, where he retrieved the scorched suitcase, and from it he took a brown leather book and placed it in her hands.

"My journal!" cried Mari. "You saved it!"

She put her arms around her father, as he said to her, "It was in your special place. I never once opened it. I just thought it was all I would ever have of you."

"This means so much," declared Mari. "Thank you, Dad!"

"You are everything to us," added her mother.

"And both of you are everything to me," confided their daughter.

Neil remained on the bridge examining his own future, but he knew that whatever happened from this point forward, Mari would somehow work it out. He was well aware of the new road that stretched before both of them. He knew she would survive no matter what, with or without him. Yet, that was why he loved her. Now he was accepting his lot, though a lonely road seemed to stretch out into darkness. A soft beeping signal caught his attention, so he left the bridge. Mari was there to greet him with her journal clutched to her bosom as he stepped out of the companion-module.

"Neil," she said, with an air of confidence and resolve in her voice, "I have sorted it out. My eyes have seen many new things and I have come to understand things a little more. I believe I know what it is that I desire most. I love my family and I know they care about what happens to me. This ranch has been and always will be home, it is a part of them and a part of who I am. So, now I have come to see the thing I must do. Only time will tell what the future will be. Some things change but other things do not. We must learn to accept—"

"I just want you to be happy—" returned Neil.

"Please," she said, "I have more to say. It was here in this place where I experienced the freedom of the open land. It was here in this place where I once had a life that was most precious. Now I know the direction I must choose, Neil...I will go wherever you go, I want to come with you."

Neil, certainly had not expected this. Looking earnestly into her eyes, he said, "I love you, Mari, with all of my heart. And I want you more than anything else, but are you sure about this? You have lost so much."

"I can't love you from afar," said Mari. "You know my values, you know my faith and my wishes, and you are aware of the demands of the One I follow. That has not changed. You once asked me to be a part of something. If you will respect me and what I believe, then I want to be a part of what you have started. This is my decision, but I have told the ones I love I will return to them again. Someday they may understand why I must take this step. This something I want to do."

"I will abide by your wishes, but you must know I have created an odd life," replied Neil. "We will live as fugitives, unearthly things and unscrupulous people have tried to seek our demise. Our world has changed."

"Yes," she replied, "let it be so."

"This may be a long journey," he cautioned.

"Perhaps, but a necessary one," she replied, "only God knows what the future holds."

"I would be honored to have you," he replied. "We will make this journey together."

Both of them returned to William and Jennifer, and Mari reassured her parents by saying, "My love is with you. That will never part. Now I must go, but I will return."

"We will always look for you," replied her mother, with emotion filled eyes.

"Are you okay with this, Mr. Cygnet?" asked Neil.

"This is what she says she wants," replied William, "so we will let it be as she says."

"What will you do now?" asked Neil.

"I don't know," said William. "It might be time to move on."

"What would it take for you to stay?" asked Neil.

"I don't know," William replied, "we've lost a lot of personal things. I believe it will take some time."

"Things can be replaced," added Jennifer.

"I would like to help if I may," added Neil.

"That would be very nice but you don't have to," replied Jennifer.

"I feel there is so much I owe both of you," said Neil.

"We have Mari," replied Jennifer, "that is the most important thing. You must take care of her."

"Indeed," replied Neil, "I will."

"Make sure you do," added William, sternly.

"With all that is in my power," restated Neil.

There was an awkward silence, then William said, "We'll find another place to stay for a while."

"We shall return, you have my word," said Neil.

"I will look forward to it," replied William.

"It is done then," said Jennifer, giving her final approval.

"Not quite," said Mari, bending down to pick up Meadow. The cat had been wandering aimlessly around the yard and occasionally rubbing against her ankles. "She must come along too."

William and Jennifer were invited aboard the ship, where they were able to see for themselves part of the new world their daughter would inhabit.

Before they parted company, Neil said to them, "I have something I must give to you Mr. Cygnet."

William's face revealed his surprise, even Mari didn't know what Neil was up to when he put a sturdy envelope into his hands.

"What is this?" said William, mystified.

"Open it later," replied Neil.

When the time was right the vessel departed the ranch. Very shortly thereafter a police cruiser arrived, for something unusual had been seen in the sky near the Cygnet ranch. William and Jennifer would speak with the authorities yet again. This time they were not afraid. The rains had come, the heat had abated, and the land was satisfied. The natural beauty of the land was as glorious as ever, remaining the one constant in the ever changing lives of its inhabitants. The earth felt firm beneath their feet and they felt more rooted than ever.

Chapter Thirteen: Connection

Somehow we all are connected,
No matter where we are or what we do,
As are faith, hope, and love.
Mari

Nothing could be trusted. Although space was as seductive as ever, it could be said that such a domain was the last place two wounded people wanted to seek shelter. The home planet beckoned, and so did a patch of land in the Phoenix Island group located in the Pacific called Nikumaroro. This was Tuesday, September 1, and the ship had come to rest on a part of the uninhabited island that supported a dense grove of coconut palms, a place where narrow stretches of beach were covered with pieces of razor sharp coral.

When the companion-module doors opened, Neil and Mari stood at the very top of the ship. The immediate view down and over the sloping hull revealed a small lagoon with blue water and a lonely stretch of beach. As the module made a full clockwise rotation they could see more trees and sandy soil on which stood the ruins of a long abandon settlement. But the most inspiring view was the one they first saw, although it was extremely bright and oppressively hot, nullifying any memories of the drought in Wyoming.

Mari's physical strength had returned but she discovered a new sensitivity to brilliant sunlight. Neil, being aware of her need brought her down to D Deck. From the various compartments and storage units he was able to produce a white wind breaker with a hood and even a pair of sunglasses. The wind breaker would prove to be too hot on such a day as this so Mari wondered what else she could use for shade. There seemed to be almost anything one might need stowed away in the compact storage area and she delighted in the odd assortment. Neil informed his inquisitive companion that he needed to return to the bridge to check on the ship's status before the outing could take place so he let her rummage through the compartments on her own. Everything was neatly stowed away, retained by clips, stashed in pockets, or secured in slots. In her search she came across something of special interest and she removed it from its clip. It was creamy white in color, of very little weight, and visually enhanced by an attractive lace pattern along its folded outer edge. It even opened up like an umbrella, more like a parasol, and it was precisely the right size to shield her from the penetrating solar rays. She put it over her shoulder and twirled it around playfully.

When Neil retuned to the deck, she proudly exclaimed, "Look what I found, this would be perfect for shade!"

Neil had a curious look on his face, then smiled as he replied, "Mari, that is an antenna."

"Another antenna?" she complained with disappointment. "But, it looks so much like my old parasol!"

"I am sorry you lost so many things in the fire," he said, regretfully. "I can only imagine what you must feel."

"I know, but don't worry," she assured him. "Anyhow, this is pretty!"

"I never thought of it from that perspective," replied Neil, amused by her observation. "It was developed as part of an on location emergency signaling device. In the end we came up with a different option. See the mesh on the top and the finely printed wires underneath?"

"Oh," she replied, "but it looks so much like a parasol!"

"I suppose you could use it," said Neil, "we do not have need of it anymore. Anyhow, there is one more thing before we go. I need to check on the calibration of the field modifiers in the interlock system."

Mari continued to muse about the parasol but soon she noticed something wasn't quite right, it didn't have an appropriate handle, only a long slender rod that connected to its folding array. By now Neil had unlocked and opened up a rather plain looking panel, but inside was a maze of neatly routed wires and tubes. Mari was attracted to a colorful set of blinking lights and came over to watch as he went about his work. In the process she noticed four small crystalline cylinders with a threaded hole in the end. These were set into four separate slots on one side of the compartment. Each cylinder was of a different shade of blue and numerically labeled, so she asked, "What are those?"

"What are what?" he asked, still busy observing numbers on a small screen.

"Those blue things," she replied.

"Those?" he asked, as he casually pointed to the attractive blue objects.

"What are they for?" she asked again.

"They are high energy discharge devices. We use them to energize the interlock couplers after repair procedures."

"They look like they could be handles for something," asked Mari.

"No, they are not," replied Neil. "An inappropriate use of them would be unpleasant."

"I guess there are some things that are better left alone," admitted Mari, wincing at the thought.

"Especially in the locked compartments," added Neil.

"I'll be sure to ask before I get into any more of your closets," acknowledged Mari.

"That would be wise," remarked Neil, as he closed the panel. "Now let me see that antenna." She handed it to him and he closed it, opened it up again, then closed it. After giving it an overall glance of approval, he handed it back to her. "You can use this if you like, it's harmless enough and it does kind of suits you."

"Are we going for that walk now?" she asked.

"Shortly," he replied. "I have something else for you, which might also be of some help."

They paid a visit to the medical unit, where he retrieved an unusual looking item from one of the compartments, saying, "This is a Quantum Medical device or Q-Med, it was developed to harness the ship's energy for field use in an effort to provide relief from fatigue. Our experiments indicated that it was of limited use. It also has a rather short range and its effectiveness became diminished when used any distance from the ship. But I suggest we try it out, it might be of some help in this situation because we won't be going very far."

The Q-Med looked like a bracelet and was composed of three parts resembling two hinged rings with a spiral on one end. Neil gently slid it onto her arm then fastened the open rings together.

"It even has a pretty design on it!" declared Mari, rather admiring its features.

"Hmm, yes," agreed Neil, wanting to move on. "We can now take our walk."

Meadow was at their feet and meowed as if asking to go out with them, but Mari felt it might be better for her to remain inside, so she gave the cat a stroke down her sleek body and said she would be back soon. As they walked towards the lagoon Mari began to talk about her experience with the Ambhuri but she still had difficulty recalling all of her experience. There were certain gaps in her memory, but somehow she seemed comfortable with not being able to recall all of the missing pieces. Neil thought she might be a little too at ease about the whole thing.

The leisurely journey on foot eventually took them through the remains of several abandon buildings. They stopped to examine the languishing structures, where long ago this lonely spot in the ocean was called Gardner Island. Things had changed and at present there was not much left to see. From there they pressed on toward the small lagoon. Mari now seemed refreshed and energized, expressing she was as hopeful as ever about the future. Neil, though, had become dispirited. Mari could tell something was on his mind so she asked him about it.

"I must confess," he said, "that I have failed."

"Failed?" she asked. "How?"

"I was not able to save my sister," he replied. "I was not available for my colleagues when they needed me the most, and I was not there for you. All I ever wanted, all any of us ever wanted was to embark on a quest of discovery, free of petty entanglements, political, and otherwise. To be free of the heavy baggage of what humanity has come to call civilization."

"Things happen over which we have no control," informed Mari. "Some things are better left to Sovereign hands."

"Maybe for you," he replied, "but I don't see the hands of which you speak."

"Even so," she assured, "they are there."

"We were the perfect team," said Neil, speaking of his colleagues. "Marcus had a way of keeping us unified. We shared the same vision and saw the promise of a new technology. We understood the risks, but I never imagined this. They trusted me—you trusted me—then in an instant my friends were taken away and my hope for any kind of future dropped out of sight."

"There are many things we can't know," she reminded him, "but the future is still before us. We must go on."

"The Seruzians are out there somewhere," Neil replied, "I barely escaped, now they are most likely plotting our demise. Mere hours ago I embraced the future—"

"Neil," countered Mari, "you couldn't have known about the snare set for you within the alien ship and you couldn't have predicted the actions taken by our own world."

"I regret ever starting this project," said Neil, rethinking all that had happened. "I have been such a fool. Things can be replaced, but people, the people who trusted me cannot. Now my life is like these ruins, ruins which echo the failed human endeavors of the past."

Mari replied, "Even if your friends had known the outcome, I think they would have wanted you to continue with what they helped create. You saw a brighter day for our world. They knew the risks, just as you did, now you are the only one who can turn their vision into a reality."

"At one time I was sure of things," said Neil. "I thought we could save the world. In the end, I couldn't even save you. But here you are, and now we are on the run. And in this race I can no longer fathom the turns."

"But, Neil," cried Mari, "you did save me! If you had not arrived when you did I might have died when I fell from my horse, or I might have been swept away without a trace in the wilderness by the Seruzians. Without your intervention at the lake my life might have ended there. If you had not returned me to my home the Ambhuri might not have been able to reach me. If you had not met with the Ambhuri on Cloud Peak I might not have been returned to you. You accepted me and you have shown me love. I see life with different eyes now. I am the same person but I see so much more. I am still discovering new things, so are you, and somehow I believe all these things will work out in some positive way. The truth will be discovered."

"How can you know that, Mari?" questioned Neil, still cynical. "People have died because of me."

"We will find our place," she said. "We can find it together. It will not always be so dark. A person must walk in the light he has at the time."

Neil gazed off into nowhere in particular, and said, "I am still searching, Mari, the answers do not come so easily anymore."

"No," she agreed, "they don't."

"You, Mari, at least you have your cat," replied Neil, a bit jealous.

"Neil?" she replied.

The jungle path opened up to a sizable lagoon of fairly shallow water. Soon they began to find small pieces of metal scattered on the beach, and out in the water was a broken skeleton of twisted parts. Pieces of rusted metal protruded sharply out of the water and Neil insisted on taking a closer look. As always, he was drawn out of intense curiosity and she was moved by her desire to help.

"Do you see that reflection out there in the water?" said Neil, intrigued.

"Yes," returned Mari, "what could it be?"

"I need to have a look," he returned.

Mari was determined to remain on the beach, but cautioned, "Be careful, it might be deep in some places."

He waded out into the water until he was about fifty feet from the shore. Mari sat patiently on a large rock while looking at some interesting shells she had collected during their stroll. Neil discovered a lot of debris under the water and now his hand was reaching for a reflective object protruding from the surface. A portion of the bright metal stuck above the surface with most of it submerged on a jagged piece of iron further concealed by the water. He picked up the piece to scrutinized the details of what resembled two pieces of aluminum fastened together by an industry long ago. Farther away he noticed three larger pieces that might be of the same composition and called out to Mari from across the water, saying, "I want to bring this back to the ship for analysis."

"Do you need any help?" she shouted.

"No," he shouted back. He wandered around in the water a bit before deciding to find his way toward the shore. He had only taken a few more steps when his right foot became snagged on something under the water. Instantly, a crushing weight came down on his boot to capture it like a bear trap.

Mari looked up from what she was doing and saw Neil struggling with something in the water, and shouted, "What's wrong?"

"My foot is caught," he replied.

"Hold on, I'm coming out there!" cried Mari, as she entered the water.

"Be careful," cautioned Neil, "we don't need to have you stuck out here as well."

Mari had to take careful strides over some rather large metal parts in the nearly invisible field debris under the water. After only twenty feet or so, she remarked, "There's an awful lot of junk out here."

Neil called out, saying, "I was trying to avoid a big metal plate down there and something must have shifted. Be careful!"

"I will," she called in return. "How ever did you get out that far?"

"One step at a time," said Neil.

"Will the water short out this thing on my arm?" remarked Mari, finally reaching the spot where Neil was caught.

"No," said Neil, "the water will not affect it."

Mari immediately reached down into the water and tried to wrestle his boot free, but in doing so she discovered how tightly it was secured under the beam. "Maybe we can get you out of the boot."

"It's sufficiently wedged," he replied, with a groan.

Mari felt around in the water again, and said, "I'll try to lift that thing up." So she pulled repeatedly on the beam but it resisted her efforts.

"Stop, stop," cried Neil, wincing with pain. "Somehow it's clamping down even harder each time we try to move it. I don't even think the two of us together will be able to make much progress. It might be better for you to go back to the ship, there is an automatic prying device in storage compartment number 5 on D Deck."

The lengthy steel beam was rusted from years under the water, yet enough remained to give it substantial weight. Pressure from all the other parts of the derelict structure resting on it only contributed to the difficulty of moving it.

"It's no use," cried Neil. "Go back to the ship—"

"No," cried Mari, refusing to give up. "Let me try one more time."

"If you say so," he replied, caving in to her persistence, "but I have my doubts."

Neil reached down into the water and grabbed the beam to assist as Mari positioned her hands under it to get a firm grasp. Neil used all of his available strength as both of them tried to lift the beam. Together, they were valiant, but the metal would not yield to their efforts.

"I think we need the prying device," advised Neil. "I'll be okay until you return."

Mari would not be deterred. Taking a moment to think things through, she maneuvered herself around to get a better hold on the beam. A new sense of determination took hold of her, and before he had a chance to speak another word or even reach down into the water to help, she expertly and, with what appeared to be relative ease, simply lifted the heavy beam off of his boot. Neil stepped backward with a sigh of relief as she let the beam fall back under its own weight with a potent splash.

"Mari!" cried Neil, with considerable surprise and no small appreciation. "How ever did you do that?"

"I don't know," she replied, "I just got a good hold on it."

He reached down into the water and tried to lift the beam again using what strength he had just to see if he could move it, then admitted, "I can't even budge it."

"It was heavy," she admitted.

"Extremely heavy," said Neil, mystified. "How—?"

"I don't know," she said. "I just did."

He reached back into the water to pick up the gleaming object of his fancy, then grunted, "All because of this."

"We've got to get you back to shore," advised Mari. "I've got to have a look at your foot."

"There is more of this stuff out here," said Neil. "Something does not make sense. These pieces can't be part of a shipwreck."

"Come on," advised Mari, "forget about that, we need to get you out of this water,"

"Ho!" he exclaimed, recoiling from the pain resulting from the attempt to walk on the foot. "Yes, you are quite right."

"Come on," said Mari, "I'll help you."

"Long ago some people believed," remarked Neil, as he threw the part back into the water, "a certain renowned flyer might have crashed her plane here, but I guess we'll look into it another time."

Mari glanced at him with a puzzled look, but her immediate concern was to get Neil back to shore. She helped him through the water, carefully dodging the scattered metal parts, but by the time they reached the rock on the beach that she had been using as a bench Neil was in considerable pain.

Still mystified, Neil had to ask again, "How did you move that thing?"

"It kind of surprised me too," replied Mari. "It must have been lighter than we thought."

Neil wasn't convinced, saying, "No, the beam was of great length."

"It was heavy," she admitted, "but for a moment it didn't even feel that way."

"Are you sure?" he quizzed, although the pain was evident on his face.

"Are you okay?" she asked.

"I think I can make it," he said, determined to get back to the ship. "We have the

144

means to deal with this in the medical unit."

He walked a short distance but suddenly lost his balance and Mari caught him. Then she urged, "I don't think you can walk by yourself, why don't you let me help." Neil picked up the parasol and held it over her as she supported some of his weight, but the more he walked the more intense the pain became so they stopped again. This time Mari said in earnest, "Let me see your foot."

He sat down on a log and she removed his boot and sock. There were abrasions on the skin accompanied by an ample amount of swelling. After closer examination, she said, "I think it's broken."

"It feels like it," said Neil. "We need to get back."

"I've only had a few first aid classes," she said. "At one time I thought about nursing, then I changed my mind. But, I did some reading."

"You would have been good at it," replied Neil, observing her careful manner.

"Do you think the Q-Med could help?" asked Mari. "Maybe we could use it on your foot. I could hold your foot or something if we aren't too far away."

"Possibly," he admitted, "I don't know, it wasn't designed for this type of thing."

"Maybe you could crank up the energy on the ship somehow with the Remote," said Mari, putting her hands firmly around his ankle to demonstrate. "It might help. We could give it a try."

"Ah, ha," he cried. "you have a substantial grip."

"Let's try," she said, insisting.

Giving in to her suggestion Neil used the Remote to wake up the ship. After initiating several commands the Q-Med received a substantial energy boost. Immediately he felt an internal heat that went through Mari's hands into his foot. She felt the warmth as well and asked him how he was doing.

"There appears to be an inner energy transfer," he replied. "I find it is actually beginning to feel much better." He made another adjustment to the ship. "This is intriguing. We must have underestimated the effectiveness in this kind of situation."

Intuitively concluding the time was right, Mari let go of his ankle, then asked, "How is it now?"

"I don't feel any adverse effects," replied Neil. "It may be that you have only eliminated the pain, or perhaps you may have actually healed the break, I cannot tell which." The swelling had diminished substantially so Neil stood up and put his full weight to bear on it. He walked around and to his great surprise it felt much better.

Mari picked up the parasol, and asked, "Do you think you can walk back to the ship?"

"Yes, I believe I can. What made you think of doing this?"

"I don't know, I just wanted to help."

"Mari, I believe you may be the other part of the equation. There is something else at work here."

"How could that be?" replied Mari, hoping he might see the larger picture.

"During our initial research Gordon was working with certain biological systems, which he found to be influenced by the primary field generator. He was trying to determine how such devices could facilitate healing but proximity was a problem." He then observed that Mari looked extremely tired, and asked, "How about you, how are you doing?"

"I want to get out of this sun," she said. "I believe I will feel much better when I'm back on the ship."

"It appears you are able to channel the field energy with considerable efficiency," said Neil. "Something I had not anticipated."

"It just felt right," she replied, "but you know more about those things than I do."

As they reached the companion-module, he said, "To the good, or otherwise, our lives have become increasingly dependent upon this vessel, but there is more work I must do."

"You mean, work 'we' must do," reminded Mari. "I'm in this thing too you know."

"And," said Neil, "I am delighted."

Chapter Fourteen: Meeting

As we enter ever deeper into the unknown a certain beauty can be found there;
Discovered in each new sun rise,
In the distant heavens,
And where the Earth is found meeting the sky.
Mari

At the request of various local authorities the people of Stone River agreed to have a meeting to assess past events in an effort to discover what was taking place around them. Governmental agencies were seeking answers and the local population wanted to know what was going on. They wanted to know about the curious and unusual sightings, the prolific military presence, the cause of distress to animals, and especially the events involving Mari. This created a high degree of suspicion and rumors were abundant.

The town council had decided to host the meeting at 6 p.m. on the evening of Saturday, September 5, and it was to be held in the cafeteria of the Stone River High School. The mayor was away on business, but City Council President David Blair would conduct the meeting. Gen. David Staffer also inserted himself into the mix to help guide the question and answer session. A local newspaper journalist was on hand as well as a television crew. The military had the last word regarding the media and the reporters had been asked to remain outside the school building. Although an initial protest was filed on the part of the press they finally agreed to the conditions. The television crew set up for a live broadcast hoping to be the first to break the story if there was one. The print journalist milled around interviewing the small contingent of military personnel stationed on the school grounds and anyone else he could catch before they entered the school. The TV cameraman set up his equipment and took a wide shot, then panned to the young reporter on site in front of the school, after which, he zoomed in for a tight shot and focused on her photogenic face.

Right on cue the station's most attractive agent of information, Lauren Wilson, began her segment of the broadcast by answering the news anchor's question, saying, "Yes, I'm standing outside the Stone River High School and we have been in contact with Gen. Staffer. We tried to get direct access to the proceedings inside but we were denied so we'll bring the information to you as they feed it to us. We know a local woman by the name of Mari Cygnet is at the center of some of the controversy. She is not here but her father William Cygnet is attending the meeting this evening. Also, the people here want to know why there is so much secrecy on the part of governmental sources. They want to know if the Cygnet family has any knowledge of what's going on here and if their daughter is involved with the strange activity concerning the Thunder Peak. Some people believe her family knows much more than what they are actually saying. We'll keep you updated as things progress."

The meeting was the only activity planned at the school for the evening and the only member of school personnel in the building when everyone started to arrive was Del Toller. He was usually scheduled on weekends to do cleaning and minor repair. Occasionally he would be asked to set up for special events and on this particular evening he had the added responsibility of opening up then locking building after the meeting was over. At one point Del had been invited to attend but he refused, however, he did keep track of the latest gossip concerning Mari. After all, he claimed to have seen her waiting for aliens in the woods.

A handful of business people from town, a few ranchers, as well as local residents arrived promptly. All were now waiting for things to get under way. William knew full well he would be the center of interest, and his presence was brought about by an earnest request from the police chief. He had complained to his wife about it but gave in to the increasing pressure. He arrived quietly, while managing to avoid the reporters, and took a seat in the back of the room at the end of a short row of folding chairs, hoping to keep his talk short then sneak out early.

Business got underway a few minutes past the hour as city council President, David Blair, called the meeting to order. The busy community leader had volunteered for the task of conducting the hastily arranged meeting, and because only 23 people showed up he decided to keep the gathering informal. Blair began the session by asking some of those present to voice their opinion or speak out regarding what they had personally observed. His original intention was to let Gen. Staffer do most of the talking, but it soon became evident that everyone was primarily interested in hearing what William had to say about what happened to his 'adopted' daughter. Gen. Staffer was in favor of having William confronted by his friends from the community rather than to have him questioned directly by officials. Staffer thought this kind of peer pressure would be the most effective means to get the man to talk. He could speak from personal experience but felt he was on the outside of pertinent information. There also was the undeniable fact that two other military personnel and three locals witnessed the 'thing' take Mari from White Lake. Another aspect was revealed when Jennifer confided in her friend Clara about Mari. Then Clara, when cornered unexpectedly by investigators, related some details that seemed unbelievable.

Staffer decided to get right to the point by speaking to the group about the importance of community cooperation. He looked directly at William, when he said, "Tonight we have with us Mr. William Cygnet. Your neighbor here was kind enough to join us tonight. I'm hoping he might say a few words, so please Mr. Cygnet, will you tell us about your recent experiences? I'm sure everyone would like to know how certain recent events have affected you. We know you must have first hand knowledge, particularly relating to the disappearance of your daughter. We would like to know what you saw on your property on the nights in question. Please, come forward." There was dead silence in the room and William just sat in his seat looking rather stunned. Staffer urged him again. "Come up to the front William, please tell us what you know."

William stammered, "Well, I...I don't know what to say—"

"You of all people have a story worth telling," replied Staffer, "we would like to hear it."

William sat glued to his chair, then Blair entered the conversation, sounding a little cross as he said, "Now, William, we are waiting. I've known you for years, we all respect you and we all need to hear your side of things."

"Mr. Cygnet," urged Staffer, in a tone that reflected his own impatience, "would you enlighten us?"

William stood up as Staffer cut in with his most important sounding voice, saying, "Just step forward now, step right up here and address these fine people."

Reluctantly, William made his way to the front of the room. He looked around at all the faces staring back at him, and said, "I really don't know what to say. I'm as mystified as all of you. I want answers too." He thought for a minute and turned to Staffer. "Yes, General, I do want answers! Starting with, where were the authorities when that mob arrived at our place and beat me up? Why did they burned my house down? Why did the fire department arrive so late? Why was Mari treated like a criminal and shot by your soldiers? We've been in this community a long time and we deserve better than that. "

Staffer found a shred of contrition, but pressed on, saying, "William, I know you must be under severe mental strain at this time. We can't begin to know what you have been through, but we wonder if you are telling us everything. You have seen some of these things first hand and I'm sure you can at least give us an account of what you witnessed. We are only trying to help. Of course, as you may be aware, I also have some first hand knowledge under my belt so I'm in a position to verify certain aspects of what's happening here. But we are still piecing things together. The fact is, we want you to tell us what you know."

William, still feeling apprehensive, replied, "All of this has been hard, and you don't know what my wife has gone through, that's why she's not here tonight."

Staffer pressed yet again, saying, "We have two soldiers who witnessed what took place at the White Lake. They reported the fact your daughter was seriously wounded. We learned later she may have died and that she was taken by the same object we dealt with on Thunder peak. Yet, if she was dead, how can she be alive? There is also word of her being taken from your home in some mysterious fashion. Further more, what about the fact that Mr. Toller saw her being ushered aboard an alien craft. He said she was waiting for them to arrive on your property. Given this information, would you tell us why they were meeting with your daughter? And just what is your relationship to this alien force? What is really going on, Mr. Cygnet? I hope you are not withholding important information!"

William was so distracted and nervous he hadn't noticed that Del had opened the door on the left side of the room and was now casually leaning against it and listening to the proceedings.

"I...I'm not hiding anything," sputtered William, "and I don't know about Toller, but I will say Mari was gone for a while but then she returned. She's okay now and she's free to do what she wants. I just want things to return to normal again like everybody else. All I can say is, Mari is my daughter and she's okay."

All the eyes in the room were still on William when Chief Harwood broke in to say, "William, it would be to your advantage if you would cooperate. People around these parts don't like secrets. Certainly you must know where your daughter is. Certainly she—"

"Yeah, Cygnet," interrupted Del, briskly shutting the door and stepping into the room, "You need to tell us where Mari is!"

There was a collective murmur from the room as William glared at Del. He was surprise to see him, and said, "You! What right do you have to say—"

"No, Cygnet," cried Del, with evident hostility erupting in his tone of voice, "she was out there on purpose, I saw it. She went with 'em! You ain't telling the truth!"

William was almost shouting when he said, "Truth? What would you know about truth?"

Del spat back, "No, you got it wrong, you ain't sayin' it like it is!"

"I want both of you to calm down," said Staffer, stepping in, and directing his attention to Del. "William was speaking, we need to hear him out."

"All right then," grumbled Del. "Have it your way. We'll talk later." Miffed, he promptly left the room and the door slammed shut.

Staffer went over to the door but found it to be locked, then he confronted William, saying, "See what you are causing? Its time to come clean."

William looked around at all the faces, and said, "Mr. Toller and I don't exactly see eye to eye, but I really don't have anything to do with him anymore. I just want to say one more time, our Mari is okay. She told us that when the time is right she'll be back. Then she'll tell everyone what they need to know."

"When will that be, Mr. Cygnet?" questioned Staffer.

There was a long silence, William finally replied, "I don't know, but it will be when she's ready."

Suddenly the door at the front of the room behind where William was speaking opened up. It was Del again, and he had a folding chair in his hand, which he promptly set up by the doorway. Then he closed the door, sat down, and casually crossed his legs with a decidedly defiant look.

"Well, I'm so glad you decided to join us again, Mr. Toller," said the general, a bit surprised, but trying to be polite.

Del didn't say anything in return, but remained sitting in the chair with a trace of his familiar unnerving grin peeking out from behind his black mustache and beard.

"We're going to let William finish speaking," continued, the general. "You will get your turn, Del, then maybe you can say what's on your mind."

"Yeah, you bet I will," replied Del, no longer grinning.

"Now Mr. Cygnet," said Staffer, extending his hand in a gesture indicating it was William's turn to speak.

"What else is there to say?" said William. "Maybe you ought to have Del take the floor now, he should have—"

"All right, I will take the floor!" cried Del, standing up, simultaneously brandishing the pistol he had hidden under his belt.

"What the—" cried Staffer.

"I'm in control of this meeting now!" demanded Del, with a steely look.

"What is this?" demanded Staffer. "Put down that gun! You can't get away with this, there are troops right outside this building!"

Del pulled a phone out of his pocket, then with his eyes riveted on General Staffer he casually replied, "That may be so but I don't care about them."

"You better care!" informed Staffer. "Our forces can take you out in the blink of an eye and if had a gun I'd do the same."

"I don't think so," answered Del in defiance.

All those present were unarmed for it was thought a show of weapons would only inflame already damaged community trust. So now Del freely paced the floor. At times he would stop to aim the gun at various people in the room, all the while his occasional grin seemed to reveal more and more teeth.

"It doesn't matter what you think," replied the general.

"Oh, it does," said Del, now holding up a phone. "All I have to do is press a little button on this here phone and boom!"

"What do you mean?" demanded Staffer.

"Look above you, Mr. General," said Del. "What do you see?"

"What should I see?" countered Staffer.

"It's what you don't see," scoffed Del.

"Riddles?" offered Staffer.

"Up there above them tiles is some explosives," informed Del, "and I can talk to it with this here little phone. All them doors, they're all locked and I got the only key. If anyone tries for it, well, they won't get too far. Any funny business from them troops out there and guess what?"

Fear crept through the room and Staffer was now cursing himself over the fact he was unarmed, but he stood keenly watching Del pace the floor with the gun.

"What do you think you are doing?" countered Staffer.

"Shut up!" shouted Del. "You, General, and you Cygnet, you put your phones on this here table. Now everybody else, you bring them phones up here. I mean everybody bring 'em up. Remember what's up in that ceiling."

Del waved his gun as his eyes darted around the room, selectively sighting and pointing the weapon at his captive audience, driven by the bidding of his own twisted vision. A few people managed to conceal their actions and sent messages before giving up their phone, including Staffer, who told the troops outside to be ready for an eventual conflict but to hold their fire. Each captive came up and reluctantly dropped their phone on the table then quietly shuffled back to their seat.

"This is insane!" cried William, tossing his phone onto the pile.

"What do you think you're going to get out of this?" questioned Staffer. "What do you want?"

"What do I want?" answered Del, in what had become a consistently defiant tone.

"Yes," quizzed Staffer, "what?"

Del looked directly at William, and said, "I'll tell you what I want. I want Mari! I want her here right now. You, Cygnet, you and the general here are going to make it happen, you are going to get her here. Otherwise, you know what can happen!"

Not backing down, Staffer said, "We don't even know where she is, that's why we're here this evening. I don't know any more than you do."

"I think you can get her here," insisted Del, "or else."

"If you set off those charges," informed Staffer, "you'll be killed right along with the rest of us."

"Maybe, maybe not," countered Del, "remember, I'm the one giving the orders. Now sit."

Staffer sat back down, saying, "You think you're so lucky?"

"I don't got to have luck," replied Del flatly. "So now, Cygnet. Yeah, you, I want you to call Mari. You're going to get her here."

"She won't come here for the likes of you!" scowled William, squarely confronting the armed man.

Del's arm straightened out as he pointed his gun directly at William, and said, "You're going to call her, and Mr. General here will make sure she gets here."

William frothed back, "You have been harassing us long enough. Someday you'll—"

"Someday what?" prodded Del, reminding everyone about the phone in his hand by putting a finger near the screen.

Staffer faced Del, saying, "Mister, you better think about what you're doing. Think about the lives in this room."

"Someday Del—" barked William, becoming more agitated.

"No, Cygnet, this is the day," shouted Del. "You're gonna make a little call."

"I don't know where she is!" cried William, standing up from his chair. "You're not going to touch my daughter. I just knew you were the type."

"Yeah," goaded Del, "what type is that?"

"You think you got smarts?" cracked William. "You're a sniveling no good—"

"Now, Cygnet!" spat Del.

"Even if I knew where she was," resolved William, "I wouldn't tell you!"

"You're gonna do it!" shouted Del, with new fury.

"If you know what's good for you—" cautioned Staffer, rising to his feet.

"He'll never know what's good," cried William.

"Shut up old man," cried Del.

"Put down the gun," demanded Staffer once more, trying to get through to the agitated man.

"Now Cygnet," growled Del, "the call!"

William pointed an accusing finger at Del, saying, "No, you stop this nonsense. You're not touching my daughter!" But Del's itchy finger got the better of him and a loud report pierced the air. William fell to the floor as cries of horror filled the room.

"Quiet," shouted Del, "or you'll get the same or worse! Remember what's up there in that ceiling!"

William lay on his back clutching his chest near the left shoulder as a man sitting on the end of the second row of chairs from the front appeared eerily unruffled, yet keenly aware of the moment as he gazed at William. Then, almost casually, he said, "This man needs a doctor."

"Are you a doctor?" growled Del.

"No," said the man in the chair.

Del snapped back, "Then you keep quiet!"

There was silence in the room for several minutes as everyone anticipated Del's next move. A groan from William caught the attention of every ear. Then a woman in the midst of the group sitting in the chairs found the courage to raise her hand. Del saw the hand go up and suspiciously pointed the gun at her, saying, "Put down your hand."

"Please," said woman, "I'm a nurse, let me see him."

"No!" countered Del, with defiance.

Then the woman bravely stood up to plead again, saying, "I'm a nurse, I work in the ER, please let me help, he could die!"

"Look," cried Staffer. "Do you really want murder on your hands?"

"My name is Deb," pleaded the nurse, "please, let me help."

"Let her see him," advised Staffer, "she knows what to do."

Del's eyes nervously shot around the room, then he motioned for the woman to assist William, saying, "No funny business, just that nurse. The rest of you, you stay in them chairs."

The woman cautiously worked her way through the group to where William lay and knelt down by his side. After a brief inspection of the wound it appeared that the bullet had traveled completely through his body, possibly missing vital organs, but it left a double wound. Deb spoke up again, saying, "He's seriously injured and loosing a lot of blood. He needs a doctor right away."

"No doctor!" cried Del. "You get that daughter of his. General, you take your phone. You call your people. You get Mari here."

"What makes you think you can get away with this?" exclaimed Staffer. "Eventually those troops out there will storm this building!"

"If I hear one little noise anywhere outside this room or if someone jumps," cried Del, "I got this phone! So quit stalling, you make it happen, you use your phone or I will use mine and it ain't going to be pretty."

Staffer carefully removed his phone from the pile on the table and made a call, relaying Del's request concerning Mari.

The task of locating Mari began. Her location was unknown even to the well outfitted armed forces, but they would put to use all the connections available. The local media sources were also given information about the emergency and instructed to get the word out. The reporters were only too willing to accommodate the request. Now they had their story, so it suddenly became the hottest news of the day.

The television camera was advantageously pointed at the school, when Miss Wilson walked into the frame again, and said, "We have just received word from our military sources that there's a hostage crisis here at Stone River High School. We have been told to make it known that the immediate presence of Mari Cygnet is requested at the Stone River High School. She must arrive as soon as possible. I repeat, the immediate presence of Mari Cygnet is requested at the Stone River High School. We have also been told someone might have been shot inside the school and that explosives have been placed inside the building somewhere. Also, the name of the man holding the hostages is Delbert Toller. He is also refusing to let a doctor in to see the wounded man. He's demanding to see the young woman at the center of the controversy and demanding she come to the school immediately. I repeat, and these are the exact words, 'the immediate presence of Mari Cygnet is requested at the Stone River High School.'"

At the same moment, on the other side of the globe, the *Aurora* was parked on an obscure but carefully chosen island near the continental shores of Australia. Neil and Mari were on the bridge. Mari was holding Meadow as they discussed their current situation and direction of departure from their temporary landing site.

Neil remarked, "I need to somehow find out what the Seruzians are up to. And, I want to know just what part the Ambhuri play in all of this. I still find no reason to trust either of them, though I am aware of your indebtedness to the Ambhuri."

"I wish you would open up a little more about your encounter," returned Mari, stroking the cat. "You are becoming like my father. You can talk to me, Neil, you know I will listen."

"I am trying to sort things out," answered Neil. "And, what about you? You have revealed very little of your experience. What about that?"

"I don't have anything to draw on, Neil," insisted Mari. "It's a blank. I can't say anything about what I don't remember."

"That may be so," Neil returned sharply, "but—"

"I don't remember," retorted Mari, trying to hold back the frustration welling up inside. "Please, believe me! It's different for you, you say you do remember but you still won't tell me."

"There are reasons," countered Neil.

She could see the pain in his eyes, but there was something deep inside as though he was closely guarding something, yet she didn't know how to draw him out. Two vastly different life encounters had created an invisible wall between them, though it was their connectivity that kept their differences at bay. All at once, in the midst of their intimate and personal turmoil, which at the same time brought them together and pulled them apart, Mari suddenly began to experience vague yet upsetting feelings. Thoughts regarding her family entered her mind, so she said to Neil, "I really feel the need to call home. I need to check on things. Somehow I think I should make the call now."

Without any further remarks, Neil retrieved the number, then put a communicator in her hand. The connection was made. Her mother answered with a timid, "Hello?"

Mari answered back, saying, "Hi, Mom, how are you?"

Her mother's voice was notably distressed, and quivered when she replied, "Oh, Mari! Oh, I'm so glad you called. Your father's been shot!"

"What!" exclaimed Mari, not believing what she was hearing. "Shot! Mom, how?"

Neil was startled back to reality.

"I was watching the news about the meeting and the military put the word out," moaned her mother, "and I called Rev. Sterling and he's going to drive me up there."

"Meeting?" replied Mari. "What meeting? What are you talking about? What about dad?"

"In the cafeteria," informed her mother.

"What's going on?" asked Mari.

"What's happening?" asked Neil.

Mari motioned for Neil to put it the call on the speaker system, so Neil listened as her mother said, "Oh Mari, Del has taken hostages at the high school!"

"Del?" cried Mari, in shear disbelief.

"Your father's there," continued Jennifer, "and Del shot him!"

"Why!" cried Mari.

"Your father's hurt bad," replied her mother desperately, "but Del won't allow a doctor in. I'm afraid for him and, Mari, Del is asking for you, he's demanding that you come to see him!"

"Me? What for? Mom, why didn't you call me?"

"The army is there and the news people and I lost the number and I just found out—"

"What does he want me for?"

"They wanted your father to talk, and there's a general from the army, and the police, and now they're hostages. Del is going to blow up the school and he's going to blow up everyone in it if you don't come to the meeting!"

"Blow it up? Mom, that's crazy!"

"That's what he says."

"Do you know how Dad is?"

"I don't know, Mari, but it could be real bad."

"Mom, you tell them I'm coming. Tell them I'll see Del if that's what it takes."

"Mari, please, come quick as you can. I'm going to the school with Rev. Sterling."

Neil had been absorbing information from the news links on his monitors, then he entered the conversation, asking, "Jennifer, how soon will you be at the school?"

"In about fifteen minutes or so," replied Jennifer. "I see the Pastor's car now."

"Okay, you go to the school," said Neil. "Please be careful. I will contact the local TV station to tell them Mari will be there soon. That will be about...8 p.m. your time."

Mari glanced at Neil, then said to her mother with determination, "Yes, Mom, you be careful and you tell them I'll be there. Tell them I'll talk to Del personally just like he wants."

"Mari," whispered Neil, "you're not going in there!"

The look in her eyes told him everything, but she replied, "I know what I'm doing."

"Where are you now?" asked her mother. "They say the roads are all blocked around here."

"We're somewhere near—" answered Mari. "Never mind, please don't worry, we'll be there soon."

"Oh, please hurry!"

"Use this number to call us back if you need to. I love you!" assured Mari, and the conversation ended.

"I don't want you to go in there," stressed Neil.

"I must do this!" insisted Mari. "I've got to see my Father."

"I would rather have you stay with the ship," added Neil. "I will go in. I can help your father."

"No, I have to do this," she insisted again.

Neil realized she was not going to budge, but then he leaned over one of the consoles to call up some technical information, data which looked hopelessly complex to her.

"What are you doing?" asked Mari.

"Its something I have been working on," replied Neil.

"Why are you doing that now?" demanded Mari.

"I am checking some info," said Neil, "we will be under way momentarily."

"We have to go now!"

"We will, just give me a second."

"You'll let me go in there?"

"I have reconsidered," returned Neil, reluctantly, "but you must know this is all about control. Del wants control...he is in control...albeit illegitimately."

"You think?" returned Mari.

"Listen, he is our focus now," added Neil, "but we have the advantage. Also, because you insist on going in there, I feel you should wear something other than a flight suit. Perhaps a nice dress or something."

"Why?"

"A softer, less threatening look."

"Oh, I get it," returned Mari, now entering the companion-module. "I'll see what I can find."

Neil energized the ship, then he mumbled under his breath, "I hate meetings...they're always so...disagreeable."

All available troops were ready to advance on the school if necessary. Frank Niverson had also received word concerning Mari and was on his way. Rev. Sterling picked Jennifer up from the motel and he made it through all the road blocks, arriving at the school in less than twenty minutes. One of the soldiers on the scene escorted them over to Lt. Bristol and Jennifer affirmed that her daughter was indeed on her way to the location.

Troops went to work securing a landing area in the parking lot between the school and adjacent football field. As the remaining minutes ticked by, Gen. Staffer was given word that Del would be permitted to talk to Mari by phone at 8 p.m. But when Del was told about the arrangement he became angry and still demanded that Mari meet with him personally.

The antenna on the broadcast van was fully extended, as it reached skyward Lauren readied herself for another live update. Their information was limited, however, the TV journalist's image clearly played across the monitors in the van and through the air. She stepped into the frame, and bravely spoke, "The situation here is still tense. The military remains secretive, but it looks as if they're preparing a place for some sort of large aircraft. It might be landing here at the school, maybe a helicopter or something. We will keep you updated."

Lt. Bristol was concerned the incoming craft for which they were clearing a space might only complicate the situation and was prepared for hostile action by Del. Considering the timing of events the lieutenant was wondering if Mari would actually show up. So now, Bristol, in conversation with Jennifer and Reverend Sterling, looked up into the emptiness above them then down at his watch. He observed it was exactly 7:58, and said to Jennifer, "It looks as if your daughter might be late. It also looks as if we might have to handle the situation without her. We'll take action if we need to. Your daughter is coming isn't she, Mr. Cygnet?"

"You can trust Mari," replied Jennifer.

Rev. Sterling gave a nod of support, and said, "I believe she's a person of her word."

A soldier came running up to Bristol to inform him they had a visual on a distant object. The lieutenant was about to bark another command when everyone heard a faint rumble directly above their heads and looked up into the sky. Soon every eye was on the rapid straight line descent of a churning mist as it fell from the upper atmosphere with a vertical stream of vapor trailing above it.

Lt. Bristol exclaimed with sarcasm, "I don't know what that is, but Staffer is going to have fit. He's going to love this one!"

The troops hurriedly vacated the large expanse of asphalt as they nervously eyed the object. Within seconds the *Aurora* touched down with a melodic rumble in the parking lot of the Stone River High School. It was exactly eight p.m.

Lauren Wilson broke into regular programming again with a shout, "Something has landed! We are going to try and stay with this."

Diaphanous shapes retreated back to a thin vaporous cascade over the vessel. The silver spars receded into their nests, and with great caution the troops approached the vessel with their guns drawn.

The television camera man wiped droplets of water from his camera lens and a very animated reporter continued her coverage, "The air is clearing now and I think we can get a good look at this thing. There is steam or something on it and it looks like it might be hot! I'm going to try to get us closer."

Those in the school cafeteria knew nothing about what was transpiring outside, they did however, hear a series of strange sounds just beyond the walls. This caused Del to make wild threats against the army and anyone else who might be interfering with his plans.

Meadow was sitting on the console by one of the viewports and meowed loudly as if to give Mari a complement when she entered the bridge.

"What do you think?" said Mari, "Or is this too much?"

Neil was a bit taken aback by the lacy white dress, but after studying her fashion statement, he said, "Perfect."

"I'm hoping for a distraction," said Mari.

"I believe it will be," admitted Neil, now admiring her appearance.

"Good!" she replied, confidently. "Are we going to use the Ring?"

"No," replied Neil. "I'm afraid it is still a bit slow and Del might have time to react. He might respond by detonating the explosives before the Ring actually reaches him. It needs work, as does the Atmospheric Bridging, we will have to deal with things as they are."

"I will do what I have to do," said Mari. "I want to make sure I can help my father and see that the others are okay."

"Things are going to be somewhat covert on your part," said Neil, speaking to the facts. "I have been working on something. Please, follow me."

"I'll go in the school unarmed if I have to," said Mari, as they entered the module.

"You will not be unarmed," replied Neil.

Neil opened one of the now familiar storage compartments on D deck and plucked the antenna from its clip, and when Mari saw it, she said, "Of course, a parasol will go very nicely with this dress."

"I made some alterations to it," added Neil.

"But, really, Neil," added Mari, "I think the dress will be enough."

He grabbed a crystal cylinder that looked a lot like the ones he told Mari not to touch, and snapped it onto the support rod. He pointed the antenna away from them, and said, "You gave me an idea. Now, all you need to do is open the antenna like this, or parasol as you fondly call it, and point it at the intended target like so." He brought the parasol down to a horizontal position then further explained. "When you are ready, just press this red button. It should forcefully stun any attacker within thirty feet, incapacitating the recipient for about 90 seconds or so. The device will not set off the explosive charges in the room, but I must give you a word of caution, do not change any of these numerical settings."

"It's a stun-gun?" exclaimed Mari, somewhat confused.

"A formidable one if need be," said Neil. "Use it if necessary. Remember, the low setting is important. Anything higher could be lethal."

"Lethal?" she replied, looking at Neil with her eyes open wide.

"Also," he continued, "it will only operate while it is in the open position and it is very directional. I leave it to your discretion, but if and when you do use it, I will be able to detect the discharge and the ship will automatically initiate the Sapphire Ring. The Ring will effectively neutralize the explosives and any further hostile action. Remember, this antenna is a viable weapon so use with caution." Neil folded up the antenna and handed to her.

Mari gingerly took it from him, and remarked, "Don't worry, I'll keep it on low."

"Do you have the Q-Med?"

"Yes," she said, pulling up her sleeve.

"I will communicate our intentions with the armed forces," added Neil, "but I would like you to assure those with whom you speak that we must be allowed to work without their assistance. Oh, and by the way your 'parasol' does go very nicely with that dress."

"Antenna!" reminded Mari.

"Of course," returned Neil. "Hmm, you get it."

All eyes were on the shiny white cylinder when it descended, but the elegant young woman who emerged from it with an open parasol over her shoulder was not what anyone had expected. She closed the parasol and confidently came striding up to the waiting soldier and saw to it that she met with the lieutenant. Bristol was caught off guard, for he had expected something alien in appearance, not a woman who appeared as though she had just stepped out of the past.

"Are you Miss Cygnet?" asked the lieutenant.

"Yes, I am," replied Mari.

"We have been informed you are to be part of this operation. Is that correct?"

"Yes."

"Do you understand what's going on in there?"

"Yes, sir, I do."

"You must know that Mr. Toller is holding hostages?"

"Yes, I understand the circumstances, unless you are not telling me everything."

"If all the information provided to us by Mr. Clayborn has been complete and accurate then, yes, we will remain forthcoming. We have told you everything we know up to this point."

"We have been totally honest with you."

"Well, then," instructed the lieutenant, "first, we insist you contact the man by phone, that way you'll be able to remain outside the school until we can remedy the situation."

"No," replied Mari, "that won't be necessary. I'll go in alone as he wishes. I'll see him personally."

"Are you aware of the danger?" warned the lieutenant. "He's irrational and you could find yourself taken hostage as well. You could make an already unstable situation even more volatile."

"I am aware of that," replied Mari, "but my father is in there. I must see him first."

"You might want to leave that thing out here while you go inside," advised the lieutenant, pointing to the parasol.

"No," she assured Lt. Bristol, "I'll be taking it with me."

Mari saw her mother and Rev. Sterling standing by his car as she was escorted over to the school. The army set things in motion by putting through a call to Del by means of Gen. Staffer's phone. Del was informed of Mari's presence and that she was just outside the building. Del responded by instructing Gen. Staffer to let her in, but not before he threw a key on the table. The general picked up the key and went to the doors leading to the hallway, then to the outside doors and unlocked them while Del kept his gun trained on Staffer.

Outside, Lauren Wilson narrated what was about to take place, "The young woman has finished meeting with her mother and some of the others and it still looks as though she is determined to go inside. She doesn't look like someone from outer space but we still don't know much about her. Things are unstable at this point and there's still no word on the condition of the rest of the hostages."

Gen. Staffer was given the word by a light knock on the door and he pushed it open just wide enough for Mari to slip in. Every captive eye was on her as she entered the cafeteria. There, about fifteen feet away, she saw her father on laying the floor in a pool of his own blood. Mari instantly went over to him and knelt down by his side. Del nervously stayed by his chair keeping an eye on everything. Although he detested the diversion he kept quiet. The nurse was still attending William and didn't hesitate to inform Mari on how he was doing. She tried to sound positive but expressed the urgent need for further medical attention because of blood loss.

Mari bent down close to her father and whispered, "Hi, Dad, how are you doing?"

"Not so good, Mari, " he moaned, rather weakly, barely able to talk.

"Make it quick over there!" shouted Del.

The general slowly worked his way near Mari and knelt down as if to help, then he put his hand on Mari's shoulder and whispered in her hear to informed her that he could disarm Del if she would distract him, but she whispered back, "Please, don't do anything yet, wait for me to speak with him first."

General Staffer replied, "But, Miss—"

"Hey," cried Del, suspicious of the conversation. "Break it up!"

Staffer slowly stood up and backed away, saying, "I was only trying to help, this man needs a doctor right away."

"Back to your seat," ordered Del.

"I was only trying to protect you, Mari," groaned William.

"It's all right, Dad," replied Mari, "please don't talk."

Mari activated the device hidden under the sleeve of her dress and opened up her father's shirt to examine the wounds, then she put one hand on the chest wound and the other one on the exit wound on his back.

Del saw she was taking her time, so he called out, "Hey. Are you a nurse or what? Hurry it up!"

"Have you no feelings?" cried Gen. Staffer. "This man is in critical condition."

Mari leaned over her father again, whispering, "I love you, Dad." Then she took a handkerchief from a pocket in her dress and wiped the blood off his shoulder. She adjusted his shirt and fussed with his collar to make it just right as she said to Deb, "Thank you so much for the brave thing you've done." Mari stood up, and as if in a carefully choreographed motion she gracefully opened the parasol and propped it over her shoulder. Turning to Del, she took several petite steps in his direction.

Deb stayed with William to monitor his condition. As Deb kept watch, William began to appear so relaxed it looked as though he might be succumbing to the trauma, so she thought to check the wound to see what Mari had done and opened his shirt. She was startled. She looked around to see if anyone else was watching, but Mari had the undivided attention of the room. Deb glanced one more time at William's shoulder and at the point where the bullet had entered. She saw that the skin was no longer torn. What had been an open wound was now completely healed. William was breathing much easier. The nurse pulled his shirt collar back in place and stayed at his side. She looked around the room again at no one in particular trying to restrain the impulse to smile broadly.

"Why did you shoot my father?" asked Mari

"He got out of line," snapped Del.

"You could have killed him," replied Mari, now inching closer. "Do you think that will make me do what you want?"

"You're here aren't you?"

"Your friends have caused me pain and now are you going to do the same?"

"If I have to!"

"What do you want?"

"I want you, little girl!"

"What about all these people? Now that I'm here, aren't you going to let them go?"

"First," demanded Del, "let's talk about you. I always knew you was different, you know, bein' deaf, readin' lips an' them funny motions and all. I saw you with them aliens. Are you from outer space? I hope you ain't one of them."

"I may be a deaf," said Mari, twirling the parasol and sweetening her voice, "but I'm human like everyone else in this room."

"Human or not, I got you here," said Del. "Now you need to come over here and prove it so I can know for sure. Do them little green men got ears?"

"There are no green men," said Mari. "You can't hold these people hostage like this."

"In case you haven't noticed," replied Del, "that's what I'm doin' and now I've got you."

"Well, since you've got me," countered Mari, "why don't you let the others go? They have families too."

"It's all or nothin'," said Del, as he advanced provocatively in her direction. Mari instinctively stepped back. "What's wrong little lady, are you afraid? I just want to talk."

As Mari toyed with the parasol, she coaxed in her most delicate feminine voice, saying, "Please put down the phone, then I'll come over to you."

Del thought it over for a second then, surprisingly, he obliged by putting the phone in his pocket. He kept his gun trained on her as his eyes looked her over, then he said, "You even talk better somehow, but you got to behave little girl. I see you got all dressed up, you and that umbrella and all. But remember, I got this gun."

"Of course," replied Mari, now gushing with charm and stepping forward just a little. "I got all dressed up just for you."

She playfully lowered the parasol and after another twirl she pressed the red button. Instantly, a short but narrowly focused burst of energy erupted from the device, the force of which threw Del across the floor, slamming him into the back wall. He slumped down in a daze, though he was still clutching the gun. Mari wasted no time in pulling his arms behind his back where she tightly held his wrists until he dropped the gun. Gen. Staffer would have assisted her but a loud snap and a deep rumble from outside the building distracted him. Suddenly a wall of sapphire burst into the room. Staffer was rendered immobile and crumpled to the floor as well as everyone else in the room except for Mari who was free to move around at will.

Most of the troops outside the building suffered the effects of the Ring, but they quickly recovered and rushed into the building to secure the cafeteria then assisted everyone out of the building. Del was immediately taken into custody and handed over to the local authorities. Mari assisted her father and soon he was reunited with her mother who had been anxiously waiting all this time with Rev. Sterling. Like Mari, both her mother and the Rev. escaped the effects of the Ring for Neil had adjusted it for them. An army doctor had been called to attend to William and they would have retained him for observation but Gen. Staffer interceded.

Neil emerged from the ship when notified by a signal from Mari. Everyone watched with renewed suspicion as a man in casual clothes and a long dark raincoat came strolling up to Mari and her parents, but William appreciatively welcomed him, and said, "I'm not about to say I understand any of this, but I'm glad to see you, Mr. Clayborn, you're okay, This may be a crazy time to admit it but I've made up my mind, we're going to rebuild the house, we're going to stay."

"That is very good to hear," replied Neil. "If I can be of any assistance please let me know."

"You are welcome to help if you want," said William, with sincerity.

"I have some unusual means at my disposal," reminded Neil.

"I will accept whatever help you have in mind," said William.

"There may be some people who will question my involvement," cautioned Neil.

"I can deal with those people," answered William.

"And the publicity?" asked Neil.

"So be it," replied William. "I have some experience with that now."

"Then it shall be done," affirmed Neil.

Late as usual, the backup units began to arrive and along with the added military force came Frank Niverson.

Gen. Staffer joined the group, and said to Neil, "It goes without saying, your presence here has saved the lives of many people. Still, we don't even know who you are. And though I want to express our appreciation we still need some answers!"

Frank added himself to the cluster of people surrounding Neil and Mari but he kept quiet and remained outside the circle, he just stood there for a long time with his arms crossed staring at Neil. Then he uttered, "The Pacific, July 22...you were there...and by the way, I had a great time at your mountain resort!"

Neil gave him a poker face, then addressed Staffer's question, saying, "I am aware of your desire for more information, and we sincerely wish to cooperate, but you must be patient."

"You are not outside the law," replied Staffer. "You can't just do as you please."

"What about those of us who died on the mountain?"asked Neil. "Although, I tend to believe our intentions were misread."

Staffer silently acknowledged the point, but said, "What are you doing here? Where are you from?"

"Just where 'are' you from?" echoed Niverson.

"We are Americans," answered Neil.

As the conversation between Gen. Staffer and Neil continued Frank's men were investigating the ship. The cameos had remained illuminated so the ever changing display had drawn a great amount of attention. One of the troops inspecting surface material exclaimed in disbelief, "This appears to be of some type of crystal composition."

Confused, after examining one of the cameos, another soldier blurted out, "The Statue of Liberty?"

Lt. Bristol went to see what was going on and Frank followed him, and asked, "What do all these pictures mean, Niverson? What do they expect us to believe? Is this a deception of some kind?"

"I don't know, ask that man over there," said Frank, pointing to Neil.

"What about this," Bristol continued, observing the next image, "Lions, a shield, and the sun?"

Frank studied the images for a moment, and said, "Apparently they're symbols."

"That's obvious!" exclaimed Bristol, with notable sarcasm. "What is *Aurora*?"

"I believe I'm not versed in the physics that could explain it," informed Frank.

"Just what kind of 'it' are we talking about?" questioned Bristol.

Frank looked around at all the activity, then fixed his gaze on Lt. Bristol, saying, "They have apparently discovered a kind of Holy Grail."

"Holy Grail?" asked Bristol. "Of what? Art?"

"Technology," replied Frank.

"Some kind of nuclear power?" asked Bristol.

Frank glanced over at Neil again then shook his head, saying, "Not in the way you may suppose."

"Then, what should I be thinking, Mr. Niverson?" asked Bristol, cynically.

"This is a very dynamic machine," answered Frank.

"Okay, it's a machine!" spouted Bristol.

"Of remarkable power," replied Frank.

Bristol's eyes got rather large, "How much power?"

With some resignation Frank conceded to the implications, "More than what is implied. It appears the evidence leads us here to Wyoming yet I feel we are missing something."

"What do you mean?" replied Bristol, confused.

Frank didn't answer and went over to one of the men conducting the investigation of the ship to give him specific instructions to scrutinize every detail and to gather as much information as possible no matter how insignificant. He then rejoined Neil and the general, and breaking into their conversation, said, "Now let's be specific, Mr. Clayborn, what is this really about? Or are we not privy to such information?"

The general added, "Why are you here?"

"You are not alone in your curiosity," replied Neil. "You could say we have dealt with a new technology. And, because of certain advances there are other issues that must be addressed. There are others whom neither you nor I understand at this time, but you and I are on the same side. I want to believe that in the not too distant future we might be able to work together. We all want the same thing."

"What is that, Clayborn?" asked Frank.

"The truth," replied Neil.

"That's what we want from you," echoed Lt. Bristol. "Is there a fleet of these things?"

"The answer is no," affirmed Neil.

"And what about her?" asked the lieutenant, nodding to Mari.

"This woman is as human as I am," replied Neil, pulling her close to his side.

"It's difficult to for us to accept the fact you are alone in this," the general probed. "We have seen other objects traveling with you almost from the time you first appeared. What about the thing we shot down? You destroyed it. Why? You seem to be in league with them."

"I don't know the origin of the others," replied Neil. "They are not of us nor do we assemble with them. We are searching them out to discover who they are as well. Because of the existing circumstances we will not return to the mountain. We must move on. And, with that said, gentlemen, the time has come for us to go."

"Go?" asked Frank. "Where?"

"Out there," replied Neil, pointing up.

Lt. Bristol, Gen. Staffer, and Frank Niverson followed Neil and Mari as they headed for the ship. Before entering, Neil said, "We are not the enemy, our work is a product of this land, a land which is the last best hope for this world. Perhaps the founding fathers got it right. This country has the potential for much good. Someday there may a greater understanding between intelligent beings no matter where they are from."

Neil reached to shake Gen. Staffer's hand as the companion-module quietly appeared behind him.

"How then can we know you will act in good faith?" asked the general.

"We give you our word," said Neil as he and Mari stepped into the module. "And, please, step back from the ship a bit. We shall be away shortly."

The doors closed and the module receded into the ship.

"What exactly qualifies as their word?" asked Frank cynically.

"What can we do?" said the general. "We are not about to stop them."

"They were right in our hands!" declared Frank.

"And right under our noses," answered Staffer.

"What if they had outside help?" said Frank,

"All of this is...I just don't know, Frank," said Staffer. "Yet, we have no choice, we must let them go. They now own their freedom."

"It does have its price," replied Frank, looking back at the general.

It took some doing, but reporter Wilson and her camera man finally got the equipment working again after the Ring had disabled it. Lauren looked into the lens, saying, "We're back! We were knocked out by some sort of beam. The hostage situation has been defused and Mr. Toller is in custody. Apparently Miss Cygnet's father was the only one shot but his wounds must have been minor. At least we can let you see things as they are happening."

The ship of gossamer sails came to life and effectively departed the school parking lot. It arrived at the Cygnet ranch a short time later and hovered over the cold heaps of debris from the charred structure that had collapsed into the foundation. A mysterious red light from the ship focused down into the pit of debris with great energy. Then flashes consisting of all the colors of the rainbow blazed in rapid succession producing a thick cloud that shrouded the violence of the energy. When all had subsided, the ship departed and the clouds and mist drifted away, revealing the familiar Victorian structure replete in all the grand scale of the original.

In the following days life in Stone River would fall into a rhythmic flow once again. In time the sightings would diminish, yet the small town would retain a certain notoriety as the news of such unusual events spread. The local people wanted everything to be normal but now it seemed as though only the weather was normal.

Chapter Fifteen: Hands

We float among the stars and our horizons are expanding,
But all things are really the work of His hands.
Mari

The *Aurora* could circumnavigate the far reaches of space at the feather weight of a single thought. However, Neil and Mari were on the run, unable to know what each hour, day, or distance would bring them. Because of this Neil hesitated to reveal to his companion the true extent of his dread concerning the future or the darkness of the Seruzian Principality. At present she seemed to be taking things in stride, learning and absorbing experiences at a rapid rate. Even Meadow was adapting to life aboard ship and always seemed to be at Mari's side.

At this moment they were sailing through the thermosphere over the northern polar region accumulating data on the earth's magnetic field and the makings of the aurora borealis and those dancing colors of the night when an alert indicated an unknown object was approaching. A scripted message appeared on the viewport directly in front of Neil, which read: "Ambhuri. Immediate contact."

"This may be what they were referring to at the time of your return," observed Neil.

"They're following up on their last message," replied Mari.

"Covert location," appeared on the screen.

"What do you make of it?" asked Neil. "You have some exclusive knowledge."

"Most likely they want this to be secret," replied Mari.

"Sounds familiar," quipped Neil. "And you trust them?"

"I'm not one of them, Neil," she reminded him, "they only helped me."

"I am searching for answers," he replied.

"You know I am with you no matter what," she affirmed. "I belong here."

"Then I shall polish up my welcome speech," remarked Neil. He sent a reply: "Contact granted. Please follow us."

The Kuskokwim Mountains of Alaska seemed appropriate, so they located a particularly desolate portion of the mountain range in which to land the ship. The Aurora touched down in a cold but tranquil valley in the pre-dawn hours of another terrestrial day. Soon an alien craft was settling on the rocky soil of the United States about 75 feet from the *Aurora*. Two beings boldly emerged from the silver craft into the brisk air and began to approach. Neil and Mari stepped off of the receiving platform of their own vessel into the shivering cold northern air. Eventually all four living beings arrived midway between the two vessels.

The visitors were humanoid in appearance and small in stature, no more than four feet in height, with grayish skin and somewhat large eyes. A head covering kept some of their features hidden. Then, in perfect English, with a voice most notably masculine yet with overtones of a young boy, one of the visitors began to speak, saying, "We are Ambhuri. My name is Tallis. I am commander of this vessel and this is Sola my second in command. We have greatly anticipated this moment in time."

"We honor your desire for further contact and we welcome you to our world. I am Neil Clayborn and no doubt you already know my companion Mari. I must reveal to you that I am extremely grateful for the fact that you have chosen to heal her body and restore her life. I am more than thankful for her return."

"I also thank you for saving my life," added Mari, "and for returning me to my own world."

"You are both most welcome," replied Tallis.

"We appreciate this opportunity for what I hope is a peaceful dialog," stated Neil.

"We have looked forward to this day, Neil Clayborn," said Tallis. "We have waited patiently for the time when we might communicate face to face."

"The time has arrived for truth and openness," said Neil.

"That is our aim," replied Tallis.

"First of all," replied Neil, "may I be so bold as to ask your point of origin?"

"Of course," replied Tallis. "We are from Ambhur, a planet which orbits Shalar. It is a star much like your own sun. Our planet is located in a region far distant from this world towards the central portion of this galaxy. We do not interfere with the progress of other worlds. So it may be said in that way we have not interfered with yours."

"I welcome such a non-interference policy," replied Neil, "yet, I believe we have experienced some form of intervention on your part. What of that?"

"What is it you wish to question?" asked Tallis.

"Although I would have it no other way," answered Neil, "why did you choose to intervene in the matter concerning Mari?"

"We admit this to be a departure for us," replied Tallis, "but I can assure you our decision was singular and this case was unique. It is about the timing of events."

"I am aware of how out of step we are with the progress of contemporary technology on our planet," said Neil. "Because of this we seem to have triggered a chain of events with many more adverse consequences than we anticipated."

"Everything is connected," said Tallis. "Now you have become aware of yet another domain that does not seek peace or truth."

"That would be the Seruzian Principality?" injected Neil.

"Yes," said Tallis, with sadness in his voice, "and that is precisely why we are here. They have become a part of the consequences of which you speak. It was because of these developments that we chose to make an exception. These circumstances are unique and singular, for the technology you possess cannot easily be managed alone. It is because you have shown honorable dealings with other life forms that we chose to intervene."

"Will this lead you to one day take possession of us as the Seruzian Principality has declared to do?" asked Neil.

Sola responded, by saying, "We have a higher code of honor. We will not take what is not ours, but the Principality will interfere where they deem it beneficial to their own ends. This planet has much value and we fear they will expand their presence here. They do not value life as you or I."

"We have uncovered one of the Seruzian devices imbedded in our soil," informed Neil. "Do you know its purpose?"

"They have many objectives," Tallis answered. "Valuable resources are below the surface of your world. They could make use of your geology, for there are many substances of interest to them."

"Could these devices be located in other regions of this planet?" asked Neil, considering wider consequences.

"We have not detected them in other places," replied Tallis, "yet the possibility does exist,"

"Is the device of which you speak in your immediate possession?" asked Sola.

"No," answered Neil, "it was buried within the mountain when we abandoned Star Harbor."

"Then it may be secure for now," said Tallis. "But I find it unfortunate, for it could have been of a distinct advantage to you. However, we do not need nor do we seek their technology, we have nothing to do with it whatsoever."

"What then do you seek from us?" asked Neil.

"Peaceful coexistence," answered Tallis, "a spirit of cooperation and a desire to share common interests at your discretion. We are not impatient for we know this will take place naturally over the course of time."

Neil replied, "Our world has representatives in place who are most willing to make contact with other worlds. The necessary preparations have been made on their part, I could direct you to them so that this cooperation may proceed under different circumstances if need be."

"We are well aware of the others but that time has not yet come," said Tallis. "We have chosen to initiate contact with you alone because we must warn you concerning some of the objectives of the Seruzian Principality. We are confident that you, Clayborn, may be the only one standing in their way that is capable of resisting them. You may be the one we have been waiting for, but there needs to be further revelation. There is much to show you."

"What do you mean by 'the one?'"

"It has been our hope to find someone from your planet that would possess the appropriate technical capabilities and also understand the realities involved with a venture into deep space. Someone who might extend peaceable relations between our worlds."

"I have not been given any great authority on my planet so how can you know I am the one you seek?"

"You alone have come into possession of great power," answered Tallis. "Further revelation on our part is necessary because of it. You must be apprised of Seruzian capabilities and their efforts."

"They have already gone to great lengths to acquire our ship," added Neil. "Of what further revelation do you speak?"

As Mari listened quietly to the on going conversation she began experiencing some difficulty with the earrings. Unusual static mixed with unintelligible voices were interfering with the auditory signals. She didn't know what to make of it but felt it unnecessary to interrupt the conversation between Neil and Tallis.

169

Tallis answered, "We prefer that you join our host ship, which is now among a small armada assembled not far beyond your solar system. From there you would follow us to an outpost some distance away. The assembly of which I speak will take place there. I will say, even before you left the confines of your mountain the Seruzian Principality had shown a marked increase in aggression. It is of great importance for you to meet with us. We fear it may be difficult for you to confront the Seruzian force on your own. So we must again deviate from our non-interference policy, but this would be in the form of information only."

"Then you must foresee their future intentions for us?" questioned Neil.

"We have assessed your capability," said Tallis, "which is unique, although it may not prove to be enough to effectively resist them in a protracted conflict. They began their interference by shadowing your activities as soon as your existence was known to them. In turn we have shadowed them. At that time we made a decision to become involved only if they became hostile toward you. As they have intervened in your affairs so we have intervened in theirs. You can be assured they will not rest and will seek every opportunity to better their own interests. So you see, returning your companion was a risk for us, but this is because you are at risk from them. The time is short."

"I was deceived by them," added Neil. "I can only hope you do not speak with the same deception."

"I realize you only have what we have told you thus far," said Tallis. "And you also have examples of our previous encounters. The Seruzian intelligence will work quickly to thwart any cooperation between our worlds. There is urgency."

Neil answered, "I would highly regard such information, though I must ask but one more question—"

A signal from the alien ship alerted Tallis, and he cried, "I am afraid we may not have come together soon enough! The Principality may have read into our motives. We must meet another time."

The Remote at Neil's side also signaled the approach of an airborne object and he replied to his visitors, saying, "Another time then!"

The Ambhuri ship sped away at low altitude following the frozen mountain valleys. Within seconds a single Seruzian craft swooped down to pursue the fleeing Ambhuri. Soon the *Aurora* was trailing the two ships. All were at low altitude and traveling only a few hundred miles per hour. The Ambhuri ship was well ahead of its Seruzian pursuers, dodging rough mountain peaks and diving through open valleys, but this track was not sustained, for the Ambhuri ship suddenly darted into the upper atmosphere and from there it entered space. Their speed steadily increased as they headed out into space on a course for Saturn. Nearing the planet the Seruzian ship fired a small projectile at the their Ambhuri target. A precise strike damaged the Ambhuri ship and it lost its amber glow and began to coast.

"Now we know their intent," said Neil.

"Things just got more complicated," sang Mari.

"I believe the Ambhuri may need our assistance," replied Neil, as the attacking ship drew near to the disabled vessel.

A long narrow boom began to extend from the tail section of the Seruzian ship until it connected to the Ambhuri ship, much like the midair refueling of contemporary aircraft. With the Ambhuri ship secured to their own the Seruzian ship maintained its course until it entered a high orbit around Saturn. At the same time two more Seruzian ships appeared and approached the *Aurora*.

"Well, there you have it," said Neil, stating the obvious.

"True to form," commented Mari, in agreement.

"I would call this interference," commented Neil.

"I don't think those other ships are here for our protection," declared Mari.

"They are not," declared Neil,

"What can we do now?" asked Mari.

"They have not made a move on us yet...we may need to make a run for it," replied Neil, "perhaps I should have made those final adjustments."

Worried about any further complications, Mari asked, "What adjustments?"

"It involves the integration of our systems," added Neil.

While Neil was still trying to figure out what action to take the larger of the two Seruzian vessels launched a small green sphere, which struck the *Aurora* with a substantial jolt.

"We have just been penetrated by some sort of charge," informed Neil, as small green lighting strikes formed over the *Aurora*'s external fields, causing the primary field drive to shut down as well as each of the ship's other vital systems. "Somehow the control system has been affected and the interlock coupler has been disengaged! They hit a weak spot but we still might be able to reengage the field drive."

Mari put her hands to her ears, and cried, "My hearing is gone!"

"The energy wells still have power but the ship is not responding," cried Neil, jumping up from his seat to access another console. While doing this he began to suffer the loss of his own motor control and he collapsed to the deck.

The emergency lights came on and Mari knelt down to assist Neil. "Must restart, must restart," he repeated. At the same time Mari began to experience something she had never encountered before, weightlessness, for the artificial gravity units had ceased to function. Oxygen production was the next thing to cease operation. The cabin pressure began to decrease, this was accompanied by a subtle hiss as the breathable air within the bridge compartment was being vented into space. The *Aurora* was now totally out of control and caught in a high orbit around Saturn, closely matching that of the captive Ambhuri ship. If circumstances were not to change, the *Aurora* and its crew would remain caught among the outer rings of the planet indefinitely.

Neil, Mari, and everything not secured, including Meadow, began to float freely within the compartment. A mechanical voice burst from the communications system, saying, "Prepare for surrender. Your ship will be boarded. You cannot escape."

The ports were now transparent and Mari could see the massive alien vessel begin to slowly maneuver toward them. A yawning rectangular opening large enough to receive the drifting *Aurora* was looming before them. Feeling true panic for the first time, she cried out, "Neil, they're getting closer!" Mari grabbed the hand rail on the side of the companion-module as Neil made a series of exaggerated motions with his right hand instructing her to look for something. She pushed off from the rail and drifted down to the deck and held on to the nearest handle and brought herself around to help Neil grasp the arm of the pilot seat.

The ship, now turning on its own odd axis, provided occasional sight of the alien vessel and planet below as both appeared and disappeared in the viewports. Meanwhile, as time and breathable air were running out Neil knew he must communicate vital information to Mari. Carefully, he mouthed the word, "Search." And, with his one good hand he made some very limited gestures in sign language, accompanied by some pulling and pointing motions, in hopes she would understand his directions.

"Search?" she repeated, in confused desperation. "Pull?"

Neil seemed to be gesturing toward the location of one of the paintings, saying, "Search—ship—pull."

Mari frantically looked around her as the emergency lights grew dimmer. Still unsure, she kept questioning Neil, saying, "Search? Search for what?" She was determined not to give in to her increasing panic. The inanimate ship, her struggle for breath, Neil's helplessness, plus the scared and floating cat were no comfort. Her eyes darted frantically from instrument to instrument. Something had to be done, but she couldn't imagine what it could be. Then she saw that one of the few remaining emergency lights now illuminated the painting of the harbor. Although it didn't seem to make any sense she maneuvered herself up to it and turned to Neil for confirmation. In response, he excitedly rocked his fist indicating "Yes" and made pulling motions, saying the word, "Bottle."

She gripped one of the nearby handles on the console to steady herself by the picture. Then, blindly following orders, she wrapped her fingers around the small bottle at the bottom of the frame and tugged on it. It resisted her effort and remained firmly attached to the frame. She used a little more force this time and it pulled away from the frame about two inches. It was firmly attached to something inside the frame and came to a stop with a resounding click. She let go of the bottle and it snapped back into place, but when it did the entire frame and picture came forward, stopped, then traveled under the console. In its place was an illuminated panel with buttons, levers, and mechanical dials. This came forward and locked into place.

There was a set of instructions printed on the panel: "Manual restart of interlock system via Fluidic system as follows: 1. Pull out crank and lock in place. 2. Move lever number 2 into position B to register clock at 15 second mark. 3. Turn crank 100 times then fold and lock. 4. Push lever 3 into position B and allow clock to count back to zero until chime. Press green button. 5. CAUTION! Only if necessary—repeat cranking procedure every thirty minutes to facilitate continued operation of computer. 6. If system does not engage immediately, repeat steps 1 through 5. 7. Use alpha-numeric key board to enter operation codes if restart is accomplished and triplex system does not come on line."

"Seriously, a hand crank?" questioned Mari, nearly out of breath, but again catching a glimpse of the alien ship overtaking the stricken *Aurora* spurred her on. Diligently she unseated the crank and locked it into place and followed the instructions. The crank turned with relative ease as it made a muffled ratcheting sound. Although the air was getting thinner by the minute, she thought of home and asked herself, "What window will this open?" She completed the 100 turns and locked down the crank, carefully she moved lever number 3 into position. The clock began counting down the seconds. When it reached zero there was a short beep tone, the green button lit up, and she didn't hesitate to push it.

The Seruzian vessel was now in the optimum position for retrieval of the stricken ship. A grappling arm began to telescope from the rectangular opening to assist in the capture. Suddenly a distinct rumble coursed through the *Aurora* and ended with a resounding thump. The display screens lit up one by one and the bridge lights returned to full their brightness. There was a momentary shudder as the primary field powered up and the internal gravity returned. Everything that had been floating in the compartment, including Neil, Mari, and Meadow, fell rather hard to the deck. At the same time the computer reported with voice, script, and musical tones: "Field drive recovery. Interlock engaged. All systems active."

The sails appeared, and Neil made frantic motions telling Mari to hit the throttle control, yelling as best he could, "Now, Mari, now!"

She grabbed the controls and the *Aurora* immediately responded by rapidly accelerating away from the Seruzian ship. Much to their relief, a fresh supply of breathable air began to circulate. Mari's ears again filled with sound, Neil's CMR reactivated, and Meadow crawled into a cubby hole under one of the consoles.

"Too close, too close, that was much too close!" declared Mari, inhaling as much of the newly oxygenated air as her lungs could handle.

"I concur," agreed Neil, catching his breath and recovering full motor control of his body. "Now, as long as we are outrunning them, I want you to stay with the controls."

"All right," replied Mari, "if you say so."

"I have some work to do," said Neil.

"Aren't you going to take over in minute or so?" she cried, noting the three Seruzian ships trailing them. "They're not far behind us!"

"They are the predators," remarked Neil, "and unfortunately we are the prey."

"Yes, but—" complained Mari.

"Look at that," remarked Neil, with some surprise, "they appear to be backing off. They're pulling back."

"They're probably up to something," added Mari.

"Most likely," said Neil. "Therefore, we may have some time."

"Time?" asked Mari. "Aren't you going to take over now?"

"No," he replied, "I must go below to make those adjustments I was talking about. Keep an eye on things up here until I return."

"No, wait!" cried Mari, not believing what she was hearing. "You're leaving me?"

"I am going to service the induction rings," he countered. "It must be done."

"Why, why now? Are you going to fix those ABCs or something?"

"No, that's something totally different, I will be back shortly," he assured.

"But I'll be the only one on the bridge!" she exclaimed.

"Don't worry, it will be okay," he returned. "Trust me. And look, Meadow is in the seat next to you to keep you company!"

The cat had a squinty know it all expression as she crouched and glared at Mari.

"This time I might actually worry," she replied.

"The first thing you will notice is a slight drop in the power reserves," added Neil "Oh, and there may be a few connection alarms."

"A drop in the power?" she cried, trying not to hear any of her own alarms now going off inside of her head.

"I will work as quickly as I can," said Neil. "If things go as planned all systems should return to normal levels. Just keep us at speed and let me know if there are any big changes. If you see those ships again and if they should fire on us use the automated weapons system to return fire. I will be right back."

"If, if? Oh, great, I can't believe this," sighed the frantic woman at the controls. "And you, you're going off to tinker with something?"

The module doors closed and Neil was gone. Finding herself alone at the helm, leaving the solar system behind, running from alien vessels, and having to strike back at another spacecraft while screaming through space was not what she signed up for. Although, it was a much better prospect than the jaws of a dark and hostile alien ship.

When the module doors opened Neil went straight to one to the locked compartments on D Deck, from it he retrieved a twelve inch long cylinder. Then after opening a small hatch in one of the bulkheads he entered a short tunnel which led to the perimeter of the vessel. In this way he could access the drive components, the interlock system, and various control modules. This was the heart of the engine that produced the energetic fields that propelled the ship. The major components were the three large induction rings. Each ring was four inches thick, twenty-four inches wide and one hundred forty feet in diameter, nearly the diameter of the ship and composed of numerous crystal compounds. The rings were unified and stacked one on top of the other. The upper and lower ring remained stationary but the center ring rotated, changed direction, or stopped in order to alter the flow of power according to the demands of the system.

Neil found a small keypad, where he entered codes to stop the automatic motion of the center ring. Once the ring was stopped and manually repositioned Mari received alerts on the bridge concerning a drop in available power. The next step involved unlocking and removing the seven existing glass disks positioned at measured distances around the ring. After plucking the disks from their respective slots he replaced them with crystal sapphire disks from the cylinder and locked them in place. Each was specifically designed for its predetermined location within the ring. Before placing the seventh and final ring in its corresponding slot he removed the leather band from his finger and carefully peeled back the natural hide. By doing this he uncovered an inner band of gold and pure sapphire. Once it was freed from its leather skin he carefully inserted the band into the circular groove cut into the last disk and placed the disk into the induction ring and secured the mechanism. Once he was finished with the placement of the disks he closed the compartments and headed for the bridge.

Upon his arrival, Mari explained what happened while he was gone, saying, "You were right, I saw a slight change in the power readings but they finally returned to normal."

"Very good," he replied, taking the pilot seat.

The screens began to display a three dimensional graphic, this represented the changes and silently announced with a script: "Completion program initiated. Wave induction rings registered. Modified disks in submission. System at 100 percent input / output capacity. System is on standby."

"Stage III of this project is now complete," announced Neil. "All of the ship's systems are now fully integrated. We hoped to do more testing before this final step, but now, for better or worse the ship is now complete. The Seruzians continue to play their little game of deception and aggression. Now it will be a new game. We shall play by our own rules."

"You just said, 'for better or worse?'" returned Mari. "What could possibly be worse? I thought you were making things better?"

"The rings have now been reconfigured," he answered. "This will make all the systems more efficient."

"How will that help?" she asked.

"I did what needed to be done in this situation," informed Neil. "I must add, this may only be a temporary reprieve in Seruzian hostilities. It is now time for us to return to Earth."

"I'm afraid of what we might find there," replied Mari.

"Nevertheless," said Neil, "we must see what awaits."

Space was clear; this was good sign because they needed time to calculate their next move, then Mari asked again, "What about that thing you were talking about? You know, for better or worse?" Neil didn't have time to answer, for suddenly the bridge was filled with another alert. Ten Seruzian ships were approaching at great speed. So once again Neil took the *Aurora* away from Earth. Now they were running like a fox from a stampede of hounds and horses with nowhere to hide. Worry spread across Mari's face. "How long can we keep up this pace?"

Neil didn't answer her question for he was working with the changes regarding the ship. Then, without saying a word he reduced the speed of the *Aurora*. The alien ships slowed in response but continued to edge closer.

"Neil, why are we slowing down?" said Mari, trying to fend off panic. "Are we loosing power?"

"No," he replied.

"You're not going to surrender are you?" cried Mari, beginning to panic.

"Not exactly," he replied, still letting the *Aurora* decrease in speed. The alien ships began to close the distance until they were in visual range. Eventually, Neil brought his ship to a complete stop.

Mari, now beside herself, exclaimed, "I hope you know what you're doing."

Seizing the opportunity, the enemy ships took an offensive posture by assuming equally spaced positions, thereby three dimensionally surrounding the *Aurora*. The Seruzians sent a warning; the commanding mechanical voice was saying, "Surrender and live. You cannot flee. Surrender or die."

"At least they're predictable," mumbled Mari.

"They are," added Neil, "but we are learning."

"Not fast enough," countered Mari.

The *Aurora* received still another demand, that said, "You have caused severe damage and loss to the Principality. You have brought upon yourselves an equally severe penalty. No further hostilities will be tolerated. You will surrender."

"Penalty," cried Mari, having her sensibilities put to the test. "Who do they think they are?"

"Our captors," quipped Neil.

"Of course," scoffed Mari.

Neil sent a response, saying, "We have only defended ourselves against your aggression. We desire to go in peace and to proceed unhindered."

There was no response from any of the alien ships and a standoff began to take shape so the crew of the *Aurora* waited for the enemy to make the first move. Fifty minutes passed with no indication of what would be next.

"They know how to wait," remarked Mari.

"Apparently," concurred Neil.

Two more hours passed as the standoff continued, and Mari observed, "It doesn't look like they want to talk."

"It does not," stated Neil, closely monitoring incoming information regarding the alien craft.

A cascade of unpleasant feelings found their way inside Mari's head and, though she already knew the probable answer, she approached Neil, saying, "What do you think they are really up to?"

"They are trying to wear us down," replied Neil.

"Waiting for us to give up?" asked Mari.

"That would be consistent," answered Neil.

"Wouldn't it be better to try to outrun them again?" questioned Mari.

At this point Neil decided to communicate once more, saying, "We request that you allow this ship to proceed unhindered. We will take no hostile action." He then turned to Mari. "Possibly, that was not assertive enough." Mari gave him an impatient glance, to which he replied, "Now I shall see what happens if we initiate the next move. I will alter our position slightly."

He nudged the *Aurora* slowly toward an open space between the ships, but the vessel by which the *Aurora* would pass responded by firing two small projectiles. There was a direct hit, this caused some severe jolts, otherwise there was no damage to the ship.

Neil mumbled something unintelligible, then Mari asked, "Do they want us to fight them?"

"Possibly," remarked Neil, flatly.

This time after the hit on the *Aurora* Mari noticed there was a slight rise in the level of available power, it was only minor but it was there. Normally, this did not happen, so she said, "Neil, I think there's something wrong here, our reserves show a slight increase. If anything, there should have been an expenditure when we took the hit. I haven't seen this before."

"I will admit the readings are a bit tricky at this at this point," remarked Neil, "but I believe it is time for us to make a definite move."

"Could they have affected our systems like before?" questioned Mari, hoping things were not deteriorating.

The bridge lights dimmed. Neil entered a detailed command, which engaged the new weapon system and in turn adjusted the central induction ring. Additional information was graphed on one of the small screens nearby as a totally new alert began to sound throughout the ship, one that Mari had never heard before. A script flashed on the ports: "Initializing system for Alpha-Omega Primordious Acquisition Weapon. AO PAW I. Low level discharge 30%. Recharge 110%. Engaged. Waiting."

Neil finally responded to Mari's concern, saying, "This is an operational attribute of completion. We now have at our disposal a weapon which was incorporated into the original design as conceived by Gordon, but it was never activated because we have always had reservations. It was the last thing on our list of tests because there were a number of unknown factors. Therefore, I will begin at the lower registers. We must proceed with a certain amount of caution."

"Caution?" said Mari. "Why can't we just go ahead and blast our way out?"

"The data was never conclusive," replied Neil, "that is, we were never sure if the thing would work. I have been working on the equations, trying to resolve some of the discrepancies, thus reducing the margin of error. I have decided to accept the existing margin."

"What happens if it doesn't work?" asked his nervous companion.

"There could be some unintended consequences," replied Neil.

"Is that the 'worse' you were talking about?"

"It could be catastrophic in nature," replied Neil, seeming a bit detached.

"What kind of 'catastrophic' are we talking about?"

"In non technical terms?"

"Just tell me!"

"I am reasonably confidant it will function as intended."

"Or?" demanded Mari.

"We might become a very brilliant and far reaching fireball," added Neil, as his viewport displayed some fluctuations in the power levels. "Or, we might blow up the universe. Well, maybe not the universe but—"

"I'm sorry I asked," replied Mari, now more unsure than ever about what the man was up to.

Another message was sent from the *Aurora*, giving their foe an opportunity to respond, saying, "If you do not allow us to exit peaceably we will do so by force."

There was still no response from any of the Seruzian ships so another thirty minutes elapsed in silence.

"Couldn't we fire a warning shot with the old weapon system," offered Mari.

"That may be something to consider," replied Neil, now fastening his eyes on Mari with a longing she had not seen before. So he readied the secondary weapon system and set his sights close to one of the Seruzian vessels. But, before he could fire and without any further communication, or without any further warning, all ten vessels simultaneously fired on the *Aurora*. An intense barrage totally engulfed the terrestrial ship.

"Of course they would take advantage of our situation," announced Neil, "but the deflection system is working and we are holding our own."

The ship vibrated violently under the deluge as the computer scripted with cool detachment: "Deflection status. Energy expenditure at 10%."

"This is crazy! I say we use the big weapon while we still can before we go dead again," pleaded Mari, now desperate. "I don't care what happens!"

Still under attack by the alien vessels Neil selected one of the craft as a target and switched to the PAW then activated the initializing sequence. After a short count down a multi colored haze engulfed the *Aurora*, so the alien ships promptly ceased firing, seemingly puzzled by what was happening to their victim. From their point of view their prize was finally succumbing to their fire power. But then a column of energy burst from the *Aurora* and contacted one of the alien ships. Subsequently, it became totally engulfed by the projected beam. In reciprocating fashion the column withdrew back into the *Aurora* and as a result the enemy vessel was simply gone. Neil targeted the next ship and fired. That ship vanished as well. The remaining Seruzian ships commenced firing back with a vengeance and despite the fact that a vicious onslaught ensued the *Aurora* remained unaffected. A fourth alien ship was targeted and it also vanished. In the end the six remaining vessels ceased their fire and made a hasty retreat.

"We shall pursue them," informed Neil, and he thrust the *Aurora* after the fleeing ships.

"I don't get it," exclaimed Mari, as she read the information concerning the *Aurora*'s core systems. "I'm reading that our energy reserves are up dramatically."

"Conversion," answered Neil, tersely.

"But what happened to those ships?" questioned his mystified companion. "Where did they go? They just disappeared!"

"They have been absorbed."

"Where? Into space?"

"The Wells."

"Our Energy Wells?" asked Mari, in astonishment. "Their ships are—"

"Yes," quipped Neil, "more fuel in the tank."

As Mari scrutinized the data regarding the fleeing ships and the increased energy reserves of the *Aurora*, she suddenly became aware of the new pulse within the ship. The chase was on and the *Aurora* drew ever closer to their to the six alien ships. In their retreat four of the six ship split off and shot away from the formation. Moments later one of the two remaining ships tore away so Neil drove the *Aurora* hard after the one remaining ship finally gaining on his target. He fired a low energy version or the PAW and the alien craft immediately lost propulsion. This sent the vessel coasting helplessly out of control.

Mari was relieved, but demanded, "So, Neil, what else haven't you told me about this ship?"

"It was a matter of security," he replied, "something we kept secret from the beginning of the project. I felt if you did not have any knowledge of it you would not worry about it. Sorry to be so tight lipped."

"So, what do you have hiding under that other picture?" asked Mari, referring to painting titled Discover, for she was still in need of some answers.

"It's complicated," replied Neil, "but please, trust me, in due time I will explain."

"You can trust me, you know," reminded Mari.

"Thank you, I know I can," said Neil. "All right...it's the Valve."

"Hmm," replied Mari, hoping for a bit more information.

Neil was mute. The bridge soon began to revert its normal status as the two occupants contemplated the breathtaking ease with which the *Aurora* dispatched the enemy ships. Neil considered what adverse events might transpire on their journey to their home planet, but their fears were unfounded. Upon reaching the home planet, and as they circumnavigated the globe, it was a relief to discover that their ship was the only unusual object in the Earth's atmosphere. Neil began asking questions aloud, perhaps he was only asking them of himself, but he said, "What have we encountered? A measure of fortune or something else entirely?"

"I don't know, I need time to process all this," answered Mari, feeling a similar range of emotions, "but what about the Ambhuri? What will happen to them?"

"We shall soon find out," reported Neil.

The space around Saturn was empty so the *Aurora* headed out of the solar system in search of the captive Ambhuri ship. A sweep of a not too distant section of space between Earth and the center of the galaxy provided evidence of alien vessels. They discovered that the Ambhuri ship was in tow at sub light speed. As the *Aurora* approached the armada a single Seruzian vessel moved out of the formation to confront the terrestrial ship. They made their intentions known, saying, "Do you look for death? What brings you here?"

"The welfare of the Ambhuri," Neil replied.

"How is it your concern?" came the reply.

"We make it our concern," replied Neil.

"You destroyed Seruzian property," came the accusation.

"You sought possession of our vessel," returned Neil.

"We acquire what we will," said the unknown Seruzian contact. "You retain no rights in this sector."

"We challenge your actions, let the Ambhuri go."

"You are interfering in what you know not."

"I will say again," returned Neil, resolutely, "let the Ambhuri go."

"On what authority do you make such a demand?"

"On what authority do you detain the Ambhuri?"

"It is foolish to defend the Ambhuri. You have not valued Seruzian property, but you are free to go, Clayborn. If you depart now we will not retaliate."

"We will not leave the Ambhuri."

"Who chose you to be their advocate?"

"We alone are determined to defend them."

"Not a wise choice," came the Seruzian response.

Neil sent no further reply and waited. Then, although no further communication took place, the Ambhuri ship was released, and one by one the Suruzian ships broke away from their hostile formation and departed. Neil nudged the *Aurora* closer to the loan Ambhuri vessel in order to assist by any means necessary. An audio message came through to the bridge, and a familiar voice said, "This is Tallis. It seems, Clayborn, we are now the ones from whom gratitude must be expressed. You continue to surprise us. We received sensitive information regarding the Seruzian Principality, therefore we have noted that the Principality has come to fear you. We are in your debt."

"I consider you as friends from across space," replied Neil. "I hope this friendship will continue. I could not let the Principality carry out their plans concerning you. As I measure their intent, I do not find it peaceable."

"You may not know what you have wrought or see your place in the host of planetary affairs," said Tallis, "however, your direction is right. You must remain on your guard, you must watch, and you must listen. It now appears as though you have the substance to resist them. We perceive you are aware of the paths of truth and deceit. When the time is right we will seek contact once again."

"We shall look forward to that day," said Neil.

No longer captive, and without further communication, the Ambhuri ship departed toward its point of origin.

The *Aurora* had not traveled a great distance in galactic terms, nevertheless, the souls within it had come far. Meadow crawled out from under the console and jumped into Mari's lap. She petted the cat and decided it was time to inform Neil of something that happened much earlier, saying, "I didn't feel I should interrupt you at the time, but I was experiencing some hearing difficulties during our conversation with the Ambhuri in Alaska. I heard static and some unintelligible voices break into the earrings. With all the other complications I forgot about it."

"Have you ever encountered such a thing before?" asked Neil.

"No," replied Mari, "only then, and it didn't last long."

"Anything else?" asked Neil.

"Just noise," said Mari, "static, and what seemed to be conversation."

"Perhaps it may have been a malfunction of some sort," replied Neil. "I will look into it."

Although Mari was given to periodic musings, she possessed a positive spirit, but now her thoughts became darker as she became increasingly introspective. Now, wondering anew about what had just taken place, an intense foreboding crept into her heart. So it was in the softest of voices, that she asked, "What will become of us?"

"I can't answer that question," said Neil. "Do you have any second thoughts about accompanying me?"

"No," she said, "but I have no words to explain my feelings. All I know is that the Ambhuri are kind and the Seruzian seek to destroy. I used to know what we faced on Earth with the powers that be. Space is so vast and I find that evil reaches deeper than I ever imagined."

"And now I question our future," replied Neil.

"We can't know the future," said Mari, "we only have the present."

"That is so," he remarked.

"Although it seems so dark, I only look for a measure of grace," she added.

"What do you see, Mari?" he asked.

"I thank God for his mercy and grace in times of need," she replied.

"I hope you are right," he said, "but I don't see as you see. I find I no longer have faith in things as I once did."

"My faith is not in things," replied Mari, "but in the Maker of all things."

"Admirable reasoning, Mari," replied Neil, "but I look for something tangible."

Three kinds of ships were speeding in three different directions. All would return to their points of their origin. The occupants of the single ship heading toward the Earth thought of home with the hope of peace and safety. The Seruzians were returning to their own dark dominion to brood and to plan. And, the Ambhuri ship was left to proceed unmolested toward its own secure habitation.

On the Ambhuri ship, Sola posed a question for Tallis, saying, "Why did you not further enlighten our terrestrial friends?"

"Of what do you speak?" asked Tallis.

"Of the great power they possess," revealed Sola.

"I believe they are aware of it," commented Tallis.

"Do you think they comprehend its full extent?" asked Sola.

"Sola," replied Tallis, "we have seen the malevolence of the Seruzian Principality encounter a most unique entity. There now exists the footfalls of two living souls born into the realm of galactic space on which providence has bestowed the privilege to hold fast the secret of inimitable power, which may change the destiny of those mortal beings as they journey outward among the celestial spheres."

Chapter Sixteen: Grace

Life is like an ocean of unfathomable depths,
So blue and so deep,
So wrapped in mystery.
I have not forgotten that which guides my soul,
For I know I shall sail the ocean and roam the heavens in realms of grace.
Mari

Saturday, September 19, was born bright and clear on the eastern coast of the United States. Although, at this time it was early in the evening. The entire compass of the terrestrial planet could be considered a homestead, with the solar system as their back yard but, Neil and Mari found that simple dreams could become intricate constructions with hundreds of doors leading to even greater complexities. The *Aurora* had become a vessel of refuge and the earthen sphere of ocean, mountain, valley, and open plain was an ever more bountiful source of supply for the most basic of human needs.

High rocky terrain with emerald valleys provided temporary hiding places as well as the great oceans that lapped the shores of the many delightful islands scattered about. It seemed they could never stay as long as they wished. Peace was hard to come by, so it was of great fortune for them to find a resting place earlier that day on one isolated, uninhabited, and unexpectedly lush patch of land in the Caribbean.

At present Mari was catching up on some much needed rest while the *Aurora* remained nestled within a stand of gorgeous palms. Sleep was at times difficult and relegated to no specific pattern. Complete relaxation was not always possible. Their vagabond life seemed to effect Mari the most. Creatures on the run and involved in an effort to evade unknown predators don't consciously adhere to any specific schedule. Yet, it was at this one spot where an interlude of relative tranquility had finally overtaken them. After spending some quiet time in her own quarters, Mari felt so exhausted that she fell asleep the instant her head touched the pillow of her bunk.

Neil had remained on the bridge to reflect. Because of the way things had transpired, there were few people among his old acquaintances who could help support the exacting weight of what now rested on them. He eventually concluded it was necessary to reconnect with his old friend Jacob Smithson. With that resolved, he decided to relax in his own quarters before continuing their flight. Meadow joined him there by curling up on his lap, something she had been reluctant to do until this time.

The afternoon was indeed tranquil, Mari's blanket was soft and the bunk quite comfortable, so she slept soundly as the hours passed quietly by. But then she awoke with a discernible fright. Her heart was pounding out of her chest. Feeling disoriented, she sat up, beads of moisture covered her face, her eyes sped franticly around her quarters as if to verify where she was and her head was filled with an aggregation of thoughts. Where was she? Then she realized she was still on the *Aurora* in her own bunk, and there was no need for alarm.

"A nightmare!" she declared, as she breathed a sigh of relief.

Getting up, she washed her face and allowed for some time to carefully brush her hair. Her quarters were complete and accommodating with everything she needed, yet she felt she had to get out of the confines of the small cabin for some air so she left a message for Neil on the communication system. She picked up the parasol and grabbed a small bag of her favorite fruit before summoning the companion-module. Once outside, she located a natural path that led from the ship to the beach, a place where the water was peacefully caressing the shore. This lone stretch of sand happened to be in partial shade with intermittent spots of sunlight streaming through the foliage of nearby trees. Shadows were getting longer and the rays of light sparkled on the sand in what seemed to be a perfect island paradise.

Standing transfixed under the open parasol with the sun at her back she let her eyes wander along the shore that arched around in a semi-circular sweep. It seemed magical, so she took off her shoes to allow her bare feet to sink into the warm sand, working it between her toes. The fruit made her think of home as she tried to savor each piece. Among the stones and pebbles sprinkled along the beach she spied a conch shell as it caught some of the stray evening light. She picked it up to marvel at its design and put it up to her ear. She heard what seemed like the rush of the ocean, a sound she never had the pleasure of until this day. Enchanted, she wondered how it came to be on such a lonesome shore. The ocean had been its home, when, once upon a time the shell had been inhabited by a living creature. With a certain empathy she tossed it back into the water and watched the ripples spread and dissipate from the resulting splash. While ruminating about the life within the sea she turned around and saw Neil coming down the path toward her. He saw her standing there with the parasol over her shoulder and he raised his hand in greeting so she returned his gesture with a welcoming smile.

"May I join you?" he called.

She used sign language to answer him with a definite, yes, then spoke softly, saying, "Of course you may."

He saw her shoes neatly set aside so he pulled off his boots and gently rested his hands on her shoulders. A long look into her inquisitive eyes finally prompted him to ask, "How are you doing?"

She sighed, and said, "Okay," then her eyes cast down to the soft white granules as she pushed the sand around with her feet.

He sensed there was something she was not saying, so he probed further, "What is it?"

"I don't know, it's just—"

"You can tell me."

"I guess I'm feeling a bit homesick."

"Hmm, true, we are on the road a lot."

"It's not that."

"What is it then?"

"It seems I am missing things," she sighed, closing the parasol and laying it on the white sand.

"And what might those things be?"

"I miss my family. I miss King. I miss my church, you know, the normal things. Sometimes I even miss the tavern. I know it sounds stupid, I guess it's all those connections one has in life."

"Any regrets over this odyssey?"

"No, not really," she said with a groan. "But it seems like so long ago when I told myself I needed to get out on my own. You know, to see the world...oh, yes, and then did I ever!"

"Sounds as if you are having second thoughts to me."

"No, Neil, its just that...I had a nightmare during my little nap."

"What was it about?"

"It was—"

"Yes?"

"It was just an uneasy feeling I can't put my finger on."

"About us?"

"No, it wasn't exactly."

"I would hope we would be the least scary part of this whole thing."

"It's not like that."

"Can you recall anything about it?"

"Not much, but I felt afraid. You weren't there and there was something going on. I don't know what it was, but I didn't know what to do about it."

"Nothing specific?"

"I guess all our recent encounters have me on edge."

Neil thought to encourage her, saying, "I don't need to remind you that you have been through some heavy seas, storms that would have shipwrecked a lot of people many times over. But, I want you to know I could not have survived without you. You have been amazing, you are strong, and you possess a unique kind of insight. The *Aurora* is more capable now and so are you. And, don't worry about me."

"The world is smaller and the universe is bigger than I ever imagined," said Mari. "I have always tried to stay optimistic, but lately there are times when I don't feel that way. I sometimes struggle, even with my own faith. How does the desire for power infect all creatures? How shall we use what we have and still be responsible? How shall we hold on and let go all at the same time?"

"The Ambhuri? The Seruzian? Our own world?" answered Neil, with more questions. "I did not choose to be the 'one' Mari, as the Ambhuri have said. Maybe I am not what they think I am. I may not even be what I think I am. Right now though, I realize I could use some help, say, some kind of guidance. Perhaps you might pray for me. He hears you."

"I have, I will, and He does. He will extend His hand to all who seek Him."

"Then, maybe 'He' is the 'One.'"

"He is," she affirmed, "He is." Then she put her arms around him. "Hold me close, Neil, and don't let go."

"I am so glad you are here, Mari."

"I love you."

"Why do you love me?"

185

"Because."

"Just because?"

"Just because I do."

"Then it shall be fine, it will as you always say, all work out somehow."

Mari said nothing more as they stood together in the sand, holding on to each other as if a great storm was about to sweep them off the beach. At last, when they sat down, Neil picked up a small stick and used it to write in the powdery grains: "I love you, Mari Abigail Cygnet." After which, he kissed her on the forehead, and said, "There is a beautiful light within you."

This corner of the world seemed to be a place where the universe was at peace. The sand felt soft and warm by virtue of the afternoon sun. The air was perfect, the sky was intensely blue, and the shadows of evening were lengthening. Neil picked up the stick again to draw a circle around them, then he helped his companion—this seemingly fragile creature of mysteries—back to her feet within the confines of the circle. Neil gently unwound the her fingers from his own and pointed to the ship, and said, "It is time."

Mari gave an affirmative reply with her hand, saying, "Yes."

Then both of them turned to catch one last look at the sea before retracing their own footprints back to the ship.

Preparations were now complete, but before leaving the island Neil had one more thing on his mind. In the circular hall of the crew quarters on B Deck, Neil said to Mari, "I am aware of something which delights you."

"What would that be?" she questioned, somewhat surprised.

"I have something for you in one of the compartments over there," he said, "something you might like to have."

"What ever are you talking about?" she asked, mystified. Neil unlocked the panel then motioned for her to open it. Mari opened the door and discovered a violin case inside. Pulling it out, she said, "What is this?"

"Surely you must know!" he replied.

Within the case was a polished instrument which looked as though it had never been used, and she exclaimed, "It's beautiful!"

"It was mine," said Neil, "now it is yours. "It will be better off in your hands."

"Mine was—"

"I know."

"Anyhow," she said, with a slight giggle, "I think I drove everyone mad."

"You have my permission to drive me mad," he replied.

"I shall do my best," she said. Her eyes sparkled as she hugged him. "But I do hope I won't drive you mad."

"Ah, but you already have," he replied.

"What, how can that be!" she declared.

"Some would call it love," he replied.

In due time the many chambered regions of the sea would be probed, but at this moment the surface of the ocean and the atmosphere above it proved to be the center of focus. The ship's lone occupants enjoyed each other's company more and more with each passing day as they shared the intimate joy of discovery. The information they gathered proved to be of great importance, although some of their excursions were characterized by an almost carefree playfulness. They were able at times to rise above their extraordinary circumstances and find an inner connection.

The *Aurora* was making the globe smaller and allowed them to roam at will. Dusk was upon the Atlantic coast of United States and the restless ocean was the subject of a careful search. They were now traveling northeast towards the island of Bermuda at a mere 45 miles per hour at an altitude of only twenty feet above the water. This allowed them to cruse along at their leisure. The ports and scanning sensors provided an exceptional view of what might be ahead. Visibility was diminishing though, for it was becoming cloudy with a light fog and a storm was gathering strength farther east, where huge gray churning clouds were becoming ever darker. The ephemeral sails were barely evident over the vessel as the ship slid easily through the atmosphere under very minimal thrust. Now it would be the spectacular glow of the sapphire hull, the shift and shimmer of the cameos, and the pulse of the antennae on the luxuriant vessel as it reflected off the waters below that might give them away to any stray ocean traveler.

"This is amazing, everything is functioning exceptionally well," remarked Neil, "even in glide mode the internal disposition of the Energy Wells, frequency of the Rings, and resultant power curves are within acceptable range, all indicating a smooth transition!"

"Internal power curves?" remarked Mari. "Smooth transition?"

"All are within optimal range and holding," added Neil. "Incoming external data is unbroken, processed, and graphed as we speak."

"All science all of the time?" replied Mari, signaling other thoughts.

"Not all of the time," returned Neil.

"How about taking time to observe the beauty?" suggested Mari.

"Oh?" replied Neil, lightly patting her on the shoulder. "I do that a lot."

"Hey!" warned Mari, as she cast a playful glance his way. "Careful, I might just drive you mad."

"With the violin?" he queried.

"Of course," she answered with a twinkle in her eyes.

"You may play it any time you like," he replied, still gazing out through one of the viewports and petting Meadow lounging on the console next to him.

"Now?" she inquired.

"Except for this fog the ocean is remarkably clear in this region, " replied Neil, not listening.

"Is that unusual?" asked Mari, only half interested.

"Perhaps not," he suggested.

"Then, we're alone?" asked Mari, rather knowing the answer.

"Quite alone," he affirmed.

"No one else for millions of miles?" she added, with glee.

"Perhaps only tens or hundreds," returned Neil, voicing the facts.

"Just you and I?" she asked again.

"Yes, Mari," he returned, wondering about all the questions. "Why?"

"I could play it now," she teased, "or maybe we could—"

"What ever do you have in mind?" asked Neil, now attentive.

Mari snuggled in close as the hypnotizing images of incoming data danced on the screens, then she said, "Well, what I was going to say—"

Suddenly an alert signal chimed with an announcement, "Intermittent signal. Atmospheric displacement. Isolated magnetic fluctuation, 8,709.207 feet ahead."

This caused Mari to grumble, "Now what?"

Neil adjusted his glasses, saying, "I have no idea, this is a very odd reading. There is something a little more than a mile ahead. It appeared for a few seconds then disappeared. The anomaly was graphed as a perfect sphere for a second, registering about 525 feet in diameter."

"A sphere?" questioned Mari, suddenly anxious.

"I have never seen this phenomenon before," said Neil,

"Was it solid?" asked Mari, totally mystified as the computer illustrated an energy field and its properties three dimensionally.

"No, it was not," he replied. "It read like some sort of a bubble as it displaced the existing atmosphere. It also had its own magnetic properties, spherical, but with no other substance."

"Seruzian?" voiced Mari, now worried.

"Unknown," replied Neil. "Wait, there it is again. We have an indication of some sort of mass accumulating within sphere."

The screen in front of them indicated the formation of a solid object, but wondering what to make of it, Mari questioned, "Could it be like a hologram?"

"No," replied Neil, "see that reading? Now look at this. I don't believe it, now there is a ship within the sphere!"

The *Aurora* slowly closed in on the phenomenon. As the anomaly continued to remain in their sights they eventually came to a full stop a short distance behind the stern of a fully rigged ship of sail.

"Do you think its real?" asked Mari.

"All indications reveal that the vessel has substance," informed Neil. "This is unknown territory. There is no way of knowing what caused it to appear."

"Dare we get any closer?" asked Mari.

"The phenomenon does not appear to be affecting us or the surrounding environment," said Neil, quite glued to the data. "Okay, now the sphere is gone but the ship remains. It appears to be drifting with the influence of wind and the current but heading almost due north. I'm having trouble penetrating the hull with our sensors to read the contents. So far there is no evidence of anyone on board. "

They crept to within thirty feet of the vessel and cast a beam of light on it because of the increasing darkness. From the viewport they could clearly make out the name of the ship in large white letters as it spread in relief across the stern with a spanker sail above it hanging in shreds.

"Well, the *Starlet* appears to be an excellent example of a tall ship," informed Neil. "We have a square rigged vessel with three masts and lots of canvas. Although, I am detecting substantial damage. Many of the sails are torn up...this thing has taken quite a beating."

"What could have done all that?" asked Mari.

"It could have been a severe storm or it could have been the result of something else," replied Neil.

During their tight circuit around the stricken vessel they found the ship taking on a slight list to starboard. Part of the outer deck railing amidships was broken away on the port side. At the bow they discovered the anchors remained secured in their places and the figurehead that loomed under the bowsprit was still intact. The gallant carving thrust forward to portray an angel holding tightly to a single ghostly white star. The cherub had pale pink skin, wings, and a flowing gown. From there they swung around to the starboard side where they found that the mizzen royal yard arm was gone from its mast and lay on the deck below in a tangle of ropes. No flags or any other type of identification could be seen.

At this point in time anyone on board the vessel would surely have noticed the presence of the *Aurora*. Nevertheless, after returning to the port side they made known their intentions, so Neil's amplified voice could be heard, saying, "Hello! Is there anyone aboard? Hello! We are here to help."

"Do you actually think there could be someone on board?" she asked.

"If there are people on there," added Neil, "they must be somewhere down on the lower decks but I see no evidence at this time. It could be that the sensors are inhibited by the twitchy energy spikes surrounding the vessel. I also find there is no record of such a ship as this. Yet, everything appears authentic."

"Why would the crew just abandon it?"

"I have no answer, but as far as I can tell, the movement of the vessel is now influenced only by the existing weather conditions. But we must assume the sphere could return at any time."

"Could we go aboard and search for survivors?"

"Perhaps that would not be wise."

"Do you think the Seruzians have anything to do with this?"

"Again," returned Neil, "I don't know, even if this ship is not of alien origin, should the sphere materialize, or should the vessel disappear while either of us are there, we might find the ourselves in a real bad situation."

"Isn't there anything we can do?" returned Mari.

"It would be possible to energize a staircase down to the open deck," said Neil, "that way I could board her. But, since there is no way to know how the *Aurora* would react to any sudden change in the phenomenon, it would be risky. Yet, by all the indicators at our disposal the wooden ship appears to be stable for now."

"I'll go aboard and quickly look around to see if anyone is there," volunteered Mari, with a somewhat strained look on her face. "You could stay with the *Aurora* and keep an eye on things, then if it gets dicey, you could get me off before something happens."

"Mari, I am surprised you would want to go on that thing without any accompaniment."

"Well, not really, but what if there are people on board, people who need our help?"

"You would not want to be alone to encounter the Principality on there, nor would I want you to disappear with the ship. Oblivion is not a good place."

"I so agree, but what if we don't try, what if there are people trapped in there?"

"I will not have you go on there alone," cautioned Neil. "I will not have something happen to you. You must stay here. I will go."

"But," she reminded him, "you know the *Aurora* better than I do, if something should go wrong I trust you to find a way to help me."

Neil thought it over, then replied, "I can't believe I am saying this, but there is a way for both of us to go aboard. Our communication system and field frequencies seem to be unaffected, thus making it possible for us to use the Remote. Of course there are no guarantees, but I think the *Aurora* is able to remain close at hand for a quick retreat. I would suggest taking weapons."

"I won't argue," she said. "I don't like this, but I feel we have to try."

"Are you sure?" he asked again.

"Yes," she replied, still determined.

"Can I ask another question?" remarked Neil, knowing how determined she was.

"Of course," replied Mari, having made up her mind.

"You know that 'grace' you are always talking about?" asked Neil, beginning to see the bigger picture.

"Yes?" she replied.

Neil gazed at the data displays, and replied, "Well, a little 'grace' would be appreciated right about now."

"I've already made a petition," informed Mari.

"Hmm," replied Neil. "I thought perhaps you might have."

A long narrow staircase formed between the two ships extending down from the *Aurora* to amidships on the wooden vessel. They decided against the silver exploration suits and opted for more conventional yellow rain gear. He also insisted that each of them carry a hand weapon called a Blasion, something similar to a pistol, but a curious device that was quite small and relatively thin that fired a highly charged laser guided bead.

After climbing down the lighted steps of the staircase they jumped the fourteen inch gap between it and the floating ship. After their feet touched down on the damp planking of the main deck Neil retracted the staircase and powered up the fields in order to park the *Aurora* about a hundred feet clear of the *Starlet*. There it would remain, keeping itself stable and motionless as telemetry was sent to the Remote.

The *Starlet* rolled with the waves in the moisture laden air as they crossed the deck and headed forward on the starboard side with their lanterns blazing. Occasional distant lightning bolts cracked through the air, brilliantly illuminating the oncoming storm in the ever darkening sky. Their progress was slow at first because the deck was in a mad disarray of ropes, pieces of canvas, deadeyes, rigging and other unidentifiable debris scattered about. For Mari, strange sounds were everywhere. It was an entirely new, although, eerie experience, yet she knew she must concentrate on task at hand. Amidst the slapping and creaking noises generated by the ship as a result of the wind and waves, she detected an unusual sound. It was as if small metal parts were striking one another ever so lightly. The sound was intermittent, somewhat flat, but delicate in tone. It was the musicality of it that caught her attention, but for now she put it in the back of her mind along with all the other odd sounds.

"This is a mess!" exclaimed Mari, as she carefully followed behind Neil.

"At least everything is stable on the *Aurora*," replied Neil, as he checked the Remote once more.

"That's good to hear," quipped Mari, trying to remain positive, "I hope it stays that way."

The central deckhouse was strangely empty. Neil made photographs using a camera capable of recording wavelengths above and below the range of visible light in an attempt to record as much information as possible. He would use this later for further study without having to actually remove any objects from the ship. Arriving at the forecastle they found the single hatch under its deck wide open. This was also empty with no trace of humanity, it was as if someone had tried to strip the cabins of anything not fastened down. Turning back toward the stern they carefully worked their way along the entire length of the ship on the port side. When they arrived at the stern Mari discovered the source of the tinkling sounds. Several old forks and spoons had been hammered flat and suspended from strings to form a crude wind chime. It hung from the railing on the poop deck close to the short companionway leading up to it.

Up on the poop deck at the stern they discovered that the ship's wheel had been lashed in place securing the ship on a straight-line course to nowhere. Their search eventually returned them to the main deck, where they took several steps down a short companionway into a series of small cabins below. This lower deck was about three and a half feet below the main deck and the ceiling of the cabin formed the deck of the stern four feet above.

Next they entered a portion of the cabin which made up the saloon or dining area and had several smaller rooms connected to it. From there they entered the captain's cabin at the rear, a cramped space, yet it provided a reasonable living area which was divided into three rooms. This proved to be somewhat cleaner and more organized than the rest of the ship. Stray items rested in neat piles around the cabin and a heap of old clothes lay in one corner, and four bowls and some spoons were on a small stand in another. A jumble of broken wooden toys spread across the floor, there were also crude drawings on torn pieces of paper neatly placed on a nearby chair. In the center of the cabin stood a medium sized table that had a raised edge to keep things from sliding off with the roll of the ship. Two small benches were pushed underneath.

While Mari looked around, Neil took his investigation back to the place where the mizzen mast came up through the cabin deck on its way to the deck above. A small desk was built around the mast and remained covered with multiple charts and a sextant. He discovered the ship's log in a small drawer under the desk, so he leafed through the detailed entries of Captain James Godwin and found that the ship was of American origin. The last pages of the log were missing or badly damaged, and the last legible fragment appeared to be written in haste. It was smudged, but it read: "We are soon to leave this ship and everything that is dear. The crew has fled. A dreadful shadow has fallen and I can no longer...if anyone reads...harken...." After more gaps and smudges: "...they are returning...cannot get to my wife... child... may God help you find your way off... wretched. May...God's...Grace...when you leave...." The last entry was dated, "July 22, 1883."

Neil called out to Mari, saying, "Come in here and look at this!"

Mari heard his voice echo through the cabin and she emerged from the sleeping quarters, saying, "What did you find?"

He read the log to her, then Mari, wondering if she heard his last words correctly, repeated, "1883?"

"If this date is correct we are standing on a ship that has traveled through time!" exclaimed Neil.

"How is that possible?" asked Mari.

"Jacob has some theories," remarked Neil, "although this could be something else."

"This ship seems so real!" exclaimed Mari.

"In the past certain ships have been discovered adrift with no living souls on board," replied Neil. "Vessels have actually been found completely intact, looking as though everyone had taken leave but never returned. No trace of the crew nor any passengers were ever found."

"Now you're scaring me!" declared Mari.

"Further examination of the log may reveal some answers," said Neil.

"That would be nice," understated Mari.

"Do you believe in ghosts?" asked Neil, paging back through the book to photograph the information.

"No," replied Mari, instantly, "well, I don't know. This whole thing is creeping me out."

"It could be an elaborate trap," Neil cut in, thinking out loud, pausing to check the camera.

"A trap?" replied Mari, with alarm.

"Although," returned Neil, "I think not."

"I hope not!" exclaimed Mari.

"This could be a planetary anomaly," returned Neil, "but the Seruzian Principality could use a condition such as this to their advantage."

"Okay," returned Mari, even more apprehensive, "now I don't know what you're talking about but I don't think we should stay here much longer."

"Do you want to leave now?"

"Yes...no...I mean we just need to be sure there is no one else here and get this over with."

"We can only guess at what happened here, indeed, we need to hasten our search."

"How is the *Aurora* doing?" asked Mari, hoping for some good news.

Neil checked the Remote, reporting, "No negative readings."

"I pray it stays that way," replied Mari, now checking her watch. The mechanical time piece was still working and providing the correct time. Then she handed him a wrinkled piece of paper. "There were several of these drawings in the sleeping quarters. Look at these odd shapes scribbled in the sky."

Neil thought the amateurish drawings looked rather appealing, but replied, "I can't tell what those shapes are above the ship, clouds maybe? Actually, it's not a bad drawing."

Mari's attention was suddenly pulled away, and she put her hand to her ear, saying, "I'm hearing distant static again."

"Like before?"

"Yes, just static this time, no voices."

"We must be vigilant."

"It's gone now."

"So what else did you see in there?" added Neil.

"I'd like to have you to take a look at a picture I saw on the wall in the other room," replied Mari.

"Just one moment," replied Neil, as he quickly photographed the last of the log entries and drawings of the ship.

All during the search there had been a slight breeze, accompanied by strong gusts of wind, which created a myriad of creaking sounds within the hull of the ship. Then, quite unexpectedly, there was a marked stillness. No wind at all, no groaning, or complaint of the ship. But, amid the uneasy silence, Mari's ears detected something else, and she said, "What was that?"

"What do you mean?"

"I think I heard footsteps."

"I did not hear anything. Was there static in those earrings again?"

"No static, it sounded like someone running on this ship!"

"Might it be your imagination?"

"No, I don't think so."

With added caution, they took the companionway up to the main deck to look around. They were not on the deck long before there was a very distinct crash of metal objects coming from somewhere forward on the deck below, which was a portion of the ship they had not yet searched.

"I definitely heard that!" declared Neil.

"Something was knocked over or kicked around," observed Mari, as her pulse quickened. "Someone must be on board!"

"Or some-thing," remarked Neil.

They both drew their weapons and stayed close. There was a square opening in the main deck that would allow them to climb down a ladder to the intermediate deck below, and when they did it greeted them with the stench of spoiled food and other unsavory odors which seemed to permeate everything. The deck was not divided up and the planking ran nearly uninterrupted along the full length of the ship except for two large hatches amidships, which allowed access to the hold below.

They worked their way forward through an appalling collection of clothes, food stores, tools, boxes, and ropes. Several rats skittered past their feet at which Mari managed to retain her composure. She was much relieved when the rodents disappeared into the dark recesses of the deck. Neil discovered a large quantity of books in several large storage crates, they were vintage with no yellowing and looked new. Only grain such as corn and wheat properly secured in unopened barrels appeared uncontaminated. Anything stored in a bag had been infiltrated by the rodents and their contents were scattered about the deck.

The relative calm soon began to give way to more wind and rain and the agitated sea increased the roll of the derelict ship. Water began finding its way through the decking as the vessel returned to its mournful complaining. Neil lifted the cover of the opening to the hold below and was assaulted by air that reeked with standing water of unknown depth. He called down into the water logged cavern but received no response. With nothing of consequence to be seen or heard he let the cover slam shut.

Their investigation soon brought them to a collection of pots and pans and other cooking utensils scattered across the deck.

"This could have been the source of the noise," observed Mari.

"I would agree," returned Neil.

A path through the cookware led Mari's eye to the bulkhead in the bow just ahead of her. There was a ladder leading up to a small hatch in the deck above, and next to it was a door that was partially obscured by the surrounding wood, making it nearly invisible but for a small latch. Mari advanced to the door and lifted the latch. The door easily swung outward and the room ejected yet another offensive odor. Her beam hit the hull to the right as she entered the space and the movement of coiled ropes hanging from pegs above her gave her a start. After searching the beams that supported of the deck overhead she found only more rope and dangling deadeyes.

Aiming at floor level, she directed her gaze to the left side of the compartment. Putting her hand to her mouth, she resisted the compulsion to scream, and backed out of the doorway. In her haste she tripped over the raised threshold of the hatch and nearly fell backward. At the same time the ship made a sudden roll to port as it heaved on the crest of a voluminous wave. With a look of terror in her eyes, she cried out, "Neil, come over here!"

Together they entered the room. There, propped against the outer wall of the hull by three wooden kegs they found the body of a middle aged female in a sad state of deterioration.

"How long do you think she's been in here?" questioned Mari.

"This is not what I hoped to find," remarked Neil, trying to stuff his emotions.

"Who could this be?" whispered Mari. Suddenly there was a noise just outside the room. "I heard something." Mari lit up the deck, but she could see nothing. "I thought I heard footsteps again just like before."

"Okay, but let's take a minute to check things out here," said Neil. He glanced at the Remote again and things still appeared to be stable on the *Aurora* so he took time to examine the scene. The clothes on the body were well worn, but consistent with the time period of the ship. Mari removed a piece of cloth covering the right hand and she was shocked to find a small gun. Yet, there were no indications of a serious wound, a struggle, or any trace of blood on the clothes that might reveal the cause of death.

"We cannot do anything for her now," said Neil, "but we do need to find out what else is going on."

"The poor woman," said Mari, grieved by the sight.

"May she rest in peace," added Neil.

"I can't wait to get off this thing," groaned Mari.

"Agreed," replied Neil.

Neil photographed the scene and closed the door to the compartment. Next they headed back to the stern by way of the intermediate deck to climb up the ladder they used earlier to climb down, deciding to take one more look through the captain's cabin at the stern. By now the weather had changed from drizzle to blustery sheets of rain. Their weapons were ready as the moving shafts of their lantern light bathed the blackness before them. Neil was the first to enter the captain's quarters again and his lantern surgically probed the corners for any sign of something amiss. Mari decided to investigate the sleeping quarters again and cast her light inside, then, once again her heart skipped a beat. Neil arrived at her side and flashed his beam next to hers, now both lights shone brightly on a small frightened figure huddled next to one of the bunks. The frightened being did not have the appearance of an alien, but looked very human, and was certainly not a ghost.

Mari put away her weapon and knelt down on the deck to greet what appeared to be a youth, saying, "Hi, Honey, don't be afraid. We are here to help you."

There was no response on the part of the one huddled by the bunk except to withdraw from Mari's advances. Now it could be seen that this was a young girl clothed in old brown overalls, a faded gray shirt, and well worn shoes.

"What is your name?" asked Mari. There was still no response. "Can you tell me your name?" The girl made no eye contact so Mari crept closer. "My name is Mari, what is yours?" Mari then signed to Neil to stay back a little as she again pleaded. "Honey, won't you please tell me your name? We want to help you."

The one huddled by the bunk spoke in a barely audible tone, saying, "Name?"

"Yes," replied Mari, "please tell us your name."

"Grace," said a small voice. "My name is Grace."

Neil just stared incredulously at Mari as she spoke to the girl again, saying, "Grace, oh that's a very pretty name. My name is Mari and this is my friend Neil. We have come to help you. Are you okay?" There was no response. "Grace, where are your parents?" Mari saw that her lips were moving but she couldn't make out the words so she addressed the frightened girl once more. "Honey, where is your mother and father?"

A pair of lonely eyes turned to Mari, saying, "Father drowned."

Mari was saddened by the statement, but replied, "Oh, we're so sorry. Where is your mother?"

"In room," she replied.

Mari was grieved but not surprised, and though aware of the girl's distress, she still sought confirmation, saying, "Is the lady down below in that room your mother?"

"Mother won't wake up," replied Grace, slowly. "Mother is sleeping in the room."

"Is there anybody else here on this ship?" asked Mari.

"No one," replied Grace. "No people here."

"Where did they go?" asked Mari.

"Alone, just alone," replied Grace.

"Will you let us help you?" asked Mari, gently prodding.

"Help my Mother?" asked Grace, timidly.

"I'm sorry," replied Mari, "but we can't help your mother. Your mother is in heaven now, she is in a better place."

Neil whispered into Mari's ear, "I did not realize it at the time, but I think the captain must have been referring to his daughter when he mentioned Grace in his log. It's obvious that we can't just leave her here alone."

Mari whispered, "She appears to have Down's Syndrome, I hope she—"

Grace blurted out with her loudest voice yet, "Get off this ship! Mother said to get off this ship when the nice people come to find me."

Mari made use of the opportunity, and replied, "Yes, Grace, we will help you get off this ship. We would love to have you come with us." The roundish face brightened slightly and Mari thought to ask another question. "How old are you, Grace?"

The girl answered, "Eighteen—I am eighteen."

"Oh my!" exclaimed Mari. "Can you stand up for me please?"

Now on her feet, the girl's physical condition appeared to be rather good considering the terrible circumstances. She willingly followed Neil and Mari through the cabin as drops of rain rapped on the windows of the ship. They took the steps of the companionway up to the main deck and once there they were greeted by the rain and wind. But Grace let out a terrible scream and tore away from them like a freighted animal, and before they realized it, she was climbing the ratlines of the mainmast with astonishing speed until she reached the crow's-nest. She remained there, clutching onto the mast and rigging.

Mari began calling up to the girl, "Grace! Please come down, it's dangerous up there."

No amount of convincing would change her mind. Then Neil thought to glance back toward the stern of the ship. What he saw spiked his adrenaline. The stern and all of the structure beyond the mizzen mast seemed to be fading away. But Neil was questioning something else, saying, "Why would she be so afraid of us now?"

"I don't know much about ghost ships," said Mari, "but doesn't the *Aurora* look a bit scary out there?"

Neil observed how their ship was glowing quite elegantly in the mist, but considered Mari's observation and turned to her, saying, "Sometimes I forget. Even so, we have to get her down from the mast."

"She must be scared," said Mari. "We have to do something!"

"I have an idea," replied Neil. "I will need you back on the *Aurora*."

By using the remote he brought the *Aurora* closer to the *Starlet*, as Mari complained, "I don't know about this."

"You get on board," replied Neil. "Once there, I want you to retract the staircase. Move away from the *Starlet* and wait for my signal. I'll go up there and try to meet her on her own terms."

Grace recoiled at the maneuver and became even more alarmed as a long set of steps began to form down to the deck. Mari was still unsure, but followed Neil's direction. When she was aboard she retracted the staircase and found her way to the bridge.

The thought of climbing the rigging of an unfamiliar ship at night in the rain was not at all appealing to Neil, but with both feet on the rope ladder he began to climb. He suffered little apprehension in most situations but this time he couldn't shake off an old nemesis—a fear of heights that would grip him at unpredictable moments— perhaps it was the rolling of the ship, or just hanging on to wet braided rope in the dark, or the torrents of rain along with the thought of the distance one would fall with only a slip of the foot.

"We want to help you, Grace," cried Neil, as he neared the crow's-nest. "Please come down to the main deck."

"No," she cried, with more determination. "Not going down!"

"Will you let me climb up there with you?"

"No," she said, firmly.

Grace kept an eagle eye on him as he finally reached the bottom of the platform, but she didn't protest when he finally climbed up on her perch. They were now very close to each other and they had to brace themselves against the wind. A stunning birds eye view of the entire ship was to be seen at this location. This also allowed him to see the stern of the ship as more and more of it began to fade from view, dissolving away into the blackness.

"I bet it's very nice up here on a sunny day," remarked Neil.

Grace brightened and her face suddenly produced the very essence of wisdom beyond her years. A great gust of wind filled what was left of the sails and the movement of the ship became more pronounced. In what became a dramatic shift of position, the ship rolled to favor the port side amid more lightning strikes and distant rumbles.

"You are very nimble up here, Grace," admitted Neil, as he steadied himself. "You must know this ship very well!"

Grace looked at him confidently saying, "Father taught me."

Loud groans erupted from the wooden vessel as if it might break apart. The lantern on Neil's belt swung freely and occasionally flickered on the pleasant child-like face before him but even here her eyes seemed both kind and mysterious.

Mari received more instructions from Neil to reduce to minimal field power and use the running lights, then to initiate a tilt towards the *Starlet* at about a fifty degree angle downward. As this was accomplished the energetic fields of the *Aurora* were no longer casting an eerie blue light on the surroundings, instead, it glowed from within. Every vivid detail was illuminated. The cameos fluttered and the antennae blinked happily as it made several slow revolutions clockwise like a gleaming carousel. Mari and Meadow were within sight on the bridge and Mari waved as she walked along the deck to stay within view.

"That's our ship, Grace," said Neil. "We can help you get off of this bad ship."

Grace seemed to be mesmerized by the sight, saying, "Pretty!"

Neil reassured her, saying, "Mari will be back soon to take you to where it is safe and warm." Neil then communicated to Mari. "Now level out and move in close and energize the staircase. Put the ship on auto stabilization, then come out to meet us. We can do this."

The *Aurora* ceased rotation and leveled out as Mari gently eased in closer, still remaining above the rolling ship near the port side. The staircase formed at the base of the hovering craft and extended to within inches of the crow's-nest of the *Starlet*. Fear was showing in Grace's eyes, but soon Mari came walking down the steps. The roll of the *Starlet* occasionally took the mast away from the welcoming staircase, and though the *Aurora* was quite stable and compensated for most of the movement of the floating ship, the timing had to be right for them to jump the changing space of the gap.

Mari reached out from the platform, saying, "Come with me, Grace. It's not good for you to stay here."

"Please, go with Mari," urged Neil.

"The sounds," signed Mari, "I'm hearing them again."

Neil signed back that he understood.

Although still fearful, Grace approached Mari. Suddenly there was a loud crack and an unnerving thud. The yard arm just below the feet of the two people on standing on the crow's-nest had just broken free of the mast and impacted on the open deck below. More of the stern was also giving way to nothingness, creeping closer by the minute. Mari reached out to Grace again and this time the girl responded. Their fingers touched and Grace held onto Mari's hand as they stepped onto the platform of the staircase. Hand in hand they climbed up the illuminated steps to the vessel above with Neil trailing closely behind.

Once everyone was safely inside the ship the staircase dissolved away and the *Aurora* became rigged with its own set of sails. A thin white fog rapidly formed over the nineteenth century vessel on the water and within seconds the sphere returned. In a brief but intensified flash both the sphere and the *Starlet* disappeared.

While Mari brought Grace clean clothes, some food, and tended to her needs, Neil researched the early entries of the captain's log. Within the photographic evidence he found the date Grace was born: February 20, 1865. Furthermore, he discovered that the ship had apparently entered the anomaly for an undetermined amount of time on that date then somehow sailed out of it again. This suggested Grace could have been born in another time period other than 1865. Years later, on July 22, 1883, the *Starlet* crossed the exact spot again and encountered the same anomaly that brought it into the present.

Grace and Mari were now sitting on the floor the galley. Meadow had taken to Grace immediately and was on her lap as she paged through a book on Wyoming. Neil eventually headed down from the bridge to join them. Handing the earrings back to Mari, he said, "I tested these and I could not find anything amiss, but I did tweak them a little."

"I definitely heard something out of context back there on the *Starlet*," replied Mari as she secured the earrings to her ears. "I admit I really miss these things when I don't have them."

"It is possible you may have picked up the static from the anomaly or it could be something else entirely," said Neil. "I re-tuned some of our communications equipment. Hopefully, we will pick up the aberrant signals during the next occurrence."

"I hope she will be all right," said Mari, thinking about Grace and her future.

"She seems to be okay for now," replied Neil.

"She appears to be accepting all this," said Mari, "but I don't know what she's really thinking. She doesn't talk much and only makes simple statements. She also seemed a bit listless, so I let her look through some of our picture books."

"It's difficult to ascertain all of her abilities or disabilities without doing some tests," said Neil, "but I want her to feel more at home before we push for answers."

"Her parents must have impressed her with a desire to learn," said Mari. "There are some positive signs."

"Things are not so simple," added Neil.

"We will just it one day at a time," said Mari, "all of us are complex beings so who are we to judge?"

"True enough," added Neil.

"I asked her about those drawings," added Mari. "She admits to drawing them, but she won't talk about it. I think she just needs some time."

"Time, maybe she has all the time she needs," said Neil. "She may know something about time we do not. Although, I find that in some strange way, I identify with her. Like her, I seem to be caught between worlds and held captive. I know what could be, I see the potential of tomorrow, then life moves swiftly along and all I can do is watch it drift by. I do not know the direction of all this. Maybe things are just getting to me, Mari."

"I know what you mean...it has been a long day."

"We all could use some real sleep."

"There is something about her though," remarked Mari, "I don't know what it is yet, but it's something positive, something about hope."

"Yes," agreed Neil. "I find it to be so."

Chapter Seventeen: Enmity

Good and evil abide in this world,
But enmity is like death.
How is it that we live so far from perfection?
Mari

October 11, started out as a day of leisure on their South Pacific Island of choice. It was a warm Sunday afternoon, Grace and Mari were engaged in a game of tag and Neil was sitting comfortably under two small trees in an unusual state of relaxation. Grace had just been tagged by Mari, so Grace was in hot pursuit. The surf was surging in and the view along the beach was as enticing as one might find, but Mari wasn't thinking of that, she was more intent on not letting Grace catch her. In a youthful burst of energy Grace came sprinting out from some trees. This took Mari by surprise. Grace touched Mari on the back, and shouted, "You're it!" In turn Mari bolted for Grace, but with a squeal of excitement Grace dodged the attempt. Mari eventually managed to catch up as they both ran in the direction of the ship and reaching out she tapped Grace on the shoulder. Grace immediately turned and made a desperate lunge toward Mari. Mari ran and would have gained some distance had she not caught her foot on a piece of half buried driftwood. The normally agile woman made a gallant effort to catch herself but was unsuccessful. Grace burst into laughter over the way sand flew up into the air from the misstep. Mari had landed on her back, flopping down like a rag doll, unhurt, but completely out of breath from running and the subsequent fall. Recovering, she exclaimed, "Grace, you're wearing me out!"

Still excited, Grace ran up and touched Mari on the back, saying, "Your it, Mari!"

"I know Honey," admitted Mari, "but I need to rest a minute."

"I can run fast!" said Grace, holding still for a moment. "I like to climb trees too."

"I know you can," said Mari. "I couldn't even climb up that last tree you found!"

"Are you okay over there?" called Neil, concerned about the acrobatic spill.

"I'm okay," replied Mari, shaking the sand out of her clothes. "The only casualty is my pride."

"I can climb good!" said Grace, again.

"Yes, my Dear," replied Mari, "you can."

"I like you Mari," popped Grace. "You play nice!"

"You're a lot of fun too, Grace," replied Mari.

"You make me laugh," returned Grace, with a giggle.

"This certainly was a lot of fun," returned Mari, "but I think it might be time to get back inside."

"Let's go!" shouted Grace, ready to run again. "I'll beat you there!"

"You're on!" cried Mari, as her spirit returned.

Grace ran ahead and was the first to enter the module, then she willingly returned to her quarters with the cat not far behind. Eventually, everyone ended up in the Galley.

"Grace said she was hungry," remarked Mari, "so I thought this was would be a good time to eat."

"If that's the case, I will stay," said Neil.

"She has a good appetite now," said Mari. "I think it helps to go outside. She's doing better than expected. And, if I might say so, so am I."

"The air is good for us all," returned Neil.

"Food 185.57 degrees," announced the oven.

"I could get used to this culinary unit," said Mari.

"I have observed how you are quite at home in here," said Neil.

"The coffee is ready," said Mari.

"Then it is complete," complemented Neil.

"Of course," replied Mari.

"I cannot thank your parents enough for the food drops," said Neil, admitting to a certain dependency.

"They're glad to do it," she added.

"Food ready," came a voice from the oven.

"I like the computer," said Grace, sporting an infectious grin.

"You do?" said Mari, surprised by the announcement. "And, why is that?"

"I like to hear words and music," replied Grace. "It talks and sings. Mother read from the Book. She sang to me too."

"She did?" replied Mari.

"What kind of book did she read to you?" asked Neil.

"Mother and Father called it the 'Good Book,'" replied Grace.

Mari raised an eyebrow and glanced at Neil, then asked Grace, "Did your mother read from that book often?"

"Always," replied Grace. "Mother and Father did."

"They were wise," said Mari.

"The food smells wonderful!" exclaimed Neil.

Totally without a prompt Grace added, "The Good Book says we should always be thankful!"

Mari responded to the admonition, and said, "Grace, would you like to pray for the food?"

"Okay!" answered Grace, and she quoted from Psalms, saying, "'Thou openest thine hand, and satisfiest the desire of every living thing....'"(1)

Mari acknowledged with a resounding, "Amen."

Grace, as they soon discovered, was quite well mannered. As the days continued, her skills began to improve in unexpected ways and she remained very pleasant company, yet, she kept many things to herself, speaking selectively, never revealing how her mother died nor how her father's life ended so tragically at sea.

It was an extraordinary ship; an admixture of technologies, a unique system of power and of control, but anything contrived by human ingenuity could not endure without accruing certain deficiencies. The critical systems of the *Aurora* required routine monitoring and periodic maintenance to remain at their full operating potential. Neil also knew that neither he nor his crew had the necessary capabilities to meet every technical demand. He needed someone who was part engineer, part inventor, part mechanic, and part magician. Perhaps not the latter, but someone with the skill to leap across the boundaries of convention. The person he had in mind was Jacob Smithson.

Smithson had originally planned to work with Neil on some of his early projects but impulsively took another direction. He also planned to get married and to settle down, to start a new life, then unexpectedly the wedding plans fell through. He was on a different course and as time passed his correspondence with Neil stopped all together. Then there was yet another issue—after the infamous mining disaster the man Jacob once knew had been declared dead.

Jacob took a professorship at a major university out east. He also possessed a heart for people in need, so at this time in his career he was on sabbatical, and taking time to become involved in a science and education program in Afghanistan. Presented with the right opportunity, Jacob was a man willing to take risks, and this brought him to a particularly volatile section of the country, where various factions were fighting among themselves.

Neil put a call through to him but it was received with considerable skepticism. His suspicions were not allayed, even though Neil eventually convinced him that they needed to speak face to face. Because of previous commitments, Jacob insisted on meeting at the home where he was now living. This was a traditional residence located within a small village, one recently decimated and reduced to rubble by conflict, where few wanted to redeem it. At present Jacob had the entire dwelling to himself as the host family had taken leave to visit with some ailing relatives for a few days.

The *Aurora* slid undetected through the night, silently cruising by stealth at a low altitude until it made an inconspicuous landing in the vicinity of the house. This happened to be within the confines of two open walls of a collapsed three story building. Near this, and en route to the dwelling, spread a low mound of refuse containing the shattered remnants of former lives.

Neil could barely contain his excitement over the up coming reunion but Mari couldn't help feeling uneasy about the visit. She voiced her concern, when she said, "It still seems to me like Jacob would be more receptive at a later date. Isn't there any other way to do this?"

"He assured me of his cooperation, at least for a brief meeting," Neil replied. "Time is of the essence, and I don't think it would be appropriate to just park the ship by his door then jump out and say, hi!"

"I know that," snapped Mari, a bit on edge.

"This is important," replied Neil, tactfully. "Besides, you will not be far away."

"I want the same thing you do," she scolded. "Sometimes everything else disappears and all you can see is the thing at hand."

"All I am saying is—" countered Neil.

"And," Mari injected, "all I'm saying is that I have other concerns."

"Yes, I am aware," he replied, realizing her concern, "and I should not be long."

"You know I'll help in any way I can, but you know I'm still learning about this ship," she replied, still hoping he might see it from her perspective.

"I know," replied Neil, "but its in good hands."

"I'll get through this I guess," she answered.

"It has been a long time," he replied. "I want to be sure Jacob is ready before I reveal certain things."

"It's just a feeling I have," she added. "There's so many unknowns."

"Like that dream of yours?" he replied.

"You know how I feel." She didn't have to say any more, for the look on her face told him everything.

"I am trying see this thing form all angles, including yours," said Neil, justifying his position. "Jacob is where he is because he hopes to improve the quality life for the people here."

She acknowledged his point, saying, "I realize the situation, but you know—"

"I desperately want to rebuild our team," replied Neil. "I am not going to some alien planet or some ship deep in space, I am going to visit his humble abode. I must find out where his present loyalties are then I must persuade him to resume something he abandon long ago."

"I hope he finds you to be the friend he remembers."

"Such is my hope, Mari, you will like him when you meet him."

"If he is a friend of yours, I know I will."

"I will make this as short as possible."

"I am on your side," reminded Mari.

"I know you are," said Neil. "If alien forces seek to break down our planetary door, then I believe Jacob will be of immeasurable assistance, also I believe he might be able rekindle his love for a new frontier."

"Just remember," returned Mari, "I'll be glad when you are back aboard this ship."

No other human presence could be detected in the area when Neil made the short journey from the ship down several dusty streets to the house. The house was quiet, a dim glow was coming from a small first floor window adjacent to the front door, this somehow made the home seem more inviting. Neil confidently knocked on the door, and it wasn't long before Jacob opened it. The man stood in the doorway with a flashlight in his hand looking rather gaunt in the artificial light. His casual attire was a bit unkempt and his dark hair was slightly ruffled. He also appeared somewhat shorter than Neil remembered, this was partially due to the fact that Neil was now standing on his own two feet. Jacob nearly blinded his guest with his flashlight, even so, he politely greeted the person at his door, saying, "Hello, may I help you?"

Neil happily dodged the bright beam, and replied, "Good evening, Jacob."

"Who are you?" said Jacob.

"I'm your friend, John Shepherd," replied Neil.

"This must be a joke!" said Jacob, not believing his eyes. "First I got the phone call—"

"This is no joke, I am John," said Neil.

"If you were John you would not be walking up to my door," returned Jacob, "nor would you be speaking as clearly as you do. Besides, if I remember right, the man is dead."

Neil knew Jacob would most likely be expecting to see or hear the arrival of a land vehicle and expecting him to arrive with a few other individuals assisting with his mobility, so he said, "You would be expecting a wheelchair, but I can explain."

"So you think you are John Shepherd?" replied Jacob, with increasing sarcasm, "What about that old nick name?"

"It's Neil, of course," said the man outside the door. "I stopped using for a time, remember?"

"That's right, you may resemble John, but no, you have yet to convince me."

"Then give me a chance."

"I say, it can't be!"

"Jacob, please let me explain."

"Why should I believe you?" countered Jacob. "First, you call me up...I should have hung up on you. Then you tell me you're not dead, now you come walking up to my door! I'm sorry I invited you here."

Jacob shut the door rather hard in Neil's face, leaving him standing in the dark, but Neil wouldn't give up at the rebuff. He banged on the door again. The door remained closed, but he waited patiently a minute or so, then he knocked again. Suddenly the door opened, and Neil said, "Please, I have come a long way to see you."

"If you are telling the truth," retorted Jacob, "great strides in medicine must have taken place!"

"Okay, how about this," said Neil. "Remember that time when we were kids and you had a tree house? You used to hoist me up in that sling you made. We would talk about space travel. Do you remember when we talked about floating among the rings of Saturn?"

"There are a few other people that know about that story."

"All right, do you remember when we talked about building an engine of light, like the one in your dream one hot August night as you slept in a tent in your back yard? You told me you saw a large orange spiral with men walking around on it. It then became a blue ring of light that grew in size and the men spoke to you about a mathematical formula and you wrote it down. One day you shared it with me, but you made me swear to never tell another soul how it came about."

Jacob paused as if to reconsider his assessment of his old friend, then he said, "I have told no one about that story, only Neil would know what you have said. So, how did you make him tell you? Perhaps he broke his promise before he died."

"I will tell you all you want to know!"

"Please do!"

"I think you will want to hear this."

"Only if it's the real John Shepherd speaking," countered Jacob.

The man's defenses were dwindling and his curiosity was getting the better of him so he finally let Neil into the house. Neil notified Mari, giving her the signal to take the ship to the agreed location approximately one hundred miles distant. She would remain there until she received the signal to return. Although Grace took all this for granted, the pilot was not totally at ease. Mari would only be happy when Neil was united with them again. The preselected landing site was in a small valley in a desolate area with scrubby trees and rocky terrain. Here Mari and Grace would wait for the call.

However implausible it might be, Jacob was finally ready to accept the fact that this might actually be the man he once knew. The conversation was difficult at first but soon began to flow more freely, for there were many things they needed to catch up on. Indeed, their friendship had remained intact and soon it was as though not a single day had passed during their separation. Neil was gratified and it was not long before they resumed the dialogue which was so abruptly severed years before.

"John," said Jacob, "I must now confess, I'm glad you came. I had somehow forgotten how close we were and how we always seemed to read the mind of the other. But, forgive me if I reserve some doubt."

"I understand," replied Neil. "We made a great team back then. We can be again you know. And please, call me Neil...I'm using that name again."

"Okay, Neil," said Jacob, "our time together was great."

"It was indeed," replied Neil,

"But also sad because of your sister," Jacob added, still probing.

"Thank you," replied Neil.

"How did that happen exactly?" replied Jacob.

"Are you testing me?" returned Neil.

"Perhaps," said Jacob.

"She was shot," replied Neil. "Remember?"

"Ah, yes," replied Jacob, becoming satisfied with the answers. "So, then, your parents, they never recovered from your sisters death did they?"

"No," answered Neil, "and as time passed it was no easier."

"I'm sorry," said Jacob."

"So," replied Neil, "how are you holding up out here?"

"I look to the future," remarked Jacob.

"We all would like to see something better," agreed Neil.

"But now I'm thinking about the past," said Jacob. "Given the facts concerning the mining disaster, how did you survive? I heard everyone died!"

Neil answered, saying, "Things are not as they seem. First of all, it was no accident. It was designed as a cover for the next phase of our project."

"A coverup?" remarked Jacob, wondering what could be behind such drastic measures.

"There were many reasons."

"Such as?"

"That's what brings me here today."

"Okay, what is the reason?"

"The answer to that is product development."

"Of course, but certainly it must have involved the others?" inquired Jacob. "How are Gordon and Marcus? Are they still with you?"

Jacob hit a nerve, then Neil replied, "Not all things have gone well for us. There is a burden I need to share when the time is right. Things have changed."

"You can tell me anything," encouraged Jacob. "I have always respected you, I'm still your friend no matter what."

"Thank you," said Neil, contritely, "I am still learning."

"One's decisions may not always be right at the time," counseled Jacob, "but we must not dwell on the past. At some point we must move on. There is a greater good, and good things can emerge from failure."

"Your words are true," admitted Neil.

"Of course I'm right," replied Jacob, with a bit of a chuckle. "If you are planing to be in the area for a while why don't you stay the night?"

Both of them were at ease now, then Neil hastened to say, "Thank you for the invitation, but I can't stay long. Time is short and there so much to tell you...I hardly know where to start."

"You can start anywhere you like my friend."

"I am here to—"

"You aren't on the run are you?"

"Not in the way you might think," said Neil, with his eyes fixed on Jacob. "First, I must reveal another matter. As part of the secrecy regarding our project, I have taken on a new name."

"You are a fugitive?"

"I can explain."

"A new name you say?"

"Yes, Neil Clayborn."

"Ahh, Clayborn you say? So what is this, espionage then? What are you telling me?"

"Please believe me."

"Are you working for the government?"

"No."

"Then why the secrecy my friend, that is, if you are my friend? Why are you telling me this? Are your ideas so good that someone is out to steal them?"

"We have developed something very attractive."

"But, to change your name completely?"

"I was dead, remember?"

"I guess, but what could be so important? What is the explanation?"

"I assure you I am still the same person you once knew. Yet, I must speak of two other people. Treasures that I did not expect to find. So much has happened—"

"You have already blown your cover," added Jacob, trying to be encouraging, but still not knowing what to think. "You might as well proceed. I will listen."

"You are so right," said Neil. "Then, I must say, there is a special someone, well, her name is Mari."

"Finally, after all this time!"

"There could not be a more wonderful person."

"Ah, Neil, you're in love, yes, I can see it!" exclaimed Jacob.

"In some ways she is a lot like Celeste—"

"Go on," encouraged Jacob.

"She is so much more than I could have hoped for," Neil returned, with evident excitement.

"You are married!"

"No, Jacob, but I must say our work has brought us together...a lot."

"An extended courtship then?"

"We have an excellent relationship, yet one that is rather shall we say, complicated."

"These things always are."

"I have respected her values," informed Neil. "I haven't, or I should say we don't...I don't know her...I mean, I can honestly say that the flower is still pristine."

"I see," replied Jacob.

"I would have it no other way," added Neil, "but—"

"You say there is another?" questioned Jacob.

"Yes, there is!" replied Neil. "Her name is Grace."

"Neil?" questioned Jacob, with a discerning frown.

"No, it's not like that!" replied Neil, defensively. "This one has an extraordinary history for such a young person. Part of her narrative includes certain disabilities, also there is the subject of your recent research, and with your help we might possibly help solve the enigma of her past."

"My research?" questioned Jacob.

"Yes," Neil concurred, "I am talking about time travel!"

"Time travel?" returned Jacob, now wondering what his friend was up to, yet struck by the tantalizing nature of the subject. "In that case you have definitely piqued my interest! But seriously, Neil, I am wondering about you, aren't you stretching things out a bit."

"Have you heard any news from the States lately?" asked Neil.

"No," replied Jacob, "I guess I haven't. I have been awfully isolated here, it's been taking all of my time."

"Have you heard about the incident concerning the recent solar eclipse?"

"Oh, yes, it was all over the news. There was something about objects in the sky."

"Have you heard about Wyoming?" probed Neil.

"Only the reports of some strange sightings in the US and Canada," replied Jacob. "I didn't pay much attention, but it did get me thinking about certain things. You see, I've given up on some of those grandiose ideas."

"Life has a way of redirecting one's perspective," suggested Neil.

"It does," said Jacob, now contemplative.

"I pursued those ideas, Jacob," informed Neil.

"So," replied Jacob, "you must be helping the authorities make sense of it all back home?"

"That would be questionable at this point," replied Neil. "You could say I plan to be of more assistance in the future." Neil stood up from the comfortable chair to stretch his legs. "I have come across great danger in my recent travels, I can't elaborate, but our work has definitely been tempered by it."

"Please, tell me," inquired Jacob, "what danger?"

"I will get to that," said Neil. "First I want to tell you about some of the positive things, developments that have changed everything we know!"

"I see you have worked miracles already!" replied Jacob. "Are you close to developing some prototypes then, say, of those propulsion systems we envisioned?"

"Actually," replied Neil, "those early ideas were a kind of springboard for what developed. But, I must now talk about the present, you, Jacob, are an excellent engineer and scientist. I have always desired for you to share in what is happening. Now I must confess I really need your help. That's why I am here, though we are not yet at the point of desperation."

"I know we've had some radical ideas," acknowledged Jacob, "but look at what you have done so far! Are you ready to develop a prototype?"

"The prototype, Jacob, has already been built," replied Neil, as new excitement emerged in his voice. "It works, and it works very well!"

"Our theories were correct?"

"Beyond imagination! I am talking about the far reaches of space."

"You propose to go into space?" replied Jacob, amazed at what he was hearing.

"Jacob, I have already been there!"

"Surely you jest, Neil, it would take great strides to execute such a thing!"

"Precisely," assured Neil, "and I need you to come with us out of this place so you can embrace this new technology. You could do so much more. In the end, you would be helping so many more people."

"You have my attention, but I don't know exactly when I can leave. I have commitments to the people here for a few more months. They are really moving forward because they want to improve their lives and their country. I am making a difference in the world and now we are pressing boundaries here as well."

"I have a great respect for what you are doing, Jacob, these people really do have needs, yet you could do so much more. That's why I beg you, please consider the things I have said."

"Certainly you have caught my interest," said Jacob, remembering his research, "but there are things I must consider."

Mari had seen to it that Grace was comfortable and tucked her in. And, after looking through some books on the stars and planets, Grace had fallen asleep on her bunk with Meadow at her side. Mari had returned to the bridge to monitor the ship and the external surroundings. She was determined to remain vigilant while she waited for the signal from Neil. All was well, but she felt like she was just treading water. At length, and now feeling confidant everything was under control, she decided to sit down to organize her thoughts and opened her journal. This kept her mind occupied with something she loved as she periodically glanced up at multiple screens and readouts. The time passed quickly as she let herself become absorbed in writing. After about forty-five unbroken minutes she glanced up, only to find that all the screens on the bridge had gone dark. The interior lighting was still operational but everything else appeared as if it had been switched off. She jumped to the controls and immediately checked each screen, hoping something might to return to life. After several unsuccessful attempts she consulted a check list of emergency instructions Neil had given her in case there were any changes in status. While doing this, the ever present hum of the ship ceased and all of the interior lights blinked once and went out. Now Mari was in complete darkness.

"What is this?" she cried. "Come on, this can't be happening!"

But, in the next instant the emergency lights came on and the registry screen near the pilot station that supplied vital information concerning the status of the ship came to life. It displayed a message, saying: "Connection error. Communications integrator module disconnected. Fluidic computer and mechanical restart from bridge not operational. Power systems active. Informational provision—IDU."

"Communications integrator module?" mumbled Mari. "IDU? What, no hand crank?"

A menu of options appeared on another screen so she consulted the list. She spoke audible commands, she used keyboards and touch screens, hit more buttons and moved more levers, she tried everything she knew but got no response. The reserve power was active but inaccessible. It was as if the ship had been paralyzed, all reminiscent of what happened during the Seruzian attack. Power was available to run some of the systems such as the emergency lights and the companion-module, yet when she tried to transmit a signal to Neil, the communication system failed to perform the task and none of the menu options seem to make sense. Then she remembered Grace, who was still in her quarters so she ran down to check on her. Grace was just waking up and totally unaware of what was going on, so Mari instructed her to remain in her cabin until she came back for her, but this meant that Mari was now on her own to search for the glitch.

The conversation with Jacob remained congenial, but Neil had been trying to clarify his intentions. In response Jacob was still trying to explain his situation, saying, "There's a lot going on here and it would be difficult to end things right now."

Leaning forward in his chair, Neil said, "I must stress urgency, though it may not seem logical."

"I don't see how I can jump out of my obligations," replied Jacob.

Neil kept to the point, "I say these things because—" Just then a beep tone interrupted him; an automated warning was telling him the ship was no longer transmitting or receiving radio signals of any kind. "Hmm, there seems to be a small problem."

"Nothing serious I hope?" asked Jacob.

"This is odd," said Neil, nervously rising to his feet and trying to establish a connection, he pointed to the Remote and emphasized his frustration over the loss of connection. "Some systems need updating, but this is somewhat disconcerting."

"Phones!" declared Jacob. "I get that stuff all the time out here."

Neil's eyes met Jacob's, and he said, "There is still so much more to reveal." Then after several more tries at reestablishing a connection he put the device back on its clip and sat down.

"What you are saying sounds so remarkable," remarked Jacob.

"Could you find someone to take over for you?" pleaded Neil, still trying to find an alternative.

"That may be the only solution," answered Jacob, "but it might take time to get them here. So, tell me, specifically, why do you need me so badly?"

A series of scuffling noises on the outside of the house by the front door caught the attention of both men. It was with one violent kick that the front door burst open sending the latch skidding across the floor. A man in a black military uniform now stood in the open doorway. He had a black ski mask over his face and he leveled an automatic weapon at Neil and Jacob. As the intruder marched into the house he was joined by a second man whose face was covered by a dark green mask. An automatic weapon was in his hands. Long knives were at their sides and only dark steely eyes were visible through the slots in the masks.

"Where is Jacob Smithson?" shouted the man in the black mask.

Neil and Jacob did not reply immediately so the man screamed again, "Where is Jacob Smithson? Tell us now or we will kill you both."

"I am Smithson," replied Jacob, giving in to the demand.

Neil inconspicuously activated an emergency signal on the Remote in hopes the glitch would eventually be resolved and Mari would respond.

"Who are you?" demanded the man, now glaring at Neil.

"A friend," replied Neil.

The man in the black mask barked another command, "Hand over your phones! Everything out of the pockets. Weapons, knives, everything. Now!"

Reluctantly, Neil pulled the Remote off its clip and held it out at arms length.

"Take it, AM," cried the man in the black mask to the other.

"Yes, MU," replied AM, and he grabbed the device.

Jacob slowly pulled some small items out of his pockets, a few coins, a pocket knife, a scribbled grocery list, a pen, and finally his wallet. He threw them down on the floor as AM scraped them up. Neil gave up a stubby pencil and a small piece of neatly folded paper but not the Blasion, which was hidden in a special pocket inside his shirt.

"Everything!" MU barked again.

"My phone is over there," said Jacob, nervously pointing to a small table by a wooden chair.

"Hands in the air," shouted, MU.

Neil and Jacob complied with the demand. AM handed the items to MU and the man tried to activate Jacob's phone, but the battery was dead. Finding it inoperable, he threw it into a far corner of the room. There was a steady glow from a small blue light on Neil's device, but MU ignored it and put the Remote in his shirt pocket as he shouted to his captives, "Face down on the floor!"

Neil and Jacob did as they were told. When MU turned to shut the door Neil pulled out the Blasion and got a clean shot at AM who was nearest in the line of fire. The man was knocked backward and he fell unconscious to the floor by the resulting discharge of the bead. MU turned around, he saw Neil with the weapon and lunged to the side as Neil fired at him. The shot hit a tall cabinet directly behind the intruder and it blew apart. Some of the fragments hit the armed man in the back with enough force to knock him down. Once MU was on the floor Neil grabbed his gun and pulled the large knife out of its sheath. Jacob jumped on him and held him down.

"I have some rope in the cabinet over there," said Jacob.

Neil fetched it and tossed the short strands to Jacob as he kept his weapon trained on the downed man. Jacob attempted to tie MU's hands together behind his back but MU managed to jerk free and went into a roll. He grabbed Jacob and pulled him down. Now MU was on top of Jacob, and as the two men struggled Neil fired at MU again but hit the empty sheath at his side. The discharge was partially deflected, leaving MU mildly stunned, but it was enough to cause him to let go of Jacob. Unfortunately, Jacob had also received some of the discharge, yet managed to get to his feet. MU lay on his stomach in a semi conscious state so Jacob proceeded to bind the man again.

"What is that thing?" groaned Jacob, feeling lethargic from the effects.

"Something new," said Neil, apologizing. "I am sorry for my poor marksmanship. Are you okay?"

"Yes," cautioned Jacob, "please, take better aim next time."

"I haven't had much time to practice," admitted Neil. "It's not much of an excuse I'm afraid."

"Well, I guess there are worse faults," said Jacob, as he handed the Remote back to Neil.

Neil tried to make another call, but had to admit he still didn't have a connection.

"Dropped calls!" complained Jacob.

"This may be the ultimate dropped call," returned Neil.

Then, to Neil's surprise, the Remote indicated satellite communication. It was Mari's voice, saying, "Neil, I got through! I'm using the emergency phone and it and it took some time to get it working."

"Good," affirmed Neil, "what is going on? I'm reading a communications failure over there."

"There's a message about some kind of integrator module," replied Mari. "The core screen is saying something about a disconnection."

"If that's true, Mari, then all computer related functions would be down."

"Yes, and I don't know what to do. Nothing works!"

"Everything is down?"

"The emergency lights are working and one small screen."

"Did it say anything about an IDU?"

"Yes, what is that?"

"It's an Instructional Diagnostic Unit. You will find it in the specialized instrument compartment on D Deck. You can take it to where ever you are working and it will guide you."

"Okay, but then what?"

"Go down to D Deck, there you will need to locate hatch B-10. You will find the integrator panels there. I can talk you through the diagnostics and repair. We have a situation here, so call me back when you are down there."

"What's going on?" she asked, now concerned about Neil. "Are you in trouble?"

"Don't worry about us," came his reply, "things are under control."

"Okay," she replied, "but give me a minute."

"Call me back as soon as you can," said Neil.

Jacob made a thorough search of the two men as Neil went over to the front door and looked around. He saw nothing unusual so he closed it and put a chair in front of it to keep it closed. Jacob suggested they call the local authorities, but Neil thought it best to question the men to get more information first to see what they were dealing with. However, MU remained uncooperative. Neil returned to the door again in an attempt to place a larger piece of furniture against it, but another violent attack thrust the door open. The chair hit Neil and knocked him to the floor and the Blasion flew from his hand, where it landed conveniently close to MU. Now two more figures stood in the doorway. Both wearing the same kind of black uniform. Their pistols were drawn as they charged in to take possession of the room, letting their heavy backpacks fall to the floor. One of the men immediately pinned Neil down with his foot as the other kept his gun trained on Jacob.

MU gave the order to bind Neil and Jacob, then said, "OM, what took you so long? Now cut these ropes!"

"We had to deal with some uncooperative people," said OM. "But now their blood runs in the street."

Once freed from the rope, MU jumped up, grabbed the Blasion off the floor and put it in his pocket, then he retrieved his knife and swung the rifle over his shoulder.

"What happened to AM?" growled OM.

"I don't know, but we're going to find out," said MU, glaring at Neil.

The men forced Neil and Jacob to sit up and kept them about ten feet apart. MU took a stride up to Neil and grabbed his hair with one hand and pulled out his knife with the other. After poking him in the back several times with the knife, MU said, "I have you now Mr. American!" He flashed the blade in Neil's face and after a few playful cuts to the air he pressed it against Neil's throat.

"Let him be," said Jacob, "he has done nothing."

"Silence!" cried OM, aiming his pistol at Jacob.

"He's done plenty and so have you!" retorted MU. "I could end this now."

MU sliced the air again with the knife, then thrust its sharp point into the calf of Neil's right leg. Neil groaned in pain but managed to retain his composure. OM and the one named SY, attended to AM lying on the floor but he couldn't be roused.

MU searched Neil and grabbed the Remote and stuffed it into his pocket. He also searched Jacob but found nothing. The Remote began to beep softly so MU pulled it out of his pocket, but slipped the device back in again, saying, "I will deal with this later."

Mari became concerned when there was no reply to her repeated attempts to contact Neil. He had insisted things were under control but now she wasn't getting an answer from him. Previously, they had agreed that if things didn't seem right she should not leave a voice message, instead, she was to send a coded text, so she sent, "Check the house."

Now she was left on her own to find the fault within the complex systems of the ship. During her search for the malfunction she spied a label pertaining to the Specialized Instruments compartment just as Neil had said. Within it she found an array of small tools neatly imbedded within a molded form. Some of the tools looked familiar, others were not, but next to these she found a device about the size of a brick. It had a display screen and the initials IDU on the top. She carefully removed it and discovered that it adhered to any surface she put it on. Then she placed it on the wall next to its own compartment to see what it would do. It began to display specific instructions pertaining to its location. Using the icons on the touch screen she entered a search for the CIM. Within seconds it provided instructions on where to find the appropriate panel in the access tunnel.

She took the device with her to the end of the tunnel, where she located the integrator panel and opened it. Inside she discovered a transparent circuit board dangling from three red, white, and blue tubes. The board was labeled CIM. It was obvious that it had become dislodged from something. There was a slot labeled A12 that would receive the rectangular board, but there were also two other empty slots exactly like it, labeled A13 and A14. She remembered the last time she suggested clipping something together with which she was unfamiliar and the words of caution that were offered up. Not wanting to short out the entire system she opted to proceed with caution so she went back to the IDU for more information and began talking to herself, saying, "If this thing is so important, why isn't the socket for it marked?"

A few seconds later the IDU began to produce instructions accompanied by audio information. It indicated the problem and instructed the user to go back to the tool cabinet to find an instrument designated CIM-PL-7. She then went back to the compartment and removed the instrument from the bedding and returned to the open panel.

As MU roamed around the room he remembered the items in his pockets and pulled out the Blasion. He examined it, then pointed it at various things, even at Neil and Jacob, but no matter what he did it would not fire. Each time he attempted to use it, the triggering mechanism would click, but nothing happened. In frustration he growled at Neil, "How does this thing work?"

Neil stayed silent so MU pulled his out knife and brought it within an inch of

Neil's face, and said, "Do you want me to carve you up? Now tell me how this thing works!"

"It has sensors," said Neil. "I am the only one who can use it."

"Fix it!" demanded MU.

"I cannot," replied Neil.

"Yes, you will," demanded MU, "or I will use this knife on you in an interesting new way."

"It is preset by the manufacturer," replied Neil, hoping to deflect any further inquiry. "I cannot change it."

"Probably CIA," grunted MU, pressing the flat blade of his knife against his captive's forehead. Still not finished, he dragged the point along Neil's left cheek just below his eye with enough pressure to draw blood. "See, I don't need your fancy weapon. This knife will be just fine to carve up a spy!"

"What will that prove?" taunted Neil.

"Ho!" cried MU. "It will prove you are weak, but I will deal with you later, Mr. American."

MU returned the blade to its sheath then gave a signal for the other two men to go up to the second floor. The sound of breaking glass and the crash of furniture soon reached the ears of Neil and Jacob.

"What do you think you will gain by all this?" asked Neil, trying to solicit information.

"First, I will tell you who we are," replied MU, now addressing Jacob, "because we are going to make an example of you. We get two for one this time. The world will soon know of the AWM. We will become strong. Soon everyone will know about the Anti Western Militants, but right now you will know me as MU 24. I will even tell you that man on the floor over there is AM 28. SY 33, and OM 27 are now right above your heads."

"What do you want from us?" asked Neil, defiantly drawing attention away from Jacob.

"Now we have two Americans to show to the world," said MU. "We will reveal the error of your ways. We know about America, we know its evil ways, we know its perversions."

"You are brothers to the destroyer of worlds," replied Neil, contemptuously.

"And you are someone who knows very little," countered MU "You will see the destruction of your own world. Our world will become strong."

"You will destroy your own world," replied Neil. "You are slaves to inferior ideas."

"We are no one's slave," snapped MU. "And you, Mr. American, have a smart mouth. It will be silenced. But first, you must tell me why are you here with this man, Smithson?"

"I am his friend," said Neil.

"Ah, so you are his friend," MU replied. "Well, good for us but not so good for you."

SY and OM finally came down from the second floor, the masks were off and they spoke together in low whispers as they came toward Jacob. OM grabbed Jacob, then SY took hold of Neil. Next they forced both men up the narrow staircase to the second floor. First Jacob, then Neil was to follow. After taking a few steps up Neil attempted to wrench himself away from SY. As a result both men tumbled down the steps. Neil managed to free himself momentarily, but SY grabbed him again and forced him back up the stairs, spurring him on with several kicks and a strike to the back with the butt of his gun.

The captives were finally taken into a room located in the front corner of the house, which had been completely stripped of its furnishings. Neil was compelled to sit against an outer wall directly below a window and Jacob was pushed to an inside wall directly across from Neil. A single light source revealed that the only two windows in the room had been draped with black cloth to block out the view. Each cloth had the AWM designation crudely painted in the center of it. Another such cloth was hung on the blank wall directly behind Jacob. After Neil and Jacob were positioned on the floor their captors set up a camera and a light in front of Jacob. By now their intent had become crystal clear to restrained men.

Mari tried several more times to get through to Neil, but she was getting no results so she turned her efforts to the repair at hand. Something at the bottom of the compartment got her attention. It looked like a small solid block of glass, which was not connected to anything, so she removed it. It was unimpressive yet had several equally spaced indentations on one side. She held it next to the IDU and it quickly identified the part as a regulator module and indicated the specific location within the compartment. Mari was then able to snap it back into place without any difficulty. Now there was one less thing to worry about. She was about to follow the instructions for the connection of the dangling board when she heard a muffled click. She stopped and held her breath to listen.

Sure enough there was another click but she couldn't determine where the sound was coming from. There was another click, then another, and another. The sound now seemed to be coming from the exterior of the ship, so she stopped what she was doing and crawled out of the access tunnel into the main circular chamber surrounding the companion-module. She lowered the light level within the compartment then crawled over to one of the floor level ports to see out but there was nothing but the dark of night. By then the clicking sound had stopped.

Now directing his rant at Jacob, MU said, "We have come to make an example of you to the world. We will bring in a new wave of followers to our cause."

OM turned the camera on and focused it on Jacob, and said, "Westerners like you must ask forgiveness for your corruption."

"Yes," said MU, "now we will show Monody 3845 how we will make you comply. We will start with you, Mr. Smithson."

"Who is Monody?" said Jacob.

"You are not to ask questions," bellowed MU, with contempt.

"You will do as we say!" insisted SY, striking Jacob across the face.

216

As this was transpiring, Neil was struggling with the ties around his wrists. The progress was slow, but he kept working on the restraints, then he asked, "Who is Monody?"

OM came up to Neil and struck him twice with a tightened fist, saying, "Shut up, we will tell you when to speak."

Mari was about to give up searching for the strange sounds and return to the repair problem when she saw a light flicker off in the distance. Someone was walking with a hand held light, moving about in the dark, casting the feeble beam hear and there. Then there were two, then three lights, all moving toward the ship. Mari began to see three shadowy forms. Now five people were approaching, two of which were of small stature. The group stopped momentarily to pick up stones and rocks then they began throwing them at the ship. When the stones hit the hull they made the clicking sound she heard earlier.

The pelting multiplied. After a few minutes the stone throwing ended and the group drew closer until they were standing under the ship. A young boy came up to one of the struts and began striking it with the rock he had in his hand as the others held their lights on him to watch in apparent amusement. The proximity of the strut was directly below the port through which Mari was looking. She could see most of the individuals below, but they couldn't see her because of the reflective properties of the ports. As she watched the group gather, it wasn't long before they seemed to be arguing with one another. Their flashlights momentarily revealed their faces and actions but their voices couldn't be heard. One young boy, having run out of stones, took off his shoe and began striking the strut with it as the others looked on with laugher. Mari wanted to keep an eye on the mischief but the urgency of the repair drew her back to work.

The dwelling had grown exceptionally quiet. OM left the upper room to return to the first floor as MU and SY stayed behind to guard Neil and Jacob. Perhaps only twenty minutes had passed when OM returned. Frustration was mounting within each of the men. OM grabbed Neil and made him stand up as if to move him to another location, but a strict command from MU made him keep Neil where he was so he was thrust back down to the floor.

"If you want to kill somebody why don't you kill me," groaned Neil. "Let Jacob go."

"That he may continue in his western ways?" taunted MU.

"I made you an offer," Neil retorted. "Take me, let Jacob go."

"We have a plan," said MU.

"He is of no use to you," replied Neil.

"No," cried Jacob from across the room, "let him go."

MU came up to Neil, saying, "You argue about who should die? I'm thinking about the ones we may deprive of your presence. Do you have a family? A mother, a father, sister, brother?"

Neil did not answer.

"Is there a woman?" asked MU. "Ha, a woman! Or is it a man? Is it Jacob? So now you keep quiet Mr. American. Yes, your ways betray you. That is why we need to make an example of you. I wonder who will mourn for you?"

Neil kept working with the restraints on his wrists as MU continued his rant, saying, "Who should it be Mr. friend of Jacob. Shall we will give those loved ones a present Mr. smart man? What if we give them your head? Don't you think that would be nice?"

The man remained a hair's breadth away from Neil stroking the handle of his knife. Neil began to feel the ties begin to slip, allowing him to finally free his hands. Then, Neil seized the opportunity to lunge at his captor. A struggle ensued, but OM was immediately on top of both men and managed to yank Neil back to the wall then held him down. Neil's left pant leg was pushed up in the scuffle and an unusually observant SY noticed a thick blue patch near his ankle.

Up to this point the intruders had not yet discovered the two miniature versions of the CMR device. Each of them adhering to Neil's body, one was on his upper torso, the other was on his lower left calf. SY tore away the patch on Neil's leg, then demanded, "What is this? Do you smoke?"

"Search him again," said OM, as he restrained his victim, "see if there's anything else."

SY patted and probed until he discovered the other patch on the right side of the chest and ripped it off.

"What are these things?" demanded SY as Neil began to lose physical control. The men were startled by what was happening to their captive,

MU questioned Jacob, saying, "What's wrong with him?"

"He's ill, maybe he needs those things so he can walk," said Jacob.

MU grabbed the strange patches away from SY to get a closer look, and said, "Tell me what these things are!"

Neil could not speak clearly and SY let him have a blow to the stomach as an indication of things to come. Each of the men took turns examining the devices, but they ended up in the pockets of MU's coat. The man fished around in the other pockets to find the Remote. He was fascinated by the technical devices he so despised.

"Why do you Americans trust in these useless things?" cried MU. After a few more minutes of play he attempted to break the device but it resisted the bending and the blows. In a fit of anger he threw it at Neil, where it hit him in the face and bounced to the floor. "Call your people, Mr. American, it does not matter now. Maybe they will hear you die!"

Neil struggled to get at the Remote, meanwhile, the men turned to Jacob and beat him. Finally, a heated discourse took place between the captors, they shouted, argued, and pointed at Jacob and then to Neil. SY pulled out his knife and waved it over Jacob. Neil managed to secure the Remote between the floor and his mouth. In this way he could hold it and touch it with the limited use of his right hand.

The arguing stopped and MU barked out orders to his men. He shouted at Jacob, ordering him to renounce his defiling activities and western education. SY went to the left side of the man as MU took a stance at his right and pulled out his blade. He placed the sharp edge against Jacob's throat.

As Neil struggled to activate the Remote with his free hand he could only watch in horror as MU gloried in the vulnerability of his victim. At the touch of a single icon on the small screen the Remote auto-dialed an encoded message.

Mari was determined to finish the repair regardless of what was taking place outside. She crawled back to the open panel and got back to the task at hand. She squeezed the tabs with the designated tool and plugged the dangling board into the A12 slot on the back of the compartment as indicated by the IDU. After that she made sure the part was firmly in place. Now the repair was complete. But even after the procedure was accomplished there was no change in the status of the ship. Mari knew she had followed the instructions precisely and she couldn't figure out why there was no immediate report or indication of what was or was not working. She reviewed and double checked everything. Her face revealed her anxiety as she checked the IDU again, which presently indicated that the system was detecting the repair. This prompted a sigh of relief on her part because there was no evidence of a short or malfunction. The stone throwing and clicking sounds began again and Mari wondered how much longer they would remain occupied with their mischief. As she nervously waited for something to happen a tone sounded and the IDU screen flashed a new message, saying that a system reboot was in progress.

She rested against the bulkhead and took a breath, wondering what was going to happen next, but within moments another message appeared indicating complete restoration.

Now on a mission, she put the IDU back into the tool compartment and crawled out of the access tunnel, then immediately headed for the nearest communication station to make a call to Neil. But by the time she arrived at the station on the companion-module bulkhead an alarm began to sound. The screen in front of her flashed with a message: "Remote emergency signal activated." So she punched the call button.

The pulse of a small blue light caught Neil's eye. The Remote was telling him there was communication on one of the emergency frequencies between the ship and his device. The device was also indicating an incoming call. He tapped an icon and maneuvered so that the Remote was close to his ear. He heard Mari, shouting, "Neil? Neil?"

But in return all Mari could hear was a mixture of agitated voices and someone shouting commands. She shouted back, "Neil. Are you there? There's an alert here. What's happening?"

Neil struggled to get the words out, saying, "Mar-i, come...quick!"

"I'm getting underway now!" shouted Mari. "Neil, what's going on?"

She heard more shouting in the background, then heard Neil cry out, "They...have...Jacob!"

"Who? Who has Jacob?"

"Mari!"

"What's happening?"

"Come!" cried Neil. "Now!"

There was a crackle in her speaker along with a grotesque cry for help followed by intense gurgling screams then an unspeakably grievous moan. "Neil!" shouted Mari, desperate to hear his voice. The connection went dead.

In the illumination of the single camera light Neil watched in horror as Jacob was being dragged out of the room. Half way down the staircase the men lost their grip and the body tumbled down the remaining flight of steps. Neil was wondering how long it would be before they would come for him. An unholy silence crept into the room as he tried to determine what was transpiring on the first floor. It seemed as though all he could hear was his own heart beating in the stillness, then it was broken by the sound of heavily booted feet steadily marching in unison up the dark narrow staircase.

Grace and Meadow were there to greet Mari when she arrived at Grace's quarters and Mari immediately instructed her to come up to the bridge with her. Grace took Meadow in her arms and did as Mari asked. When they reached the bridge it was still bathed with emergency lighting. A few small screens were displaying images of the people outside which revealed a large crowd gathering around the ship but there wasn't time to speculate.

Mari activated an automated sequence that instantly brought all the systems up to full power. This also brought the interior lights up to full intensity. Each of the viewports had gone into transparency mode when the ship was down and would be the last to shutter back to data screens. The people on the outside could now see two women looking back at them from inside the vessel but Mari wasted no time in preparing for departure. She directed Grace to take a seat as Meadow jumped on one of the consoles. The fields reached full power, the sails unfurled, and the individuals standing near the ship were blown to the ground by the resulting pressure wave. The struts retracted and the *Aurora* was away.

Mari engaged the semi automatic option to control the ship because she could use this feature to increase the previously selected speed along the flight path and still remain on course. She was unfamiliar with how the increase would influence the automatic controls, although she did understand the manual operation procedure. She also set into motion a complex sequence of events which initiated the defense capabilities. Grace sat quietly and coaxed Meadow onto her lap. She seemed to be aware of the situation and obediently stayed in her seat, watching the view screens project data as well as every move of the woman at the controls. The ship became facile in Mari's hands, though this time they were not traveling slowly in stealth, but attaining speeds of just over 1200 hundred miles per hour at an altitude of less than 200 feet in the dark of night.

When the ship reached the vicinity of the dwelling it automatically slowed. Their destination was coming up fast and Mari needed to manually slow the vessel down further under the assisted control. A clear path opened up as the ship closed in on the dwelling. She waited until the last moment to initiate breaking power but the vessel did not immediately respond to her commands.

AM was still unconscious on the first floor but the three other men had returned to the upper room of the house. They all stood around Neil as he lay under the window. One of the men broke out of the huddle and turned the camera and light on their subject. SY and OM grabbed Neil and yanked him into a sitting position. SY brought his knife up to Neil's throat as MU kicked away the Remote. MU grabbed his hair and thrust back his head. Then he drew his fingers sideways along Neil's throat and muttered, "This is your hour, Mr. American."

MU positioned himself with his knife in hand for the lethal stroke, tensed and ready, with the glimmer of victory in his eyes. But in the next instant there was an explosion of splintering wood and flying glass, the black cloth that covered the window wrapped itself around the crystal sphere of one of the antennae on the *Aurora*'s outer rim. It rode the sphere as the antenna penetrated nearly ten feet into the room like a saber, striking MU squarely in the head. The knife flew from his hand and he was thrust to the floor unconscious. SY and OM fell back as the camera and the light hit the opposite wall. The black cloth slid off the antenna after it came to a stop and dropped to the floor.

When the struts were down and the ship at rest, Mari activated a low intensity Ring, the effects of which burst into the entire structure. The men inside immediately became immobile. She grabbed her parasol and a pair of night vision spectacles designed to resembled a pair of sunglasses then took another CMR with her just in case it might be needed. She told Grace to stay aboard the ship and to wait for her return.

Mari cautiously entered the open doorway of the house and searched the lower rooms. She found AM on the floor still unconscious but there was no sign of Neil or Jacob. She located the staircase and the small room next to it. Inside, she discovered Jacob's body. Sickened by the brutality and afraid it might be Neil, she turned away, but on a second look she discovered it was not Neil after all. Suddenly she was alerted to a crunching sound on the floor above. SY had recovered from the Ring and was making his way out of the upper room in the dark. Her glasses allowed her to see him at the top of the stairs with gun in hand so she activated the parasol. The discharge sent SY tumbling down the steps where he landed at her feet unresponsive. She picked up his gun and threw it across the room, then climbed the steps which were now slippery with blood. Led by the light of the ship's glowing antenna she found the second floor room. She removed the guns from the unconscious men and threw them out of the building.

As Mari was assisting Neil, MU had awakened from the strike to his head and the effects of the Ring. He bolted for her, but she jumped away. She also managed to duck successive swings and thrust a boot into his stomach. The man fell backward, but he managed to recover his footing. Mari now found her back against the wall. Gripping the parasol, she flipped it open and let the discharge crumple her attacker into a silent heap in the middle of the room. Then returning to Neil she attached a

221

new CMR to his belt. He recovered his strength, and now was able to walk so she urged him to get out of the building.

"Where is Jacob?" he asked.

"Down stairs I believe," said Mari, picking up the Remote.

"Of course," he mumbled.

"I'm sorry about the landing," said Mari. "I was trying to get here as fast as I could."

"You did great," replied Neil, pointing at MU still laying on the floor. "You gave that miscreant a firm punch in the face with the ship."

"The communication system went down completely," complained Mari.

"It looks like you did a good job of it," replied Neil.

"It took some time," replied Mari, "but I think everything is back in place."

"You are here," said Neil, "and that is a good thing."

"We must go now," urged Mari.

"What about Jacob?" asked Neil, now searching MU's pockets to retrieve the two CMR patches and anything else of importance.

"I'm afraid we can't help him," Mari replied.

"Where did they take him?" asked Neil.

"Down stairs."

"I tried to stop them."

"I know."

"Maybe the Ambhuri could help?"

"No, Neil, they can't. The authorities will take care of this now. They will bring their own justice to this."

"Authorities? What justice? I must see him. Where is he?"

"There's nothing we can do for him now."

"Why not, the Ambhuri helped you?"

"Even the Ambhuri can't help this time."

As they left the upper room Neil insisted, saying, "I must see him."

When he entered the small room he saw the pool of blood and the abhorrent dismemberment of the body. He assaulted the wall, and cried, "They beat us...they took everything...they—"

"I know," assured Mari, "you did what you could."

"They killed him," shouted Neil. "Mari, they killed him!"

He broke down but Mari urged again, saying, "I know, I know, but we need to go, there is nothing we can do for him now. Some of these men might regain consciousness soon."

Neil took a blanket and covered the body and the two of them made their way back to the ship. Mari didn't want to leave Neil alone, but she was concerned about Grace because she was not on the bridge when they arrived. She said, "Will you be okay for a minute? I need to check on Grace."

"Yes, go," he assured her, then he let his own frame fall helplessly into the pilot seat. The men in the upper room were now coming around as the two men on the first floor staggered up the steps to see what was going on.

Neil was fighting with the rolling tide of his emotions as he took the controls of the ship. The landing gear retracted and he backed the vessel away from the building to pull the antenna out of the gash. Once the ship was clear he brought it to a stop near the opening. His fingers ran over his touch pad in front of him giving instructions to the computer: "Initiate Ring. Modify control sequence. Malleable field. Minor Solmissus. Controller coupling. Sensory camera."

"Accomplished," was the scripted reply.

The Solmissus formed, its tentacles began reaching for the building with serpentine movements as all four of the men, now all in the upper room of the house recoiled in fear of the artificial beast. Ten long probing and snaking arms probed the room as some of them pulled the ancient building material away from the structure. One of the arms searched the room with a camera imbedded within the probing end. AM attempted to strike the camera with his knife and managed a few desperate blows, but each one glanced off without repelling the monster.

Seconds later, the Ring swept into the room and miniature threads of light danced across the men. Images of the scene splashed across the screens in front of Neil as his hand manipulated a joystick on his console. The men were then compelled to line up side by side to face the ship. OM and SY still had their knives in their sheaths and AM had his in his hand but MU's knife lay on the floor at his feet. Each man now stood rigidly at attention while a mechanical voice reverberated through the dwelling, saying, "Remember your knives."

MU obediently picked his knife up from the floor as the other two men removed the knife from his own sheath. All four of them now gripped their weapons as if for battle. Neil moved the joystick once again so that each man slowly brought his own knife up to his own neck. Each man's blade contacted the soft skin of his own throat. The men cried out as their blood began to run in dark rivulets across the shiny blades in the blue light. It mingled readily with the droplets of water from the gathering mist.

A mechanical voice cracked through the air, saying, "Consider the blood you have shed and what your blades have wrought."

At this very moment Mari and Grace entered the bridge with Meadow. When Mari saw the visual of the men, she cried, "What's going on!"

There was no reply from Neil.

"No, don't do this," cried Mari. "Leave them be!"

She could see a cold undercurrent of insatiable hostility in Neil's eyes as he raised his voice, saying, "Leave them be? For what? These are animals. These so called men killed Jacob! They killed him, Mari, just like the thing that killed Celeste. Beasts that end life and kill the future. They kill hope. Now you take Grace, take her and leave the bridge. Get out of here and leave me alone!"

"No, I won't!" pleaded Mari in desperation. "Are you God? They will be brought to justice in their own world. Can you discern the heart? This is not the Neil I know."

Grace was sitting in one of the seats near Neil petting the cat.

"Justice?" lectured Neil. "There is no justice in this place. I will deal with them as we dealt with the Principality."

"That was survival," said Mari, "we had no choice."

"You speak of God," growled Neil, with contempt, "where is your God now, Mari? Where is He?"

"Where is your heart?" declared Mari.

"These are animals!" cried Neil.

"Look at your own hands," she cried. "Look at them! They have been given great power. Your destiny is to protect life, not destroy it!"

"I will destroy the destroyers."

"Will you repay evil with evil?" replied Mari, fiercely. "Can you live with their blood on your hands? I believe our lives have been given back to us for a reason. Think about me, think about Grace!"

Neil studied the men, watching each one cry out for mercy. Their legs buckled and they dropped to their knees. Blades that were once red with the blood of another soul had come to collect that of their owners. Neil folded his arms to gloat. Mari glared at him as images of the captors, now captive, were blatantly displayed across every screen on the bridge.

"I can say no more," said Mari, instilled with increasing fear and disgust. "Grace, you come with me."

Grace heard Mari but remained fasten to her seat, then softly speaking, she quoted from the book of Proverbs, saying, "'In all thy ways acknowledge Him....'" (2)

The man at the controls didn't want to hear such words amidst the cries of the men and the graphic images. Mari's face had a new expression, not of anger, nor of contempt, but a deep sadness as if she had just experienced a profound loss that could not be restored.

"Grace," demanded Mari. "I said, come with me!"

Neil brought his attention back to the screens. Mari stood frozen as Neil's hands returned to the controls. His fingers began to reach for the joystick again, but then, somehow, he found the touch screen and tapped it. The Ring and the controller instantly shut down, and in one coordinated relaxing of the fingers the men let go of their knives. The steel blades dropped to the floor with a unified clatter. By sheer instinct each of the men cried out and grabbed his throat to clutch the finely cut flesh. They were still very much alive, for the supple skin of their bodies had been parted only enough to draw a generous amount of blood.

As the men nursed the cuts to their flesh the invading arms of the monster retracted from the opening. A colorful a rainbow wave of particles hit the dwelling. A dense gray substance filled all the doors and windows and the gaping hole. Seconds later it solidified, making the openings as solid as the walls. The four men now would wait in their own hellish darkness until they would be discovered along with the grisly aftermath of their deeds.

The lambent object backed away from the structure and retraced its path across the broken landscape until it came to a stop above the mound of refuse laden with torn lives. Neil glanced over at Mari who had by now taken the co-pilot's seat with the gaze of shock. His eyes drifted back to the house as it appeared on his viewport, then he said, "And I feared our destruction at the hands of the Seruzian world. No need Mari, it will probably be by our own hands. The misanthropy is not lost here."

The computer announced, "ABC enabled. Spiral sequencer engaged."

Neil glared at the confirmation, then with sarcasm said, "Now it comes on line!" He manipulated the controls before him. "It is time to get...out of here."

Some of the local population living near enough to have seen strange lights in the sky quickly spread the word to others and people began assembling in the night. American military forces had also received word that something was afoot and taking the appropriate action. Specialized equipment was on its way. The Atmospheric Bridging Capability would function as designed and greatly increase the vessel's ability to traverse the atmosphere. In the next moment, after generating a cyclonic motion in the surrounding air, the ship made its most rapid vertical assent to date. The instant departure caused a virulent whirlwind at ground level and the loose debris from the vile mound were drawn up within the vortex. Shortly thereafter the debris, consisting of pieces of wood, dirt, spans of sheet metal, and a myriad of other materials began raining back down to earth.

Several individuals had braved the wind to gather at the mound in the absence of the strange object. They congregated there hoping to see more of what ever it was, but soon they were dodging the falling debris and ran for cover. Except for one lone gunman, his eyes defiantly searched the sky as he joyously fired his automatic weapon up into the falling debris. The material somehow missed him until a very thin two by six foot sheet of wood came spiraling down to not so gently contact his head. Both fell to the ground. The wood inflicted a blow just hard enough to knock him out.

A large piece of printed cloth was among the lighter materials sifting through the air. At one time it spread across the frame of a billboard, but it now was carried to and fro by the agitated air like a dislodged sail in a delirious wind. It danced on the turbulence in the night until at last gravity brought it gently to the earth. The generous span, with its printed side facing up, covered the fallen man like a luxurious cotton sheet spread out on a paupers bed. A small convoy of local military vehicles soon arrived with search lights. In their haste they drove their heavily armored vehicles directly over the debris and the printed cloth. There was a brief outcry as the life beneath the cloth became extinguished.

When the vehicles came to a stop they directed their lights across the material, curiously seeking the location of the outcry, but all they saw was an advertisement—one that had been censored—for it was the face of a woman which had been selectively, albeit, very hastily painted out.

Chapter Eighteen: Compassion

We must have compassion, for we have received mercy,
Yet our sails reach for the restless winds.
Mari

It was November, and the *Aurora* was traveling over the very part of the ocean where the *Starlet* had last appeared and disappeared. Neil was looking into the possibility of detecting the anomaly responsible for transporting the doomed vessel through time. He hoped that by solving the mystery surrounding Grace he might possibly be able to return her to the place in time before her ship encountered such unfortunate circumstances then somehow warn the captain to stay away from that region of the sea. He also considered the prospect, if it were possible, of returning himself to a time before the disastrous chain of events that led to the death of his friends and brought an end to Star Harbor. The vision of somehow changing the unfortunate course of history was intoxicating. His mind was also struck by the vivid revelation of his own capacity to inflict pain on others. He also remembered the time when he and Marcus discussed the conundrums of life and how they vowed to protect the sanctity of it. The more he contemplated his present state of affairs, the more he marveled at the optimism and kindness he saw in Mari and Grace; even as the universe seemed full of instability, with Earth inexorably caught in the middle, destined to be the victim of every malignant force.

In an effort to find a distraction from his inner turmoil he was focusing on a screen displaying weather data pertinent to their location. Other screens were displaying information provided by the global news networks. At first he ignored the chatter, but one monitor was displaying vivid pictures of a geological upheaval and human catastrophe. The commentator was saying, "Hundreds have been killed and injured in this major earthquake in Indonesia..." But the crawl at the bottom of the screen displayed: "Individuals calling themselves AWM posed as medical personnel board hospital ship..." The letters AWM reverberated in Neil's head so he switched to another feed of the story that featured a more in-depth report with the file footage of a crisp white ship on the waves of the ocean.

An American reporter on an aircraft carrier making its way to the vicinity was trying to explain the ongoing events, saying, "A faction calling themselves Anti Western Militants were able to get aboard the *SS Compassion* posing as medical personnel sent to assist the earthquake victims. Instead, they were intending to use the hospital ship to pick up nuclear material from another ship in the area. Agents from the United States posing as the party with the material were somehow detected by the AWM. Once the militants discovered the deception they threatened to kill all the people on board the hospital ship and destroy the vessel if they were not paid seventy-five million dollars and given asylum. When their requests were denied they forced the ship to sail north into the Yellow Sea looking for a suitable port and a country through which to escape."

The reporter went on to say, "The captain and his officers were held hostage, but at some point the security officers there killed six of the ten invaders and took two into custody. We were told another two still remained at large within the ship and one of the men set off strategically placed charges in the engine room which disabled the engines. That man was killed. Eventually the other man was killed in an explosion damaging the electrical system and part of the medical facilities. Also the only helicopter on board had been disabled. Now they are well within the sovereign waters of countries to the north and the ship is essentially dead in the water. They were able to overcome the hostile takeover only to be surrounded by a storm at sea, and, if that isn't enough we have received information there were reports of objects in the sky. The ship endured the first encounter with winds just under 100 miles per hour but that was before it was disabled. At this time the ship is within the eye of the storm. Fortunately the eye is rather large and the typhoon is just sitting there wobbling. That means the ship may be hit by the full fury within about three hours with winds expected to exceed 165 mph, that's equal to a category 5 hurricane."

Allen Sommers asked, "What about the accusations by certain governments concerning the ship?"

The reporter went on to say, "The country with the closest port accuses the *SS Compassion* of entering sovereign waters for the purpose of spying. They say they will seize the ship if it does not leave the area within a matter of hours. The storm is making it difficult to get help to the ship and there may be no way to make repairs or get all the people off in time to meet the deadline."

"Is there anything the US can do at this point?" asked Sommers.

"It appears tensions are rising between the United States and the other countries in the region. Any hostile action taken against the ship would be considered an act of war. The United Nations might step in but there seems to be no movement in any direction."

Grace was in a bright mood, talking, giggling, and having fun with Mari. The module doors snapped open and Meadow ran out ahead of them as they entered the bridge. Grace immediately took to the deck with the cat and opened one of her favorite books. She began to page through it as Mari found a seat next to Neil and opened her journal, but she noticed an aura of disdain hanging over him, and asked him what was wrong.

He replied, "It looks as if there is no shortage of evil. Humanity could achieve so much, but how will we survive something from space if we can't even survive ourselves?"

"What now?" asked Mari, putting down the journal.

"See," replied Neil, pointing to the reports, "on it goes, AWM is at it again. No matter what the scale, these are the ultimate bullies, murderers, not to mention a typhoon, not to mention someone saw orange lights out there. Objects or whatever."

"The Ambhuri?" questioned Mari.

"I don't know," replied Neil, "what ever the anomaly was, it entered the airspace above the ship then quickly made an exit. Can we trust the information coming from these media sources? Anything is possible. Peace and safety have fled the planet. The sources of global reporting, the recording of history, and even certain scientific data have become corrupted in a disgraceful abandonment of the truth."

"Think of all those poor souls on board!" replied Mari, now observing a broadcast showing file footage of the *SS Compassion* in less stressful times. Colorful pictures of the ship were on display, showing footage of a vessel floating majestically in a wide expanse of blue water gallantly adorned with white paint and a red cross.

Grace stood up and pointed at the screen to ask, "What kind of ship is that?"

Neil gently explained, saying, "It's a hospital ship, Grace, it helps people when they are sick."

"Is it helping people now?" asked Grace.

"Yes," added Mari, "but it's in trouble. Bad things happened and now it's in a bad storm."

"I know about bad storms!" reminded Grace.

"Yes, Honey, you do," replied Mari warmly.

"Neil and Mari can help them!" exclaimed Grace, exuberant with a childlike fancy.

Mari looked for Neil's reaction, then asked, "Do you think there's any way?"

Neil protested, saying, "I understand their plight, but there are some things that worry me. It could get complicated. We do not have all the details and the needs of our world are extremely far reaching. Can we help everyone? As someone once said, the authorities can handle it."

"I know, I know," sighed Mari, "but perhaps the authorities need some help this time."

Neil pushed himself back into his seat. "An international incident, threats, talk of war? We are probably not getting the whole story. The powers that be seem to resist entering the fight against any kind of terrorism. They complain when it happens then blame the people who are actually doing the work to alleviate the threat. There are always people willing to oppress others regardless of the exacting cost. As you can see, tyranny takes on many forms. It smothers the intellect, it kills the spirit, and stifles the will. What can be done about a populace lulled into listening to those who speak smooth deceptions into the ears of simpletons? This planet will probably die by its own hand, ultimately becoming the victims of an all consuming evil. Subjected to marauders who will take the world hostage as civilization continues on in its slow procession to nowhere, only able to recognize the warning signs when it's too late. Do you not realize we spend our entire lives striving to discern the difference between the truth and a lie? We are in a sad state."

Mari was about to speak her mind, but he continued, "We can go anywhere, Mari, anywhere, yet there are times when I just want to leave this terrestrial ball and never return. Where do we fit in? Some things make no sense. What in the name of heaven is the answer? Who's hands are we in anyway?"

"I think you should know the answer to that," reminded Mari. "We seem to have found a new kind of evil, but it is same evil as in ages past. The master of evil can even masquerade as an angel of light you know. We can't face that in our own strength."

"But what should be our course?" asked Neil.

"Look at where we are now!" exclaimed Mari. "Look at us. Are we in deep space? Guess what? We are now traveling across the sky over our own planet! And, Neil, did you know that even if you're in space you're not in a vacuum?"

They both laughed at the joke, but he countered by saying, "Anything could go wrong, especially at sea."

"I thought you had a special connection with the sea?"

"This goes beyond the sea! People and friends seem to have very short lives after I enter their world."

"We all have limitations, but look, I'm still here and Grace is still here!"

"And I am glad you are," admitted Neil.

"We are going to stay," insisted Mari, "and we want to be with you no matter where that may be."

"I could not bear to lose either of you," Neil replied. "Is there not one cup of mercy for this dire state of affairs?"

Grace was still sitting comfortably on the floor, petting Meadow, and paging through her book, seemingly detached from the conversation, but she made a declaration without ever looking up, saying, "'Let not mercy and truth forsake thee...'"(3)

"She's right you know," added Mari.

"Perhaps," grunted Neil.

"It's the right thing to do."

"Why did I look at that report?"

"Because you want to help."

"I do?"

"So?"

"I doubt whether anyone will actually request our help," questioned Neil, scanning the streams of information. "They would rather hunt us down. They probably even blame us for global climate change!"

"We have to do something!" replied Mari in frustration.

"There is an international incident developing," replied Neil, "and I am not about to start a war."

"What if we contacted them?" suggested Mari.

"You want me to make a call?" returned Neil. "I don't know...first I would need to contact someone who knows something...or someone who knows someone who knows, that is, somebody who knows exactly what is happening. Someone trustworthy, yet someone who has inside information."

"There has to be someone we can contact?" encouraged Mari.

"Well, there is someone—" said Neil, under his breath.

"Of whom are you thinking?" asked Mari.

"Staffer," replied Neil, looking rather distant.

"Gen. Staffer!" exclaimed Mari. "Are you sure?"

"Yes," assured Neil, realizing what he just said.

Grace entered the conversation again by quoting from Proverbs, "'Lean not unto thine own understanding.'"(4)

"Neil?" replied Mari, agreeing with Grace, but looking sternly at the man.

Giving in, he decided to put a call through to an office in Washington DC. To his surprise the connection was immediately directed to Staffer's office and he was speaking directly with the general, only to discover the man was more open than he had anticipated. In the end Neil made a commitment to help, and Staffer gave him a short briefing to bring him up to speed on all the essentials. The armed forces agreed to give him total control, providing he could come up with a reasonable plan of rescue or perform the necessary repairs on the ship. Immediate action would be necessary because of hostile nations, and because the weather would very shortly be an issue. It was then understood if things became unstable the operation would be handed over to the armed forces of the United States.

Grace was overjoyed at the prospect of helping people on a hospital ship, she couldn't wait to go aboard to see each person, not realizing there would be hundreds of people there. As for the ship itself, it was experiencing rough though somewhat forgiving seas in the eye of the storm. Fortunately the communications had been partially restored and the *SS Compassion* was given notice that unspecified help was on the way. Out of secrecy the captain wasn't told exactly what kind of craft it would be, only to prepare for immediate assistance and that the ship's landing pad was to be made ready with all possible speed. Reluctantly, the damaged helicopter was sacrificed to the sea.

The *Aurora* headed down toward a whirlpool of clouds on its approach to where the stricken vessel lay helpless. The huge white ship with its red crosses stood out conspicuously on the dark water as the officers and crew waited on the windy deck. The members of the welcoming party were ready for their visitors, but they looked at one another in puzzlement as a glowing set of sails covered in mist came toward their ship.

"What is that thing?" uttered one of the attending officers.

"Our forces must have some interesting new equipment!" remarked another.

"I was told it would not be military," countered the captain.

"Something from that secret base in the West, sir?" said another.

"I wouldn't know," replied the captain. "It's supposedly American, but unspecified."

The ship's captain and officers stood by as the *Aurora* touched down, resting itself securely on the helicopter landing pad. Neil was alone when he emerged from the companion-module. He humbly approached the captain and the officers and addressed them, saying, "Sir, my name is Neil Clayborn, I am here to offer assistance."

"I am Capt. Grayson," replied the officer stepping forward to greet him. "Welcome aboard."

"Thank you, sir," returned Neil.

"We are prepared for you to immediately attend to the needs of this vessel," replied the captain.

"May I first ask permission for the rest of my crew to join me at this time?" said Neil.

"Permission granted," replied Capt. Grayson.

"Very well," answered Neil, then using the Remote he sent a short message, saying, "Word has been given."

Mari and Grace were soon to appear along side of Neil. They were initially greeted warmly by the officers, but they were certainly not what had been anticipated, and they thoroughly scrutinized every inch of the new arrivals.

"I'm with Neil and Mari," piped Grace, now beaming with pride and a big grin.

"This is your crew?" questioned the captain.

"They are," replied Neil. "Mari and Grace will assist primarily with the sick and injured aboard you ship. You will find them very capable."

"I would hope so," returned the captain.

After this short exchange the three visitors were escorted into the confines of the stricken ship by one of the attending crew.

The captain muttered to his second in command as he watched the new arrivals leave the open deck, saying, "One scrawny man and two girls?"

The second officer turned to the captain, and remarked, "Only three?"

Grayson answered, "So it appears, unless he's hiding more people in that thing. We send for help and this is what we get?"

"That younger one seems like what?" commented the second officer with a smirk.

"Slow?" replied the captain.

"Must be awfully close quarters in there," commented the second officer, suspiciously.

"Real close," added the captain.

"They're all kind of strange, don't you think?" said the second officer, scoffing.

"At least the one with the dark hair is good looking," commented the captain.

Mari and Grace were directed to the medical care facility while Neil was being escorted deep within the ship. After Neil was given the opportunity to inspect the damage to the engine room, he turned to his hosts and said, "I look forward to the day when I will have expanded capabilities and thus be able to make modifications in any environment, nevertheless, some of that capability does not exist at this time. The damage here is considerable, unfortunately I will not be able to perform the necessary repairs. Our fabricating ability falls short given the amount of damage and the time available."

The officers in the group glance at one another and anticipated the captain's response when he said, "What do you mean you can't perform the necessary repairs? We were told by the top brass that you, sir, would provide some exceptional technological assistance!"

"Our fabrication technology is still somewhat raw and inadequate for this situation and due to unexpected complications we have lost most of it."

"Lost it?" replied Capt. Grayson, as small flames appeared in his eyes.

"I cannot attempt reconstruction on this scale within the structure of this vessel," returned Neil.

"What is this, a charade?" questioned Capt. Grayson. Then the captain brought himself within close proximity of Neil's nose as a condescending grin appeared on his face. "I'm disappointed. But to be truthful I didn't actually believe it when Staffer informed me of the this dubious plan. I figured they were just giving us a story. So what's up? Why did they really send you out here?"

"I am going to have to study this situation for another relevant option," returned Neil. "We will come up with an alternate plan."

One of the other officers spoke up, thinking to draw out more information so that everyone might receive a further explanation. But if he had taken a moment to think before he posed his question he might have remained silent. In this case the danger was eminent and the officer felt certain any idea might be worthy of airing, so the officer said, "Sir, how might this be accomplished?"

Capt. Grayson, and snapped at the officer, saying, "You have your duties mister, and I have mine, I will ask the questions here." The officer shut up. The captain then turned to address Neil. "Actually, you have very little time to 'study' the situation. We were told one thing by Washington, now you give us something else. What is going on?"

"I did not say we would not help," replied Neil.

"Then?" questioned the captain, ever more accusatory.

"I will get back to you," answered Neil, "some further research is necessary."

"Of course it is," scoffed the captain.

Everyone was silent as their visitors left the devastated engine room. The *Compassion* was a vessel of human cargo and it was here that the infirm had taken refuge. It was now up to three rather curious people to make things right, not for the purpose of remuneration, only desirous of necessary permission to get the ship to a place of safety.

Mari and Grace willingly followed their hosts throughout the ship. Soon they were introduced to a number of patients, all of whom had no trouble accepting the new arrivals. Meanwhile, Neil had returned to the confines of the *Aurora* to analyze pertinent information. Grace was separated from Mari and kindly chaperoned by a nurse named Lily to the cafeteria to meet with some of patients dining in the room. Eventually she was introduced to a young boy by he name of Patrick Hammond. It had been determined that the boy suffered from significant emotional trauma and therefore needed special attention.

Mari was on her own separate tour, which was now winding down and now she was leaving one of the operating rooms with the attending nurse. When they stepped into the adjacent corridor she was confronted by Capt. Grayson. The captain dismissed the nurse so he might speak with Mari alone. The nurse departed, and the inquisitive captain asked, "Did you find our facilities acceptable?"

"Oh, yes," replied his enthusiastic guest, for she was excited about the opportunity to be of any kind of assistance, "they're wonderful."

"Not anymore," contended Grayson.

"I am sorry such a thing has happened here," said Mari, "and to such a beautiful ship."

"We were the best on the sea," preened the captain.

"I would certainly agree," said Mari, politely. "I believe it will be again."

There was a pregnant pause, then the captain posed his question, "What are you really doing here?"

"I don't understand?" said Mari, duly surprised.

"Why are you here?" pushed the captain.

"We've come to help of course," affirmed Mari.

"I see," replied the captain, "but what's a woman like you doing here? What are you getting out of it?"

"I beg your pardon?" questioned Mari.

"You know," inferred the captain, with a twist of implication.

"I do?" replied Mari. "Well, I thought I was here to help."

"What kind of help?"

"We have come to assist in any way we can."

"Maybe you should think that through."

"What do you mean?"

"Who is that man?"

"Excuse me?" replied Mari.

"You know," inferred Grayson. "You must be more than just crew!" Incredulous, Mari just stared at the captain as he continued. "When or if we get out of this mess, maybe you would find more accommodating facilities here."

"I'm sorry," said Mari, "but I'm needed on the *Aurora*."

"I bet!" said Grayson. "But you can be assured, I could make it very comfortable for you aboard this ship."

A signal on Mari's Remote interrupted the conversation, and she said to the captain, "Please, excuse me, I have to take a call."

She put the Remote to her ear, Neil's voice was saying, "Mari, are you busy?"

"No," she replied. "We're just finishing up my tour."

"Very well," returned Neil, "if you can be interrupted I would like to have you join me on the *Aurora* for a few minutes."

"That would be a pleasure," replied Mari, with a sigh of relief. "I'll be right there."

"Your ship?" questioned the captain.

"Yes," replied the anxious guest, "I have to go."

"Of course you do, but think about what I said," replied the captain.

Mari nodded politely and turned to go. She rolled her eyes as she briskly made her way down the empty corridor. In her haste to get topside she became confused and in the next moment she found herself confronted by two different passageways. She took the one to the right. Within a short distance she found another passageway, and after she rounded yet another corner she was met by a crewman she had not seen before. The crewman was more than happy to show her the shortest way to the upper decks of the *SS Compassion*.

Once Mari was back on the *Aurora*, she confided in Neil, "I've been introduced to the injured patients and I've found some serious cases here. I activated the Q-Med to test it out and I found it's not responding. So, it's going to be a challenge."

"I will see what I can do," said Neil, "but getting this ship out of danger is our first priority."

"Even if you get the Q-Med to work, it looks like the medical staff would be hesitant to let me actually use it," admitted Mari.

"I'm not surprised," replied Neil, "I understand they must exercise caution. We are, as you might say, not the average fare around here."

"I was approached by the captain," revealed Mari.

"Oh, about what?"

"Us!"

"Us?"

"You and I, and the *Aurora*," replied Mari. "He thinks I should remain on the *Compassion* as part of the crew. He would make it comfortable for me!" A furrow ran between Neil's eyes. "Not to worry. But I guess I wasn't prepared for all of this. Was this whole thing a bad idea?"

"It was not," replied Neil, "I am glad you forced me to see the issue. But, we will have to work with what we have and do it quickly. I believe we can do this."

"Do you think they will cooperate?" asked Mari.

"The captain," added Neil, "seems to retain a certain animus."

"I picked that up," said Mari.

"The atmosphere here is questionable as the captain is somewhat recalcitrant," added Neil.

"You said it kindly," offered Mari.

"If there were not certain constraints," added Neil, "I believe the crew would flee. An individual may not long tolerate the constant fatigue of demoralization. As indentured subjects placate to petty demands their inherent loyalty weakens, which only instills cracks in any sound organization."

"Well," said Mari, "if all our ducks are in a row—"

"They will be," returned Neil. "These people need to work with us regardless of certain attenuating and accusatory attitudes. They don't have a choice."

"They need to let us do our job here," said Mari.

"Although, maybe the captain is right," admitted Neil, second guessing himself. "Maybe I am not thinking this thing through. Once again I may be the victim of my own arrogance."

"Neil," cried Mari, "you can't be serious! You can't let the circumstances get to you. Remember why we came. You just said we can do this!"

"I do think about why we came," replied Neil.

"I don't know all about what you're feeling," said Mari, "but I've experienced some of it. We need to be focused, there's something more to this than just ourselves."

"Something more," replied Neil, acknowledging the thought. "You always see something more. So, should I trust the One you trust?"

"That might help," said Mari. "Trust Him to help you and to help them."

"Something more to consider," returned Neil, "then it is for the needy that I shall bolster my reserve."

Mari's countenance, which had taken on a slightly ragged appearance, had mostly recovered, then she said, "This is all beyond me, but I'll do whatever is necessary. The Morning Star is always shining."

"We shall press on," returned Neil. "I will do what I can to get power to the Q-Med. The same factors are at work with the fabricating processes. I cannot remedy everything but I suspect the Q-Med might become operational once we get under way."

"I hope so, there's not a lot I can do otherwise," sighed Mari.

"How is Grace doing?" asked Neil.

"She's fine," returned Mari. "She's taking this whole adventure surprisingly well. I let her stay with Lily and a young boy with some emotional difficulties."

"She seems to have a way with people," agreed Neil. "Now, moving on, there are numerous factors to consider. I have reviewed the possibilities and I have come up with the solution."

"This will work out," said Mari. "There are other factors at work besides the hardware."

"I am considering all our options," said Neil, then he pointed to the screens. "If you have a minute, I want you to look at what I have here. I would like your assessment."

By the time Neil arrived back on the bridge of the *Compassion* to meet with the captain several deadlines were fast approaching and one of them was the inner wall of the eye of the storm. The tension was palpable as Capt. Grayson greeted him, saying, "Well, Mister, we have survived a hostile takeover and brought order to the house but now we need to see your plan if you have one?"

"Yes," replied Neil, "it is in process as we speak."

"Process?" enlightened Grayson. "I believe that's a fine piece of transportation out there on our landing pad but that doesn't answer the question. We have been advised that the fix is in your hands, so what do you propose to do? You must certainly be aware that we will never make the so called 'deadline' to vacate these waters. Who knows what will shake down next? And, I see that little woman of yours is helping out down below but your part of the bargain is lacking. It doesn't even look like you understand what we are up against. You have given us nothing so far. I wonder who is paying you anyhow?"

"There is a solution," replied Neil, "and I think we have a viable option."

"You think?" exploded Grayson. "I don't know if I like what you think. Do you know what's going to happen when the declared deadline is up? All the dogs and jackals will be cut loose and we'll be in the middle of it! In case you haven't noticed we have a boat load of sick and injured. There's a hostile country making threats, why, we even have a typhoon that could sink this ship, and you and that 'thing' out there haven't provided any answers!"

"Excuse me, sir," replied Neil, retaining his position, "I am aware—"

"Excuse you?" cried the captain, getting into Neil's face. "Well, now I'll tell you something, I'm responsible for this ship and all on board her. So far our brave men have brought things under control. I'll have you know I've nearly lost my son in this. Unlike you, he took immediate action, he proved himself to be a hero. Now he'll be crippled for the rest of his life! Do you have any idea what that's like?"

Neil's eyes sailed out through the windows of the bridge and out to the sea, where he saw the waters churning, nervously whipped to a frenzy by the increasing winds, then he turned to the captain, and said, "We are all grateful for your son's bravery and he is indeed a hero. I would—"

"You bet," Grayson cut in. "Now what are you going to do? Come on buddy, I'm waiting!"

"Given the exact weight of this ship," answered Neil, "which is just over forty-one thousand tons—"

"Well, I see you can do math!" exclaimed Grayson.

Mari boldly entered the bridge with an electronic pad, saying, "Neil, I have the information you requested."

"Thank you," he replied, putting on his reading glasses then closely examining the screen.

"I've had it with this," injected the captain. "We are running out of time."

"Indeed we are," replied Neil.

"Well, finally we agree on something," laughed Grayson, "I see you must have all the statistics. So, we are waiting!"

Mari was bristling but kept quiet.

Neil took off his glasses and earnestly addressed the captain, saying, "This ship will have to be towed."

There was dead silence all around, then the captain cried, "Towed?"

"By another ship," informed Neil.

"Others are on their way as we speak," said the captain, "but there's not another ship within 75 miles because of this storm!"

"I will tow your ship with our ship," answered Neil.

Laughter burst forth from all of the officers on the bridge, then Capt. Grayson replied, "You're going to tow a forty-one thousand ton ship through the ocean in heavy seas in a typhoon with that thing out there?"

"That is my intention," said Neil,

"You're crazy!" chided Grayson.

Mari scoffed to herself at the resistance of immediate help, but this time she couldn't resist entering the conversation, in support of Neil she fired back, "We have verified all of the equations and the plan remains sound."

"I also believe we can attain some reasonable speed," assured Neil.

"Even if you could tow this vessel at her top speed she might not take the pounding," informed the captain. "We could sustain damage or capsize without the proper stability."

"That should not be a problem," said Neil in reply. "We can deal with the external forces and stabilize the entire vessel once we are under way. I will know more of the specific details when we actually complete the connection."

"You won't know until you complete the connection?" decried Capt. Grayson.

"There is some risk of course," added Neil. "I can't predict all the variables in what we might encounter, but we will proceed with all possible speed to Pearl Harbor for repairs."

"Risk?" cried the captain. "I won't have any more damage to my vessel!"

"Nor to my own," added Neil. "You have your responsibilities and I have mine."

"My responsibility?" scolded Capt. Grayson. "That even includes you and your dubious plan."

"Look," replied Neil, now letting his frustration surface, "we could fight our way out of these waters and start a war or I could promise something I could not deliver or I could take my leave of you. Or, you can let us help you with the means at our disposal. There will be no rash action on our part. It is now your choice, you may follow our plan or you may tell us to be on our way."

"Blazes!" blurted the captain. "If this doesn't work I can see the headlines now, 'Captain humiliated after UFO fails rescue of stranded ship and starts World War III!'" All mouths were shut as Neil and Mari waited patiently for the captain to finish. "I'll most likely regret this. I might even lose my command. But, it looks as if I have no other choice in the matter, thanks to Staffer and some other so and so I can't name. I don't relish your plan, and though I hate to, I will grant you the permission. You may proceed, but if I see any indication this isn't working you stand down. You hear me? You will let our military forces handle it!"

"Agreed," replied Neil, somewhat relieved.

"It's your move, Clayborn," returned Capt. Grayson. "As Staffer told me, it is in your hands."

"Okay then," replied Neil, "I will start by providing you with a transceiver to assist your electronic systems that will take care of the telemetry needs between our ships. I then must request enough heavy electrical cable to connect our ship to your ship's electrical system."

"A direct connection?" queried Capt. Grayson. "To suck what auxiliary power we still have? Don't you have your own?"

"First," said Neil, "I will monitor the necessary information concerning your navigation and power systems. Second, we will supply all the electrical power needed for your ship. You will be able to put your emergency generators on standby."

"Then what?" added Grayson.

"There is one specific safety issue I must address," added Neil. "You must restrict the movement of personnel within the ship. You will need to keep everyone off all exterior decks and platforms, no one must be permitted on the outside of the ship once we are under way. Also, you must keep all windows, portholes, hatches, and doors closed, and you will need to secure any loose items that might be on the open decks."

"Why is that necessary?"

"I will explain things as we go along. We can do this, unless you have a better idea?"

"Will we need heavy tow lines?"

"No."

"Of course not, you have your magic wand! As I've said, Mr. Clayborn, permission is granted, but we'll be monitoring this."

Capt. Grayson gave the orders to have his crew produce the requested materials and receive the necessary instructions. Neil boarded the *Aurora*, then returned just long enough to provide the crew with a special connector. This would allow the electrical cables to adapt to the output receptacle on the *Aurora*.

The winds and the swell of the ocean had been on the increase as the eye wall was drawing nearer. The floating ship began to exhibit a more definite pitch and roll, but by now the *Aurora* was high above the stricken vessel, maneuvering around the bow and within reach of the two crew members stationed on the forecastle. The airborne vessel was hovering only inches above their heads and they were buffeted by the elements as they worked. No difficulties were encountered as they attached the cable to the receptacle, but once the electrical connection was made all personnel were ordered off the forward part of the ship. Now the *Aurora* could take a position just ahead and slightly above the bow. Then, after the *Aurora* matched the pitch and roll of the giant ship, a metallic substance began to form. This was not the Solmissus, nor was it any monster of the sea, but a type of gripping mechanism. True apprehension began to show in the eyes of the officers when the animated form began to engulf part of the superstructure and expand out along the hull of the *Compassion*. The entire fabrication connected the airborne *Aurora* to the disabled floating hull so that it became as one unit and solidified. Then an accompanying set of stairs leading from the *Aurora* down to the deck of the *Compassion* quickly formed. It was by this means that Neil returned to the deck of the immobile ship to check the mating of the newly fabricated material with that of the hull. He took readings with the Remote until he was satisfied with the data. From there he went up to the bridge to speak with the captain.

"In the name of all that's sacred, what is going on?" retorted Grayson. "Are we to be consumed before we even get started? What are you doing?"

"Providing a means of escape," informed Neil. "Adhesion has been verified, the bonding elements are holding."

"If I would have known about this I would not have given you the permission," replied the captain, doubting such events.

"This is the only way," remarked Neil.

"You should know," reminded the captain, "in a few minutes we'll be hearing from our friends to the north. By then it won't matter what happens, space ships or no space ships, they will try to blow us out of the water."

"We shall be under way momentarily," replied Neil. "The storm should give us some cover."

"As we are blown out of the water," reiterated the captain, under his breath.

Gail force winds commenced to buffet the conjoined ships, giving everyone a glimpse of the ferocity of the storm, but all was in good order aboard the *Aurora* as Neil eased himself into the pilot seat and settled in. Next he deactivated the CMR and let his body return to its natural state. Everything around him automatically adapted to be of assistance; the instruments, screens, and necessary controls all approached to serve the operator. Now cloistered there he would be in total control of both ships.

A scripted message was received by Capt. Grayson from the *Aurora*, saying, "We are ready to commence operations. The first heading will be due south and you will see the coordinates displayed on your monitor. Once this is accomplished I will await your order to proceed."

Capt. Grayson noted the time, which was less than five minutes before the deadline, then informed his passengers and crew to prepare. He radioed back to the *Aurora*, saying, "Any time Clayborn. It's a, go."

As the information transmitted to the *Aurora* provided the status of the vessel in tow a script appeared on the bridge of the *Compassion*, informing Capt. Grayson of what would follow: "Forward momentum will commenced on zero count from the sixty-second mark."

"Why no voice communication?" questioned one of the other officers.

"I don't know," replied a nervous Capt. Grayson, "that's what he requested."

At the end of the count down the sail-like sections of the field drive began to organize themselves over the two vessels until they were totally enveloped in light which rapidly accumulated a roiling mist. Everyone aboard the *SS Compassion* felt a substantial jolt as forward motion began, although once under way there was a silky smooth but steady increase in speed.

"20 knots, sir," announced one of the officers. "Now 45 knots. Now 75 knots, still increasing, sir!"

"What are you doing out there, Clayborn?" shouted Grayson.

A script appeared on the captain's screen: "All systems are within optimal range. We proceeding as planed."

"Watch that speed!" cried Grayson.

"Affirmative," was the reply.

Capt. Gayson was soon in communication with Washington to keep Gen. Staffer posted on the progress. Satellite tracking revealed an object traveling at increasing speed through the spiral of the typhoon. Gen. Staffer issued instructions for all ships to open a specific ocean corridor with all haste as the two vessels—now operating as one—traveled freely over the water. Even now their speed continued to increase, exceeding 300 knots. At this time any objects on the outer decks not secured near the stern of the *Compassion* were torn away by the wind. Unsecured cables flapped in the turbulent air, unattended ropes disappeared, and several deck chairs flew away. The fields surrounding the two ships were eventually adjusted to close the gaps and no one was lost nor did they incur any injuries.

"100% structural integrity. Ships are stable," came the message to the screen on *Compassion*'s bridge.

"Roger," radioed the second officer, "*SS Compassion* is responding well."

"Stable?" complained Grayson. "With this speed?"

Because the otherwise stealthiness of the *Aurora* had been compromised by the joining of the two ships the other ships and military air craft in the vicinity began to pick up an anomaly on their radar screens. At a screen on one of the vessels along the path a young sailor was almost afraid to report what he was observing, but he relayed his information, saying, "We have them on our radar sir. We have the *SS Compassion* traveling at—" There was a long pause as he rechecked the data. "It's now holding steady at just over 900 knots. Sir?"

His commanding officer replied, "That reading is correct. I was provided advanced information concerning this but I thought I might be misinformed. Our orders are to let them proceed unhindered."

The vessels made their exit from the forbidden waters in less than a minute before the arbitrary deadline was to expire, leaving the fierce winds of the typhoon behind them as they departed from the Yellow Sea. Racing across the Pacific in the radiance of a full moon and a bright clear night on a course for Hawaii, skimming the surface of the sea with sails unfurled in a race of their own making, effortlessly casting aside the ocean waves.

As the vessels plied the sea somewhere between Japan and their destination five objects appeared out of the upper atmosphere. Each of them had the familiar amber glow. Neil tracked them on his instruments making note of the V formation now directly above him.

Screens displayed the data: "Registering five Ambhuri vessels. Altitude marked at 3207.45 feet." The communications system followed up with a script saying: "Friends." Moments later the sound of a voice, saying, "This is Tallis. You now possess the necessary data."

"Tallis?" replied Neil, "It's good to hear from you, but please specify!"

"What you seek has been folded within the pages of your own technology long ago," replied Tallis.

"Explain?" replied Neil.

"We must say farewell for now," said Tallis. "May you find completion, Neil Clayborn."

"Farewell, Tallis," replied Neil, "my comrade from across space."

The transmission ended and the Ambhuri ships departed, disappearing as silently as they had arrived. The pilot of the *Aurora* was relieved to find the absence of any hostile Seruzian presence.

The mission was well underway but the pilot of the *Aurora* would remain alert and vigilant. While keeping track of all communications and critical systems at hand he also began to re-evaluate his personal quest. He felt driven to examine the historical markers of his life and recount the events that led him to this time and place, for there was still an uneasiness residing deep within his soul. He revisited the words spoken by Mari and Grace and began to understand the context from which they were drawn. He reexamined the scriptural truths which pointed to the greatest of all mysteries: The very Truth he rejected had all along been seeking him.

The lament of his restless and searching soul finally led him to accept the Ancient of Days. A profound conviction gripped him, for his own heart suffered from a corruption he was powerless to change or control, and his darkness was exposed to the light of the Bright and Morning Star. He thereby surrendered, and in acknowledging his need he found beneficence and deliverance. The scientist now understood the grand design of all things and the veil was lifted from the eyes of his mind. The emptiness of his own heart was filled. A new perspective had entered his vision, one wrought by the Spirit now within him. For he was now a mariner at the foot of the cross.

In their journey together the unique problem solving abilities of two different people had become intertwined, one helping the other with complimentary differences. They were now separated by task but remained in contact concerning the needs of the ships. The time had come for Neil to contact Mari once again concerning the status of the souls she was attending. But before he did so his personal screen lit up with an alphanumeric code, and it riveted his attention: "777-A02."

He entered a response, which repeated the numbers accompanied by an acknowledgment.

A new code then appeared before him: "777 A02 01 SUBMIT."

To which he replied: "777-A01-02 ACQUIRE."

Then came a voice saying, "Neil, this is Marcus."

"Marcus!?" replied Neil.

"Yes, I'm on the *Aries*," replied Marcus. "I've longed to contact you."

"Where have you been?" replied Neil. "I thought perhaps you might be dead!"

"I'm fine," assured Marcus, "and Candice is with me, but that's another story."

"Candice!" exclaimed Neil.

"We will contact you again soon," said Marcus. And the communication ended.

It was during Mari's last appearance among the patients that she was introduced to Dr Spaulding. Skepticism on the part of the medical team was evident, but after some gentle persuasion on her part Mari gained permission to use the Q-Med. The patients on the other hand, seemed grateful for any kind of assistance, due to the lack of necessary medical equipment and supplies. While she was in conversation with the medical staff the case of a thirty year old American woman suffering from severe back pain came to her attention. The woman had been injured during the earthquake and the trauma to her spine had been treated though she was still experiencing considerable pain.

"Would you permit me to see the patient?" asked Mari.

"We will allow it," said Dr. Spaulding, "but be aware, we'll be watching any procedures very closely. Mind you, this is only because we have no other recourse at this time."

"I understand," replied Mari.

As they entered the small private room, Dr. Spaulding informed Mari, saying, "We have nearly run out of pain medication but we are trying to make her as comfortable as possible."

"May I speak with her first?" asked Mari.

"Her name is Lisa," replied the doctor, "but I must warn you she has been difficult and uncooperative."

As they approached where her bed it became obvious the woman was suffering considerable discomfort so Mari introduced herself with a gentle touch. Lisa responded with a simple nod, a groan, and then a scowl.

"Could you tell me where you are feeling the pain?" asked Mari.

"Lower back of course," groaned Lisa, barely making any effort to show the location.

"If you will permit me I will try to help you," replied Mari.

The woman reluctantly nodded in affirmation. Mari then gently put one hand underneath her back and the one with the Q-Med she placed on her abdomen.

"You may feel some warmth," said Mari.

Only about a minute or so had passed, when Lisa seemed to be responding positively.

Another minute passed and Mari withdrew her hands, and asked, "How are you feeling now?"

"It seems better," said Lisa.

"Very good," replied Mari, then she turned to Dr. Spaulding, "That's all I can do at present, but I would like to check in on her again."

"Thank you so much," added Lisa, now feeling additional relief. "The pain seems almost gone now."

"I'm glad to hear that," replied Mari, "I will check back with you."

Dr. Spaulding was not sure what to think as he escorted his visitor from the room. Finally he allowed her to visit some of the other patients. Mari also visited one of the men on the nursing staff, his name was Richard Grayson, the son of the captain, who suffered the loss of both legs in the explosion that destroyed part of the medical facility. At present he was stable and recovering reasonably well. During her visit Mari informed him that the prognosis looked good and he could expect to hear from Neil in the near future.

Lily eventually let Grace stay alone with Patrick in a large cabin which had been converted into a library. The ten year old boy was suffering psychologically from the loss of his parents who had been American missionaries in Indonesia. Now the boy was headed to the United States where relatives would take him in. His parents were killed in a robbery attempt and the boy refused to speak from that time on. He withdrew, turned inward and became sullen. At first Lily was reluctant to let Grace stay alone with him but Grace's gentle manner and sunny personality soon won both of them over. And, because the movement of personnel within the ship had been restricted, both Grace and Patrick were confined to the room. Now they sat together at a small table where Grace had taken an interest in some of the picture books spread out before them. Each one was filled with illustrations of ships and planes.

"I like pictures!" announced Grace, holding up a book with a picture of a sailing ship on the cover. "Are these your books?"

Patrick nodded in response, hardly breaking through the blank expression on his face. The small selection of books actually did belong to the boy. He liked ships and took the books where ever he went but he was willing to share them. Grace was devouring every bit of the pictorial history of ocean going vessels. The boy watched as Grace turned page after page, examining the drawings and colorful photographs, occasionally expressing delight in what she saw. He watched intently as she marveled at all the modern ships, exclaiming how she had never seen a ship such as the *SS Compassion* before. Everything was new to her. After all, she was just getting to know a completely different age and time. She remarked how the *Compassion* seemed so very big, a little scary, and yet it was a lot of fun.

Suddenly, though, her visage lost its customary cheer and her face reflected sadness as she pointed to a glossy photograph of a fully rigged sailing ship. Then she spoke quietly, saying, "That's like my ship. Mother and Father were on my ship. Its gone now, I don't know where. Bad things happened. Mother is in heaven. Father is in heaven now." A moment of connectivity danced between them, then somehow she was able to move on and spoke again. "Sailing is fun. Then the dark time came and I was sacred. Neil and Mari came to help me. Neil and Mari are here to help your ship too." Patrick's expression softened and his face gradually lost some of its blankness. "I like this ship, its fun here."

The dark clouds that hung in the boy's eyes began to part, then in a tone just above a whisper he spoke about the death of his parents for the first time, saying, "My Mom and my Dad, they died too."

"Oh," comforted Grace, "don't be afraid, they are in heaven and now they are safe."

"I miss them," grieved Patrick.

Grace gave the boy a big hug, saying, "I miss my Mother and Father too."

"Terrorists got on this ship," reported Patrick, "but the security guys got them. There were some big explosions, but they got the bad guys."

"Neil and Mari helped me," said Grace. "Now they are helping your ship."

"Where do you live?" asked the boy, now revealing his inquisitive side.

"I live on a ship with Neil and Mari," proclaimed Grace. "It's a flying ship!"

"A flying ship?" questioned Patrick. "That's cool! What kind of ship is it?"

"We came here on it," said Grace.

"You did?" questioned Patrick.

"It looks like this," said Grace, then she made a big circle in the air. "I don't see it in any of these books but its round. It has lights!"

"I never saw a ship like that!" exclaimed Patrick, skeptical of her description. "Could you show it to me if we get to go on deck?"

"I can ask Neil and Mari," said Grace, with an undercurrent of excitement.

"That would really be neat," replied Patrick, with more emotion working its way to the surface. "I like you Grace, you're nice!"

Grace patted Patrick on the back in return. The boy inched closer to his new friend and soon the two of them were paging through the book together each one talking about their favorite ship. Lily eventually returned the cabin and quietly slipped in. She paused just inside the door to listen to the conversation between the two young people. Eventually she came over to where they were seated, and said, "Why, Patrick, I'm glad to see you and Grace are getting along so well!"

"We like ships," reported Patrick.

"I'm so glad you're here, Grace," said Lily.

"Me too!" added Grace, with unguarded enthusiasm.

Patrick was loosing his lifeless modality and an unconscious bond was forming between him and his new friend. Lily was surprised and encouraged at the change in Patrick and could see that the boy was beginning to return to life again. As she considered the new developments she quietly found her way over to the cabin window, where, she ever so slightly pulled back one of the curtains to peer outside. She became transfixed as she gazed upon the thin blue haze rippling just beyond the wall of the cabin.

In time the conjoined ships would be nearing safe harbor in the island chain of Hawaii. In well under five hours the ships had journeyed more than four thousand nautical miles and now began to retreat from their extreme speed. By the time they were within a quarter mile off the shore of Oahu the *Compassion* would displace water on its own. The vessels found rest near the welcoming harbor and the control of the *SS Compassion* was given back to Capt. Grayson.

Grace and Patrick had been returned to his own cabin and all was quiet when Neil and Mari arrived there, Lily greeted them at the door, saying, "I want to thank you for letting Grace stay with the boy, he's doing very well and we hate to see her leave!"

"I'm sure she enjoyed her time with both of you," added Mari.

"I wish Grace could stay!" exclaimed Patrick.

"I want to stay!" pleaded Grace.

"I know," replied Mari, "but it is now time for us to go."

"Can Patrick come with us?" asked Grace.

"I don't think so," said Mari, "he must stay here for now."

"I'll miss Grace a lot," said Patrick. "We had fun!"

"I bet you did, Patrick," said Mari, "but she has important things to do and you will soon be off to see your Aunt. She loves you and I'm sure she can't wait to see you!"

"It's not the same," said Patrick. "I miss my Mom and Dad."

"You will miss them," explained Mari, "but you will come to know your Aunt loves you too. In time you will understand."

Patrick turned to Lily, and said, "Can I come up on deck to say goodbye to Grace? Can I see her ship when it leaves? Grace says it looks really cool!"

"Can he see it?" pleaded Grace.

"Well," replied Neil, as he thought for a moment, "we might be able to work something out."

Frank Niverson arrived in Washington DC. He was soon ushered into Gen.

Staffer's office and was demanding answers, saying, "Well?"

"I just wrapped up communications with Grayson and Clayborn," said the general. "It has been confirmed that the operation went off without a hitch. I believe they pulled it off just as Clayborn said they would."

"Or pulled the wool over our eyes!" returned Frank, with his usual cynicism. "Are you aware General Staffer, we've had confirmation of more objects over the Pacific? They even joined our so called friends as they crossed the ocean."

"I've been informed," replied Staffer, "and I'm keeping abreast of it, but I'm convinced that Clayborn is not partnered with them. Although we still don't know much about those people I think they can be trusted."

"Trusted?" questioned Frank.

"Something leads me to believe their only intentions were to help us out," Staffer answered. "They provided control to an unstable vessel, cared for the critically injured, and they delivered an entire ship to a safe harbor. They could very well have taken that ship into outer space for all I know or brought us into war but they didn't. And, Frank, while we were scratching our heads they called us!"

Dawn was at hand as several tugs closed in on the disabled ship. Then Neil, true to his promise, opened up the *Aurora* for Patrick to see. The boy was able to go aboard and Grace was only too happy to show him around. His feelings for Grace were visible and he presented her with a gift in a brown paper bag with her name on it. She opened it to find a book about ships, one from Patrick's very own collection. In the end Grace and Patrick parted with a promise to stay friends. Finally, the time had come to separate the connection between the *Aurora* and the *Compassion*. One became buoyant, floating of its own accord on the surface of the ocean and the other was given to reside high in the air in a stationary position off the port bow of the waterborne ship. The fields were barely evident and so the *Aurora* was aglow in the morning sky. A crowd of people had gathered on the open decks of the SS *Compassion*, hoping to catch a first hand glimpse of something unexplainable and to bid farewell.

By now several sea going vessels were within close range of the *Compassion*. One such ship was the *Aries*. At the port railing stood a man named Ted, and next to him was Marcus Zaire, and Dr. Candice Canton was with him. Marcus held a sophisticated pair of electronic field glasses up to his eyes so that he might closely examine the *Aurora*, then he said to Candice, "Somehow I knew we would prevail."

"I had no doubt at all," affirmed Candice.

On the bridge of the *Aurora*, Neil was checking essential systems at the pilot station, monitoring communications and waiting for word on the status of the *Compassion*. Grace had both eyes fastened longingly on the big white ship on the water while petting Meadow. She couldn't help but think about Patrick. Mari jotted some thoughts in her journal just as three Navy aircraft thundered over the harbor. A sudden burst of fanfare erupted from all who were on the open decks of the ships in the small armada below.

"Is that a salute or are they just checking up on us?" quipped Neil.

"Possibly both," added Mari.

"Will I see Patrick again?" asked Grace.

"Yes," encouraged Mari, "I think you will someday."

"Marcus, and Candice are alive!" declared Neil.

"Alive!" exclaimed Mari.

"They are on one of those ships down there," informed Neil. "Marcus will contact us in the near future."

"That's wonderful!" said Mari.

"I thought the worst," admitted Neil.

"So did I," revealed Mari. "And the others?"

"Marcus did not say anything about them," replied Neil, still feeling the loss.

"Somehow, this will all work out," reflected Mari, "I know it will."

"I wonder if you have considered those things we discussed a while back?" asked Neil, as he rose from his seat to scrutinize some data on a nearby console.

"Such as?" she returned.

"Surely you must know!" exclaimed Neil. "You and I, Grace, the future?"

"Of course," replied Mari, turning to him with an almost secretive look.

"There is something I need ask you, though," added Neil.

"What is it?" she asked.

"Later," he said.

"Later?" she questioned, but with anticipation. "I'll be waiting."

Neil took off his reading glasses and gazed out of the viewport at the hospital ship with eyes that roamed to the orange tint in the sky. The edge of the sun began to appear on the distant horizon with rays spreading out in uncommon brilliance. Then he said, "Now, I must address another subject."

"Oh?" replied his companion.

"All of this has a purpose," he asked, "does it not?"

"I believe so," affirmed Mari, but wondering about where his thoughts were going.

"Well," he said. "I want to thank both of you."

"Why?" asked Mari, seeking his true point of view.

"Why?" asked Grace, who was listening.

"For helping them," said Neil, pointing to the ship below, "for being here, for who you are. I could not have done this without either one of you."

"This is where we belong," replied Mari.

"We belong," echoed Grace, cradling Meadow in her arms.

The voice of Capt. Grayson broke in, saying, "We have been cleared for port, Mr. Clayborn. We can take care of things from here. By the way, there are a lot of people who would like to get their hands on that ship of yours! Although, I believe you are up to the job."

"Thank you, captain, for that vote of confidence," returned Neil. "Everything is squared away here."

"You have been cleared," replied Capt. Grayson. "I know I don't need to say it but you may take your leave of us."

"Roger that," replied Neil, "and farewell."

"All systems are go and I am ready," announced Mari.

"As any captain would be," replied Neil, now satisfied.

"Captain?" she repeated, quizzing him.

"Anywhere, Mari, anywhere," replied Neil. "The ship is yours."

"All mine?" she said, with a twinkle in her eyes.

"Hmm," he returned. "I can imagine some sort of mutual arrangement."

"Then I would love to go where ever you may lead," replied his companion. "I'm always here."

"I know you are," said Neil, "but somehow I just wanted to hear you say it. You have become quite proficient at piloting this rather novel set of wings."

"Then I will set the course," she answered.

"You listen well," he stated.

"Hmm," she returned.

"I know what you are thinking though," he added.

"Oh," questioned Mari, "you do?"

"I cannot begin to know what the future will hold," said Neil, thoughtfully. "For it has become difficult to grasp all of what we have been given."

"It has," she agreed.

"It's not about the hardware is it, Mari?" he queried.

"No," she said, "it's not."

"Then," he asked, "is this contrivance worth the trouble?"

"I believe it is," she returned.

"Are dreams worth dreaming?" he asked, still earnestly seeking.

"I believe they are," she answered.

For a moment Neil's eyes again fixed on the sky, then he said to Mari, "I sought the origins of the universe, but in turn it led me to you. Now you have led me to something more. Other worlds may await our discovery and rightly so. Yet, I see the great need of our own world, but this time I will let events fall into Providential hands."

"Of whom do you speak?" asked Mari, seeking deeper things.

"I apologize for my deaf ears regarding your words," confessed Neil. "Perhaps if I had acted on such things sooner, much pain could have been avoided. I didn't know who to trust."

"You're forgiven, of course," replied Mari, "but what has brought all this about?"

"The Bright and Morning Star," replied Neil, adjusting the Mariner's Cross on his lapel. "And, I looked up that passage of yours."

"So," questioned Mari, now getting personal, "have you been found?"

"Your compass is true, but I was the one off course, and I am sorry," answered Neil. "I confessed that thing that separates us from our Creator, and I have discovered the One Salvor who can rescue from the depths of the sea in Whom is found unmerited favor."

"The Truth?" asked Mari, in light of the confirmation.

"He 'is' the One," answered Neil. "John Shepherd and Neil Clayborn were both dead, but they are now alive!"

Mari excitedly expressed praise to the Ancient of Days. Grace put her arms up with her hands together then made a downward arc with her right arm rhythmically moving her fingers, and saying, "Glorious."

"Perhaps," said Neil, "Wyoming?"

"Of course!" declared his able companion.

"Then onward!" replied Neil, signaling toward the rising sun.

"How did you know what I was thinking?" asked Mari.

"I just know," answered Neil, appearing at her side.

"Because?" asked Mari, questioning his response.

"Hmm," returned Neil, "just because."

Grace came over to Neil, and asked, "What do you mean, just because?"

He put his arms around them, and said, "Because I love both of you very much."

The attention of each person on the *SS Compassion* was now riveted on the *Aurora* as it hung in luminous detail against the gray curtain of clouds to the west. Lily had her arms protectively around Patrick as they stood by the port railing for the boy was anticipating the departure of his new found friend with all due excitement. Then with the work accomplished and the blessing to proceed the *Aurora* covered itself with sails and took leave of its stationary position to glide over the glistening white ship, gradually gathering speed as it traveled steadily upward and outbound to the east, disappearing into the evanescent light of morning.

"Will I ever see Grace again?" asked Patrick.

"Oh, I think you will someday, Patrick," said Lilly, "in God's good time."

"There's something else, Lily," said the young boy, turning to Lilly.

"Yes, Patrick?" questioned Lily.

"Grace is right!" announced Patrick.

Epilogue

Someday there will be another eclipse of the sun,
And with it will come the transient night,
But the astrolabe is firmly in hand.
For within His never ending circle of providence
I find something most wondrous:
Love, light, mercy, and the gift of unmerited favor,
Quite enough to guide all of our footfalls—
Between heaven and earth.
Mari

"I still dream."

BIBLIOGRAPHY

All references from the Holy Bible (King James Version)

(1)Psalms 145:16 202
(2)Proverbs 3: 6 224
(3)Proverbs 3: 3 230
(4)Proverbs 3: 5 230
(5)Romans 8: 28.. 16
(6)Proverbs 3: 5 86

L. Lynn Eckert was born in Saginaw Michigan and is a graduate of Saginaw Valley State University. He has always been involved in the arts, concentrating on painting, large format photography, and writing. He also illustrated the cover of this book.

MICK ART
PRODUCTIONS LLC
PUBLISHING

www.mickartproductions.com

www.ingramcontent.com/pod-product-compliance
Lightning Source LLC
Chambersburg PA
CBHW070049260626
47160CB00004B/1146